OXFORD COUNTY LIBRARY

JAN - - 023

P9-DGR-406

ALL THE
DANGEROUS
THINGS

ALL THE
DANGEROUS
THINGS

STACY WILLINGHAM

MINOTAUR
BOOKS
NEW YORK

This is a work of fiction. All of the characters, organizations, and events portrayed in this novel are either products of the author's imagination or are used fictitiously.

First published in the United States by Minotaur Books, an imprint of St. Martin's Publishing Group

ALL THE DANGEROUS THINGS. Copyright © 2023 by Stacy Willingham. All rights reserved. Printed in the United States of America. For information, address St. Martin's Publishing Group, 120 Broadway, New York, NY 10271.

www.minotaurbooks.com

Designed by Omar Chapa

The Library of Congress Cataloging-in-Publication Data is available upon request.

ISBN 978-1-250-80385-6 (hardcover)
ISBN 978-1-250-80386-3 (ebook)

Our books may be purchased in bulk for promotional, educational, or business use. Please contact your local bookseller or the Macmillan Corporate and Premium Sales Department at 1-800-221-7945, extension 5442, or by email at MacmillanSpecialMarkets@macmillan.com.

First Edition: 2023

10 9 8 7 6 5 4 3 2 1

For my big sister, Mallory

Sleep, those little slices of death. How I loathe them.

—ANONYMOUS

ALL THE
DANGEROUS
THINGS

PROLOGUE

Today is day three hundred and sixty-four.

Three hundred and sixty-four days since my last night of sleep. That's almost nine thousand hours. Five hundred and twenty-four thousand minutes. Thirty-one million seconds.

Or, if you want to go in the opposite direction, fifty-two weeks. Twelve months.

One whole year without a single night of rest.

One year of stumbling through life in a semiconscious dream state. One year of opening my eyes to find myself in another room, another building, without any recollection of when I got there or how I arrived.

One year of sleeping pills and eye drops and chugging caffeine by the quart-full. Of jittery fingers and drooping eyelids. Of becoming intimately familiar with the night.

One whole year since my Mason was taken from me, and still, I'm no closer to the truth.

CHAPTER ONE

NOW

"Isabelle, you're on in five."

My pupils are drilling into a spot in the carpet. A spot with no significance, really, other than the fact that my eyes seem to like it here. My surroundings grow fuzzy as the spot—*my* spot—gets sharper, clearer. Like tunnel vision.

"Isabelle."

I wish I could always have tunnel vision: the ability to selectively focus on one single thing at a time. Turn everything else into static. White noise.

"Isabelle."

Snap snap.

There's a hand in front of my face now, waving. Fingers clicking. It makes me blink.

"Earth to Isabelle."

"Sorry," I say, shaking my head, as if the motion could somehow clear the fog like windshield wipers swiping at rain. I blink a few more times before trying to find the spot again, but it's gone now. I know it's gone. It's melted back into the carpet, into oblivion, the way I wish I could. "Sorry, yeah. On in five."

I lift my arm and take a sip of my Styrofoam cup of coffee—
strong, black, squeaky when my chapped lips stick to the rim. I used
to savor the taste of that daily morning cup. I lived for the smell of it
wafting through my kitchen; the warmth of a mug pushed against my
fingers, cold and stiff from standing on the back porch, watching the
sun come up with morning dew beading on my skin.

But it wasn't the coffee I needed, I know that now. It was the
routine, the familiarity. Comfort-in-a-cup, like those dehydrated
noodles you splash faucet water onto before popping them into the
microwave and calling it a meal. But I don't care about that anymore:
comfort, routine. Comfort is a luxury I can no longer afford, and
routine . . . well. I haven't had that in a long time, either.

Now I just need the caffeine. I need to stay awake.

"On in two."

I look up at the man standing before me, clipboard resting against
his hip. I nod, down the rest of the coffee, and savor the bitter pinch
in my jaw. It tastes like shit, but I don't care. It's doing its job. I dig
my hand into my purse and pull out a bottle of eye drops—redness
relief—and squirt three beads of liquid into each eye with expert pre-
cision. I guess this is my routine now. Then I stand up, run my hands
over the front of my pants, and slap my palms against my thighs,
signaling that I'm ready.

"If you'll follow me."

I hold out my arm, gesturing for the man to lead the way. And
then I follow. I follow him out the door and through a dim hallway,
the fluorescent lights buzzing in my ear like an electric chair hum-
ming to life. I follow him through another door, the gentle roar of
applause erupting as soon as it opens and we step inside. I walk past
him, to the edge of the stage, and stand behind a black curtain, the
audience just barely obscured from view.

This is a big one. The biggest I've done.

I look down at my hands, where I used to hold notecards with
talking points scribbled in pencil. Little bulleted instructions remind-

ing me what to say, what not to say. How to order the story like I'm following a recipe, meticulous and careful, sprinkling the details in just right. But I don't need those anymore. I've done this too many times.

Besides, there's nothing new to say.

"And now we are ready to bring out the person I know you're all here to see."

I watch the man speaking onstage, ten feet away, his voice booming over the loudspeakers. It's everywhere, it seems—in front of me, behind me. Inside me, somehow. Somewhere deep in my chest. The audience cheers again, and I clear my throat, remind myself why I'm here.

"Ladies and gentlemen of TrueCrimeCon, it is my honor to present to you, our keynote speaker . . . Isabelle Drake!"

I step into the light, walking with purpose toward the host as he signals me onstage. The crowd continues to yell, some of them standing, clapping, the beady little eyes of their iPhones pointed in my direction, taking me in, unblinking. I turn toward the audience, squinting at their silhouettes. My eyes adjust a bit, and I wave, smiling weakly before coming to a halt in the center.

The host hands me a microphone, and I grab it, nodding.

"Thank you," I say, my voice sounding like an echo. "Thank you all for coming out this weekend. What an incredible bunch of speakers."

The crowd erupts again, and I take the free seconds to scan the sea of faces the way I always do. It's women, mostly. It's always women. Older women in groups of five or ten, relishing this annual tradition—the ability to break away from their lives and their responsibilities and drown themselves in fantasy. Younger women, twenty-somethings, looking skittish and a little embarrassed, like they've just been caught looking at porn. But there are men, too. Husbands and boyfriends who were dragged along against their will; the kind with wire-rimmed glasses and peach-fuzz beards and elbows that protrude awkwardly from their arms like knobby tree branches. There are the loners in the corner, the ones whose eyes linger just long enough to make you uncomfortable, and the police officers perusing the aisles, stifling yawns.

And then I notice the clothing.

One girl wears a graphic tee that says *Red Wine and True Crime*, the *T* in the shape of a gun; another sports a white shirt sprayed with specks of red—it's supposed to mimic blood, I assume. Then I see a woman wearing a T-shirt that says *Bundy. Dahmer. Gacy. Berkowitz.* I remember walking past it earlier in the gift shop. It was clipped tight against a mannequin, being advertised in the same way they advertise overpriced band T-shirts in the merchandise tents at concerts, memorabilia for rabid fans.

I feel the familiar swell of bile in my throat, warm and sharp, and force myself to look away.

"As I'm sure you all know, my name is Isabelle Drake, and my son, Mason, was kidnapped one year ago," I say. "His case is still unsolved."

Chairs squeak; throats are cleared. A mousey woman in the front row is shaking her head gently, tears in her eyes. She is loving this right now, I know she is. It's like she's watching her favorite movie, mindlessly snacking on popcorn as her lips move gently, reciting every word. She's heard my speech already; she knows what happened. She knows, but she still can't get enough. None of them can. The murderers on the T-shirts are the villains; the uniformed men in back, the heroes. Mason is the victim . . . and I'm not really sure where that leaves me.

The lone survivor, maybe. The one with a story to tell.

CHAPTER TWO

I settle into my seat. The aisle seat. Generally, I prefer the window. Something to lean up against and close my eyes. Not to sleep, exactly. But to drift away for a while. *Microsleeping,* is what my doctor calls it. We've all seen it before, especially on airplanes: the twitching eyelids, the bobbing head. Two to twenty seconds of unconsciousness before your neck snaps back up with astonishing force like a cocking shotgun, ready to go.

I look at the seat to my right: empty. I hope it stays open. Takeoff is in twenty minutes; the gate is about to close. And when it does, I can move over. I can close my eyes.

I can try, as I've been trying for the last year, to finally get some rest.

"Excuse me."

I jump, looking up at the flight attendant before me. She's tapping the back of my seat, disapproval in her eyes.

"We're going to need you to make sure your seat back is in the upright and locked position."

I look back down, push the little silver button on my armrest, and feel my back begin to bend forward at an acute angle, my stomach folding in on itself. The attendant begins to walk away, pushing over-head compartments closed as she goes, when I reach out my arm and stop her.

"Can I bother you for a soda water?"

"We'll begin beverage service as soon as we take off."

"Please," I add, grabbing her arm harder as she starts to step away. "If you wouldn't mind. I've been talking all day."

I touch my throat for emphasis, and she looks down the aisle at the other passengers squirming uncomfortably, adjusting their seat belts. Digging through backpacks for headphones.

"Fine," she says, her lips pinched tight. "Just a moment."

I smile, nod, and ease back into my seat before looking around the plane at the other passengers I'll be sharing circulated air with for the next four hours as we make our way from Los Angeles to Atlanta. It's a game I play, trying to imagine what they're doing here. What life circumstances brought them to this exact moment, with this exact group of strangers. I wonder what they've been doing, or what they plan to do.

Are they going somewhere, or are they making their way home?

My eyes land first on a child sitting alone, giant headphones swallowing his ears. I imagine he's a product of divorce, spending one weekend every month getting shuttled from one side of the country to the other like cargo. I feel myself starting to imagine how Mason might have looked at that age—how his green eyes could have morphed even greener, two twin emeralds twinkling like his father's, or how his baby-smooth skin might have taken on the olive tone of my own, a natural tan without having to step foot in the sun.

I swallow hard and force myself to turn away, twisting to the left and taking in the others.

There are older men on laptops and women with books; teenagers on cell phones slouched low in their seats, gangly knees knocking into the seat backs in front of them. Some of these people are travel-ing to weddings or funerals; some are embarking on business trips or clandestine getaways paid for in cash. And some of these people have secrets. All of them do, really. But some of them have the real ones, the messy ones. The deep, dark, shadowy ones that lurk just beneath the skin, traveling through their veins and spreading like a sickness.

Dividing, multiplying, then dividing again.

I wonder which ones they are: the ones with the kinds of secrets that touch every organ and render them rotten. The kinds of secrets that will eat them alive from the inside out.

Nobody in here could possibly imagine what I've just spent *my* day doing: recounting the most painful moment of my life for the enjoyment of strangers. I have a speech now. A speech that I recite with absolute detachment, engineered in just the right way. Sound bites that I know will read well when ripped from my mouth and printed inside newspapers, and manufactured moments of silence when I want a point to sink in. Warm memories of Mason to break up a particularly tense scene when I'm sensing the need for some comedic relief. Just as I'm going deep into his disappearance—the open window I had discovered in his bedroom letting in a warm, damp breeze; the tiny mobile situated above his bed, little stuffed dinosaurs dancing gently in the wind—I stop, swallow. Then I recite the story of how Mason had just started talking. How he pronounced T. rex "Tyranto*snorious*"—and how, every time he pointed at the little creatures above his bed, my husband would break out into exaggerated snores, sending him into a fit of giggles before drifting off himself. And then the audience would allow themselves to smile, maybe even laugh. There would be a visible release in their shoulders; their bodies would settle into their chairs again, a collectivly held breath released. Because that's the thing with the audience, the thing I learned long ago: They don't want to get *too* uncomfortable. They don't want to actually live through what I've lived through, every ugly moment. They just want a taste. They want enough for their curiosity to be satiated—but if it gets too bitter or too salty or too real, they'll smack their lips and leave dissatisfied.

And we don't want that.

The truth is, people love violence—from a distance, that is. Anyone who disagrees is either in denial or hiding something.

"Your soda water."

I look up at the flight attendant's outstretched arm. She's holding a small cup of clear liquid, little bubbles rising to the surface and bursting with a satisfying fizz.

"Thank you," I say, taking it from her and placing it in my lap.

"You'll need to keep your tray table stowed," she adds. "We'll be in the air soon."

I smile, taking a small sip to indicate that I understand. When she walks off, I lean down, digging my hand into my purse until I feel a mini bottle tucked neatly into the side pocket. I'm attempting to discreetly unscrew the cap when I feel a presence beside me, hovering close.

"This is me."

My neck snaps up, and I'm half expecting to see somebody I know. There's a familiarity in the voice above me, vague, like a casual acquaintance, but when I look up at the man standing in the aisle, I see a stranger with a TrueCrimeCon tote bag slung over one arm, the other pointing to the seat beside me.

The window seat.

He sees the mini bottle in my hand and grins. "I won't tell."

"Thanks," I say, standing up to let him pass through.

I try not to glower at the prospect of being stuck next to an attendee on the fight home—it's complicated, really, the way I feel about the fans. I hate them, but I need them. They're a necessary evil: their eyes, their ears. Their undivided attention. Because when the rest of the world forgets, they remember. They still read every article, debating their theories on amateur sleuth forums as if my life is nothing more than a fun puzzle to be solved. They still curl up on their couches with a glass of Merlot in the evenings, getting lost in the comforting drone of *Dateline*. Trying to experience it without *actually* experiencing it. And that's why events like TrueCrimeCon exist. Why people spend hundreds of dollars on airfare and hotel rooms and conference tickets: for a safe space where they can bask in the bloody glow of violence for just a few days, using another person's murder as a means of entertainment.

But what they don't understand, what they *can't* understand, is that one day, they could wake up to find the violence crawling through their television screens, latching on to their houses, their lives, like a parasite sinking in its fangs. Wriggling in deep, making itself comfortable. Sucking the blood from their bodies and calling them home.

People never think it'll happen to them.

The man glides past me and into his seat, pushing his bag beneath the chair in front of him. When I settle back in, I pick up where I left off: the gentle crack of the cap breaking, the glug of vodka as it pours into my drink. I stir it with my finger before taking a long sip.

"I saw your keynote."

I can feel my seatmate looking at me. I try to ignore him, closing my eyes and leaning my head against the headrest. Waiting for the vodka to make my eyelids just heavy enough to stay closed for a bit.

"I'm so sorry," he adds.

"Thank you," I say, eyes still shut. Even though I can't actually sleep, I can act like I'm sleeping.

"You're good, though," he continues. I can feel his breath on my cheek, smell the spearmint gum wedged between his molars. "At telling the story, I mean."

"It's not a story," I say. "It's my life."

He's quiet for a while, and I think that did it. I usually try not to make people uncomfortable—I try to be gracious, play the role of the grieving mother. Shaking hands and nodding my head, a grateful smile plastered across my face that I immediately wipe away like lipstick the second I step away. But right now I'm not at the conference. It's over, I'm done. I'm going home. I don't want to talk about it anymore.

I hear the intercom come to life above us, a scratchy echo.

"Flight attendants, prepare doors for departure and cross-check."

"I'm Waylon," the man says, and I can feel his arm thrust in my direction. "Waylon Spencer. I have a podcast—"

I open my eyes and look in his direction. I should have known. The familiar voice. The fitted V-neck and dark-wash skinny jeans. He doesn't look like the typical attendee, with his glossy hair shaved into a sloping gradient at the neck. He's not into murder for entertainment; he's in it for business.

I'm not sure which is worse.

"Waylon," I repeat. I look down at his outstretched hand, his expectant face. Then I swivel my neck around and shut my eyes again. "I don't want to come across as rude, *Waylon*, but I'm not interested."

"It's really gaining some traction," he says, pressing on. "Number five in the app store."

"Good for you."

"We even solved a cold case."

I can't tell if it's the sudden movement of the plane—a gentle lurch that makes my stomach flip, my limbs pushing deep into the seat as we rattle down the runway, this giant metal box we're all locked inside moving faster and faster, making my eardrums swell—or if it's his words that make me feel suddenly uneasy.

I take a deep breath, dig my nails into the armrest.

"Flying make you nervous?"

"Can you stop?" I spit, my head snapping back in his direction. I watch as his eyebrows raise, my sudden meanness taking him by surprise.

"I'm sorry," he says, looking embarrassed. "It's just—I thought you might be interested. In telling the story. *Your* story. On the show."

"Thank you," I say, trying to soften my tone. We both tilt back as the plane begins to ascend, the floor rattling violently beneath our feet. "But I'll pass."

"Okay," he says, digging into his pocket and pulling out his wallet. I watch as he flips open the faded leather, pulls a business card out, and places it gently on my leg. "If you change your mind."

I close my eyes again, leaving his card untouched on my knee. We're in the air now, ripping through clouds bloated with water, a beam of sunlight occasionally finding its way through the half-drawn shade and casting a ray of bright light across my eyes.

"I guess I just thought that's why you do it," he adds softly. I try to ignore him, but curiosity gets the best of me. I can't.

"Do what?"

"You know, your talks. It can't be easy, reliving it over and over again. But you have to if you want to keep the case alive. If you ever want it to be solved."

I squeeze my eyes harder, focusing on the little spider veins I can see in my eyelids, glowing red.

"But with a podcast, you wouldn't have to talk to all those people. Not directly, anyway. You'd just have to talk to me."

I swallow, nod my head gently to indicate that I hear but that the conversation is still over.

"Anyway, just think it over," he adds, reclining his chair.

I can hear the rustling of his jeans as he tries to get comfortable, and I know, within minutes, he'll be able to do so easily what I haven't been able to do in a year. I peek one eye open and glance in his direction. He's pushed wireless headphones into his ears, the steady thumping of bass loud enough for me to hear. Then I watch his body transform the same way it always does, predictable yet still so foreign to me: His breath begins to get deeper, steadier. His fingers begin to twitch in his lap, his mouth hanging open like a creaky cupboard door, a single bead of drool quivering in the corner of his lip. Five minutes later, a gentle snore erupts from his throat, and I feel a pinch in my jaw as I clench my teeth.

Then I close my eyes, imagining, for a fleeting moment, what it must be like.

CHAPTER THREE

I push my key into the front door, twisting.

It's nearly two in the morning, and my trip home from the airport is nothing more than a blur, like those long-exposure photographs that feature busy commuters with trails of color following them around the train station. After landing at Hartsfield-Jackson, I had grabbed Waylon's business card and tucked it into my purse, picking up my things and pushing toward the exit without so much as a goodbye. Then I ran to my gate, hopped onto my connection, and took another forty-five-minute flight into the Savannah/Hilton Head International Airport, my eyes boring into the seat in front of me the whole way home. I barely remember staggering through baggage claim, hailing a taxi outside the terminal. Letting the car lull me into a kind of trance for another forty minutes before being dropped in my driveway, stumbling up the steps toward home.

I hear my dog whining as soon as the key begins to turn. I already know where to find him: sitting just inside the front door, tail wagging furiously against the hardwood like a feather duster. He's always been mouthy, Roscoe, ever since he was a puppy. I envy his ability to hold on to the things that make him *him*, unchanged.

Sometimes, when I look in the mirror, I don't even recognize myself anymore. I don't even know who I am.

"Hey, you," I whisper, rubbing his ears. "I missed you."

Roscoe emits a low groan from somewhere deep in his throat, his nails pawing at my leg. My neighbor takes care of him when I'm gone: an older woman who pities me, I think—that, or she really needs the twenty dollars a day I leave for her on the countertop. She lets him outside, fills his bowl. Leaves meticulous notes about his bathroom schedule and eating habits. I don't feel bad about leaving him, to be honest, because she gives him more of a routine than I do.

I drop my purse on the counter and thumb through the mail she left in a pile, mostly junk and bills, until I feel a catch in my throat. I pick up an envelope addressed in familiar script, my parents' address in the left-hand corner, and flip it over, sticking my thumb in the gap and ripping it open. I pull out a small card with flowers on the front; when I open it up, a check flutters out and falls to the floor.

I drop the card on the counter, exhaling slowly. I can't bring myself to touch the check, to see how much it's for. Not yet, anyway.

"Are you ready for a walk?" I ask Roscoe instead. He spins in a circle, an undeniable *yes*, and I feel myself smile. That's the beauty of animals—they adapt.

Ever since I've become nocturnal, Roscoe has, too.

I remember looking up at Dr. Harris, nine months ago, during our first appointment. The first of many. I couldn't see my eyes, but I could feel them. Tight, stinging. I knew they were bloodshot, the little veins that were supposed to be invisible branching out across my sclera like a windshield after a wreck, bloodied and cracking. Broken beyond repair. No matter how many times I blinked, they never got better. It was almost as if my eyelids were made of sandpaper, chipping away at my pupils with each flip of the lid.

"When was the last time you got a full, uninterrupted night of rest?" he had asked. "Can you recall?"

Of course I could. Of course I could recall. I would be recalling that date for the rest of my life, no matter how hard I tried to push it out of my memory. No matter how hard I tried to will it out of existence, how desperately I wanted to pretend that it was just a nightmare. A terrible, horrible nightmare I would be waking up from at any minute now. Any second.

"Sunday, March sixth."

"That's a long time," he had said, glancing down at the clipboard on his desk. "Three months."

I nodded. One thing I was starting to notice about being awake all the time was the way in which seemingly little things grew bigger by the day. Noisier, harder to ignore. The ticking of the clock in the corner was deafening, like a long nail steadily tapping against glass. The dust in the air was unusually visible, little specks of lint floating slowly across my field of vision like someone had tampered with my settings, distorting everything into high-contrast slow motion. I could smell the remnants of Dr. Harris's lunch, little particles of canned tuna wafting through his office and into my nostrils, fishy and brackish, making my esophagus squeeze.

"Did anything extraordinary happen that night?"

Extraordinary.

Until I had woken up the next morning, there hadn't been anything extraordinary about it. It had been painfully *ordinary*, in fact. I remember changing into my favorite pair of pajamas, pushing my hair back with a headband, and scrubbing the makeup from my skin. And then I had put down Mason, of course. I had read him a story, rocking him to sleep the way I always did, but for the life of me, I couldn't remember which story it was. I remember standing in his bedroom, days later, after the yellow police tape had been snipped from the doorway, the silence of his nursery somehow making the room seem to expand to triple its actual size. I remember standing there, staring at his bookshelf—at *Goodnight Moon* and *The Very Hungry Caterpillar* and *Where the Wild Things Are,* desperately trying to remember which one it was. What my last words to my son had been.

But I couldn't. I couldn't remember. That's how ordinary it was.

"Our son," Ben had interjected, placing his hand on my knee. I looked over at my husband, remembering that he was there. "He was taken that night from his bedroom. While we were sleeping."

Dr. Harris had to have known, of course. The entire state of Georgia had known—the entire country, even. Then he had bowed his head the way most people seemed to do when they realized their mistake and didn't know what else to say, his neck mimicking the snap of a shutting lid. Conversation closed.

"But Izzy has always had . . . problems," Ben continued. Suddenly, I felt like I was in detention. "With sleep. Even before the insomnia. Kind of the opposite problem, actually."

Dr. Harris had looked at me then, studying me, like I was some kind of riddle to be cracked.

"About fifty percent of sleep disorder cases are related to anxiety, depression, or some kind of psychosocial distress or disorder, so this makes sense, given what you've been through," he had said, clicking his pen. "Insomnia is no exception."

I remember looking out the window, the sun high in the sky. My eyelids were feeling heavier with every passing second; my brain, cloudier, as though I were enveloped in a blanket of fog. The pen was still clicking, amplified in my ears like a ticking time bomb ready to blow.

"We'll run some tests," he said at last. "Maybe get you on some medication. We'll have you back to normal in no time."

I'm reaching for Roscoe's leash when I catch a glimpse of myself in the hallway mirror and wince. It's an automatic reaction, like jerking your fingers away from a hot stove. I should be gentler on myself, I know. I've been through a lot, but the lack of sleep has become so apparent on my face it's hard not to notice. I look like I've aged years within months, with the new bags hanging heavy beneath my eyes, droopy and worn. The thin swathes of skin beneath my tear ducts have morphed from a warm olive to a deep, dark purple, like a marbling bruise, while the rest of my face has taken on a grayish tone, like chicken that's been left in the fridge too long. I've lost twenty pounds in twelve months, which doesn't seem like *that* much, but when you're already tall and waifish, it shows. It shows in my cheeks, my neck. My hips—or, rather, my lack thereof. My hair, usually a deep, glossy brown, looks like it's dying, too, the ends split clean in half like a splintered tree that's been struck by lightning. The color growing duller by the day.

I force myself to turn around and fasten Roscoe's leash to his collar before stepping back outside, the cool night air making the skin on my arms prickle. Then I lock the door behind us and take a right, setting out on our usual path.

Isle of Hope is a tiny little spit of land, barely two square miles. I've walked the entire thing hundreds of times, memorized the way the Skidaway River slithers across the east side like a water moccasin, shiny and slick. The way the oak trees have formed a giant archway over the Bluff, their limbs getting mangled together in time like the lacing together of arthritic fingers. But it is amazing how completely a place changes in the dark: Roads that you've lived on your entire adult life look different, like instead of stepping onto smooth pavement, you're walking straight into the murky river itself. You start to notice light poles that you used to ignore, the dimming and subsequent brightening as you work your way between each one the only way to gauge distance or depth. Shadows become shapes; every tiny movement is eye-catching, like the dance of dry leaves on the ground or the legs of phantom children pushing an empty swing, chains squeaking in the breeze. Windows are dark, curtains drawn. I try to imagine the life inside each house as I pass—the gentle stirring of a child as they sleep, a nightlight casting otherworldly shapes against the wall. Spouses in bed together, skin-to-skin, bodies tangled tight between the sheets—or perhaps pushed as far apart as humanly possible, separated by an invisible cold line drawn down the center.

As for me, I'm familiar with both.

And then there are the creatures of the night. The living things, like myself, that crawl out of their hiding spots and come alive in the absence of others. Raccoons scurrying across the shadows, rooting through trash. The distant hoot of an owl or snakes slithering out of their shady places and leaving behind nothing but their own dried skin. The scream of crickets and cicadas and other invisible things that pulse through the grass with a steady determination, like the pumping of blood through veins.

I approach the marsh at the edge of my neighborhood and stop, staring out at the inky water I can hear lapping against the shore. I was born in Beaufort, just barely over an hour from here. I've lived on the water my entire life, learned to swim with minnows tickling my feet and the sound of shrimp skidding across the surface at low tide. I've tied chicken necks to a string and let them dangle for hours, waiting patiently until I felt that familiar prickle of life on the other end of the line, watching as countless animals gnawed their way toward their own demise: a sick entertainment that, even then, I didn't understand.

I breathe in the smell of the marsh now, one single whiff immediately transporting me back there. Back home. To the way the salt takes to the air, making it thick like buttermilk. To the pluff mud's familiar stench of rot like a decaying tooth. Because that's what it is, after all. That's the smell of decomposition; the liquid kiss of life and death.

Millions of living things dying together, and millions of other things calling it home.

I stare into the distance and feel my arm rise instinctively, touching the delicate patch of skin behind my ear. The spot I always gravitate to when I'm stuck in a memory. *This* memory. I try to ignore the twist in my stomach, that feeling of someone plunging their hand into my insides and grabbing them tightly, refusing to let go.

I look down at Roscoe, at the way he's standing just at the edge of the water. He's staring into the darkness, too, his eyes trained on something in the distance.

"C'mon," I say, giving his leash a tug. "Let's go home."

We make our way back, and once we step inside, I shut the front door, lock the deadbolt, and fill up Roscoe's water bowl before pushing various leftovers around in the fridge. Then I pull out a Tupperware container of spaghetti, open the lid, and sniff. The wet noodles flop into a bowl, still molded together in an oblong tube, and I thrust it into the microwave, staring at the clock as my dinner spins. Those little digital numbers glowing in the dark.

3:14 a.m.

When the microwave beeps, I pull the bowl out and bring it into my dining room, pushing aside the various papers and folders and sticky notes with midnight musings scratched across their surfaces with dried-out pens. The chair screeches as I pull it out, and Roscoe ambles over to me at the noise, resting at my feet as I jab my fork into the pasta and spin.

Then I stare at the wall, my skin prickling as it stares back.

I look into the smiling eyes of my neighbors, their pictures clipped from church directories and faculty yearbooks; their statements and alibis and hobbies and schedules pinned into place. I analyze the dead eyes of mug shots; the expressions of the strangers whose pictures I've plucked from police blotters or torn from newspaper articles that now decorate my dining room wall like some kind of high-school-girl collage—an obsession I don't know how to tame. So instead, I stare. I wonder. I try to gaze past the paper and into their minds, reading their thoughts. Because, like those people on the plane, someone out there has a secret.

Someone, *somewhere*, knows the truth.

CHAPTER FOUR

THEN

I come to in a start. It's the kind of panicked awakening that follows a slammed door or a breaking glass: not a gentle emergence but a jarring disruption. I immediately know I'm not alone. There's another body pushed against mine, warm and slightly damp like a leaky furnace. Little puffs of breath hot on my neck.

I twist around, blink quickly as two large eyes come into focus.

"You were doing it again."

I rub my own eyes with the backs of my hands and stare at my sister, her hair tangled together like strings of melted caramel. Her thumb is pushed gently between her lips as she looks at me expectantly. I try to remember her coming into my room last night, lifting the dead weight of my arm before wriggling her little body flush against mine, draping it back over her stomach like a seat belt.

I try to remember, but I can't.

"Sorry," I say.

"It scares me when you do that."

"It's okay." I wet my fingers, reach for her head, and pat down a particularly large knot, like a cat licking a newborn. "It's just sleepwalking."

"Yeah, but I don't like it."

"I can't help it," I snap. For a second, I'm annoyed. I've always been groggy in the mornings. I've always been a little irritable, like my brain is perturbed at being forced to wake up and drag itself to work. But then I remember that she can't help it, either. She's only six.

I force myself to exhale, to breathe.

"What was I doing?"

"Just standing there," she says. The side of her face is pushed into my pillow, squishing her cheek. "Your eyes were open."

I roll onto my back and stare at the ceiling, tracing the crack that starts at the base of the chandelier and branches outward like little tributaries snaking their way across the cement, collecting in the corners. An interchange of veins. I've always been a heavy sleeper, as long as I can remember. Once my head hits the pillow, I enter a slumber so deep, nothing can wake me. *Nothing.* A few months ago, I slept clean through a fire alarm blaring just outside my bedroom door. I remember stirring awake on my own, outside in my nightgown, a pungent smokiness in the air. The feeling of my bare feet sticking to the dewy grass as my father held my hand in the dark, squeezing. Apparently I had walked outside with him, my fingers clenched tightly between his. I stood there for thirty minutes, rigid and upright and entirely unconscious, watching as the firefighters doused out the flames that had taken to our kitchen, licking up the walls.

"Where was I?" I ask.

"In my bedroom," Margaret says, her pupils still flicking back and forth across my face. "You woke me up."

I feel a hot flash of embarrassment crawl up my neck at the thought of my little sister feeling someone watching her as she slept. Of opening her eyes, blinking rapidly as her vision adjusted to see me, finally, standing motionless in the dark.

"Did you try to wake me?"

"No," she says. "Mom said not to. It's dangerous."

"It's not dangerous. That's an old wives' tale."

Margaret pushes herself deeper into my comforter, and I try, so hard, to picture it: my eyes clicking open with a lifeless stare. My torso sitting upright, swiveling to the side, and my skinny legs swinging over the mattress. Hanging there, kicking, like I'm sitting on the edge of the dock, toes in the marsh, blind to the life that's lurking just beneath. Feeling the plush shag carpet on my feet as I walk across my room, open the door, and creep down the hallway.

I try, but I can't.

"What did you do?"

"Just lay there and waited for you to leave," she says. "Then I followed you into your room."

"Why did you get into bed with me?"

"I don't know." She shrugs. "I couldn't sleep. That's what I do when I'm scared."

I look at my sister, place my open palm on her cheek, and smile. Margaret, my little shadow. She follows me everywhere. Always running to me when she's afraid—even, apparently, when I'm the one she's afraid of.

"How long are you going to keep doing this?" she asks.

"I don't know," I say, sighing. And that's the truth. I don't know. I don't know how often it happens, but judging by the number of times I've woken up in strange places over the last few months, I'd say it's not infrequent. Coming to while standing rigid in our living room, the television emitting a silent blue glow. Sitting at the kitchen table with a bowl of cereal in the dark. Me in my white nightgown, lit by the moonlight, haunting the halls like the ghost of some lost, lonely girl. The doctor says it's harmless—common, even, for kids my age—but the idea of my body acting independently from my mind is a little eerie, that's all. The first time it happened, I woke up on the floor of Margaret's bedroom; she was sitting right next to me, playing with dolls. She hadn't even realized I was sleeping. "Dad said I'll grow out of it."

"But when?"

"I don't know, Margaret." I bite down on the inside of my cheek, hard, to keep myself from saying something mean. Something I'll regret. "I'm sorry, though, okay? I'm not going to hurt you. I promise."

She looks at me, considering my words, before nodding her head.

"Now let's go," I say, flinging back the covers.

I swing my legs over the side of the bed, ready to get up, when something stops me: a catch in my throat, fear lodged somewhere deep and out of reach. There are footprints on my carpet—faint, but there—a little dirt trail leading from my bedroom door to the side of my bed. I swallow, my eyes darting over to the window next. To the half acre of grass that butts up against the marsh; a gentle, muddy slope.

I rub my foot against one of the prints, hard, trying to make it disappear.

"Come on," I say at last, hoping Margaret won't see. "Let's get some breakfast."

CHAPTER FIVE

NOW

The midday news whispers in the background as I shuffle through the house, making my third cup of coffee. I've showered and changed since last night, peeling myself from the couch at the first trickle of light through the windows before making my way into the bathroom, turning on the showerhead, and craning my neck, letting the spray pelt my skin.

Then I had closed my eyes, held my breath. Imagined, as I have so many times, what it might feel like to drown.

Exhaustion does strange things to the brain, things that are hard to reason with. Hard to explain. I've been thinking a lot about torture ever since I've stopped sleeping—and not the overtly violent kind, either, like taking a rusted blade to the skin or a pair of old pliers to an outstretched finger. I've been thinking about the painstakingly normal kind. The kind that uses simple necessities like sleep or sustenance to turn us into the worst versions of ourselves: isolation, sensory deprivation, waterboarding.

I understand what it's like now, how maddening, lying awake in the middle of the night with nothing but your thoughts for company.

Of course, I have gotten *some* sleep over the past year. I'd be dead if I hadn't. I've found myself nodding off in waiting rooms or taxicabs, blinking my eyes and looking at the clock, realizing that I couldn't account for the last hour. All of those little microsleeps throughout the day: mere seconds of intense, deep, bewildering unconsciousness that seem to come out of nowhere and evaporate just as fast. Restless catnaps on my couch, waking up every fifteen minutes before dropping off again. Dr. Harris prescribed me sleeping pills in the early days, instructing me to take one every night as the sun went down. I tried them a few times, but the dosage was never strong enough, so I'd started hoarding them. Taking three or four until my eyelids finally started to feel heavy, but even then, I'd pop back awake after a couple of hours, feeling groggy and slow, unable to think. Unable to do anything.

Sometimes, the mind is just stronger than our attempts to override it.

I sit at the kitchen table now, mug between my hands, and stare at the envelope sealed before me. I had snatched it last night from the man with the clipboard with the same embarrassment I imagine hookers might feel when they collect their cash—after all, I had exposed myself to those people for pay.

Maybe not my body, but my soul, and somehow, that feels worse.

I take a sip of coffee now and flip the envelope over, loosening the clasp and sliding its contents out on the table. This is my fee: the full attendee list, complete with names and email addresses of every single person who purchased a ticket. The lead detective on Mason's case once told me that criminals often show up at public events like press conferences and memorials as a way of reliving the rush, pushing their luck just a *little* bit further—or to try and stay informed of the latest breaks in the case. By that logic, I started demanding the attendee list at every conference I've spoken at, hoping that someone in the audience might stand out. The organizers always balk when I request it—they claim it's an invasion of privacy, until I point out the attendees already agreed to the dissemination of their information in the Terms and Agreements.

It was in the fine print. It's always in the fine print.

In the end, they always agree. After all, a speaker like me could get away with charging thousands of dollars per appearance—a high-profile case, cold but not yet discarded. But instead, all I ask for is this: information. Access to something, *anything,* that I could potentially use.

My eyes scan the grid of names, listed alphabetically.

Aaron Pierce, Abigail Fisher, Abraham Clark, Adam Shrader.

It's always the same: searching for them on Facebook, sifting through profiles and trying to determine where they might live. I look for childless women, maybe. Lonely souls with too many cats and too much free time, or maybe men who set off the alarm bells that are somehow hardwired into our brains. The ones with eyes like ice cubes, cold and hard, that raise the little hairs on the backs of our necks, though we can't even put a finger on why.

Alexander Woodward, Alicia Bryan, Allan Byers, Bailey Deane.

I toggle over to the sex offender registry next, to see if they're there. Then I highlight their name if anything unusual pops up and move on to the next one, repeating the process all over again.

It's tedious, mind-numbing work, but with no suspects and no leads, this is where I am right now. This is all that's left.

Some of these names seem vaguely familiar, and I know I've searched them before. After a while, you start running into the same people over and over again. There are regulars at these things, and they always find me, somehow, introducing themselves again or just assuming I should remember them. Expecting me to engage with their questions and their small talk, as if I am nothing more than an author at their book club.

As if I should be asking them how they *feel* about my story, about the unresolved ending. About their opinions of it all.

It's the little things that bother me the most: The way their fingers rest gently on my arm, like they're afraid I might break. The way their heads cock to the side like curious puppies and how their murmurs always dip a few octaves too low so I have to lean in close, strain to hear. The floral perfume dabbed beneath their ears and their warm, stale breath making my stomach churn.

"*I can't even imagine,*" they'd say at last, "*the pain you've endured.*"

And they're right: They can't imagine. There is no way to imagine it until you're right in the thick of it, living it, and by then, it's too late.

The violence has come for you, too.

I can hear Roscoe snoring at my feet, his breath rhythmic and peaceful, until the charms on his collar clank as he lifts his head and stares at the front door. My heart sinks, watching him get up, trot over, and sit patiently by the window as a shadow of a man appears outside. I squeeze my eyes shut, take a deep breath, and lift my hand to my chest, my fingers massaging the outlines of the necklace hidden beneath my shirt. Then I make my way to the door.

I know who it is before I hear the knock.

"Good morning," I say, opening the door and staring at my husband, realizing too late that it's already well past noon. "What a surprise."

"Hey," Ben says, his eyes looking anywhere but into mine. "Can I come in?"

I open it wider and gesture for him to come inside. There's a rigid politeness in his posture, as if we were strangers. As if he didn't used to live in this very house; as if his lips haven't touched every inch of my skin, his fingers haven't explored every birthmark and blemish and scar. He leans down and pets Roscoe, whispering *good boy* over and over again. I watch their interaction, natural and calm, and wish Roscoe would curl back his lip, bare his teeth. Give my husband a menacing snarl for leaving him, leaving us.

Instead, he licks Ben's fingers.

"What can I do for you?" I ask, crossing my arms tight against my chest.

"Just checking in. Today, you know."

"Yeah. I know."

Today. Day three hundred and sixty-five. One full year since our final day with Mason. One year since I read him that story and tucked him in tight; since I climbed into bed next to Ben and closed my eyes, drifted so easily into that long, still slumber, blissfully unaware of the hell that waited for us on the other side of dawn.

"Still not sleeping, huh?"

I try not to let the comment hurt—he doesn't mean it like that, I know he doesn't—but still, I hate it when he sees me like this.

"How can you tell?"

I try to crack a smile, show him that I'm kidding, but I'm not quite sure how it comes out. Maybe a bit deranged, because he doesn't smile back.

It started as a desperate need to stay awake in case Mason came back. Someone had taken my baby, after all. Someone had *taken* him from me, and I had slept through it all. What kind of mother does that? What kind of mother doesn't wake up? I felt like I should have known—I should have had some kind of primal *feeling* that something was happening, something was wrong—but I didn't. I didn't feel anything. So for those first few nights, I told myself I'd stay awake, just in case. That maybe, in the middle of the night, I'd peek into his nursery, and there he'd be: sitting up straight in his crib like he never even left. That he would crack that gummy little smile when he saw me. That he would reach for me, fingers curled around his favorite stuffed animal, and finally feel safe.

I wanted to be awake for that—no, I *needed* to be awake for that.

Then nights turned into weeks, weeks to months, and Mason still wasn't home—but by then, I was wired differently. I was changed. Something had snapped in my brain, a taut rubber band that just couldn't take the pressure anymore. Ben had begged me in the beginning, tried to pull me away from the window where I stood, feet planted, staring into the darkness.

"*This isn't doing anybody any good,*" he would say. "*Izzy, you need to rest.*"

And I knew he was right—I knew it wasn't doing any good—but still, I couldn't help it. I couldn't sleep.

"How's work?" Ben asks now, straining for conversation.

"Slow," I say, tucking a rogue strand of hair behind my ear. I had let it air dry, resulting in a wiry halo of baby hairs I feel tickling my forehead. "I'm not getting a ton of offers at the moment."

"I would think business would be better than usual," he responds, walking over to the couch and taking a seat. It annoys me he doesn't ask permission, but then again, he did buy it. "You know, given the publicity."

"I don't want to do anything that feels exploitative."

"And that's different from what you're currently doing . . . how?"

I stare at Ben, and he stares back. This is why he's here—why he's *really* here. He must have heard about it somehow: my keynote. I knew he would eventually, just not this soon.

"Why don't you just come out and say it," I say. "Come on, Ben. Just say it."

"Fine, I'll say it. What the fuck are you doing?"

"I'm trying to keep his case alive."

"It *is* alive," he responds, exasperated. We've had this conversation so many times. "Isabelle, the police are working on it."

Isabelle. He doesn't call me *Izzy* anymore.

"You've got to stop this. All of it," he says, gesturing to the dining room. I noticed him steal a glance earlier, that subconscious flinch as he rounded the corner, like steeling for a punch, his eyes skipping over all the pictures cluttering up the space where an oil painting of our wedding once hung. "It's not healthy. Besides, it looks—"

"How does it look?" I interrupt, anger building in my chest. "Please, tell me."

"It looks *wrong,*" he says, wringing his hands. "You, standing up and doing that in front of some sick audience the day before the anniversary. It doesn't look *normal*."

"And what exactly would look better, Ben? What would look normal? Doing nothing?"

I stare at him, my nails digging into my palms.

"They *have* nothing," I continue. "They have *no one*, Ben. Whoever did this is still out there. Whoever *took* him . . ." I stop, biting my lip before I start to cry. I exhale, try again. "I don't understand why you don't care. Why you don't want to find him."

Ben shoots up from the couch, his face suddenly flushed with blood, and I know I've gone too far.

"Don't you *ever* say that!" he yells, pointing his finger at me. There's a bead of spit on his lip, quivering. "Don't you *ever* accuse me of not caring. You have no idea what this has been like for me. He was my son, too."

"Is," I correct, my voice a whisper. "He *is* your son, too."

We're both silent, staring at each other from across the living room.

"He could still be alive," I say, feeling the tears well in my eyes again. "We could still find him—"

"Isabelle, he's not alive. He's not."

"He could be—"

"He's not."

I watch as Ben sighs, pushing his hands through his hair and tugging at the ends. Then he walks over to me and wraps his arms around me. I can't bring myself to hug him back, so instead I just stand there. Dead weight.

"Isabelle," he whispers, his fingers running their way through my hair. "I hate being the one to keep telling you this, I really do. It rips me apart. But the sooner you accept what happened, the sooner you can move on. You *have* to move on."

"It's been a year," I respond. "How can you move on in a year?"

"I haven't," he says. "But I'm trying."

I'm quiet, feeling his hands on the back of my head; his breath on my ear, warm and damp, and the gentle thump of his heart against my chest. I open my mouth, ready to apologize, when suddenly, he pulls back.

"Speaking of which, there's something else, too," he says, dropping his arms. "Something I've been meaning to talk to you about."

I cock my head, unsure of how to answer.

"My therapist talks a lot about how part of moving on is being open to new possibilities," he says. "You know, getting excited for the future again. Whatever, or whoever, that entails."

"Okay," I say, crossing my arms tight, trying to ignore the hopeful twinge in my chest. I can't deny that I've thought about this: The possibility of Ben crawling back. Of apologizing for leaving me when I needed him the most.

But I can't say that I blame him, either. Losing a child makes you lose a lot of things. Your rationality, your mind.

"I wanted you to know that I'm seeing someone."

His words hit me like a stomach punch, swift and hard. I try to hide my shock, but I'm sure my expression shows it because he doesn't wait for me to respond.

"It isn't serious or anything. It's new, just a few dates, but Savannah's a small town, you know. People talk. I wanted you to hear it from me first."

"Oh," I finally manage, my nails squeezing into my sides, making it hurt. I imagine them leaving little crescent-shaped slits in my stomach like bite marks, sinking deep into my skin.

"I debated whether or not I should tell you today, but in the end . . . I don't know," he says, his hands punched into his pockets. "I didn't want you to find out some other way."

"It's okay," I say, still searching for words and unable to find them. "That's . . . that's okay. I mean, that's *good*—for you, I guess. I'm glad you told me."

"It is good," he says. I can see his shoulders relax a bit, a long ex-hale, like the tension he had been holding there suddenly melted like wax. "Even if it doesn't go anywhere, it's been good for me. It's been giving me hope, Izzy. And I want that for you, too."

My ears burn at the familiar sound, *Izzy*, my old nickname on his lips suddenly rancid and wrong. What used to be so tender, full of longing and love, now feels like a punishment: something swathed in pity, like a lukewarm smile tossed across the room when someone you used to love catches you hanging out without them.

"I'll see you tonight?" he asks, pulling a hand from his pocket and resting it on my shoulder.

I nod, smile, and watch as he pets Roscoe and makes his way toward the door, the whole time trying to ignore the tingling on my skin in the exact place where he touched me. When he closes the door behind him, I feel a slow stretch in my insides: the hollowness, growing, like a gaping black hole.

Then I dip my hand beneath my shirt, finding my necklace, and clutch the ring—*Ben's* ring—that dangles from a chain fastened tightly around my throat.

CHAPTER SIX

My house reeks of Ben even after he's left. His spiced aftershave and soapy hair gel; the sriracha turkey sandwich I know he ate in his car on the way over. I saw a dab of it on his shirt collar, a little red smear. A few years ago, I would have rolled my eyes at his clumsiness, licked my thumb and rubbed it against the stain. Maybe popped my finger into my mouth afterward, savoring the heat. A little tease before he left for work, ensuring that he would spend the day thinking of me.

Not anymore, though. Now, whenever I see him, I taste something metallic. Like sucking on pennies or licking a fresh wound, tasting blood on my tongue. It's like my body is refusing to let me forget how deeply he hurt me. When he looks at me with those gentle eyes, soft and sweet like two dollops of whipped cream, I don't melt the way I used to.

Instead, I harden.

"Losing a child is one of the most trying things a couple can go through," Dr. Harris had said the first time I showed up to our appointment alone. I didn't have to say anything; somehow, he just knew. Maybe he saw it coming. "Some make it out stronger, but most don't make it out at all."

I had wanted to fall into the category of *some*. Really, I did. Not even to make it out stronger—just to make it out alive. But that's the thing about grief: There is no manual for it. There is no checklist outlining the optimal way to move through it and move on. Ben, always the realist, simply bowed his head and swam against the current. From day one, he leaned on statistics and facts, adjusting the probability of Mason's return every single day until, finally, he decided it was time to stop swimming. We had lost the race, and it was time to admit defeat. It was time to rest. I knew it was painful for him. I knew it hurt. I knew it took everything in him to keep himself moving forward—and even more to force himself to stop—but I couldn't even keep my head above water. From the very beginning, I was dragging him down, drowning him with me, and when he realized he couldn't save us both, he decided to save himself.

Turns out, we were wedged firmly in with *most*.

I find myself wondering now if *most* at least make it a year, because we certainly didn't. We barely even made it six months.

We didn't have the most traditional courtship, Ben and I, so maybe I shouldn't be surprised that a relationship that started out with the speed and electricity of lightning disappeared just as fast—but still. We shared seven years together. *Seven*.

That's something.

I can't help but think back on it now, the moment we first met. It felt like fate, honestly; the collision, quite literally, of two people who were just meant to be together. At the time, it reminded me of the stars: how two can collide and fuse into one—bigger, brighter, stronger than before. But what I didn't know then was that when they collide too fast, they don't fuse at all. Instead, they explode, evaporating into nothing.

I had just moved to Savannah back then, three years out of college and my barely furnished studio apartment just blocks from my new office at *The Grit*. I don't even remember the exact moment I decided I wanted to be a writer for *The Grit*; it was just something I had always known, the same way doctors and firefighters carry their childhood dreams over into adulthood, cupping them so tightly they forget to look up and notice what else could possibly be out there. What else exists.

Some of my best memories involve lying on the floor of my parents' living room, Margaret and I, belly-side down on a rust-red oriental. Our skinny legs would kick in the air as Margaret flipped through the glossy pages, pointing at her favorite pictures. *Tell me a story*, she'd croon, and I would read the accompanying article out loud for her, sounding out every word. It was the kind of magazine people noticed in airports and grocery stores, with a thick matte cover and expensive-looking paper; the kind of magazine people kept as a coffee-table decoration—people like my parents—its mere existence so perfectly mirroring the type of image they aspired to uphold: sophisticated, cultured, *well-to-do.*

Their tagline, so impeccably succinct: *The Grit Tells the Stories of the South.*

I moved at the end of October, a week before my first day. I remember thinking that all these Southern cities are always a bit of the same, with their giant live oaks and Spanish moss and wrought-iron gates crawling with star jasmine—but at the same time, all a bit different, too. Unique in their own right. Savannah reminded me of home, but only the good parts, as if the squishy bruises had been extracted with a switchblade, leaving nothing but ripe possibility. And I was loving it, I really was, but five whole days of solitude—of not recognizing a single face, uttering a single word—can get a little lonely, so by that weekend, I had decided to get dressed up and venture out on my own.

I remember ambling up to a little spot by the Savannah River, my hands punched into my pockets and the smell of smoke and jalapeños making my nostrils flare. Then I walked up to the outdoor bar, my breath coming out in puffs.

"Fifteen dollars for all you can eat," the bartender had said. He smelled like salt water and marsh mud and the sour traces of warm, spilt beer. "Comes with a shucker and towel."

I fished out my wallet and handed him a twenty, exchanging the cash for a Blue Moon, a little knife, and a bucket full of oysters steamed over a grate of hot coals—but once I swung around, I immediately knocked into the man behind me, sending my beer flying.

"I am so sorry," I said, trying to stop the rest of it from sloshing down my wrist. I looked at his jacket, at the frothy liquid dripping down his chest. "Oh God, I'm sorry. I didn't see you—"

The man looked down at his jacket, soaking, and wiped the excess off with his gloves. Then he looked back at me, took in my face, and smiled, the corner of his lip pulling up gently until I got a glimpse of his teeth.

"It's fine, no worries," he said. "At least you didn't hit me with that." He pointed to the knife wedged between my fingers, the blade sticking straight out. "Shanked by an oyster shucker. Not a pleasant way to go."

I looked down at the shucker, then back at him, horrified, feeling like a kid getting scolded for running with scissors.

"I'm kidding," he said at last, his smile morphing into a playful grin. He must have noticed me blushing; my face turning a deep, dark red. "You know how to use that thing?"

"No," I lied. I don't really know why I said it. I knew how to shuck an oyster, of course. Dig the knife into the opening, twist, and pop. But this man was handsome, and I had just spent the last week entirely alone. I wasn't ready for the conversation to end; I wasn't ready for him to walk away, for me to be on my own again. "Care to show me?"

He gestured to an open table, an overturned whiskey barrel with a hole in the center to toss in the empty shells. He grabbed the first oyster he could find, wriggled the meat free, and dropped it onto a saltine, thrusting it in my direction.

"They key is plenty of cocktail sauce, a little lemon," he said, watching me. "It helps to offset the salt."

"Thank you." I smiled, popping it into my mouth and licking my lips before thrusting out my free hand. "I'm Isabelle."

"Ben," he said, giving me a firm shake. It was then that I noticed his hands were empty.

"You need a drink," I said. "Let me buy you one. It's the least I can do."

"I was actually just on my way to close my tab."

"Oh." I blushed at the thought of my flirty banter backfiring. "Well, thank you, anyway, for the lesson. And I'm sorry again about the beer."

He hesitated in his spot for a moment, glancing back at the bar, then back at me, like he was considering something very carefully.

"You know what," he said at last. "A couple more won't hurt. And let me buy *you* one. It's the least I can do, you know, since I'm now wearing yours."

I let out a laugh as I watched him walk away and order our drinks, feeling a twinge of excitement in my chest. Once he came back, I immediately launched into small talk, not waiting for him to be the one to chart the course of the conversation. We talked about Savannah and how long he had lived here; we talked about Beaufort, even though I tried, several times, to divert the conversation away from home. He asked about my family, my siblings.

"I have a little sister," I said, keeping it at that. He didn't need to know more about Margaret. Not yet, anyway.

He took the hint and changed the subject, asking next about my job.

"I'm a writer for *The Grit*." I smiled. I didn't have to fake it that time; the excitement in my voice was real. "My first day is on Monday, actually."

I watched his eyebrows raise, a little smirk stretch across his mouth. He was impressed.

"Wow," he said. "*The Grit*."

"I can't wait," I blurted out. I was three beers deep at that point, feeling talkative and loose. "I'm so excited. I haven't even been to the office yet, but I've heard it's just gorgeous. Like something out of the magazine itself. I mean, of course it is. I suppose it has to be, given their image—"

I stopped, suddenly realizing that I was rambling. That Ben was looking at me, smiling, trying to stifle a laugh.

"I'm sorry," I said. "I'm blabbering. What do *you* do, Ben?"

"I guess you could say I'm a writer myself," he said, looking down at the table. "But that's enough about work. It's the weekend."

He kept talking, but at that point, I couldn't listen. I could barely hear a word. Instead, I was looking at him, marveling at how perfect the night had turned out to be. This gorgeous man: nice, funny— and, on top of it all, *a writer*. I don't know if it was all those plastic cups of draft beer sitting in my stomach or the nearby bonfire making my cheeks warm and red or the fact that that was the first time I had felt normal, *wanted*, in God-knows-how-long, but something about that moment felt right. Something about that moment felt like if I didn't seize it, I might live to regret it for the rest of my life. So I pushed myself up on my toes, leaned in close, and gave him a kiss.

I remember his lips feeling salty and soft, the slick skin on the inside cold and hoppy from the remnants of his beer. I lifted my hand and placed it on his cheek, my fingers gently touching his hair. After a couple seconds, I leaned back and wiped my lips on the back of my hand.

"I'm sorry," I said, my cheeks flushing, suddenly embarrassed. "I'm sorry, I don't know why I did that."

"It's fine," he said, but his smile was different. A little bit bashful. "Really, don't worry about it."

"I have to go to the bathroom," I blurted out, desperate to get out of there. Away from him for just a second. I needed to recollect my thoughts, compose myself. Figure out what to say next. So I took off, stepped into the restroom, and looked in the mirror, noticing the way my eyes were a little bit dark and disoriented, the way they always got when I had too much to drink. But I also noticed the way my cheeks looked so alive, sore from all the smiling. The way my chest was flushed with red, warm not just from my coat and the fire, but from all that talking. A warmness that came from the inside. A contentment I hadn't felt in years.

I pushed myself out of the bathroom again, running my fingers through my hair as I walked back to our table. I had decided to play it off with a joke, maybe some self-deprecating jab about being a lightweight, but very quickly, I realized that something was wrong.

He wasn't there. He wasn't anywhere. Ben had left.

And that's when it hit me: The sudden awkwardness of that kiss. The way his smile had looked so different when I pulled myself away. The way he had been standing there, arms at his side, somewhat rigid. Not moving.

He hadn't kissed me back.

CHAPTER SEVEN

I push the memory from my mind and make my way back to the dining room—but before I get back to the list, I turn toward my computer and launch a new browser window, Googling myself. My name auto-populates immediately—I've done this so many times before—and once the results load, I click on *News* and sort chronologically.

As predicted, there's an article, less than two hours old, about my keynote at TrueCrimeCon. I wonder if Ben has Google Alerts set up to notify him anytime my name is mentioned. The thought is endearing for a second, until I realize that he isn't keeping tabs on me because he cares. He's keeping tabs because he's angry.

I click on the link and skim.

Isabelle Drake headlined at TrueCrimeCon this weekend, the largest true crime conference in the world, which draws a global attendance of over 10,000. The keynote focused on her son, Mason Drake, who disappeared from his bedroom on March 6, 2022, and has yet to be found.

While the case has captivated the curiosity of true crime fans across the country, it remains unsolved one year later, with no viable suspects or legitimate leads. Detective Arthur Dozier of the Savannah Police Department implores the public to exercise "patience and trust" as they continue to investigate, although Drake has taken matters into her own hands, speaking openly about the case at conferences and events across the country.

While some see Drake as a determined mother fighting to find her son, others believe her intrusion into an open investigation may come with consequences.

I stare at the picture of myself, openmouthed as I speak into the microphone. I've managed to do a pretty good job of hiding my insomnia from others: white eyeliner to make my eyes pop, extra blush for a pretty convincing kick of life. Nobody knows, other than Ben, what my existence really looks like now.

How long the days drag on; the nights, even longer.

The bright auditorium lights are reflecting off the wedding ring I still wear in public, and I snake my hand down the neck of my shirt again, feeling the cool metal of Ben's ring around my throat. It isn't his wedding ring—I couldn't get away with taking that—but a gold college signet ring with his name and graduation date engraved around the outside. I found it, months ago, tossed on top of our dresser as he packed his belongings into various boxes. I remember picking it up, feeling the familiar well of tears erupt at the thought of losing yet another person in my life that I loved.

Then, before I could think twice, I shoved it in my pocket.

I don't even know why I did it. I guess it was because he was leaving, leaving *me*, and this was a part of him that I could hold on to. Or maybe it was because *by* leaving me, he was taking the very last scrap of hope from me—hope that things would somehow wind up okay—and I had wanted to take something from him, too. Even if it was something small, something replaceable. I didn't even know if he would notice it was missing, but if he did, I wanted him to know how it felt: to look for something and never find it. To wonder where it could have possibly gone, the same way I looked into his eyes and searched for the feelings for me I knew he no longer had.

My eyes flicker across the rest of the image, taking in the crowd. I recognize some of them: the one with the T-shirt and the mousey woman in the front row, tears dripping. They're watching me hungrily, like vultures ready to pick at something not yet dead. The flash from the camera has done something strange to their eyes, making them look even more ravenous. Making them glow.

They look like they want to devour me whole and lick the blood from my bones.

I stifle a shudder and scroll down to the comments, the real meat of the story. Already, there are dozens.

That poor woman. Can't imagine. Her talk was great!

Let's not act like she's doing this for any reason other than self-promotion. She's a writer. You know there's a book deal coming.

Shut up. I hope your kid gets taken so you know how it feels.

Isabelle Drake is a baby killer. Change my mind.

I slap my laptop shut, and Roscoe jumps at the sound. Then I press my thumbs into my temples and exhale.

Isabelle Drake is a baby killer.

I know these comments shouldn't get to me; I know they're just noise. I've experienced firsthand the sick fascination people have with other people's pain. The way they cling to it like static. The way they interpret every move as the wrong move, as if they could possibly know. As if they could possibly know what they'd do in my shoes. How they would feel.

The morning after Mason was taken, I'll never forget the way our neighbors poked their noses into our yard, smelling a story. They had seen the police cruisers in our driveway, uniformed cops snooping around our house. They had offered their condolences—genuine concern, at first—their hair tousled and sleep still stuck to the corners of their eyes as they pushed a warm mug of coffee into my hands, whispering words of encouragement in my ear. But as time went by, they started to retreat. They didn't come into our yard anymore; they stayed at arm's length, watching from their porches, like someone had erected an invisible fence around our property. Like they were afraid that if they came too close, the violence would come for them, too. Consume their life as it had consumed mine. So they glared as the police tape was cut away; they whispered no longer to me, but *about* me. Because at first, they had wanted to assume that there was an innocent explanation: He had slipped out in the middle of the night, that's all. He would be found, of course he would, somewhere in the neighborhood. Lost and confused but entirely unharmed.

But after one day, two days, a week, a month, it became harder and harder to cling to any kind of hope. So without someone to blame, they decided to blame me.

That's why it's so hard to do these talks, knowing what half of the audience is thinking. Their eyes on me, scrutinizing. Waiting for me to slip up. They think I killed my baby: another Susan Smith or Casey Anthony, woefully *unmaternal.* Some of them actually think that I did it—that I smothered him in his sleep, maybe, fingers twitching after one too many restless nights—while others simply say that I was asking for it. That I didn't do enough to keep him safe.

Either way, it always comes back to me: the mother. It's always my fault.

I tell myself I don't care, that their opinions won't bring Mason back, but I would be lying if a little part of me—somewhere, deep down, the debris of self-preservation floating across the murky depths of my subconscious—wasn't trying to prove something to them. Wasn't trying to convince them that I *am* maternal. I *am* a good mother.

Or maybe I'm just trying to convince myself.

I look up from the table and glance out the window, the afternoon stretching ahead of me like a prison sentence. I'm practically counting down the hours until the sun sets again, the metaphorical marking of that grim milestone no family of a missing child ever wants to reach.

One year.

It's almost three o'clock now; Mason's vigil is downtown at six. Ben and I planned it together, albeit for entirely different reasons. He wanted something to remember—I can't bring myself to say the word *memorial*, but that's really what it is. As for me, I wanted something to draw a crowd. Like sitting on the dock with that string, bobbing the bait and waiting for something to bite.

A trap, of sorts. Like leading a moth to a flame.

I stand up from the table, pushing my chair back with a screech before walking into the kitchen and grabbing my purse. I don't have it in me right now: sifting through those names, spending another day chasing ghosts. I can't pass the next three hours in this house, alone. Mason is everywhere here: in the closed door of his nursery, the one room in this house I refuse to step inside. In the child locks still strapped to the cabinets and in his crayon-scribbled drawings still stuck to the fridge.

That's the thing about a missing child, the thing nobody tells you: They never die. In a way, their goneness makes them immortal— always there, just barely out of view. Forever alive in your mind exactly the way they were when they left you, materializing as that sudden cold spot when you walk down the hallway or a twirling tendril of smoke before evaporating into nothing, leaving behind just the faintest trace of what used to be.

"I'll be back," I whisper to Roscoe before slinging my purse over my shoulder and making my way toward the door. Then I step outside and lock it behind me, my eyes stinging in the sudden brightness of outside.

CHAPTER EIGHT

THEN

We pad down the stairs, Margaret carefully placing both feet on each step. Left, then right. Left, then right. I walk with her slowly, her fingers laced in mine.

Going anywhere with Margaret always takes a while; she's small, after all, and our house is so big. Three stories with wraparound porches on every level. I'm old enough to understand that *big* is a relative term, actually. I really have no way of knowing if it is big, comparatively speaking, since this is the only place I've ever lived. The only place I've known. Maybe everyone's house looks like this—so large that I find myself discovering new nooks and crannies during every game of hide-and-seek, no matter how many times we've played; so old that the creaks and pops and snaps of the wood have become like a family member to me, frightening yet familiar—but I don't think so. I can see the way people stare as they walk past, cameras slung low around their necks as they grip the wrought-iron fence, trying to sneak a peek through the bars. I watch them read the weathered bronze plaque bolted to the brick columns, the inscription providing a little bit of background on our home. I've read it so many times myself that I have it memorized now, reciting it out loud like

I'm ushering pretend visitors through a gallery exhibit. But I'll never forget the first time, the way my fingers moved across the cold metal as if I were reading braille.

"Built in 1840, the Hayworth Mansion was abandoned years later during the Great Ske-ske-skedee—"

"Skedaddle," Dad had said, smiling. "The Great Skedaddle."

"The Great *Skedaddle*."

I had never heard that word before, *skedaddle*, but I liked it. I liked the way it made my tongue feel, like it was dancing. In learning to read, I was also learning to fall in love with words; I liked how each one was different, unique, like a fingerprint. How some hissed through my teeth while others rolled off my lips, slippery like oil, and others clacked against the roof of my mouth like a verbal gum smack.

Each new word was a new experience, a new sound. A new feeling. And each combination led to a new story to read, a new world to discover.

"Converted into a hospital by Union soldiers," I continued, "the mansion was later renovated during the—"

I glanced at my dad, eyebrows raised.

"Reconstruction Era," he said.

"Reconstruction Era."

After that day, I started to look at our home in a whole new light. It wasn't just *our* home anymore; somehow, it seemed to belong to both everyone and no one, like we were living inside my sister's dollhouse, an identical pillared mansion Mom had gifted her for Christmas, our family nothing more than the collection of plush fabric dolls some invisible hand ushered from room to room, acting out a scene.

I thought of the prying eyes of the tourists, their fingers wrapped tightly around our torsos, playing with us. Making us dance.

I tried to imagine our ground floor, the main floor, grand piano and tufted couches replaced with rollout cots and bloodied men, their heads wrapped in gauze bandages. I had asked my mother once if any of those soldiers had died—and if so, where were they buried? She had just shrugged, told me that they probably had, and then glanced out the window and into our backyard, eyes glassy and gray. Now the ground floor houses our most important rooms: our foyer, kitchen, living room, mudroom, dining room, and Dad's office, which is strictly off-limits. The middle floor is our floor—a long hallway of bedrooms, most of which are empty—and the third floor is Mom's studio, a giant open room with floor-to-ceiling windows and French doors that swing out onto the patio. She keeps her easel up there; her paints smeared across an old wooden table, her brushes soaking in cloudy water lined up against the wall. It's my favorite floor of the house because of the views.

Sometimes, after dinner, we all go up there together and curl up in blankets on the balcony floor to watch the sunset, a salty breeze making the air stick to our skin.

"Can we have French toast?"

We hit the landing and Margaret unfurls her fingers before scampering into the kitchen. Her limbs are so skinny, her skin so tan, she looks like a fawn darting from a bullet.

"I don't know how to make French toast," I say, following behind her. "How about an omelet?"

"I'm sick of omelets," she says, pulling out a chair with a screech. She clambers on top of it, pulls her legs to her chest, and grabs the baby doll Dad brought home for her after his last business trip. She carries it everywhere now, those porcelain eyes, forever unblinking, trailing us around the house.

"I'll put cheese in it," I say, opening the fridge and stacking everything onto the countertop: a brown carton of eggs, shredded cheddar, milk, chives. I crack the eggs into a bowl and start to whisk with a fork, tossing in the other ingredients while Margaret cradles her doll, singing in the background.

"*Hush little baby, don't say a word. Mama's gonna buy you a mockingbird.*"

I light the stove and start to stir, the skillet hissing and the kitchen starting to fill with the scent of salt and herbs as I pour the creamy mixture onto the hot surface, batting away the steam. I almost don't hear the soft approach of footsteps padding across the landing, the creak of the floorboards as an invisible weight shifts away from the hall and into the kitchen. The arrival of a new voice, light and sweet like frothed milk.

"My darlings."

I turn around and take in the sight of my mother leaning against the kitchen doorframe, watching us. She looks like an angel in her white robe, the gauzy material delicate and thin. I can see the out-line of her legs and hips; the gentle slope of her stomach as she walks across the windows, light shining through.

"You two are getting so grown," she says, opening the windows to let in a breeze before striding over to the table and taking a seat next to Margaret. She rests her head in her hand, her hair a mess of thick, brown curls cascading over her shoulders, and I can see dried remnants of the always-there paint peeking out from behind the sleeve of her robe: royal blue and emerald green and blood red. A rainbow of birthmarks that never really leave. "I wish you could stay my babies forever."

She puts her hand on Margaret's cheek, rubbing her skin with the back of her thumb, and smiles, looking at us in a dreamy kind of bewilderment. Like she almost can't believe we're real.

"Have you named her yet?" she asks, gesturing to Margaret's doll, her fingers absentmindedly twisting through her hair.

"Ellie," Margaret says, tilting her head. "Like Eloise."

Mom is still, quiet, her fingers stuck in the strands.

"Eloise," she repeats.

Then Margaret smiles, nods, and the silence is broken again by her lullaby—"*And if that mockingbird don't sing, Mama's gonna buy you a diamond ring*"—followed by a burst of my mother's laughter, high-pitched and fragile, like shattering glass.

CHAPTER NINE

NOW

I hop into my car and drive downtown, gliding into a parking spot along Chippewa Square. The early March air is crisp and clean, and I decide to stroll without direction until the vigil starts, walking past the fragrant azalea gardens and a tarnished brass statue of General James Oglethorpe looking down on us all. Walking the squares always gives me a sense of peace, a sense of calm, which I know I'll need tonight. Eventually, I find myself on Abercorn, on the outskirts of Colonial Park Cemetery, staring through the giant stone archway topped with that big bronze bird.

There are over ten thousand headstones in that cemetery, a useless piece of trivia I learned on my first day at *The Grit*. I look to the left—the office, my old office, is only a few blocks north, closer to the river. I used to be able to see it every day: the Savannah River, winding in the distance through those gorgeous floor-to-ceiling windows as I sat at my desk, tapping out articles.

"Do you believe in ghosts?"

I remember looking up at Kasey, my tour guide and mentor. She was a lifestyle reporter, too, two years my senior and tasked with greeting me at the front door on my first day of work. I remember thinking everything about her was perfect that day, the surrealism of my dream come true painting everything in a warm, white glow: her blond ringlet curls and the way her talon fingernails tapped against a glass coffee mug filled with a latte dispensed from the office coffee maker. I tried to keep up with her heels clicking against the floor, a restored hardwood, as she gave me the official tour.

"Sorry, what?"

"Ghosts," she repeated. "Savannah is supposed to be haunted. The most haunted city in America, in fact. Even this very building has a ghost story or two."

I looked around, the modern office looking the exact opposite of a haunted house.

"Sometimes, people say they can feel a cold little shiver go down the back of their spine when they're the last one to leave at night."

"Oh." I laughed, unsure if she was kidding. Judging by her expression, she wasn't. "No, actually. I don't think I do."

And that was the truth, sort of. I didn't believe in ghosts—not the traditional kind, anyway, the kind they show in the movies—but my mother used to tell us stories about something else, something harder to explain. She used to tell us that all those little experiences you could never put your finger on—a tickle on the back of your neck, a nagging feeling that you were forgetting something, that creeping sense of déjà vu that flared up when you visited someplace new—were other souls trying to send you a message. Living or dead, it didn't matter. Just other souls. I never thought of it as being *haunted*, exactly. Just gently reminded. A peaceful prodding that there was something that needed to be remembered. Something important. Margaret and I used to try it sometimes, squeezing our eyes shut and attempting to will each other to sneak into the other's bedroom at night or grab a cookie out of the kitchen pantry.

I used to imagine my thoughts guiding her hand like the planchette of a Ouija board; her little body being pulled through the house by an invisible string with me on the other end, tugging it gently. It never worked.

"Well, you're about to." Kasey grinned. "Out that window is Colonial Park Cemetery. Home to over ten thousand headstones, but that's not even the creepiest part. You know Abercorn Street, the sidewalk you walk down to get to Oglethorpe?"

I nodded, tucking a rogue strand of hair behind my ear and letting my fingertips rest on that familiar patch of skin.

"That's technically a part of the cemetery, too, even though it isn't gated. There are bodies buried beneath the sidewalk, the street—*hundreds* of bodies—that people just walk over every single day."

I glanced out the window again, remembering my commute to work. Walking over those very sidewalks. I didn't like to think about it.

"Over here is the art department," she continued, a change in topic so abrupt I felt a bit of whiplash. I looked at a cluster of desks housing giant Mac computers and graphic designers. They waved at me meekly; I waved back. "On this side of the office, we have our editorial team—which, of course, includes you!"

I remember looking at my desk, imagining all the people I would meet and worlds I would explore. Dreaming up all the stories I would get to tell; stories that so perfectly encapsulate an entire way of life that's so familiar to some but so foreign to others, like where to find the best quality bird knives or a long-form feature on a Louisiana shrimper family who supplies seafood up and down the East Coast. Directions on how to make a crawfish étouffé or set a table the proper way; the evolution of country music and the well-kept secret of a perfectly tart tomato pie.

The office was amazing, truly. Everything I had hoped it would be. Even the name, to me, was perfect—*The Grit*—because there was a double meaning to it that rang so true. There was the nod to shrimp and grits, of course, that creamy, decadent, indulgent Southern staple.

But there was also the other noun, *grit*, the one that seemed to hiss through the teeth. A dirty type of determination that reminded me of cane farmers and fishermen and toiling away in the hot summer sun; the sting of a sunburn on your neck and calloused hands and digging out dirt from beneath your fingernails before going home and sitting in front of the air conditioner with a sweet tea in hand. A pebble in your shoe or a sticker chafing against your heel; the remnants of sand coating your tongue after prying open an oyster and swallowing it whole.

It was the effortless blending of those two completely different things into one perfect word. A contradiction, of sorts. But one that made sense.

To be honest, it reminded me of me.

I decide to walk toward Lafayette now, putting some distance between myself and that memory. I don't get within a block of my old office anymore. I didn't know it at the time, but my career at *The Grit* was over before it ever had the chance to start. It's hard to say that I regret them, my choices, because I don't. But when I'm down here, just steps away from where my old life was starting to begin, it's hard not to think about how different it all could have been.

How much I was forced to give up.

I approach the outskirts of the square and notice a faint twinkle in the dimming daylight: a small crowd holding tea candles has already begun to gather, and they remind me of fireflies in the summertime, the way they flicker through the tangles of Spanish moss in the trees. Others are holding flowers, placing them gently against a green fountain lit from the inside. Someone has placed a picture of Mason in the center of it all, his emerald eyes large and unblinking.

"Mrs. Drake."

I twist around at the sound of my name, already knowing who I'll find. Detective Dozier is walking up behind me, two thick thumbs hooked through his belt loops. I remember thinking he was an intimidating figure in March of last year—tall and muscular, with one of those thick handlebar mustaches I've always imagined men only grow to prove to other men they can.

"Detective." I nod in his direction as he approaches me. He doesn't bother to remove his hand for a handshake, so I don't initiate one, either.

"Wanted to let you know we'll have a few undercovers here tonight," he says, glancing around the square. A few more people have trickled in, quietly making their way to the fountain. "Watching the crowd."

"Thank you."

I look at the detective, the tendons in his neck straining as he twists his head to scan the group. This man used to scare me—the way he stood, hovering, his weighty limbs for arms hanging dead by his side; the way he stared, unblinking, or spoke with no emotion, so you never really knew what was on his mind. But in time, a certain numbness has started to creep in every time we're together, like a lethal injection of lidocaine slowly spreading through my veins. I look at him now, and I no longer feel fear or hope or gratitude or anger. I just feel . . . nothing. Nothing at all.

Maybe it's because I've watched him fail too many times.

"I would advise you not to do anything impulsive," he says to me now, his eyes still on the crowd. Then his neck slowly twists so he's back to staring at me again, reminding me of all the times he interrogated me at the station. Grilling me, hard, over and over and over again. Asking the exact same questions, worded in slightly different ways; making me repeat my statement as he studied my façade for cracks.

"What do you mean?" I ask, although I already know.

He stares at me a beat longer, ignoring my question. "I heard about your performance last night."

Performance.

"I'll have some names for you shortly," I say, although I know that's not why he brought it up. "This list is longer than the others. It'll take some time to sift through."

"Mrs. Drake, you are looking for a needle in a haystack. We are working on it. Let us do our jobs."

"Will you look into the names if I send them to you?"

"We'll look into them," he says. "But like I've said many times before, it's a waste of our time. You could be pulling resources away from working another angle. And I'm sure you don't want that, now, do you?"

"Of course not," I say. "Do you *have* another angle? Because if so, I'd love to hear it."

He's quiet, but I can see the muscles in his jaw tense. He doesn't answer, which tells me everything I need to know.

His eyes flutter away from mine and over my shoulder, back to the growing crowd gathering behind me. Then he exhales, digging his thumbs back into his belt loops.

"Your husband's here," he says at last, turning around and walking toward a cluster of trees. "I'll be in the back if you need me."

CHAPTER TEN

The first thing I notice about Ben is his wedding ring. It's snug around his finger, the way it always is when we find ourselves in public. It wasn't there earlier when he showed up on my doorstep. I know because I checked.

He walks over to me now, his arms outstretched, and gives me a hug, burying his nose into my collar. I can feel his other ring around my neck push deep into my chest, and I inhale, smelling those familiar smells: his cologne up close, the spearmint of his mouthwash, the spiced clove of his aftershave that he always dabs on with too heavy a hand. But what I'm really looking for is something else, something different.

I'm looking for traces of *her*.

"Are your parents here?" Ben asks as he pulls back. I watch him glance around the square, looking for their faces hidden somewhere in the crowd, but I shake my head.

"No, they couldn't make it."

Not the truth, really. But not exactly a lie, either.

"Let's go ahead and get started, then. It's about time."

I nod, looking back at the fountain. The sun has set beneath the trees now, and the water seems to be glowing, trickling over the metal lip like molten silver. It reminds me of the marsh in my parent's backyard; the way the moonlight makes it glisten like a pane of smooth glass.

I shiver, whether from the sudden chill in the air or the rush of memories, I can't be sure.

Ben grabs my hand, and we slowly walk to the front. People step aside, making room—too much room—like we give off some kind of aura, a magnetic field that forces everything else away. When we reach the head of the square, I turn around. Just like last night, standing on stage in that auditorium, I feel the gaze of eyes on my skin.

Scrutinizing me as I scrutinize them.

"Thank you all for coming," Ben says, his voice the perfect swirl of gratitude and grief. "As you all know, tonight marks one year since our Mason was taken."

The crowd has grown fairly large by now. There are some stragglers on the outside of the circle; curious tourists, maybe, or people too uncomfortable to get too close. I recognize a few faces—old coworkers, neighbors. Mason's day-care teacher is at the very front, tears in her eyes. Most people are holding candles or cell phones, little dots of light dancing in the air, and I watch as a young girl walks self-consciously toward the fountain and places a stuffed dinosaur on the ground like some kind of ritual sacrifice.

"We're now going to hold a moment of silence," Ben continues, bowing his head. "We ask that you use this time to lift Mason up in prayer. It is our hope that wherever he is, he knows he is loved, and that he'll be brought back to us soon."

I hear a few sniffles erupt; the strangled chokes of the sentimental ones trying to stifle their sobs. Everyone's eyes are on the ground now, but mine stay straight ahead. I want to memorize this crowd. I want to see who stands out—an unlikely face, maybe, or a total stranger who seems out of place. I see a flash of movement in the back, something red, and as I strain to catch a glimpse, my eyes land squarely on Detective Dozier's, watching me from the back. His eyes burrowing into my skull like a warning.

It's dark after the vigil is over, the center of the square overflowing with flowers and melting candles and tiny little toys that will be snatched up by the garbage collectors as soon as we leave. I'm still not ready to go home yet, not ready to face the silence of my house and another long, lonely stretch of night, so I stay in the square for a little bit longer, sitting on the wrought-iron bench overlooking the fountain.

"Isabelle?"

I twist to the side at the sound of my name, taking in the familiar face of my past. She looks mostly the same, though it's been years since I've seen her, her long, ringlet curls now clipped to her shoulders, their formerly blond color now more of a natural, burnt brown.

"Hey, Kasey."

"Oh my God," she says, her eyes bulging at the sight of me before she recovers quickly. "How are you?"

It's strange sometimes, seeing myself through the eyes of the people who know me. In the mirror, my transformation has been gradual—a daily withering away, like a slow starvation or a decaying body—but to *them*, I can see the shock of it at once, like a swift slap to the face.

"Oh, you know." I smile, not bothering with a real answer.

Her expression shifts again, like she's suddenly remembered who I am, what I've been through. She tries one more time, tilting her head and dropping her voice to a whisper as she takes a seat beside me, her hand on my knee.

"How are you holding up?"

The gesture is unexpected, catching me off guard. I look down at her hand, then back at her face.

"As well as can be expected, I think."

"We all miss you," she says at last. "So much."

I bite my cheek, trying to stifle a grimace, because I know that's not true. I know what they all think of me.

"It's been seven years," I say instead, turning to face her. "I'm sure you've moved on."

"God, that long?" she asks. "Time flies, doesn't it?"

"It sure does."

"Do you want to grab a drink or something?" she asks, her voice perking up. "I was just on my way to Sky High to meet some of the crew."

I bite my lip, remembering that restaurant everyone went to after late nights at the office. I haven't stepped foot in that place since the last time Kasey and I were there together, at *The Grit*'s annual Christmas party, only two months into my employment.

"Not tonight," I say, smiling. "Thanks, though."

"Okay," she says, standing up slowly. She looks down at me, her face a mixture of pity and concern. "Let me know if you change your mind. It's an open invitation."

I watch as she walks away, her hands stuffed into the pockets of her coat. When she reaches the edge of the square, I watch as she stops, like she's trying to decide if she should turn back around.

Finally, she does, her eyes finding mine in the dark.

"You don't have to do this alone, you know. It's okay to ask for help."

Something about her voice makes me feel like she's wanted to say that for a long, long time. Like she's thought about it, churned it around in her mind, only to lose her nerve and file it away for some other, faraway time. I don't exactly know how to respond to that, so instead I just nod and watch as she smiles at me again, something sad and resigned, before turning back around, her heels still clicking as she makes her way across the street.

CHAPTER ELEVEN

There's a cold chill in the air now, a sharp bite that causes me to stand up and walk into the cathedral across the street, a towering basilica just past the square with twin pointed arches that seem to jut straight into the stars. I've never been religious—even less so now—but it seems like a good place to go at the moment. A good place to sit and think. To formulate a plan.

It's close to empty inside, a few people sitting, praying, or wandering around the aisles with their necks craned to the ceiling. I can hear the echo of footsteps around me as I take a seat in the back, the old wooden pew groaning against my weight.

Then I exhale, close my eyes.

I can still remember trailing Kasey around the office that very first time, my eyes glassy and bright. Taking in the belongings situated on top of my desk—*my desk*—and my name, ISABELLE RHETT: LIFESTYLE REPORTER, etched onto the shiny gold nameplate.

"And here," she had said, opening an office door with a gust of bravado as we reached the pinnacle of her tour, "is the man we have to thank for it all."

I had poked my head into the editor in chief's office, ready to introduce myself, when the blood suddenly drained from my face.

It was him.

In front of me, the man from the bar was sitting behind a giant mahogany desk. He smiled at me, a playful kind of grin, like he was the big reveal on some kind of game show, only I couldn't tell if I had won or lost.

"Welcome, Isabelle."

I could feel a burning in my cheeks, knowing my face was quickly morphing into a deep crimson red, just like it had after we collided into each other that night on the water. For a moment, I forgot how to speak. I had lost my voice—it was stuck, lodged somewhere deep in my throat like a chunk of stale bread—although *his* voice was smooth and familiar, flowing easily from his lips like decanted wine.

"Hi," I finally managed to say. I remember looking down at the nameplate on his desk, his name—BENJAMIN DRAKE—embossed in gold. I had known that was the editor in chief's name, of course; it was written at the top of every masthead. But he had introduced himself as *Ben.* The most common name in the world. I had never seen a picture of him before, and of course I hadn't interviewed with the editor in chief for an entry-level position. I had no way to recognize his voice. "Thank you so much for this opportunity."

"Of course." He smiled. I looked down at his hands folded on his desk; at the gold wedding band stretched tight across his finger. The wedding band I couldn't see when he was wearing gloves. "Kasey, if you'll give us a second."

Kasey smiled beside me, slipping back through the door and closing it with a click. Once we were alone, that night came rushing back to me in a flash: our bodies pushed together close, talking for what felt like hours. His face when I had told him I was a writer for *The Grit*—and me, just assuming he was impressed. But that wasn't the right expression, I finally understood. It was shock, maybe. A realization that he had just found himself spending the better part of a Friday evening chatting up not only his new coworker, but his new employee. A twenty-five-year-old subordinate.

And then, of course, there was that kiss. The way I had pushed myself up on my toes and leaned in; the way I had cupped his cheek in my hand before taking off to the bathroom; coming back out and realizing that he was gone. Walking home alone, embarrassed and confused and a little too buzzed, replaying the night over and over and over in my mind, trying to unearth a missed signal or an overlooked sign.

"I loved it, by the way."

I blinked, trying to find the words. He was staring right at me, *talking* to me, and still, all I could think about was that kiss. Certainly, he wasn't bringing that up right now . . . was he?

"I'm—I'm sorry?"

"Your article," he clarified. "The one you attached with your application. I read the whole thing."

"Oh," I exhaled. "Oh, right. Thank you."

Applying for *The Grit* required a hefty portfolio of previously published bylines, but being only a few years out of college, I didn't have many to share. Instead, I attached a story I had written on my own about a dolphin that had been seen lingering around the Beaufort harbor for longer than normal; you could tell it was the same one because of the little bite mark on her dorsal fin. I had wanted to know what it was doing there—day after day, swimming in circles—so I asked the dockhand at the marina.

"She's grieving," he had told me.

"Grieving what?"

"Her calf."

I must have looked confused, notebook in hand, because the old man flung a greasy towel over his shoulder and kept talking.

"Dolphins are complex creatures, darlin'. They have emotions, like you and me. That one there just lost a newborn a couple weeks ago. If you look close, you can see her pushin' it around."

"Pushing what around?"

"Her calf," he said again. "Her baby."

I remember squinting then, straining my eyes against the glare of the sun. And he was right: There wasn't just one dolphin in the distance, there were two. One was alive, and one, much smaller, was dead.

"How long is she going to do that?"

I felt a peculiar mix of emotions in that moment: sympathy, yes, but also a sense of disgust at this animal pushing around the corpse of her dead baby, bloated and bobbing like some kind of gruesome pool float. It reminded me of a recent story I had seen in the news about a mother who kept her stillborn in the freezer, nestled among the vegetables.

"As long as it takes," he responded. "As long as it takes to grieve."

"That seems like a strange way to grieve."

"Nothin' about grief makes sense." He shook his head. "Not for any of us."

I later learned through my interviews that nobody knew how the calf had died. Sometimes it happens in childbirth, they explained, sometimes right after. And sometimes, male dolphins engage in a behavior called calf tossing, where they bash a baby to death in order to free up the mother for their own sexual needs—although that detail I left out. That wasn't the story I wanted to tell.

But still, there was something so magnetically macabre about it all. About these creatures, so beautiful and serene, having a darker side. A violent side.

"Excuse me."

I feel a tap on my arm now, making me jump. My neck jerks around, and my eyes adjust to find an old woman standing behind me, her leathery arm outstretched as it hovers over my shoulder.

"The cathedral is closing in five minutes."

"Oh," I say, the beating of my heart starting to slow. I look around, realizing the place is completely empty now. That the people perusing the aisles have long since left, and I've still been sitting here, oblivious. Totally alone. "I'm sorry . . . what time is it? I was just looking for a place to sit—"

"It's fine," she says, her eyes weary but kind. She must see the panicked confusion in my face—the way I'm glancing around, looking for any indication of how much time has passed—because she places her hand on my arm now, squeezing gently. "There's a group that meets on Monday nights, if you're interested."

"A group?"

"Grief counseling," she says. "Around back. You'll see a sign outside the service door."

"Oh, no—" I start, reaching for my purse. But suddenly, I remember Kasey's eyes finding mine in the dark. Her voice, gentle and low.

"You don't have to do this alone, you know. It's okay to ask for help."

"You don't have to say anything," the woman says, winking, sensing my hesitation. "You can just sit."

I collect my things and step back into the brisk night air, walking around the side of the building. The square is eerily empty now, still except for the faint flicker of the remaining candles not yet blown out by the wind, and once I reach the back of the church, I find an open service door, cheap fluorescent light leaking out onto the sidewalk.

I poke my head inside, the smell of bitter coffee pricking at my senses.

"Welcome."

I turn to the side, taking in the woman before me. She looks young, in her late twenties, with olive skin and glossy brown hair pinned back at the sides. Her eyes are large—domineering, almost— and when she smiles, two dimples emerge on her cheeks, slits like gashes deep enough to scar.

"I'm Valerie," she says, extending her hand. It takes a second, but slowly, her expression shifts, the dimples disappearing as her smile fades.

She recognizes me. Of course she does.

"Isabelle," I say, even though I need no introduction.

I peek farther into the room, noticing the metal chairs arranged in a circle and the folding table set up in the back. There are carafes of coffee, rows of pastries, all of the stereotypically sad things you'd expect to find at a place like this.

"I saw the candles," the woman says, gesturing to the open door. "It looked very nice out there."

"Thank you."

"Are you joining us tonight?"

I hesitate, glancing back at the chairs, but all I can see are the chairs in that auditorium. All of those glowing eyes, staring. Judging.

"No," I say at last, shaking my head. "I was just curious, I guess."

The woman smiles, a knowing look in her eyes. She opens her mouth, ready to speak again, when we're interrupted by a noise behind me. I swing around, my eyes landing on an older gentleman who's just shuffled through the open door. He looks apologetic for interrupting us, gesturing meekly to the circle of chairs before walking toward them and taking a seat. The smell of cigarette smoke follows close behind him, mixed with the sickly sweet scent of brown liquor.

"Sorry," I say, feeling suddenly embarrassed, though I'm not even sure why. Maybe just for showing up here, in this vulnerable place. "I should probably go."

"You're welcome to join us any time," the woman says. "We're here every Monday. Eight o'clock."

I smile and nod, flashing a grateful wave before stepping outside and walking back toward my car. I'm digging my hand around in my purse now, feeling for my keys, when my fingers wrap around something thin and hard, like a notecard. A business card. I pull it out, my fingertips running across the name embossed on thick, black paper.

Waylon Spencer.

Suddenly, I remember that man on the plane. That was only yesterday, the way he had looked at me and offered his help. It felt a little slimy then—opportunistic, right on the heels of that conference—but his words are ringing loudly in my ear now, a tempting pull.

"With a podcast, you wouldn't have to talk to all those people. Not directly, anyway. You'd just have to talk to me."

I keep walking toward my car, my mind on all the people in my life who take it upon themselves to dissect my every move: Ben, Detective Dozier. The judging eyes of the audience members whose names now sit on my dining room table, taunting me even more.

It would be nice, I think. *Not having to convince all these people of my innocence, my pain. Only having to convince one.*

I look at Waylon's business card, scanning his information. Then I pull my phone out of my pocket, before I can think twice, and navigate to my Inbox, launching a new email and beginning to type.

CHAPTER TWELVE

THEN

The air has a gelatinous quality to it today, sluggish and wet. It reminds me of gravy dripping from a serving spoon, concentrated and thick, pooling into various creases and settling there. Turning everything damp.

Margaret and I are outside by the water, the thin fabric of our nightgowns sticking to our skin with sweat. We're sitting on the grass, pretzel-style, trying to savor the little gusts of wind that occasionally find their way to us through the trees. It's usually breezy out here, but right now it's painfully still, like even the clouds are holding their breath.

"Tea?"

I look up at my sister, my eyes adjusting to the sudden brightness of the sky above us. She's arranged the garden statues in a semicircle, a plastic teacup placed before each one. We're a peculiar party, I have to say, Margaret and I, with our humidity-soaked hair, crimped and wild, and our matching white nightgowns. Necks itchy with ribbons and lace. We're two years apart, but Mom still dresses us in coordinating outfits, even when we're sleeping. Like we come in a set: life-sized nesting dolls.

I imagine opening myself up at the stomach, placing Margaret snugly inside. It feels like that sometimes. Like she's mine to protect. Like without her, I'm hollow.

I glance at the statues: a frog playing the ukulele, a baby with wings. There's a woman directly across from me, bigger than the others, her mouth hanging open and her stone eyes looking directly into mine. She used to be a fountain, I think, but she hasn't been hooked up in ages. Instead, there's some kind of black algae trickling out of her mouth. My gaze follows as it cascades down her chin, her neck. It almost looks like she's possessed.

"Ma'am?"

I look back at Margaret. She's holding out a pitcher, her eyes darting back and forth between me and the cup and saucer she's placed in front of me.

"Please," I say in my best British accent. I lift the cup and make a show of pushing my pinkie up, sky-high, because I know it'll make her laugh. Margaret giggles, tilting the pitcher with both hands. It's too heavy for her, I can tell, and the ice and liquid comes barreling out and overflows out of my cup and into the grass.

"My apologies," she says, licking the side of the pitcher before placing it back down. For some reason, it makes me smile. The way she says it, like a little adult. She heard it somewhere, I'm sure—Mom on the phone, maybe, or on some TV show—chewing it over in her mind before parroting it back.

She's always watching, always listening. Always absorbing life like a sponge, silent and porous and malleable in our hands.

"I saw the footprints."

My neck snaps toward Margaret, still standing above me, her head tilted to the side like a curious bird. I was hoping she hadn't noticed those—those faint, muddy prints trailing their way from the hall to my bed—but I should have known better. Margaret notices everything.

"Do you go outside?" she asks. "At night?"

I don't know how to answer that, so instead, I glance back toward the marsh, my eyes on the water lapping against the dock as I try to conjure up a memory dancing somewhere in my subconscious. Somewhere out of reach.

"I guess," I say at last.

"What do you do?"

"I don't know."

"Do you go swimming?"

"I don't know," I repeat, closing my eyes.

"Why can't you just sleep normal?"

"*I don't know*, Margaret."

She plops down next to me, her bare legs coppery and smooth. I watch as she pushes a few strands of sweaty hair off of her forehead before she turns to me again, all those questions swirling in her eyes.

"Is it because of what happened?"

It comes to me in flashes, like something out of a nightmare: me, creeping down the hallway, careful not to get caught. Dad, pacing the halls, white knuckles around a bottle of brown liquid while my mother lay splayed out on a mattress, white sheets staining red.

"We're not supposed to talk about that," I say.

"This house is a little creepy sometimes."

I glance back to the house, standing tall at the top of that giant hill. I've lived my entire life in this house; aged from a newborn baby cradled in my mother's arms to now a very independent eight. And as I've aged, things have changed. *I've* changed. We all have, really. We've all turned into something different, almost unrecognizable, mutating with time like the wood itself.

"Yeah," I agree. "It's so big, so old. Lots of noises."

"You ever feel like we're not alone in it?"

I think about the plaque bolted out front and all the other people who have called this place home. The statues that seem to have minds of their own and the soldiers who died here, their bodies probably scattered around the property, piles of bones buried beneath the floorboards

"It's just me. Walking around," I say, because I can't bring myself to tell her that I feel it, too: the company of something otherworldly that I can't quite name. The ever-present aura of something, or some-one, trying to warn us, scare us. I can't even bring myself to kill bugs here. Whenever I watch my dad slap at a beetle with a rolled-up newspaper or pop a tick between his fingers, I instinctively flinch and say a little prayer, knowing that each one is just adding to the body count. Tipping the scales of this place even further in the direction of death.

I twist back toward Margaret, but she isn't facing me anymore. She's facing the water, and I can see her spine protrude from the back of her neck, a skinny little centipede slithering beneath the skin.

"Try not to worry about it," I say at last.

Margaret nods, her eyes still trained on something in the distance, and I follow her gaze to the giant oak tree on the edge of our property, its mangled limbs hanging directly over the water and the Spanish moss twisted into its bark like knotted hair. It's low tide now, the water slowly retreating, and I can hear the clicking of tiny fiddler crabs as they climb over one another, their movement making it seem as though the ground is alive, breathing.

CHAPTER THIRTEEN

NOW

I tried to get some rest yesterday. To prepare.

I took a couple of sleeping pills at noon and sunk into my couch, letting my lids grow heavy. Then I felt my eyeballs roll back, a redness dripping over my vision as I stared at the inside of my own skin, my veins. As I let my mind wander for a while, getting lost in a feverish kind of dream—an open window, that prehistoric stench of the marsh—but still on the brink of consciousness.

Somewhere in between, like purgatory.

I glance at the clock before making my way over to my laptop and skimming a few emails—some true crime fans who managed to find my address; a couple of interview requests, mostly trash—and click back over to the TrueCrimeCon article I was reading on Monday. I refresh, scrolling back down to the comments to see if there's anything new.

So we're just going to ignore this woman's history, then? Her past?

Leave her alone! She's a grieving mother.

That poor child. Let's not forget he's the real victim here.

He's in a better place.

I feel a catch in my throat, my mouse hovering over the last one.

He's in a better place. It was left yesterday, one year from the day of Mason's disappearance. My eyes scan the username. It's generic, a mess of random numbers and letters with a default gray silhouette as the profile picture. I try to click on it, but it takes me nowhere.

I wonder what that means: *He's in a better place.* I stare at it, my eyes drilling into the screen until the letters start to blur and double. I get lost there for a second, staring, until I shake my head and copy the URL, composing a new email to Detective Dozier and dropping it into the body.

"*Read the last comment,*" I type. "*Can we trace the IP address?*"

I shoot the email off with a *swoosh* and close my eyes again, exhaling slowly. Then I stand up, grab my purse, and force myself to walk out the door.

I make my way inside a little corner bistro called Framboise, a place near the office I used to frequent for lunch. I'm early, intentionally, so I take a seat at the bar and order a glass of Sancerre and a crock of French onion soup—but when the food arrives, I can't bring myself to eat. Instead, I take my spoon and push down on the melted cheese, watching the brown liquid gush through the top and start to pool.

It reminds me of a footprint in pluff mud, swamp water leaking out.

I stare into the bowl, setting myself adrift for a second. I can hear the street getting noisier as the square comes alive with art school students walking home from class and young professionals sneaking away from their desks to catch a happy hour special. I vaguely register lights from outside twinkling in the distance; the clack of horse-drawn carriages pulling tourists to dinner across rough cobblestone roads. It's a rhythmic sound, peaceful. Like the steady click of a metronome or a fingernail tapping against a glass pane window.

I feel my head start to bob, heavy, like it's slowly filling with sand. Like soon my neck won't be able to hold it on its own. Like it might topple over and break.

Click-click-click-click.

"Mrs. Drake?"

I jolt at the sudden closeness of a voice, my head popping up like someone yanked me back by my hair. I glance around for a clock and try to imagine how I must have looked, staring down at the bar top, a hazy mist coating my eyes for God-knows-how-long.

Five seconds, maybe. Five minutes. My body, here, but my mind, somewhere else. Somewhere far away.

"Sorry," I say, looking up, blinking a few times to clear the fog from my eyes. "I was lost in thought for a second there—"

I have to squint to make out his face in the dim restaurant light, my eyes still bleary, and it takes me a moment to recognize him. It's Waylon—of course it is, that deep, velvety voice—hovering just above the empty barstool next to mine. I rub my eyes, trying to pull it together. The bar is busier than it was when I first sat down; my soup, still untouched beneath me, already congealed.

"Do you mind if I sit?" he asks. I can tell he's uncomfortable, like he's intruding on a private dinner instead of simply showing up at the place and time we had agreed.

"Of course not," I say, gesturing to the barstool beside me. I watch as he glances around the restaurant before self-consciously ducking his head as he sits, as if to make himself seem smaller. "Thanks for coming on such short notice."

"Are you kidding?" he asks, flagging down the bartender and ordering a whiskey on the rocks. "I dropped everything when I got your note."

I take a sip of my wine. Back when I emailed him on Monday night, I wasn't really sure *what* I was proposing—just that I was open to trying something new, something different. Something that might actually work. He had responded within seconds, almost as if he had been sitting right there on his own computer, waiting for me. Willing me to hit *Send*.

"Savannah's a cool town," he says, his arms vaguely gesturing around us. It's a well-intentioned attempt at small talk, I know, before diving into the real reason we're here.

"It is."

"Have you always lived here?"

"No," I say, hesitating. I don't really want to elaborate, but when Waylon is still quiet, still staring at me, I keep talking to fill the empty space. "No, I'm from Beaufort, South Carolina. It's another coastal city, albeit smaller than Savannah. Port Royal Island."

"What was growing up in Beaufort like?"

I stop and stare at Waylon, suspicion creeping into my chest.

"I'd prefer not to talk about that."

Waylon raises his eyebrows, and I feel my heart begin to race, beating hard in my throat. I realize now that no matter how many times I've done this, no matter how many times I've told my story, this time, it's different. This isn't detached, standing on a stage somewhere and reciting the same thing over and over again to strangers at a distance.

This time, it's personal. I have no idea what questions he might ask. I have no way to escape.

"Fair enough," he says at last, taking a sip of his whiskey. "Let's jump right in, then. Why don't you tell me a bit about that night? How it started?"

He already knows this, I'm sure. He saw my keynote—besides, you can find it all through a simple Google search, an archived news broadcast, one of the hundreds of articles that have been written about that awful March night. I imagine he just wants to hear it all in my own words, unscripted, so I tell him about how I put Mason to bed, like I always do, around seven o'clock. How I read him a story, though I'm not sure which one it was. How I had turned on his night-light, blew him a kiss from the hallway, and closed the door behind me.

"My husband and I stayed up for another few hours after that," I say. "We watched some TV, had a couple glasses of wine. I poked my head in to check on him around eleven, saw that he was still sleeping, and then went to bed."

"Did you hear anything strange during the night? Any noises?"

"No. I used to be a very heavy sleeper."

"Used to be?"

"Not so much anymore," I say, but I don't elaborate.

"So your husband could have gotten up, and you wouldn't have noticed?"

I shoot him a look, my eyebrow cocked. "He was questioned extensively, obviously. I mean, yeah, I guess he could have, but Ben wouldn't hurt our son. He had no reason to. We were happy."

"What about the neighbors?" Waylon asks. "Did they see anything?"

I shake my head, sipping silently.

"And what time did you notice he was gone?"

I'm quiet, replaying that morning again in my mind. How I had woken up early, around six, the way I always did. How I had brewed my coffee, puttered around the kitchen. Wasted two precious hours scrolling through Instagram and reading the newspaper and scrambling eggs before I had ever even thought to check on him. Because that's the thing about time: It feels endless in the mornings, the day stretched out before you like a long yawn. I remember actually feeling relieved as it continued to drag on, slow and uneventful, no noises erupting from beneath his bedroom door. No screams or whines or cries. I was grateful that he was sleeping in, that I had a few more moments of quiet than normal. Of precious time to myself.

I didn't realize that the second I poked my head into his bedroom, I would soon be racing against it. Begging it to stop.

"A little after eight."

"Any clues?" he asks, a burning intensity in his eyes. I look down at his drink, notice the way he's twirling his glass in rhythmic circles. "Prints? DNA?"

"An open window," I say. "I'm almost positive I closed it the night before. Sometimes we opened it, to let the fresh air in, but I never would have—"

I stop, exhale, take another drink.

"They found our fingerprints on the windowsill, obviously, but nobody else's. There was a partial shoeprint in the mud outside his window—it had rained that morning—but not enough to glean any real meaning from it."

"Estimated shoe size?"

"They think it may have been somewhere between a size nine and a size eleven, but we had workers, too. Lots of people who could have left it. The exterminator came the day before and sprayed in that exact spot, so we don't even know if he's the one—"

"You keep saying *he*," Waylon interrupts. "Do you know the person who took him is a he?"

"Well, no," I admit. "But the vast majority of stranger kidnappings are committed by men."

"Well, the alternative to a stranger kidnapping is the kidnapper being someone in the family," he says. "Someone close."

"Yes," I say, biting my cheek. "And the vast majority of parental kidnappings are committed by women. The mother. So why don't we get that out of the way right now?"

I look at Waylon, my eyes unflinching.

"I didn't hurt my son. I didn't do anything to him. I'm trying to find the person who *did*."

"That's . . . not what I was implying," Waylon responds, his hands raised in surrender. He looks genuinely uncomfortable, once again surprised at my sudden outburst, like that time on the plane, so I simply nod and turn back toward the bar, my cheeks burning as I scan all the different bottles of amber liquid glistening in the dim light.

"Is there anything else you think is worth mentioning?" he asks, trying to gently nudge us along again. "Clues, I mean?"

"Yes," I say, a squeeze in my chest. "They found his stuffed animal when they were searching the neighborhood. A dinosaur he used to sleep with."

"Where in the neighborhood?"

I'm quiet, sticking my finger in the glass and swiping at a speck of sediment stuck to the rim.

"On the banks of the marsh," I say finally. "In the mud."

"I'm assuming they searched the marsh, though, right? For any other clues? Or . . ."

"Helicopters, divers," I say, answering his question preemptively so he doesn't have to say what I know he's thinking: a body. *Him*. "They didn't find anything else—though, of course, with the falling tide, any of his other belongings could have been pulled into the ocean, so we may never know."

"Do you have any theories?" he asks at last. "What do *you* think happened?"

I sigh, picturing all those articles on my dining room wall; the lists of names that I scour through, night after night, hoping against hope that something important might finally leap from the shadows and make itself known.

"I have no idea," I say at last, and that's the ugly truth of it. No matter how many nights I've spent awake, poring over his case file or pounding on doors or scrubbing the internet for some subtle clue, I still have no idea what happened to my son.

I have no idea where he is.

"None of it makes any sense," I continue. "You have no idea how many times I've retraced my footsteps of that night, tried to remember some detail that might be the key to it all. Some tiny little thing that was out of place—"

"Maybe you need to stop retracing your footsteps," Waylon interrupts, his eyes on the side of my face. "Maybe you need to try a new path."

I turn and look at him, my eyes flickering over his features in the dark.

"Maybe." I shrug, turning back toward the bar. "That's why I emailed you."

We're both still as the bartender walks toward us, taking a little too long to clean the inside of a highball glass. I can see his eyes flitter over to us a few times, and I wonder if he recognizes me. I wonder how much he's heard. Finally, another patron flags him down, and he's forced to move on.

"Didn't you have a baby monitor?" Waylon asks, as if it suddenly occurred to him that the entire thing might have been caught on camera. It feels accusatory, the way he says it, but I could be projecting.

I close my eyes, bow my head. It takes a few seconds for me to work up the courage to answer this one, and when I do, I can hear my voice crack.

"Yes," I say. "We do. We *did*. It was wireless, but the batteries were dead, so it wasn't recording."

Waylon is quiet. He's thinking, I'm sure, about all the little ways this should have gone so differently. About how I should have double-checked that the window was closed, maybe even locked it. About how I should have been sleeping with one ear open, ready to run to him if he called out. About how I should have checked on him as soon as I had woken up, called the police at six instead of eight, or how I should have changed the batteries in the baby monitor the second I realized they were dead instead of waiting until it was convenient for me to run to the store.

"It's not your fault," he says instead, downing the last of the tawny liquid at the bottom of his glass. "You know that, right?"

I feel the sting of tears in my eyes, so I squeeze them shut, swallowing the rock I feel lodged in my throat. I'm not used to hearing that. Then I rub a rogue tear away from my cheek with the back of my hand and nod, smile, thank him for his words. Because I don't want to tell him that somewhere, deep down, it seems like it is. And I'm not just talking about mom guilt, that secret society reserved for mothers that batters one single notion into our brains over and over and over again: That no matter what we do, no matter how hard we try, we're doing it all wrong. That every little thing is our fault; that we're unfit, unworthy. That our shortcomings are the cause of every scream and tear and trembling lip.

This is something more than that.

It's that *feeling* again, the one my own mother warned me about. That feeling that someone, somewhere, is trying to tell me something. That I'm missing something—something big.

That I *know* something. But I can't, for the life of me, remember what it is.

CHAPTER FOURTEEN

It's late when I get home, after midnight. Maybe I can blame it on the Sancerre, or the dim lights that made it hard to discern how much time had passed, or the knowledge that there was nothing waiting for me back home other than an empty house and another long, dark stretch of quiet. Another perpetual waiting for those first little glimmers of normal life that only emerged with the sun.

But whatever it was, Waylon and I stayed seated on those barstools for a very long time.

I step into my house now and greet Roscoe at the door, scratching behind his ears before pulling off my coat and making my way toward the kitchen. Then I pour myself a glass of water before walking to my laptop.

"Give me one minute," I say to him, tapping the keys as the glow of the screen illuminates my face in the dark. I refresh my browser and check my email: no response from Dozier. Then I take a deep drink and click back to the article, scrolling down to the comments again, the liquid suddenly lodging in my windpipe, making me choke. I sputter out a gag, slamming the glass down on the table as I feel the water claw at the lining of my throat.

I cough, blink a few times to clear the tears from my eyes, and refresh it again, but it doesn't matter. It still looks the same.

The comment is gone.

"*Shit,*" I whisper, leaning back into my chair. I should have taken a screenshot. I refresh again, just to be sure, and am met with the same blank screen where that sentence stared back at me just a few hours ago.

He's in a better place.

I stand up and slip off my shoes before lacing up a pair of sneakers and fastening Roscoe's leash to his collar. Even though I just got home, I have an urgent need to get out of this house again. It feels like there's something heavy settling over it, like the sensation of a storm as it moves quickly and quietly across the sky: bloated and ominous. It doesn't feel safe.

I exhale as soon as we get outside, the cool night air filling my lungs and making them burn. We walk down our porch steps, and Roscoe veers right, the way he always does, until suddenly, I hear Waylon's voice in my head, enveloping me like a blanket of fog.

"*Maybe you need to stop retracing your footsteps. Maybe you need to try a new path.*"

I give Roscoe a tug, stopping him in his tracks.

"Let's go this way," I say, turning left, forcing him to follow. "Do something a little different tonight."

We walk silently for a while, venturing deeper into the darkness, the road like an inkblot bleeding into the distance. As usual, the houses are dead, all their lights off. There's a deafening quiet to the neighborhood, more so than usual, and it's making my thoughts ring a little louder, rattling around in my mind like loose change in a jar.

I'm used to thinking about Mason, of course. Talking about Mason. But lately, I've been thinking about other things, too. About Ben and our beginnings; about Margaret and my parents. About what happened back then and how my entire life seems to be one giant question mark. A string of ellipses and unresolved endings, the answers dark and murky, like sitting on the dock, feet submerged in the water, trying to find your toes through the muck.

And then there's that feeling again. That feeling that the answers are so close, within my reach. That someone, somewhere, is trying to tell me something—or that I already *know* something, and I just can't retain the thought. It's like waking up groggy and trying to remember a dream, the outlines of it fuzzy and fading. Racking your brain, attempting to recall words or shapes or sounds or smells, anything to get you just a little bit closer to the truth.

But after too much time, it withers away, getting erased from your memory, like the ashes of a burnt building getting swept up in the breeze.

Roscoe and I have been walking for about twenty minutes now, and although I'm not as familiar with this part of the neighborhood, I can tell that we're starting to make our way back home. We're nearing the marsh, and at this point, my pupils have fully dilated, my eyes adjusted to the night. I can see things more clearly: the outline of toys abandoned in front yards, soggy newspapers left in driveways. An overturned garbage can, the owners too lazy to secure the lid. There's trash scattered across the sidewalk, the work of raccoons, and that's the problem: Nobody ever stops to wonder what happens in the dead of night, all the things that take place when the world is unconscious. The strangers who lurk in the shadows, crouching low beneath a window or twisting the knob of an unlocked door. The animals who hunt, warm blood dripping from their teeth as they feast on the meat of another. We just assume that when we fall asleep, the world does, too. We expect it to resume exactly as it was in the morning, untouched. Unbothered. As if life just stops because we have.

But that's not true. Even before Mason was taken, I knew it wasn't true. I was always keenly aware of the evils that mask themselves in the cloak of night; the horrors that haunt the world while we sleep.

Roscoe and I are on the street parallel to my own now, just about to turn the corner, when the silence is broken by a low growl.

"Hey," I say, yanking his leash. "Stop that."

He keeps growling, the noise getting louder, angrier, his paws planted firmly on the concrete and his tail pointed back. He's staring at something across the street, a house, and when I follow his gaze beneath the streetlight, I let out a small yelp, my hand jumping to my chest.

"I'm so sorry," I say, exhaling, feeling my heart thump hard beneath my bones. "I didn't see you there."

There's a man sitting on his front porch, just a few feet away. He looks old, maybe in his eighties, wearing a thick brown robe cinched tight at the waist. His hair is gray and disheveled, his eyes distant and dull. He's sitting silently in a rocking chair, his slippered feet pushing himself back and forth. A gentle creaking barely audible despite the quiet of the night.

"Nice evening," I say, smiling. Trying to break the tension. "I don't believe we've met. I'm your neighbor, Isabelle. I live just over there—"

I start to point back toward my house, one street over, but the man doesn't respond. Instead, he turns to me and continues to stare—at me, through me. I wonder if maybe he's deaf or blind; if he can't hear or see me. If my body is just a vague blur in front of him, no different from a shadow. My voice, a gust of wind.

I wonder what he's doing right now, sitting alone on his porch at one in the morning. It seems strange, too late to be outside. But then I suppose he could say the same for me.

"All right, well. Have a good one."

I pull Roscoe, forcing him to follow, all the while feeling the man's eyes on my back. Once we make it home and step inside, I lock the door behind me with a little more urgency than normal, though I can't put my finger on why. It's not as though that man could be dangerous, trailing me in the dark.

It's only later—around three in the morning, as I'm mindlessly flipping through channels, sinking deep into the couch—when I realize what it is.

All this time, there's been an inherent strangeness to my nights, knowing that I'm awake while everyone else is asleep. Knowing that, in a neighborhood full of people, I'm completely alone. It makes me feel otherworldly, different. Like the only fish swimming across a never-ending ocean; like anything could happen and not a soul would see. But now, seeing that man—his eyes like peeled grapes as he stared into the darkness; the way he creaked back and forth in his rocking chair, a methodical rhythm, like someone had wound up a key in his back and left him to sway—I understand that there's something even more unsettling than being alone in the dark.

It's realizing that you're not really alone at all.

CHAPTER FIFTEEN

THEN

I sneak down the hallway, toes pointed, my bare feet avoiding the boards that are prone to creaking. I know them all: the soft spots in the wood that shift under the weight of my heel; the rusty door hinges that whine in the night. Margaret and I have turned this house into our own enchanted labyrinth—roaming halls, twisting doorknobs. Poking our heads inside barely used rooms and holding our breath as we trail our hands across the furniture, leaving behind nothing but finger streaks in the dust. The corridor looms before me now like a tongue rolling out of the depths of a darkened throat, but still, I force myself forward. Into the underbelly of the house.

It's quiet, but my parents are awake. I can hear them shut inside Dad's office. I can hear them whisper.

"You don't know what it's like," my mother says, her voice like silk that's starting to tear. "Henry, you don't understand."

I feel a rock lodge in my throat, and I swallow, trying to force it down. Dad works in Washington—the Rhetts have been in Congress since my grandfather's grandfather, or so the story goes—but he always comes home for the weekend before turning around and leaving again every Monday morning. He usually brings Margaret and me some kind of present when he's back—candied pralines or boiled peanuts or bags of thick, juicy scuppernongs that he picks up from a roadside vendor on his drive back from the airport—a reminder of his love for us that has slowly started to feel more like an apology. Or a bribe.

"I need you to come home," she continues. "Stay home with me. Please."

"You know I can't do that," my father says, his voice low and stern. "Elizabeth, you know that. You've always known that."

"I don't know if I can do it anymore. I'm starting to feel . . . I don't know. The girls. Some days, I look at them, and I—"

"Yes you can," he says. "You can do this. The girls are fine."

Margaret brought it up again at dinner tonight: those footprints on my carpet, muddy and fading like my memory, my mind. I can still hear the clank of my mother's fork as she dropped it; my father, staring at us, probably imagining me wandering into the marsh at night. My white nightgown sticking to my ankles, my calves, my thighs. The water moving higher and higher until it poured down my throat.

"Maybe if we could just get some help," my mother says now, her voice perking up. "If *I* could get some help—"

"No."

The room grows quiet, but it's the kind of quiet that's heavy, dangling over them like a piano suspended by a string, threatening to come crashing down in an instant and bury them in the debris. And that's when I hear my mother sigh—a sigh of resignation, maybe. Frustration. Of knowing that no matter what she says, no matter how hard she pleads, come Monday morning, he'll be gone again, and she'll be left to deal with us alone.

"Elizabeth, this was the deal," my father says. "My job is in Washington, yours is here. I thought this is what you wanted?"

"It was," she whispers. "It is."

"You can stay home," he says. "You can paint. We can keep growing our family."

Another bout of quiet, but this time, different. Intimate and fragile. I think I can hear the groan of a chair, the sound of rustling clothes. The almost inaudible suction of two lips pressed together, moving in unison. I take a step backward, trying to make my way back upstairs, when the board groans beneath my feet—and suddenly, I can tell that the movement has stopped. I can feel their eyes on the other side of the door, watching me freeze in fear, like a deer on the wrong side of two headlights barreling fast.

I hold my breath, stand perfectly still, until I hear the screech of a chair being pushed back, my father's lumbering footsteps growing loud.

My heart plummets as the door swings open.

"Isabelle."

I stare up at my father towering above me and feel impossibly small. He looks at me for a moment, quiet, before opening the door wider. Inside, I see my mother sitting on the arm of his office chair, nightgown hanging off one shoulder so I can see the pop of her clavicle. She stares at me in the doorframe, her eyes waxy and red. She's been crying, I can tell, and I feel guilty. Guilty for making her feel like this.

I think of her words to my father, a hushed whisper. A desperate pleading.

"You don't know what it's like. You don't understand."

"I couldn't fall asleep," I blurt out, realizing they might be thinking it right now: that I'm doing it again. That I'm walking the halls of the house in my sleep, standing here with my eyes open and an emptiness on the other side.

My mother stands up and glides across the room, joining my father in the doorway. She continues to stare, examining me. It's the same way she looks at me sometimes when I wake up in the dark, standing in the bathroom with the faucet running or holding a spatula in the kitchen. The same way she tilts her head to the side, like she's studying me. Like she's trying to determine if I'm real.

Like she's afraid.

CHAPTER SIXTEEN

NOW

That man from last night, sitting on his porch. Something about him has been irking me, bothering me, sticking to my side like a burr digging in its spikes.

I walk into the dining room, streaks of orange light illuminating the house and a mug of coffee pushed hot in my hands. Then I stare at the wall, that giant canvas covered in pictures and maps and article clippings; Post-it notes with late-night ruminations that have never amounted to much. He didn't look familiar to me in any way; he didn't seem like anybody I know—and that's when it hits me.

He *should* look familiar. He *should* be somebody I know.

I know everyone in this neighborhood. They're all right here, right in front of me. I've researched them all, walked house-to-house and pounded on doors. I've listened to their alibis and apologies and forced myself to smile, nod, thank them for their time. And through it all, I've never come across that man. I've never seen him. If he lives here—so close to my home, his house practically parallel to mine—I should know who he is. I should know everything about him.

But I don't.

I hear the squeak of wheels in my driveway, and I twist around, registering Roscoe perking up from his corner.

"Be nice," I warn as a car door slams outside, and a low growl begins to rumble in his throat.

Footsteps start to approach my house before a knock on the front door sends Roscoe into a frenzy. I walk over quickly, swinging it open to find Waylon on my doorstep, a briefcase in one hand and an equipment case in the other.

"Good morning." I smile, gesturing for him to come in. After dinner last night, I had agreed to another conversation—on the record this time. He smiles back at me now, hesitating before he steps inside, and I get the distinct feeling that he's nervous today. It seems strange, given how laid-back he was last night, but I suppose being in my home is different from meeting at a neutral location.

But then I realize: It might be the dog.

"Don't worry, he's friendly," I say, pushing Roscoe out of the way. "He does this with strangers."

"It's no problem," Waylon says, kneeling down to let him sniff his fingers. Once he stands back up and steps inside, I watch as he glances around, taking everything in.

"Beautiful home."

"Thank you."

"Is this where you've always lived?"

I know what he's asking, masking it in polite formalities. He wants to know if this is where it happened, where Mason was taken.

"We moved here about seven years ago."

I see him drink in the living room again, his eyes searching for any evidence of *we*. Men's shoes kicked off by the doormat, maybe, or a baseball cap resting on the island. Family photos of the happy couple, Mason nestled snugly between us.

He doesn't find anything.

"My husband moved out," I say, clenching my fists. I'm not wearing my ring, either. I was when we met that day on the plane, but I didn't think about it this time. After all, a podcast is only audio. "This whole thing is hard, you know, on a relationship."

Waylon gives me a sad smile, like he's trying to understand. "I'm sorry."

"Would you like some coffee?"

I take off into the kitchen because I don't know what else to do. Without the mask of the dim restaurant lights or the three glasses of wine to further dull my senses, I feel suddenly exposed here in my home. Like Waylon is not only looking at me, but through me, seeing all the dark and dangerous things coiled up on the inside.

"No, I'm fine," he calls out from the living room. I'm already topping off my own cup, hands shaking. "I've had a few today. Any more and I won't be able to sleep."

I stifle a snort. If only he knew.

"You can put your things down over there." I gesture to the dining room, where I've cleared off the usual clutter from the table. "There's an outlet if you need to plug in your equipment."

"Do you mind if I poke around first?" he asks. "With podcasts, description is important since the listeners can't actually see what I'm talking about."

I stare at him, my hands pushed hard into my mug. He wants to see Mason's room. He wants to *go inside* Mason's room.

"Or we can just get started," he continues, sensing my hesitation. "Why don't we do that?"

I smile, nod, and make my way over to the dining room table. Waylon follows, and I can almost feel the intake of air as he turns the corner, silently processing what's staring back.

"Wow," he says at last, standing before that wall of pictures. His eyes are wide, like he's admiring some abstract work of art. "You did all this yourself?"

I shoot him a self-conscious smile. "I have a lot of time on my hands."

He nods, letting himself stare for another few seconds before setting down his case and opening the latches, his eyes occasionally darting back over to the mess of articles and pictures as he pulls out his equipment: two microphones with attachable pop screens, two pairs of headphones. A miniature stereo, battery pack, various coils and cables that he proceeds to untangle and plug into different-colored outlets. Within minutes, there's an entire sound studio set up in my dining room.

"I know it seems intimidating, but I promise, it's not," Waylon says. He hands me a pair of headphones, and I take them from him, surprised at their unexpected weight. "It's just for sound quality. It removes background noise like the air-conditioning, cars honking. Dogs barking."

He smiles at me and winks, and I smile back, disarmed a little, before putting the headphones on until the padded leather is snug around my ears. Waylon puts on his own and leans into the microphone.

"Check, check."

His voice is crystal clear, like he's speaking to me through a tunnel. The sound is amplified and crisp, and I can't help but be surprised.

"That makes a big difference," I say, speaking into mine.

"Sure does." He flicks a switch on the stereo, and I notice now that there's a green light blinking. "So, Isabelle Drake, thank you for having me in your home today."

"You're welcome," I say again, aware now that the conversation has officially started. That whatever was said *before*, when this light wasn't blinking, wasn't being recorded—so, therefore, didn't count.

"I'm sure all of you know Isabelle's story," Waylon says, leaning into the microphone, that familiar voice taking on a more official tone. "But for those uninformed few, here it is: Isabelle's son, Mason, was taken from his nursery in the middle of the night exactly one year ago. His case is still unsolved."

"That's right," I say, feeling suddenly self-conscious.

"The police have no suspects, no leads, and practically no clues. So far, they've been completely unable to weave a story together of how the events of that night progressed."

Waylon is silent for a moment, letting his point sink in for our invisible audience. Then he looks up at me, a little smirk tugging at his lip.

"And that, listeners, is where we come in."

CHAPTER SEVENTEEN

We spend the first few hours rehashing what I shared with Waylon last night, going about the conversation as if it were happening for the first time, unfolding naturally—only this time, with that green light blinking.

"Did you hear anything strange during the night? Any noises?"

"What time did you notice he was gone?"

I answer in the same ways, telling him the truth. Telling him everything. And he nods, eyebrows scrunched, like he is just as enthralled to be hearing it again. It's late afternoon by the time we're finished, the entire day somehow gone in a blink right here at my dining room table.

After we've covered it all, Waylon reaches out and flips the switch, turning the green light off.

"I think we're done for the day." He smiles.

I watch as he packs up his things, a methodical movement to his routine, like he's boxed up this equipment a million times before in this exact same way—which he has, I suppose—and it suddenly reminds me that I'm not special.

That this story, Mason's story, is just business to him. It's work.

"I have something for you," I say, remembering the copy of the police records I made for him this morning. I lean to the side, digging them out of my bag. "I've told you everything, but I don't know. Maybe reading through it will help."

I hand the stack over to Waylon, watching as he takes the folder and flips it open, his eyes scanning the first page. Then he thumbs to the second, the third. I know what he's looking at right now, skimming everything slowly, methodically. I've done the same thing myself hundreds of times. The missing persons report is in there, Mason's picture and physical description: brown hair, green eyes, striped pterodactyl pajamas. Twenty-five pounds, thirty-three inches. Eighteen months old. There's a copy of his *MISSING* poster, too; I remember making it on my laptop, feeling dazed at the pointlessness of it as I dragged his image to the center of the screen, cropping it tight. It had reminded me of applying for his baby passport the year before when I was trying to convince Ben to take a trip overseas—of laying him down on a thin white blanket, trying to calm his squirming as I snapped a picture of his face. It seemed like such a strange but necessary formality, because in truth, kids that age all look the same: fleshy cheeks, wispy hair. Lips wet and writhing like a gasping fish.

I watch Waylon flip the page again. Maybe he's looking at the crime scene photos of our house now—empty crib, open window, partial footprint outside in the mud—or reading the dozens of interview transcripts with Ben and me: those first conversations, panicked and frantic with our fingers intertwined on our living room couch, followed by countless others at the police station. They kept us separated those times, estranged by the walls of the interrogation rooms, trying to catch one of us, or both of us, in a misstep. A lie. I remember looking at the wall between us, knowing that Ben was just on the other side of it. I could sense him there, the way you can somehow sense a body hovering behind a closed door. The misplaced air.

I remember closing my eyes, trying to hear what he was telling them—about Mason, about me. It seemed so imperative that our stories aligned, word for word, but I wasn't sure why they wouldn't. We were both home; we were both sleeping. We didn't hear a thing.

"Thank you," Waylon says, handing it back over the table. I can't help but notice now how painfully little there is; how quickly he was able to scan through it. Because that's all of it, right there in his hand. That's everything they've got—or, at least, everything they'll share with us—wedged between two cardboard flaps, thin enough to fit in a purse.

"Keep it," I say. "I have my own copy."

"Would you mind if I reached out to some of these people?" he asks, tapping the edge of the folder before slipping it into his briefcase. "To interview? Friends, family, Ben—"

"My family is off-limits," I interrupt. "Please don't bother them."

"Fine," he says. "Fair enough."

"Friends are fine," I say, even though I don't have many of those anymore. "Neighbors are fine. Ben . . ."

I stop, wondering how to word this delicately. I reach for the mug before me, even though it's empty, my fingers worrying their way around the edge.

"Ben isn't going to cooperate," I say at last. "And honestly, he won't be happy I'm doing this, so I would appreciate it if you didn't reach out to him. Or at the very least, save him for last. Give him less time to try and talk me out of it."

"Okay," he says. "But, you know, you're both his parents. It would seem a little one-sided if you were the only one who participated."

"I know. I know how it looks."

"It looks bad. It looks like, you know, like he doesn't want to help."

"And people say it looks like I'm exploiting my missing son for fame," I say. "So I've just learned not to care what people think it *looks like*. Everyone grieves in different ways."

I'm reminded again of that dockhand back in Beaufort; his watery eyes as we watched that dolphin pushing her dead baby around the harbor with her nose.

"That must have been hard," Waylon says, shifting gears. "You two, trying to deal with this together . . . but, you know, on your own."

I look up at him, that simple explanation tearing a hole through my chest. Because that's exactly what it felt like: the two of us, together, but also completely alone.

"Yeah," I say, my fingers hovering over Ben's ring, still tucked discreetly beneath my shirt. "We just handled it differently, you know? I had a hard time sleeping. I had a hard time doing anything, really. All I wanted to do was be involved in the case, in every little detail. And Ben . . . well, I don't know."

I force myself to swallow, take a deep breath. I can feel my eyes tightening; the blood vessels squeezing.

"He thinks I could be doing more harm than good, going out on my own like this. And he isn't alone, either. Other people think that, too."

I think about Detective Dozier; the disapproval in his tone as he mentioned my keynote—no, my *performance*.

"The detectives told us after a couple months that Mason probably wouldn't be found alive," I continue. "That, statistically speaking, they were more likely to find . . . *remains*, probably."

Waylon is silent, an apology in his eyes.

"They advised we try to find a way to make peace with it, but I just couldn't. I couldn't give up like that."

"I don't think anyone should expect you to."

"No," I say, shaking my head. "I don't think so, either. But Ben wanted to try, you know. Try to make peace with it. Not move on from Mason, obviously, but move forward. He tried to throw us into therapy, grief-counseling groups, and I just wasn't ready for that. I made it pretty hard for him."

Waylon nods, glancing at the collage of pictures on the wall: my entire home a persistent and painful reminder of everything that was taken from us. Everything we lost.

"When did you start doing that?" he asks, gesturing to it.

"A few weeks after he was taken, I guess. When the official investigation started to slow down."

I remember feeling surprised at how easy it was for everyone around me to move on. The first talk I gave was in a high school gymnasium, just days after the news had broken. Ben and I had set up the chairs ourselves, a couple dozen metal folding ones organized in rows, and it had been packed—the entire city showed up, bodies crammed tight as they leaned against the tumbling mats, leeching on to my every word. They were willing to do anything to help, *anything*, but when I held another one a week later, the crowd had visibly shrunk. We had volunteers who truly cared, for a while, manning tip lines and passing out fliers, but it only took a few months for the intrigue to fade for them, too. For them to tire, attach themselves to some other story, like ours had expired and suddenly made them sick. That was the first time I ever considered responding to the true crime requests piling up in my Inbox. Even though I didn't understand it— their fascination with violence, with pain—at least they cared.

"It started small," I say, standing up and walking closer. "Just moving a few things from the table to the wall, so I could see it all more clearly."

And then it had spread, taking on a life of its own. Creeping toward the corners, mutating and expanding and growing like a tumor that had spiraled out of control.

"Has it gotten you anywhere?"

"Into trouble, mostly."

"How so?"

I sigh as my eyes scan it all. The articles, the pictures. The giant map of the city, remembering the initial shock I felt when I finished sticking in those little ruby pins, stepped back, and took it all in.

"These are sex offenders," I say, pointing to the pins. I'll never forget the rising dread as I saw them sprawled out across our street, our neighborhood, like a swarm of insects erupting from a beaten hive. The way they seemed to multiply outward and spread like cancer until the entire thing was bleeding red. "Every single registered sex offender within thirty miles."

"I imagine they were interviewed, right?"

"Sure, the serious ones," I say, pointing to the spreadsheet printed out and tacked next to it. My eyes skim down the grid of names and addresses, page after page after page. "Criminal sexual misconduct with minors, child pornography, rape. But there are hundreds of them. *Thousands*. The cops barely even scratched the surface."

Waylon stands up and steps closer, too, probably thinking the same thing I was the first time I let it truly sink in: the magnitude of it. They're everywhere, it seems. Our neighbors, coworkers. Friends.

"What did you do?" he asks, barely a whisper.

I'm quiet, still eying those little red pins. My mind on Detective Dozier at the vigil and the way he had sunk back into the trees, watching.

"I would advise you not to do anything impulsive."

"There was this older man who used to work at the grocery store," I say at last, a cold detachment in my voice. "He always liked Mason. He used to keep these stickers in his apron pockets and hand them to the kids at checkout. He was sweet. I liked him. I always made it a point to get in his line, you know, make small talk . . . until I found his name on the list."

Waylon is quiet, letting me continue.

"I told Dozier, but he wouldn't listen. He said it wasn't enough—a lesser charge, no probable cause—and at that point I just felt like everyone had stopped trying, stopped caring, so I went to the store one night and confronted him myself."

I still remember the look on his face: the wrinkles in his cheeks stretching when he saw me and smiled; his arms outstretched like he was going in for a hug. And then: the terror. I couldn't stop myself. As soon as I saw him, I couldn't stop. The screaming, the thrashing. My fists flying and connecting with anything they could find until the other employees were able to shake off the shock and rush over, hold me back.

"It was public indecency," I continue, my eyes still drilling into the wall. I can't bring myself to look at Waylon and see the judgment there. "Apparently, he had stumbled behind some bar after too many drinks and peed in front of a cop. That was it."

I'll never forget his body on the floor, a trembling ball of limbs. Looking back, I don't even know if I truly believed it was him. Maybe I did—maybe some small part of me had seen the way he looked at Mason, those stickers in his pockets, and assumed the worst—or maybe I was just looking for someone to blame. An outlet for the anger that had been roiling inside me.

It had been there so long, it was bound to boil over.

"Any mother would have done the same thing," Waylon says at last, but it sounds like a courtesy. Like he can't think of anything else to say.

"Yeah, well, he didn't press charges, so the cops went easy on me, but they've never really wanted me around after that," I continue. "Ben moved out shortly after. I guess it was his final straw."

The house is uncomfortably quiet, and I start to chew on my nail to give my hands something to do. I feel a rip, a sharp sting. Taste blood on my tongue from where my cuticle tore.

"Why do you do this for a living?" I ask at last, an exasperated laugh escaping my lips. "How can you possibly stand it, listening to these stories over and over again? I always think about that, you know, when I go to those conventions. I ask myself how people could *possibly* get enjoyment out of listening to a story like that. Like mine."

"Oh, yeah," Waylon says, pushing a loose strand of hair away from his forehead, embarrassed. "I got into it because, uh, because of my sister's murder, actually."

His words send a knife through my chest. I inhale, trying to breathe through that familiar, painful twisting.

My sister's murder.

"I'm so sorry," I say. "I didn't mean—"

"No, it's fine," he says. "I get it. It's a morbid career."

"What happened to her?" I tread lightly, realizing now that after all of our encounters together—after our conversation on the airplane, our email exchanges, our meal at Framboise, and now this—I have never stopped to wonder what Waylon's story is. I've been so used to being the one with a tale to tell, the one with a tragedy, that I've never even thought to ask. "Your sister?"

Waylon shrugs, shoots me a sad little smile.

"That's the question," he says. "The one case I've been working on since I was twenty-three years old."

The sun is sinking quickly now, and I glance outside, watching the sky brighten into an unnatural orange one last time before the light is bound to disappear again. With that one single admission, I realize that, for the first time in three hundred and sixty-eight days, I'm not approaching the impending night with the same sense of dread that always comes when it's time to buckle up, settle in. Ride out the long, lonely hours with nothing but my thoughts, my memories. My mind.

Instead, I feel hope.

I feel it, I really do. Just the faintest little glimmer, but it's there. Because now I understand something crucial. I understand that Waylon and I may be more alike than I thought. Both of us are victims of the violence, spending our lives in the dark searching blindly for answers; both of us tainted by tragedy, defined by our loss, unable to do what everyone keeps telling me to do: just move past it, move on.

I understand that, unlike the others—unlike the detectives and the neighbors and the true crime enthusiasts—this isn't just business for him. It isn't entertainment. It isn't work.

For him, it's personal.

CHAPTER EIGHTEEN

THEN

Our air conditioner died this morning. It was *overworked,* Mom said. It's too hot.

For some reason, that reminded me of the horse-drawn carriages we sometimes see downtown, the horses' thick bodies pulling the weight of a dozen people in oversized wagons. The heat of the sun on their necks, muscles bulging. Bits in their mouths, and the smell of manure baking on the concrete. We had seen one collapse once, stumble in the middle of the street and fall to its knees. The tourists had screamed as the coachman jumped down, pried open its jaws, and poured a bottle of water down its throat as blood oozed from a gash in its leg and pooled between the cobblestones.

"Is it dead?" Margaret had asked, looking up at my mother. The horse's belly was moving, but just barely: slow, heaving breaths that made its nostrils flare.

"No, it's not dead," she had said, turning us around, hands on our necks as she led us in the opposite direction. "It's just too hot. It's overworked. It's . . . tired."

Margaret and I are sitting back-to-back on the hardwood floor of my mother's studio now, hair pulled into ponytails, though I can feel my baby curls escaping the grip of the elastic and gluing themselves to my forehead, stuck to my skin with sweat. Mom put us up here earlier, setting out an assortment of paints and blank canvases, entertainment that she knew could last for hours. The morning stretched by in a warm, slow rhythm, and I can tell by the shifting sun that it's late afternoon now, another day gone.

"I'm hot," Margaret says, fanning herself with her hand. I turn around and see a bead of sweat drip down her chest, disappearing down the neck of her nightgown. We're each wearing one of my father's old work shirts on top of our pajamas, backward, sleeves rolled up to our elbows to create makeshift smocks.

"It'll be fixed soon," I say, feeling the tickle of a no-see-um on my leg, nipping at my skin with invisible teeth. I had swung the patio doors open earlier, letting in a warm marsh breeze that did nothing but bring the bugs in.

"How soon?"

"Tonight," I say. "Maybe tomorrow. Once Dad gets home."

"I can't wait that long."

I glace in her direction again and notice that her cheeks are flushed red, like she's got a fever or something, but I know it's just the heat: July in South Carolina is brutal. It can make you feel a little crazy, like you're being cooked alive.

"Can we sleep outside?"

"No, we can't sleep outside."

Margaret nods, looking back down at her latest painting. It's a mess of squiggles, childishly abstract, and I feel my chest squeeze a little, remembering her age again. Her innocence.

"You can sleep in my room," I say, an apology for snapping at her. "We'll open the window, get the breeze from the marsh. It'll be cooler at night."

She smiles at me, reassured, and begins to hoist herself up to get a clean canvas.

"I'll get it," I say, resting my hand on her arm and standing up myself. "Sit tight."

I step over the milky water glasses and old paintbrushes strewn across the floor and walk across the studio to my mother's easel. There are dozens of her paintings up here, almost all of them of us, like our own private gallery: Margaret sitting in a circle of statues outside, holding a teacup in the air; Dad smoking from my grandfather's old pipe, clouds of smoke billowing out. The blank ones are in a stack by the wall, but before I can get there, something catches my eye.

I stop walking; there's half of an in-progress painting peeking out behind the others. I move toward it and slide the top one to the side so I can see it more clearly, and when I do, I can barely breathe.

"Izzy?" Margaret says, sensing the sudden stillness in the air, my body rigid and unmoving on the other side of the room. "What is it?"

I don't answer; I can't answer. I'm staring at the painting, fully in view now, a worm of worry writhing in my stomach. It's our backyard, that swath of green grass leading to the gentle hill that slopes into the creek. The long, wooden dock spooling out into the water and the oak trees on either side of it, their gnarled branches reaching out like wiggling fingers. It's nighttime, the moon high in the sky, and in the very middle of it all is a girl: long brown hair, white nightgown, arms hanging heavy at her side as she stands ankle-deep in the marsh.

"Look," Margaret says, and I jump at her sudden closeness. She's standing right next to me now, though I didn't even realize she had moved. She's pointing at the painting, the girl. "Look, Izzy. It's you."

CHAPTER NINETEEN

NOW

The early morning fog is still burning off the blacktop, hovering over the ground like a ghost. I leave my house at the first hint of dawn, deciding to walk over to the old man's house in the daylight. It only takes a few minutes now that I know where I'm going, and once I arrive, I size up it from the sidewalk, a little brick bungalow that would be easy to overlook. It's smaller than the other ones on the street, partially covered in overgrown shrubs and wild magnolia trees in desperate need of a trim. The paint is chipping off the siding, mold growing on the concrete sidewalk that leads to the front door.

On the porch, the rocking chair is empty, swaying gently in the wind.

I watch it, rocking on its own, and almost make myself believe that I had invented the entire encounter. Invented *him*. There's just something about the way he was sitting there, staring into the darkness. The way he was looking at me as if he didn't even seen me at all. I start to wonder if he was just a figment of my imagination, some kind of glimmer from my subconscious, so used to being alone so late at night that it just snapped its fingers and materialized some company out of the shadows—because if I'm being honest, I have done that before.

Seen things, heard things, that weren't actually there.

It is amazing, the kinds of tricks that the mind can play on you after two, three, fours nights without sleep. The kinds of things it can make you believe. The jarring *ding* of my doorbell, but when I step out onto the patio, seeing it empty; Roscoe's incessant barking, but when I shoot him a look, finding him fast asleep. A fuzzy outline moving in my peripheral vision, getting closer, but when I snap upright and twist my head, open my mouth and begin to scream, realizing that it's nothing more than the dim afternoon light making shapes out of an empty corner.

That still, I'm alone.

But no, I know he was there. Roscoe was growling, staring straight at him. I had seen him with my own two eyes, heard the creak of his rocking chair.

I had spoken to him—he just didn't speak back.

I walk quietly up the porch steps and look at the chair. The wood beneath the rocker rails is heavily worn, the paint buffed away from years of use, indicating that it's been in that spot for a long, long time. I inch closer, close enough to touch it now, and trail my fingers down the armrest, feeling the splintery wood on the pads of my fingers. I have a sudden memory of Margaret in this moment—the way we would sneak into forbidden rooms, our fingers dragging across various surfaces, touching things that weren't meant to be touched—but then, like a dream, it leaves me again.

I look down at the chair, glancing around, making sure nobody is watching. Then I turn around slowly, lowering myself down.

Once I'm sitting, I rock back and forth wordlessly, the way he was. I look out at the street, at the very spot where I was standing before, and notice that, from this vantage point, I have a relatively clear view into part of my backyard. You have to look in just the right spot—a little clearing between some trees, beneath the streetlight, past a fence—but there, *right there*, is the back side of my house, that little tuft of neglected grass looking even more yellow from a distance. Only a few feet to the right, obscured behind some branches, is Mason's bedroom window.

I can feel my heartbeat increase a little, a hopeful beating in my throat. Maybe that man saw something. Maybe he was outside that night, late, and saw someone in the backyard, creeping toward the window. Maybe he could *identify* someone—

My thoughts are moving so fast, so frantic, I almost don't hear the groan of the front door opening beside me; the presence of someone new stepping outside.

"Who the fuck are you?"

I look up, startled, and see a man standing on the porch beside me—only this man, I recognize. I can't recall his name, but his features are hard to forget: red hair, late fifties, with freckled skin and the kind of skinny stature that makes his hip bones protrude. I spoke to him once—a year ago, now—and I remember thinking he was polite, friendly, but entirely unhelpful.

Forgettable, even, until this very moment.

"Hi," I say, standing up and realizing with a stitch of embarrassment what I must look like; how strange it would be to walk outside and find a woman rocking in your rocking chair. "I'm so sorry, let me explain—"

"Jesus, it's you." He seems relieved to recognize me, but at the same time, he doesn't. He sighs, running his hands through his hair, and I watch as a tuft of it flops back over his forehead. The motion triggers something in me again; a memory that I can't quite place.

"Hi, yeah. Sorry," I say. "We met last year when I was going door-to-door about my son, but I can't recall your name. I'm Isabelle."

I hold my hand out, smiling, and watch as the man stares at me, his thin lips set in a straight line. It's silent for a few seconds, my arm hovering in the air, and once it becomes clear that he's not answering, I retract it, clear my throat, and continue.

"Listen, I was just wondering: Does an older gentleman live here? The other night—"

"Get the fuck off my porch."

I stare at him, taken aback, and fully register the way he's looking at me now, scrutinizing the dark bags beneath my bloodshot eyes. My tangled hair and the smudges of last night's makeup still caked to my ashen cheeks. He looks angry, maybe even afraid, and I suppose he has every right to be.

I would be, too, finding someone lurking this close to my home.

"I'm . . . I'm sorry," I say again, stumbling over myself to try and find the words. "I'm sorry for just showing up like this, I'm sure I gave you a scare. It's just that the other night, I saw someone, and I was wondering if *he* might have seen someone—"

I stop, realization dawning on me slowly. Monday night, at the vigil. That quick flash of color in the distance that caught my eye as I was scanning the crowd—not unlike a bob of fiery red hair ducking down low, weaving its way through the pack.

"Where were you on Monday night?" I ask, eying him carefully. "Were you downtown, by chance?"

"I'm gonna warn you one last time," the man says, taking a step closer. "Get off my porch before I call the cops."

I think back to what Detective Dozier told me: that sometimes, perpetrators can't help themselves. That they have to revisit the scene of the crime or a public gathering—like patrolling the back of a vigil, maybe, or sitting on the porch at night, staring at a window they once entered in the dark.

"What is your name?" I ask again, firmer this time. My eyes dart past his face and toward his front door, barely cracked to reveal a sliver of his living room: a splash of beige carpet and a mustard-colored couch.

"You're trespassing," he says, ignoring my question, and I take in the little twitch of his lips, almost like he's afraid. "I could have you arrested in a second after what you did to that other guy."

I feel a spasm in my chest and force myself to continue.

"Who was the man on your porch?" I ask, ignoring his threat. Taking in the windows next, realizing that they're shuttered. That all the lights inside are off. "And why were you at my son's vigil on Monday?"

"*Get off my porch.*"

"Why can't you just *talk to me*?" I ask. "What are you hiding?"

"GO!" he screams, charging at me a bit. It isn't threatening, more of a little lunge, and suddenly, despite how badly I want to lunge back—despite the fact that every muscle in my body is screaming at me to push past him and run inside—I think again of Dozier's warning.

"*I would advise you not to do anything impulsive.*"

I think of that man at the grocery store, the way things had escalated so quickly the second I lost my cool. I can feel the adrenaline in my arms, my legs, twitching at the thought of finally finding the answers I'm looking for—finding *Mason*—but my mind is telling me that if I do this, and if I'm *wrong*, I won't be able to do anything to find Mason from inside a jail cell.

"Fine," I say at last, my fingers curling into fists. I can feel my nails digging into my palms as I retreat down the steps. "I'm leaving."

I make my way back home, my heart racing by the time I step inside. I immediately walk into my dining room, my eyes tracing the map. I'm almost positive I won't find a pin there—if either of those men were on the registry, this close to my home, I'd already know—but still, I look at the neighborhood, the area clear where his house would be. I skim the spreadsheet next, anyway, looking for 1742 Catty Lane: the numbers I had seen bolted to the porch columns when I had approached the house. I flip through the first page, then the second. The third, fourth, fifth—just in case I somehow missed it. Only once I look at them all—every name, every address—do I deflate a little.

He's not there.

I grab my phone and navigate to my email, refreshing my Inbox. Still no response from Dozier. Then I click over to his contact information and make a call, listening as the line rings and groaning when his voice mail picks up instead.

"Hi, Detective, this is Isabelle Drake," I say once the line beeps. "I sent you an email on Wednesday, and I just wanted to make sure you got it." I drum my fingers against the table, trying to decide how much to reveal. "I also had a question about one of my neighbors at 1742 Catty Lane. I had an encounter with him this morning that was . . . unsettling."

I decide that's good for now. Enough detail to maybe pique his interest, prompt him to get back to me—I asked him a question, after all, which requires a response—but not too much.

"Okay, thanks," I say. "Talk to you soon."

I drop my arms, exhaling slowly as I crane my neck back, staring at the ceiling. Just as my eyes close, I feel my phone start to vibrate in my hand, and I snap them back open, hoping to see Dozier's name on the screen.

Instead, it's a text from Kasey.

"*Good to see you the other night,*" it reads. "*Offer still stands.*"

CHAPTER TWENTY

The Grit always threw extravagant holiday parties—or, rather, Ben always threw extravagant holiday parties—and my first year, almost two months into my employment, we went to Sky High, one of Savannah's nicer rooftop restaurants, with string lights illuminating the dining area and a perfect view of the riverboats as they slid beneath the bridge.

I've been thinking about that night ever since I ran into Kasey at the vigil: the two of us adorned in sequins and sipping champagne while overlooking the bridge, its two cable peaks swathed in lights resembling oversized Christmas trees in the dark. We were standing beneath a heater together, a faux fur shawl wrapped around my shoulders, when Ben walked in with a woman on his arm.

"That's Allison," Kasey had said, swirling the champagne in her flute and watching the little bubbles rise to the surface. "Ben's wife."

That was the first time I had heard her name: *Allison*. Allison Drake. I had seen pictures of her in Ben's office, of course, on that very first day when I had stepped inside. Pictures of the two of them, together, intertwined on the hull of a sailboat or sprawled out lazily in a field of lush, green grass. But in those pictures, despite the fact that

I knew she was real—logically, of course, I knew she was real—she was still only two-dimensional to me. I knew she existed in the same way I knew rare, exotic animals existed from the pages of *National Geographic*—she was a concept, a curiosity, nothing more than colorful ink slathered across glossy paper. Everything I thought about her had been imagined, concocted in my own mind rather than based on any truth or fact. I couldn't hear the chirpy hum of her laugh or smell the floral perfume that seemed to swirl beneath my nostrils the second she stepped out onto the roof. She didn't have a name, *Allison*, or hair that bounced or hips that swayed or any of the other human things about her that suddenly seemed to hit me so hard.

"She's pretty," I said. And she was. Her features were dark, like mine—chestnut hair, brown eyes, olive skin—though she was wearing a formfitting black dress with a slit to the knee, which made my gold sequins seem childish in comparison. She was tall and naturally skinny, her bare arms toned in just the right places. Her eyes winged with black liner, and her lips a deep, bloody red. "What does she do?"

"I don't think she does anything," Kasey said. "She stays at home."

"Like a stay-at-home *mother*?" I felt my chest lurch, the champagne threatening to claw back up my throat. I never considered the possibility that Ben might have kids.

"No, no kids. She just stays home. I mean, why not, right? His paycheck must be fat."

"I don't know," I said. "That seems . . . boring."

Kasey shrugged. "Would you work if you didn't have to?"

I watched as they floated from person to person, giving out handshakes and hugs. Ben was wearing a fitted navy suit, looking more handsome than ever, and I could barely peel my eyes from him. The way he effortlessly mingled with my coworkers and their plus-ones; the way he seemed to say just the right thing to every single person, making them smile or laugh or nod along in agreement. And especially the way he held Allison, his hand on the small of her back, guiding her along everywhere he went.

"I'm getting a refill," Kasey had said, knocking her champagne back and taking off toward the bar. I had nodded, barely even registering her voice, until I found myself standing completely alone as they made their way toward me. I was suddenly aware of how painfully solitary I must have seemed in that moment: standing alone beneath a space heater, no plus-one to rub my goose-bumped arms or chivalrously drape their suit jacket over my shoulders.

"Isabelle," Ben had said as he ambled up, flashing his teeth through that perfectly symmetrical grin. "Are you enjoying yourself?"

"I am," I said, trying to make it convincing. "This is a great party. Thank you for throwing it."

I waited for him to introduce me to Allison, or for her to introduce herself, but instead, a stubborn silence settled over the three of us. My eyes darted around, looking for Kasey to save me, but she was nowhere to be found.

"You must be Allison," I said at last, caving first. I thrust my hand out in her direction with too much eagerness. "It's lovely to meet you."

"Likewise," she said, placing her dainty hand in mine. "And I'm sorry, I hate to run off on you so suddenly, but I need to find the restroom—" She leaned in close, her mouth to my ear, and I could smell the warm spearmint of mouthwash on her breath. "To be quite honest, this dress squeezes me in all the wrong places. It was a horrible choice."

She leaned back and winked in my direction, flashing a smile as she placed a hand on her stomach. It was one of those self-deprecating jabs that perfect people do—trying to call attention to a tummy bulge or physical flaw that just isn't there—and I smiled back, feeling conflicted. On the one hand, I felt a strange sense of satisfaction at being the one she chose to share this secret with—at the two of us having had a *moment*—but on the other hand, I hated how nice she seemed. It made me feel infinitely worse.

I watched as she placed one hand on Ben's cheek while handing him her glass with the other before stepping away and gliding toward the restaurant. My eyes trailed her all the way across the rooftop until she disappeared inside, but when I turned back around, Ben's eyes were on me.

"So, how are you enjoying *The Grit*?" he asked. "Is it everything you hoped it would be?"

I could tell from his expression—his forehead tilted into mine, eyebrows raised—that he was alluding to that night, *our* night, at the oyster roast. That he was acknowledging what happened between us for the very first time. There had been other moments, though. Every now and then, just as I would be starting to think that my memory of that night was somehow wrong—that maybe my mind had fabricated the way he had looked at me, that subtle twitch in his lips as I pulled back; that maybe the beer sitting stale in my stomach had contorted the evening into something it just wasn't—little glimmers of truth would shine through, like the sun peeking out from behind a cloud of smog. He would assign me a story about a bladesmith who made artisan oyster knives, their handles handcrafted out of black walnut and mother of pearl; I would walk back to my desk on a Friday afternoon, running late to an office happy hour, and find a crisp Blue Moon waiting patiently for me on my desk, the cap cracked off and the neck slick with sweat.

It was like he was shooting me an invisible wink from across the room, one that only I could see.

"Everything and more."

I knew I shouldn't have said it—or at least, not like *that*. I knew what I was insinuating, how he would take it: that *he* was everything, to me, and more. But there was something about knowing that the two of us were sharing a memory in that moment, enveloped in a sea of other people who wouldn't understand, that made me feel more drawn to him than ever before.

It was the knowledge that he had Allison—beautiful, charming, nice, funny Allison—and he still seemed to have an interest in *me* that made me feel both light and airy and simultaneously sick with dread at the exact same time.

In truth, I didn't want to feel that way about him. Honestly, I didn't. That job: It was my dream. It was *mine,* finally, and I didn't want to do anything to give that up. So in the weeks that followed, every time I passed his office, my eyes would skip over his door, like a stone tossed over a glassy river. I tried to focus. I tried to pretend it wasn't him sitting on the other side of it. I tried to forget. But deep down, I knew it was too late. I knew there was nothing I could do to stop it. It was inevitable, Ben and I. We had chemistry. A reaction had started—a spark, ignited—and both of us would soon be pursing our lips and blowing on it gently, giving it life.

Strengthening a kindling into a full-blown fire.

CHAPTER TWENTY-ONE

I ignore Kasey's text and decide to shoot a message off to Waylon instead. After all, if Dozier won't help me look into my neighbor and that man on his porch, I know Waylon will.

"Busy?" I text, and within seconds, my phone is ringing, his name on the screen.

"Hey," I answer, my voice unusually bright. "That was quick."

"Yeah, I was just wondering if I could swing by on my way out of town. Say goodbye."

"Goodbye?" I ask, panic creeping into my voice.

"It's Friday," he says, hesitating. "I had my hotel until the weekend. I need to head home."

"Oh," I say, my chest deflating. "Right. But we're not . . . we're not *done* here, right? You haven't changed your mind—?"

The thought makes me feel suddenly frantic: the idea of, after losing everything that I've already lost, now losing this. Of course, it wouldn't be the first time an attempt at answers left me with nothing, but for some reason, this one feels different, important. The most important thing I have left.

"No, no," he says quickly. "Of course not. I'll continue doing my work from home, get some interviews in over the phone. We'll be in touch, and I'd like to come back . . . maybe in a few weeks?"

The line goes quiet, like Waylon is waiting for me to say something.

"I just can't, you know, stay here indefinitely," he says at last, sounding embarrassed. "I have some advertiser money, but other than that, I'm self-funded. These hotels aren't cheap."

"Stay here." I interrupt him before I can even realize what I'm doing, what I'm saying. "You can stay with me. In my guestroom."

The line is quiet for a beat too long.

"That's really generous," he says at last. "But I can't . . . I can't do that. I don't want to impose—"

"It's not an imposition, really." My mind is spinning as the words come out; I know this is a bad idea, but still, I can't stop. It reminds me of that first night with Ben on the water; the lie about the oyster-shucker that I had just blurted out of nowhere because I was tired of being alone. "I have this whole house to myself. It doesn't make sense for you to spend your own money when I have all this space."

Waylon is quiet again, and I can almost hear him thinking. Trying to find an excuse, maybe. A kind way to tell me that what I'm suggesting is crazy—we barely even know each other. We're practically strangers, he and I. I know there's an air of desperation in my voice, and on some level, I want to open my mouth and reel the offer back in—tell him that he's right, that we can do everything we need to do over the phone—but on another, deeper, level, I don't want him to leave.

I don't want to be alone. Not now. Not again.

"Okay," he says at last. "Okay, yeah, if you really don't mind."

"I don't mind," I say, a mixture of relief and dread flooding through me. But still, the thought of another person in my house, another life, makes the weight on my chest release just slightly. "Why don't you come over and unpack? Make yourself at home."

We hang up, and I walk into the kitchen, opening the fridge and scanning the inside. Of course, I know what it's like to share a space with a man, but I've lived alone for six months now, and there are things that we'll need to work out: things like groceries and cooking and refrigerator space and privacy; how long he's staying, what's acceptable. What's not. I make a mental note to clear out some space in the pantry for him when my eyes catch the stack of mail still sitting on the counter.

I notice my parent's card again, that check still sitting untouched on top. I walk over and pick it up, eying the little bouquet of daisies on the cover. Inside, it's completely blank.

Fitting, I think, tossing it into the trash. We've never quite known what to say to each other, my parents and I. Not for a while, anyway.

I pick up the check next and fold it in half, stuffing in into my purse. I know I'll deposit it eventually—I'll have to soon, with no real cash coming in—but until then, I don't want to look at it. I don't want to think about it. It feels like blood money to me. Like a payment for this prolonged silence—only I know it isn't my silence they're buying.

It's theirs.

CHAPTER TWENTY-TWO

THEN

Margaret clambers into bed first, her hair wet and smelling of lavender shampoo. We had a cold bath tonight, lowering ourselves in gently, our legs prickling when the ice water hit our skin.

"How much longer?" Margaret asked. Dad had been tinkering with the air conditioner since he got home a few hours earlier, but still, it wasn't fixed. I could hear him muttering cuss words beneath his breath as he slammed around various tools, the sleeves of his work shirt rolled to his elbows. His collar damp with sweat. "It's so hot."

Mom turned to us then, her elbow resting on the edge of the tub. Her curls were in a ponytail draped over one shoulder, the ends swirling and sticking to the sweat on her chest. It reminded me of the algae that I sometimes saw growing on the bottom of the dock, stringy and green, like strands of hair pulsing with the waves. When I was younger, I used to think there was a body stuck beneath it, mollusks for skin.

"Not much longer," she said, trailing her fingers along the surface of the bathwater. She scooped up a handful of suds, clumped together like a tumbleweed of sea foam coasting across the beach on a particularly windy day. "We'll be comfortable soon."

"By morning?"

"Sure." She smiled. "By morning."

We got out of the bath and put on our matching nightgowns, little yellow daisies, our sweat immediately pushing back up through our pores, skin like squeezed sponges. The heat is oppressive tonight, especially inside. It makes the entire house feel like an oven. Like we're trapped in it.

Margaret plops on top of the mattress now while Mom rips off the comforter and tosses it to the floor. I walk over to the window, unlatching the lock and hoisting it open. Immediately, I smell the marsh, that prehistoric stink, but it isn't as strong as it normally is. The water is twinkling in our backyard, deeper than usual, and that's when I notice a full moon reflecting off the surface like there's some kind of orb submerged underneath. The intensity of it is masking our yard in an eerie kind of glow—somehow both dark and bright at the exact same time—and I remember that Dad had told me about this once. It's called a spring tide. When the earth, moon, and sun all find themselves in perfect alignment, something extreme happens.

I turn around and find Margaret nestled in bed, her body like a pill bug, curling in on itself. She looks so small like that, so compact. I know that sleeping together will only make us hotter, body heat radiating, but I also know that Margaret's mind is her own worst enemy. She feels safest in the company of others.

"Don't forget to say your prayers," Mom says now, sitting on the edge of the mattress. I slide into bed beside her, already feeling the heat from Margaret's limbs searing into the sheets. She has her doll in her arms, those unblinking eyes staring straight into my soul. "My two beautiful girls."

"You forgot Ellie," Margaret says, lower lip jutting out.

I look up at my mom and register her expression—her tired eyes and drooping smile; those thin, delicate fingers that rise to her sweat-dotted lip like she's trying to tamp something down, keep it from escaping.

"Yes, well," she says, clearing her throat. "Of course we can't forget about Ellie."

Margaret smiles then, pinching her eyes shut and placing her palms together, fingers stiff like they're stuck together with glue.

"Now I lay me down to sleep, I pray the Lord my soul to keep."

I glance over at the thermostat glowing in the corner, watching as the degrees tick upward—eighty-four, eighty-five, eighty-six—wondering how high it could go. How much more we could possibly take.

Then I look back over at Margaret, her eyes still shut.

"If I should die before I wake, I pray the Lord my soul to take."

My mother smiles, kisses us on our foreheads, and clicks off my bedside lamp before standing up and walking into the hallway. The room is enveloped in darkness now, the shroud of night, but I'm still looking at Margaret. At the way the moonlight is streaming in through the window like a spotlight, casting its glow directly on her.

CHAPTER TWENTY-THREE

At first, my house felt strange with Waylon in it, the comfortable companionship we built up this week seeming to dissolve as soon as he stepped through the door. We spent the first couple of hours dancing around each other, sidestepping one another, like late-night lovers who forgot each other's names.

He's offered to cook dinner tonight, a thank-you, I think, for opening up my home. He went out for groceries earlier, and now that he's started cooking, we've slipped back into that easy camaraderie I've felt all week. I think it's the way I'm kicked back in the kitchen, watching as he hops around, tending to the bubbling skillets and boiling water. Cooking feels like a chore when it's done out of necessity—not for the taste or presentation, but for survival alone—but when you throw another person into the mix, it turns into an activity, a pastime. Enjoyable, even. An intimacy in the mundane.

"Red or white?"

Waylon pulls two bottles of wine out of a large paper bag, hoisting both into the air. I point to the red, and he nods, uncorks the bottle, and glugs a healthy amount into an empty wineglass, pushing it in my direction.

"Thank you," I say, taking it by the stem. A relaxed silence settles between us as he unloads the rest of the groceries, and I can't help but think about how we met on that airplane; the bizarre juxtaposition of *then* and *now.* I never would have imagined that in just one week, we'd somehow find ourselves here: no longer strangers, but partners. Maybe even friends.

"What was the case you solved?" I ask, suddenly remembering. "You mentioned that you solved a cold case. On the plane."

"Oh yeah," he says. "Another missing child."

He diverts his eyes as he chops a few cloves of garlic, and I wonder if he's avoiding my gaze for a reason. If he knows that whatever comes next is something I won't want to hear.

"The case was going on thirty years," he continues after a prolonged silence. "The family had *no* answers. I mean, none. No clue what happened. But we were able to find out."

"And what happened?"

He looks at me, finally, an apology in his eyes.

"She died," he says in matter-of-fact numbness. "She was taken by a town crossing guard. Kept in his basement for a few months before he killed her and buried her in the woods."

I swallow, my eyes darting over to the window, in the direction of my neighbor's house.

"How did you find him?"

"We found a witness," Waylon says, pouring himself a glass now, too. "Another kid who actually saw her get taken. He was terrified at the time—he was, like, seven—so he never came forward. I talked to everybody in that town, *everybody*, and finally, I found him."

"So, what, the cops just believed the thirty-year-old testimony of a second-grader?"

"No," he says, sighing. "But I gave them the tip, and they were able to get a warrant. They searched his house—Guy Rooney, was his name. He'd been living in the same place his entire adult life, ever since he got divorced in the seventies, and they found some of her . . . *things* . . . in his basement. Things he was keeping."

I nod, chewing on the inside of my cheek, still staring out the window. The sky is beginning to morph colors now, a slathering of black and blue, like a juicy bruise.

"He confessed on the spot," Waylon continues. "Brought the cops to the woods, almost like he was relieved to get caught. Get it off his chest. All those years later, he remembered exactly where she was. Where he buried her."

"And nobody had any idea?" I ask. "That that was going on in his house?"

"None at all," Waylon says. "That's what's so terrifying. He and his ex were on great terms, co-parented their kids. She evens remembers being over there once and noticing that the basement door was padlocked. The girl was probably still down there . . . but, you know, she never thought anything of it."

I shudder, trying not to wonder what would be worse: no resolution to Mason's case, or a resolution like that. The story makes me even more curious about my neighbor and that man on his porch; there has to be a reason why he seemed so guarded this morning. Why he didn't want me going near his house. Why they both refused to speak to me, and why he was at the vigil on Monday, watching from a distance.

"But that's enough about that," Waylon continues, changing the subject. "Let's eat first. I hope you like chicken marsala. It's my specialty."

"You have a specialty?" I ask, finally tipping my glass back and taking a drink. I'm still trying to figure out how to introduce the topic of my neighbor; I know that without any concrete evidence, a spot on the registry, or even a name, it's really nothing more than a feeling at this point. An instinct. "Don't ask me to cook for you, then. My specialty is spaghetti. Chicken nuggets when I'm feeling fancy."

Waylon looks at me and smiles, but it's a sad kind of smile. He's thinking of Mason, I'm sure. The types of dinners I used to make for him: cut-up hot dogs and Kraft macaroni and cheese, tiny little finger foods served on plastic trays with cubby holes meant to keep them from touching.

"Family recipe, I should say," he continues. "I can't take too much credit. I'm Italian."

"Italian," I repeat, fidgeting with the glass. "I'm not quite sure what I am, to be honest. Southern? Does that count?"

"I think it does." He grabs a skillet and shakes it around a bit, filling the kitchen with the aroma of garlic and olive oil, oregano and shallots and salt. "Your family has always been from around here, then?"

I look up at him. Every time he mentions my past, my family, it's in such a casual manner—like he doesn't care about getting to know the story, but instead, he just cares about getting to know me. I can't tell if it's genuine yet, if he *really* doesn't know, or if he's just good at faking. I'd like to find out.

"Yeah," I say. "Though I'm sure you already knew that."

He looks thrown off, like he's about to apologize, but before he can, I let out a laugh and take another sip.

"I'm teasing. Yes, born and raised in Beaufort. My dad, too, and his dad, and his dad. As far back as it can go, I think. The Rhetts were like royalty in that town."

I'm sure he catches the *were,* the intentional use of past tense, but he doesn't ask.

"What brought you to Savannah?"

"I came because of a job," I say, sinking deeper into my chair. I'm getting comfortable now, the easy back-and-forth of conversation in my own home something that has felt so far gone lately, so foreign. I've missed it. "But I stayed because of a boy, as stupid as that sounds."

"Ben?"

"Yes, Ben."

"How did you two get together?"

"The job." I laugh, glancing out the window again. I can't help but think about the fact that if someone happens to walk past my home, glimpses inside the illuminated window, it won't be one body they'll see sitting at the table, eating alone. It'll be two. "He was my boss. I'm a walking cliché, I know."

"I wasn't gonna say it." Waylon smiles.

"But we didn't meet at work," I add. "We met before then."

"So you quit the job so you could be together?"

"Pretty much. Sounds awful when you say it like that."

"Did you like the job?"

"I loved it," I say. "But I loved him, too."

Waylon tosses some mushrooms into the skillet, and it hisses back to life. We're quiet for a while, and I watch as he cooks, mixing in the Marsala wine, the chicken broth, the heavy cream. People always judge me when they find out about that—and to be honest, if it had happened to anyone but myself, I'd judge them, too. I never thought of myself as *that* kind of girl: the kind who would intentionally shrink in order to fit neatly into the life of another.

But it wasn't like that with Ben. It wasn't.

I never even thought of what we had as an affair. That seemed too strong a word—too dirty, too *wrong*—and I think that's because the relationship that had started to unfold between us was situated some-where in the murky in-between: not wrong, exactly, but definitely not right, either. It was something that defied definition, something only we could understand. We didn't cross any concrete lines; we didn't break any rules. We never had sex—we never even kissed, apart from that night on the river, which, in my mind, didn't even count.

I never thought of myself as the *other woman* with Ben, because I wasn't—but at the same time, I was. I know I was.

To Allison, I was. Or at least I would have been, had she known.

It seems naive now, maybe willfully so, but at twenty-five years old, I had painted a picture in my mind of what *cheating* was, and it practically mirrored cable television: cheap motel rooms paid for in cash, burner phones, sleazy encounters that ended with shame and tears and lies. But it wasn't like that with Ben, it never was. It was coffee together every morning, our faces pushed close in our favorite corner café. Memorizing each other's orders and writing nicknames on the cup. It was inside jokes and multi-hour conversations, seamlessly switching between laid-back small talk and sharing our innermost thoughts, our deepest desires, as if we had known each other for years instead of months. Sharing a cocktail after work when everyone else had gone home, followed by late night text messages—*I can't sleep*—the unspoken suggestion that he was lying awake, next to her, but still, thinking of me. In a way, the PG nature of our relationship made it even more intimate, more real. It was like a high school love that wasn't yet cheapened by sex, something innocent and pure. It didn't make me wonder if the physical aspect was all that he was really after, all that mattered. It didn't make me wonder if he was just that kind of guy—*a cheater*—and it didn't force me to look at myself in the mirror and decide if I was proud of who stared back.

At the time, it almost seemed valiant, to be honest: Ben's refusal to get physically close. Like that very first time on the water, he had walked away and continued to do so every single time. I used to obsess over the way his mouth would hover inches from mine when we were deep in conversation; the way he would pull back slightly, licking his lips, like he was trying to taste me in the air between us. The way he would glance over his shoulder just one more time when he left the office at night, eying me at my desk, branding me into his brain before he went home to her. It made him seem like a good man, a noble man.

The kind of man who, if I could just *have* him, would always treat me right.

The irony, of course, was lost on me then: that he wasn't being a good man to Allison, leading me on like that. He wasn't treating her right. But in my mind, that was different. *She* was different. They didn't have what we had.

They weren't *us*.

I had underestimated one thing, though, and that was the danger in letting him fill every single crevice of my life. He was like water, pooling his way into my empty spots. He was my personal life and my professional life—he was *everything* to me—but I knew, deep down, that I wasn't everything in return. I knew that despite what we had, Allison still had more. She had his last name, after all. His ring on her finger. She had his body in bed. I had come to think of him as a library book, entering my life on rented time. Something that I could enjoy for a few hours, curled up and comfortable, devouring as much of him as possible before our time was up. And because he wasn't mine, I couldn't scribble in the margins or write my name on the spine; I couldn't leave my mark on him in any discernable way. Sometimes, when he stood up from his barstool—the room around us dark and quiet, his glass bone dry—I could feel him draining from me slowly, like blood seeping from an open wound.

When he opened the door and stepped out into the night, I was left with an overpowering emptiness, like I ceased to exist.

"I went freelance," I say now, trying to make it sound exciting. Trying to convince Waylon that I do, in fact, work. "I got to write for all kinds of publications. I even traveled around a little, got to see different parts of the country."

Waylon nods, dumps of a box of pasta into the boiling water.

"Freelance is nice." His tone is polite, poised, like he's comment-ing on the weather. "Working for yourself. There's a freedom to it."

"Ben was married when we met," I blurt out, turning to the side. I don't want to see the look on his face, the appraisal in his eyes. I don't really want to be telling him this—it's not something I'm proud of—but I know he'll find out eventually, if he hasn't already. He's going to be talking to my friends and my neighbors. Detective Dozier. I'd rather him find out from me. "But I didn't . . . we didn't, you know. We weren't *together* when they were together."

"They get divorced?" he asks, his voice clipped. We're getting personal now, the mood veering quickly from easy small talk to something deeper. Neither of us is looking at the other.

"No," I say, letting the silence stretch out for a beat too long. Then I turn toward him and take a deep breath. "She died."

CHAPTER TWENTY-FOUR

Ben hadn't come into the office for three straight days.

I was starting to worry, wonder if maybe it had something to do with me. Maybe someone had found out—*but found out about* what, *exactly? We hadn't done anything wrong*—or maybe he was having regrets, avoiding me. Trying to figure out how to end whatever it was that we had started. He wasn't answering my texts; he hadn't told me about any upcoming vacations. He didn't have any work trips on his calendar.

All I knew was that on Monday, he was there. And then he wasn't.

"Did you hear?"

Kasey shuffled past my desk, a pencil tucked behind her ear. I peeled my eyes from his closed office door, the darkness of his windows, and moved them over to her, alarm creeping into my chest. Kasey always had that look about her: easy to read. Her emotions were scribbled between the lines of her face like notes on a scrap of loose-leaf paper, and right now they were telling me something was wrong.

"No," I said. "Hear what?"

"Allison died."

"What?"

"Allison Drake," she said. "Ben's wife. She *died*."

"*What?*" I gasped, my hand shooting to my chest like I'd been shot.

"Yeah. She died."

"*How?*"

"Suicide," she whispered, her mouth on my ear. Her breath was warm and earthy, the way it always was when she drank her coffee black. I wondered if this was what she had been doing all morning—chugging caffeine, making her rounds, spreading the latest office gossip like a jacked-up journalist, reveling in the fact that she knew first. "Or accidental overdose. Either way, it was pills. Like, a shit ton of them."

I felt the words clot in my throat; I opened my mouth, tried to speak, but nothing came out. Kasey raised her eyebrows, tilted her chin down.

"I know, right?"

"That can't be right," I finally said. "Why would she—?"

"I know," she said, shaking her head. "I have no idea. I guess she had a problem we didn't know about. That happens with housewives sometimes. Too much time on their hands."

I conjured up the only real memory I had of Allison: the two of us, standing close on that rooftop, her fingertips on my forearm as Ben stood to the side, watching us both. The way she had leaned into me, shared a secret and a wink. Made me feel like I was suddenly on the inside of something special.

"She seemed happy."

I felt stupid the second I said it. I knew that one moment we shared together couldn't possibly be enough to know her—to *really* know her—but what I was really thinking was: How could she *not* be happy? She had Ben.

Kasey shrugged. "We all have secrets."

I watched her walk away, taking a few steps to the next row of desks and leaning down, whispering again. Then I glanced back at

Ben's office, thinking about all the times I had imagined them to-gether: Ben and his wife. Every night after we'd parted ways, I would walk into my apartment, the emptiness making it feel even lonelier than normal. I would sit at my kitchen counter or slump over in my too-small bathtub, lukewarm water barely grazing my chest, and wonder what they were doing together at that exact moment: having a cocktail on the porch, maybe, or cooking something sophisticated for dinner while I would be reheating a coagulated Lean Cuisine I had neglected for too long in the freezer. I would imagine them fuck-ing on expensive granite countertops, water boiling over and spilling onto the floor. It made me want to scream.

But in that moment, a realization settled in my stomach like swal-lowed vomit, putrid and sour: I knew nothing about her. I knew nothing about *them*. The inner workings of their lives were a com-plete mystery to me, and now Allison was dead. Ben's wife was *dead*. Which meant that Ben was now a widower.

We all have secrets.

I wondered what Kasey meant by that, what she was suggesting. I wondered if she meant that *Allison* had secrets—a pill problem, an addiction, that steered her in the direction of taking her own life; a depression that had spiraled out of control, guiding her hand as she tipped the bottle back while Ben was at work—or if she meant that someone *else* had secrets. Secrets that perhaps she had unearthed.

Secrets she could no longer live with.

CHAPTER TWENTY-FIVE

There's an atmospheric shift in the air at the mention of Allison, her death. Like the way dogs start to whimper when a storm is near, sensing the impending danger. The electrical charge.

Waylon plates our food, his eyes cast down as he walks into the dining room, sliding a plate in front of me.

"This looks delicious," I say, picking up a fork. "Thank you."

"Of course." He eases into the seat next to mine, unfolds a napkin, and drapes it over his lap. Then he exhales, looks me in the eye. "So, that's heavy."

"Yeah," I say, stabbing at a mushroom. "It was awful."

"Suicide?"

I spear some pasta, twirl, my eyes on my plate. "Yeah, I guess. Or an accidental overdose, it was never quite determined. They didn't find a note or anything."

"What do you think happened?"

I drop my fork, the clatter of metal against glass making Roscoe jump from beneath the table, jolting my chair. I look up at Waylon, at his large eyes staring straight into mine.

"If you had to guess," he adds.

"I don't know." I exhale, trying to steady my hands. They're shaking, for some reason. A gentle tremor. Maybe it's the talk of Allison, the unresolved guilt I've always felt over her death. Or maybe I'm just hungry; too much caffeine on too empty a stomach. "I guess, if I *had* to make an assumption, I would say accidental."

I don't really know if I believe that, but for some reason, it makes me feel better.

"What about Ben?"

"You know, he never actually told me what he thinks," I say, realizing it for the first time. "We never talked about her much, and of course, I never wanted to ask. But he was torn up about it, obviously."

"Huh," Waylon says, looking back down at his plate. I glance up at him, notice the way he's picking at his food, like he's trying to dissect it.

"Anyway, I just wanted to bring it up," I say. "Before you hear it from the neighbors. Or Detective Dozier."

"Yeah," he says. "Yeah, thanks. That's good to know."

"But there wasn't any foul play suspected or anything like that. I want you to know that, too. It was an open-and-shut case."

"It's just . . ." He stops, seems to consider whether or not he should keep going, finish his thought. Finally, he spits it out. "Doesn't any part of you think that her death was very . . . convenient?"

"What do you mean?" I ask, although I know what he means. I just want to hear him say it.

"Just, you know. It looks bad. He was having an affair—"

"It wasn't an affair."

"There was another woman. Then his wife dies under suspicious circumstances . . ."

"It wasn't suspicious. It was an overdose."

". . . and now his *son* disappears under suspicious circumstances, and you two are no longer together . . ."

"Okay," I say, placing my fork down with measured control. "Look, I understand it's your job to ask questions, I do. But Allison had an overdose. It happens. And Ben and I separated because our world was ripped apart, okay? We were happy before Mason was taken from us. We were *fine*."

I stare at Waylon, daring him to keep pushing it. I can see his lower lip quiver—the threat of retaliation, another question that I can't answer—but instead, he clenches his jaw, like he has to physically restrain himself from speaking.

"It's hard for a couple to survive something like this," I continue, regurgitating the words from Dr. Harris. Like because he said them, it makes it fact. "It's hard for a *person* to survive something like this."

"Okay, I'm sorry. You're right."

We eat in silence, the clanking of silverware somehow amplifying the awkward stillness that has settled over the house.

"Tell me something about Mason," Waylon says at last, changing the subject. It seems intentional, like he wants to pivot away from this sore subject and toward something better, lighter. "Something personal."

I look down at the table, remembering just yesterday all the equipment that sat here blinking between us. It had reminded me of those first recorded interviews at the police station, the antiquated cassette player with spinning wheels like eyes. Of Detective Dozier on the other side of it, and the way he'd pace, trying to unnerve me.

"Let's see," I say, picking up my glass, twisting the stem between my fingers. "He loves dinosaurs. He's obsessed with them, really. We have this one book—"

"Isabelle," Waylon interrupts, leaning forward in his chair. "Something personal."

I bite my tongue, feeling my heart pound in my chest. I'm so used to calculating my statements, trying so hard to please whoever is on the receiving end of them—saying only the right things, the *good* things—and how, still, it never seems to matter. Waylon appears to see through that, though. He somehow knows when I'm not being entirely truthful. When I have something more to say.

I look up at him again, at the kindness in his eyes, and wonder if this time really could be different.

"Honestly?" I say at last. "He was tough." The admission feels like a sudden exhale after holding your breath for far too long.

"How so?" he asks.

"He was a colicky baby, always crying. I mean, nothing could soothe him. *Nothing.* I was home alone a lot, with Ben at work, and I remember there were times, during those first nights—"

I stop myself, deciding that it may not be in my best interest to be *too* honest. Not yet, at least. To describe the unusual way Mason came into this world or the panic of those early morning hours in too much detail. The desperation that started to creep into my chest when I found us alone in the dark, his writhing little body in my arms, limbs like twigs that could so easily snap. I can still remember those muddy, sleep-deprived musings; the kind that didn't even feel real. The kind that no mother would ever admit to herself, let alone utter out loud. Mason would shriek in the night and they would flare up so suddenly, so *violently*: dark little fantasies of all the things I could do to finally make him stop. And I would let them in, if only for a second. I would let myself entertain them for a beat too long—but then, in the mornings, I would simply ignore them again, pretend they were never even there to begin with. I would feel my cheeks burn hot with shame as I lifted him out of his crib and smothered him in kisses, casting them back into the recesses of my mind where the other banished feelings lived: naughty and nocturnal, curled up in that dank cave of my subconscious, skulking around until the sun dipped below the horizon again and it was safe for them to crawl back out.

"It's just hard," I continue. "Being a mother. It's not what you expect it to be."

Nobody ever warns you about the spite that comes in the night when you're operating on two hours of sleep. Nobody ever tells you about how resentful you begin to feel toward a person you created. A person who relies on you for everything.

A person who never asked for any of this.

Waylon shifts in his chair, uncomfortable, before taking a deep sip of wine and returning his attention to his plate. I'm sure he was imagining something different: one of those rosy memories mothers relay with stars in their eyes, making everyone else feel botched. I don't really know what drove me to say it—the intimacy of this dinner, maybe, of sharing a meal with someone in my own home for the first time in months. Or maybe it's because Waylon has been the first person in so long to really listen to me, to *believe* me, and we've been tiptoeing toward this type of raw honesty ever since that day on the plane when he placed his card on my knee.

Whatever it is, it feels good, the admission, even though I know it's not what people want to hear. It feels honest.

Finally, something honest.

The fact is, I've never been able to be honest. Not to Ben, my parents, the other mothers at day care—*especially* the other mothers. Even before Mason was taken, before I met Ben, I always had secrets, swallowing them down every time the urge to repent came gargling up my throat like bile. I learned fairly quickly that when people asked how I was doing, how I was *holding up,* they didn't actually want an answer—not a real one, anyway—so I simply ignored that little needle prick that stuck in my jaw, the threat of impending tears, and plastered on a smile, giving them the answer I knew they expected: that everything was good, everything was fine.

In fact, no. Everything was *perfect.*

CHAPTER TWENTY-SIX

Waylon and I are still in the dining room hours later, the table pushed to one side so we can sit on the floor and stare at the wall. Mason's case file is between us, along with the two bottles of wine—both of them empty. We've since moved on to liquor: a whiskey on the rocks for him, and for me, a vodka soda, a single slice of lime bobbing on top.

"Did you ever leave a spare key outside?" he asks. It's late, almost one in the morning, and there's a little slur in his speech, barely there, like his tongue is numb. His eyelids are heavy, and although I'm sure the alcohol isn't helping, mostly, I think he's tired. He's ready for sleep. "One that someone else might have known about?"

"No," I say, shaking my head. "Ben was always opposed to that. Ever since I found ours missing from under the Welcome mat."

Waylon raises his eyebrows, but I shake my head.

"That was years ago," I say. "Mason was, like, six months old."

Waylon looks back down, nodding, and I can still remember its grimy outline making my stomach squeeze. Ben had assured me that we had probably just misplaced it—maybe it fell out of my pocket on one of my walks with Roscoe or slipped through the wooden slats of our porch—but still. It spooked us: the thought of somebody else being able to lift up that flimsy piece of fabric and let themselves into our lives so easily, almost as if we had invited them in ourselves. It made me realize that we were too trusting; that, too often, we just assume nobody is out to hurt us. That nobody is watching when we walk around our houses at night, blinds open, the lights from inside illuminating our every move. That when we step outside and lock our doors, stash the key beneath a flower pot or wedged behind a rock, they're not going to walk up behind us and dig it back out.

That the violence isn't always looking for a way in—always poking and prodding at our lives, searching for a soft spot to sink in its teeth.

"What about the baby monitor?" he asks next, and I shoot him a look.

"The batteries were dead. Remember, I told you—"

"Sorry, yeah," he says, rubbing his eyes. "What I mean is, did the monitor keep any earlier recordings? Like, did they save? Like a security system?"

"Yeah, they did," I say. "It was connected to WiFi, so the video synced to our cell phones and laptop. You control it all from an app."

"Do you still have that old footage?"

"I should," I say, speaking slowly. The police had asked for footage of that night, the night he was taken, but since the batteries were dead, I couldn't help them. They never asked for *earlier* footage, though, and I never really thought to look. It didn't seem important, looking inside the house. I had spent all my time looking outside of it. "Why?"

"Just in case there's something on there to see," he says. "In the days leading up to his kidnapping. You never know."

I nod, push myself up from the floor, and walk over to the table, grabbing my laptop. I bring it back over to Waylon, who's taking another sip of his whiskey, his eyes inspecting something at the bottom of his glass. I open the laptop, type in my password, and find the folder housing the old recordings, buried deep in my hard drive. There are hundreds of files in there, organized by date, each one storing a night of Mason's life.

"I guess I'll start about a week earlier?" I ask, looking at him. He shrugs, nods, so I double-click on the file labeled "Thurs_ Feb_24_2022" and hold my breath as a video loads.

It starts in the morning, six a.m., with Mason sleeping. My breath catches in my throat as I watch from the corner of his nursery, where the camera is mounted, his little body lying still on the mattress.

"He's cute," Waylon says, and I look over my shoulder at him watching the screen. He smiles at me. "Big head of hair."

"Yeah," I say, that familiar sting in my eyes.

After a couple of minutes, he starts to stir, and a few seconds later I see his door crack open, and I watch as I walk into his bedroom, leaning into his crib and picking him up. I plant a kiss on his cheek, bouncing him around and making him laugh, before we walk back out the door and leave the room empty behind us.

"I was hoping we might be able to see his window," Waylon says, pointing at the screen. "But it doesn't look like it. Not from this vantage point."

"No," I say. "The camera is mounted behind his crib, facing the door. The window is next to his crib, so it wouldn't show up here."

I click on the timer at the bottom of the video, fast-forwarding through a couple hours of empty room. Around midday, I watch as I drop Mason back off for a nap, then later that night, as I carry him over to his bookshelf, choose a story, and read it to him in a rocking chair in the corner, lulling him to sleep.

We're both quiet for a while until I clear my throat, trying to push down the tears I can feel crawling their way up.

"Thanks for doing that," Waylon says, his voice soft. "It was worth a shot. But hey, I'm going to bed. And you should, too. We'll pick this up in the morning."

I nod, give him a close-lipped smile, and watch as he stands up and puts his glass in the sink, slinking off down the hall and closing the door behind him. I hear the faint shuffles of movement in the guest room—pulling back his comforter, removing his clothes—and wait until the light clicks off, the crack underneath the door going dark.

I look again at my laptop—at Mason, now back in his crib. I could sit here for hours, watching him sleep.

I stand up with my laptop and make my way to the table, taking a seat. Then I click on the timer and drag it again, speeding through the night, watching Mason as he twitches in fast motion. The room grows darker, a gentle glow emitting from his nightlight in the corner, until suddenly, it starts to brighten up again. Daylight coming. Then, at six o'clock the following morning, the recording stops.

I lean back in my chair, thinking about what I just saw. It's so simple—just a day; just a regular, normal day—but at the same time, so hard to process. It's mind-numbing sometimes, thinking about how different my life is now. How lonely, with Mason's nursery just an empty room collecting dust; a skeleton stripped of life.

I glance at the clock on my wall—one thirty a.m.—and back at my laptop, deciding to watch another.

I click on a random day, going back a couple of months, and watch again as my life unfolds before me like a dusty old carpet, getting unspooled after years of neglect. I do the same thing as before—watch the parts with Mason in them, fast-forward through the rest—and when that one is done, I choose another. I watch Mason as a newborn, so impossibly small, then decide to jump forward and watch as he teaches himself how to rock on his knees in his crib, getting stronger. These are the little moments that I had missed—the moments tucked behind a closed door, unfolding while I slept—but now, I don't want to miss any of them. I don't want to miss a second.

I'm on another video now—from early December, three months before he was taken—and watch as Ben rocks him to sleep this time. He's whispering something into his ear, over and over, before walking him to his crib and resting him inside. I watch as he walks away, turns off the light, and I start to fast-forward again, getting ready for the timer to end and the video to stop—until suddenly, I catch a movement.

I pause the video and look down at the timer: 3:22 a.m. I look back at the frozen image, squinting, trying to figure out where the motion was coming from, and then I realize: It's coming from the crack underneath his door. It's coming from the hallway.

I start the video again and notice a subtle shadow moving across the door, like someone is out there, walking. Ben going to the bathroom, maybe, or grabbing a glass of water. But then I watch as the door slowly starts to open, and I see myself step inside.

Mason must have been crying, I think, even though he looks fast asleep. I tap the volume louder and hear nothing but his sound machine, a mild swishing, like pushing your ear into a conch shell and hearing your blood rush. I lean closer to the screen, hypnotized, as I see myself walk into his nursery, toward his crib—and then, suddenly, I stop moving.

"What am I doing?"

I say it out loud without even realizing because it's so strange, watching myself like this. Seeing me standing in the middle of Mason's bedroom, unmoving—and that's when the memory hits me, hard.

My hand shoots to my mouth, stifling a gasp.

"What was I doing?"

Margaret and I, lying in bed, her cheek pushed into the pillow as she stared at me, eyes wide and afraid.

"Just standing there. Your eyes were open."

I watch for another minute, waiting for my body to do something on-screen, but still, I don't move. My feet are cemented in place; my eyes, open, staring straight ahead.

"It scares me when you do that."

I want myself to move so badly; I want myself to do something, *anything,* other than just stand there, comatose. The whites of my eyes glowing in the camera like an animal caught in headlights. Finally,

I can't take it anymore. I click on the timer and start to fast-forward, watching as my rigid body sways in a jerky rhythm as the clock ticks forward.

3:45, 4:15, 4:45, 5:05.

Finally, at 5:43 a.m., I watch my body turn around and walk back into the hallway after two hours of standing in place, shutting the door behind me. Then I stare at Mason—asleep in his crib, oblivious to it all—for another seventeen minutes until the video cuts off and the screen goes black.

CHAPTER TWENTY-SEVEN

It's a groggy morning. I wake up slow, like my brain is trudging through mud. I can taste the sleep on my breath, thick and heavy, and feel a phlegmy film on my tongue, like the kind you peel off a boiled egg. It takes a few blinks until my eyes are fully adjusted, the world coming to in a blurry kind of haze, but when it does, I instinctively know that something is wrong.

The first thing I notice is the quiet. There are no cicadas shrieking outside my window, no birds signaling the start of a new day. It's almost as if the world has stopped turning and I'm caught up in the stillness of it, floating. There's the smell of the marsh, too. It's stronger than last night, almost overpowering, like the water somehow seeped in through my window and spilled onto the carpet.

I imagine it for a second: the tide, getting higher, until it reaches the house. Climbing up two stories, brown water pouring through every crack and crevice and window and door. Trapping us inside, taking us down. Drowning us all.

I clear my throat. "We slept in."

My voice has a croakiness to it, like an unused instrument, and

I roll over to face Margaret. I expect to see her face pushed into my pillow—those big, blue eyes staring back into mine—but she's not there.

"Margaret?"

I sit up. That's why it's so quiet, I realize. Margaret isn't here. Usually, when I wake up before her, I can hear the steadiness of her breath; a gentle snore vibrating in her throat. The graze of her limbs rubbing against my old, scratchy sheets.

I glance over to my attached bathroom, but the door is wide open. She isn't there, either.

I fling my legs over my bed, push my feet into the carpet, and feel a wetness gush through my toes. I yank my feet away and look down, the little puddles that had collected from the pressure sinking back into the carpet like footprints on damp sand.

"Margaret?"

I get out of bed and start walking toward my bathroom. The carpet is moist, and for a second, I think again about that strange vision—the water from the marsh pouring into my bedroom—but I know that's not possible. It could never get that high. I turn on the bathroom light and squint at the brightness, noticing more water on the floor—one giant puddle creeping toward the walls—and a few dank towels heaped in the corner. Already, they're starting to sour.

Was this from our bath? I wonder, taking a step closer. Maybe we made a bigger mess than I thought. I imagine Margaret clambering out, water spilling from the side of the tub before Mom grabbed a towel and dried her off, tossing it in the corner. Pulling on our pajamas and turning off the light, leaving it for tomorrow.

But then I see myself in the mirror's reflection, and I know that's wrong, too.

I look down, grabbing the fabric of my nightgown in my hands. I'm wearing a different nightgown from what I had on last night. I *know* it's different. I remember, because I remember the little daisies on Margaret's, her body like a flower field as she lay on my mattress. Mine had daisies too, only bigger, like Mom meant for our clothing to signify our age.

But now, the one I have on is just a clean, crisp white.

"*Margaret?*"

Something is wrong. I *know* something is wrong. I can sense it, a throbbing in my bones, like waking up after a growth spurt. Like my body is threatening to rip straight through the skin.

And then there's that *feeling* again, that niggling in my brain, daring me to remember.

I lift my arms and place them on my neck, feeling my jugular pulse. I'm trying to relax, slow my breathing, and that's when I feel it: something behind my ear, beneath my jaw, that little patch of delicate skin. I lower my hand and look down at my fingers, at the faint smear of brown, and lift them to my nose, inhaling slowly.

I'd recognize that smell anywhere, like death and decay.

It's pluff mud.

I throw my hair over my shoulder and lean into the mirror, trying to catch a glimpse at my neck. And there, just beneath my ear, are three little streaks. Like fingers.

I run back into the bedroom, feeling my heartbeat climb in my throat. Then I dash into the hallway and run down the stairs, taking them two at a time. My thoughts are swirling around me now, thick and heavy like a cloud of gnats. The spring tide and the water on the floor and the footprints on the carpet. Me, eyes open, walking into the darkness. My mother's painting, my toes in the marsh.

Margaret, always following me, even when she's afraid.

I hit the landing and turn into the kitchen, expecting to see her there: Margaret, sitting at the table, doll in her lap. I'm waiting for her to register my appearance. For her expression to sour, her eyes to roll, shaking her head: "*You were doing it again.*"

Instead, I see my parents.

They're sitting at the kitchen table, two mugs of coffee between them, their eyes cast down to the floor.

"Dad?"

They don't look up; they haven't even noticed me. For a single, unsettling second, I feel like I'm dead. Like I'm just another ghost haunting this place, my body stuck in the walls like rot.

"Mom?"

I see my mother's shoulders stiffen, like my voice was a cold, hard slap against her skin. Like she had to physically brace herself from it, protect herself, from me. Her fingers tighten around the coffee mug, hard enough for me to see the whites of her knuckles appear beneath the skin. She lifts her head up slowly.

"Where's Margaret?" I ask, but suddenly, I have a feeling that I don't want to know the answer. My mother's expression makes that perfectly clear: the haggardness of her eyes, glassy and red, like that night in my father's office. Like she's been crying again. Like she's afraid.

"Your sister had an accident."

I look at my dad. His speech is steady and smooth, the way it always is.

"What kind of accident? Is she okay?"

My mother shoves her chair back violently, and I jump at the screech of legs against tile. Then she stands up and pushes past me, eyes straight ahead, and walks up the stairs before slamming her door shut.

"What's wrong with Mom?"

My dad sighs, drops his head again. Then he pushes his palms into his eyes, hard, and I watch as he lifts his neck and forces himself to look at me.

"Isabelle, the police are on their way. I think it would be best if you went to your room."

CHAPTER TWENTY-EIGHT

NOW

"Izzy has always had . . . problems. With sleep."

Dr. Harris, leaning forward in his chair, studying me like a lab rat. Ben, to my side, his hand on my knee.

"Even before the insomnia. Kind of the opposite problem, actually."

The memories fill me up slowly, like I'm drowning in them: blinking my eyes—three, four times—my father's face materializing up close in the dark. His hands on my shoulders, eyebrows bunched.

Standing in the grass, my palm clasped in his, the orange glow of flames as they traveled up our house as we slept. The warmth on my cheeks like an infection, eyes ablaze.

Waking up in the kitchen, all the lights off. A puddle of milk spilt on the floor.

My mother, that hazy confusion. The kink in her neck as she stared at me, trying to determine if I'm awake. If I'm real.

But most of all: Margaret.

"How long are you going to keep doing this?"

I remember the footprints in my bedroom; the way I had tried to hide them, rubbing my feet against the dirt, smearing them into the carpet. Begging them to disappear. That stone statue, eyes wide, retching up something dark. My parents had taken me to a doctor, of course. But according to him, it was nothing to be concerned with. He said it was common, harmless. Most kids grow out of it by the time they're teens.

"Isabelle?"

I hear the voice, but my mind is still elsewhere. Somewhere far away. It's on Margaret, the way her little body felt as it was pushed up against mine. A mess of slippery limbs and the smell of sweat in the sheets.

"Now I lay me down to sleep, I pray the Lord my soul to keep."

Waking up the next morning, that mud smeared on my neck like little fingers reaching up, pushing me back.

"If I should die before I wake, I pray the Lord my soul to take."

"Hey, Isabelle."

I blink a few times, turn my head. Waylon is standing above me, looking concerned. I forgot he was here.

"Did you stay up all night?"

I blink again, look around. I'm in my dining room, sitting at the table, my laptop dead in front of me and case file papers strewn across the floor. I glance at the wall, at all those eyes staring me down, and suddenly, it no longer feels like I'm studying them; it feels like *they're* studying *me*. Like that audience at TrueCrimeCon, they're looking at me expectantly, just waiting for me to slip. To reveal something dark and dangerous, like *I'm* the one with the secret. Like *I'm* the one with something to hide.

Which, I suppose, I am.

I glance out the window—it's light outside—then back to Waylon. He looks like he's freshly showered, ready for a new day, and I clear my throat.

"No," I say, trying to reorient myself. I have no idea how long I've been sitting here. "No, I . . . fell asleep on the couch. In my clothes."

"Okay," he says, still eying me. "Do you need anything?"

"No," I say again. "I'm just going to . . . I'm going to shower. Get dressed. Sorry."

"Can I make you something to eat?"

"Yeah," I say, standing up, suddenly embarrassed. "Yeah, that would be great. Thank you."

"Sorry, I didn't mean to . . ." He stops, and I can tell he feels uncomfortable. Like he was just caught snooping through my bathroom cabinet, reading my prescriptions. Witnessing something that was meant to be private. "You were just sitting there, staring. I wanted to make sure you were okay."

"Yeah, I'm fine," I say, pushing my hair out of my face, trying to smile. "Didn't mean to scare you. I just zoned out for a second."

I excuse myself and make my way into the bathroom, locking the door behind me. Then I walk over to the sink and turn on the faucet, letting the water run, and stare at my reflection in the mirror. I look awful; worse than usual. My makeup from last night is caked into my creases, my eyes their usual angry red, but there's something else in my face that looks different, haunted. A paleness to my skin that seems unnatural, like someone siphoned my blood in the night.

I lift my hands to my cheeks, touching them gently, then snake my fingers back to my neck, behind my ear, feeling that smooth patch of skin beneath my jaw. It's starting to come together now, like the slow orientation after waking up somewhere new—although suddenly, I'm not sure I want it to anymore.

I think of all those feelings that have been flaring up over the last twelve months; feelings of inexplicable guilt, of *knowing* something that I just can't retain. All those little moments with Mason— those dark, shameful moments that I refused to acknowledge in the morning—and the way I saw myself on that laptop screen, standing above his crib in the dark.

The similarities between *then* and *now* that suddenly seem so obvious.

I think of his stuffed dinosaur found on the banks of the marsh;

the familiar smell of pluff mud in the morning and the icy silence from my parents that never seems to melt. The wary way Detective Dozier looks at me every time we're together, and how Ben fell away from me so fast, almost like I did something. Something unforgivable.

Almost like he knows something that I don't.

"You need to get it together," I whisper, closing my eyes.

Then I take a few deep breaths and splash the cold water over my face, trying to shock myself back to life.

CHAPTER TWENTY-NINE

We decide to go downtown after breakfast and walk off our budding hangover. Waylon hasn't mentioned this morning: the way he found me sitting there, staring. When I emerged from the bathroom, hair wet and makeup slathered beneath my eyes, he was whistling in the kitchen, scrambling eggs.

"That must have been tough for you," he says now as we weave our way through the city, cardboard cups of coffee in hand. "Seeing that video."

"Yeah," I say. He's talking about the one we watched together, the one where nothing really happened, but all I can think about is the way I looked on the screen in the one I watched *after* he left for bed: my body, upright and rigid; my eyes glowing like two hot coals. I'm glad he wasn't there for that. I'm not sure how I would have explained it. "It was a little unusual, watching it all back. Kind of nice, though. Getting to remember."

"I bet," he says, looking down at his shoes.

I wish I had videos like that of Margaret: bird's-eye accounts of her going about her days. Just something to help me recollect the little things that are, by now, long forgotten: the exact shade of her hair, somewhere between blond and brown with hints of honey when the sun hit it just right; the smell of her skin, and the way even her sweat had a subtle sweetness to it. That infectious giggle that always erupted from somewhere deep in her chest. Mason is fading from me now, too, and I know there's nothing I can do about it. I just have to let it happen, let my memory betray me, turning them both into shades of their former selves. It's getting harder and harder to remember it all: his scent, his laugh. His details. Every day, my memory of him grows fainter, like a stain disappearing slowly under the pressure of running water, my thumb massaging the fabric.

Soon, he'll be gone completely. Like he never even existed at all.

"Hey," Waylon says suddenly, tapping my arm. "Isn't that Ben?"

I look up in the direction of Waylon's gaze and see that he's right: Ben is a few feet in front of us, holding the door open for an elderly couple as they shuffle out of a breakfast diner. Sometimes I forget that he lives downtown now; he bought a fancy new condo near *The Grit*'s office right after we separated.

I try not to think about it, really. I don't want to know what he does in there; who he entertains.

"Yeah," I say, my eyes on the side of his face. He's turning left, in the direction we're going, so I think we're safe. He shouldn't see us.

"Who's that?"

Right as Waylon says it, I see a woman walk out of the restaurant and grab ahold of Ben's arm, her fingers digging into his bicep. She's grinning, obviously proud of her place at his side. The way I used to be.

"I don't know," I lie, but I know who she is. It's Ben's new girl-friend, the one he told me about. It has to be. She looks vaguely familiar, though I can't put my finger on why, but my hunch is confirmed as I watch Ben lean over and graze her lips.

I feel a squeeze in my chest—anger, jealousy—and clench my jaw as his hand snakes down her spine, resting on the small of her back.

"He's got a type, huh?"

"What do you mean?" I ask, turning to look at Waylon. He stares back at me like I'm crazy.

"What do *you* mean?" he asks. "Don't tell me you don't see it."

I glance back in their direction. They're walking away from us now, hand-in-hand, but I can still see glimpses of her profile—the slightly upturned nose; the wide smile and youthful glow—and I suddenly realize that Waylon is right.

"She looks like Allison," I say, the realization hitting me hard. *That's* why she looks so familiar. I knew there was something. "Allison, but younger."

The primary features are there, the ones that would catch your eye at a distance. She's tall, slim. Bronzed skin and dark brown hair—but then my stomach drops with a vicious jolt, like an elevator with a snapped cable, barreling down.

I suddenly realize that Waylon isn't talking about Allison, because he doesn't know Allison. He's never seen Allison.

I don't know how I've never noticed it before.

"Allison?" he asks, as if reading my mind. "Isabelle, she looks like *you*."

CHAPTER THIRTY

I didn't want to go to Allison's memorial. It felt wrong, like dancing on her grave. Like I was gloating, disrespecting the dead, reveling in the victory of some game she didn't even know she was playing.

Ever since I had learned of her existence—that day at the office, those pictures of their perfect life displayed proudly on Ben's desk like trophies—I had looked at her with a strange mixture of jealousy and resentment; of wonder and awe. I had wanted to *be* her, and in order to be her, I had wanted her gone. But now that she was gone, I wasn't sure how I was supposed to feel about it.

The entire magazine was going, though, paying their respects, and I couldn't think of a way to get out of it that wouldn't either seem cold-hearted or crude.

"It'll just be an hour," Kasey had said as we walked up the side-walk, yanking down the hem of her dress. It was too tight for the occasion, the kind of thing I would have worn to a bar, but I couldn't blame her. Nobody ever seems to have the right outfit to commemorate death. "It's not open casket, so it's not like you have to *look* at her or anything. Thank God."

She was mistaking my nerves for some kind of inherent fear of funerals, but it wasn't that. It was never that. It was this idea that I couldn't seem to shake: that now that Allison was dead, she *knew*. Allison *knew* about Ben and me. Our secret. As soon as we walked inside, I got that feeling again. The one my mother used to warn me about: eyes on my back, Allison's eyes, trailing me around the house as if she were in the ceiling itself, watching.

We stood in the foyer, looking around, before spotting the bar table and making a beeline, grabbing two flutes of champagne. It felt like an odd thing to serve at a memorial, too celebratory and light, especially considering the circumstances. But I needed something to take the edge off. Something to help me breathe.

"Ben's in there," Kasey said, gesturing to the living room. "*Accepting condolences.*"

"Should we go in?"

"I guess," she said, taking a sip of champagne, wincing. It looked cheap, an unnaturally fluorescent yellow. "Her family's in there, too. I guess we should say something."

"Allison's family?"

I had expected it, obviously—of course her family would be at her memorial; this was their house, after all—but I wasn't prepared for it. For the reality of facing them: her mother and her father, her siblings, her grandparents. Of looking them in the eye, trying to fake a lip quiver, maybe even squeeze out a tear. Of reciting the words I knew I was supposed to say—*I'm so sorry for your loss*—but knowing, deep down, that their loss was my gain.

"Yes, Allison's family. Who else?"

I exhaled, took a long sip from my own flute, and licked my lips. "I think I'm just going to go outside for a second. Get some air."

I remember pushing my way through the crowded dining room, throwing shy smiles at my coworkers. It was strange, seeing them there, dressed in black. Their demure expressions and ill-fitting clothes; the way they stood huddled together, shoulders tense, in packs of three. It was almost like I hadn't even realized they existed outside of the walls of the office, even though we had socialized together so many times before. It reminded me of one time in Beaufort when I had run into the liquor store and bumped into my childhood pastor; he was clutching a handle of vodka at nine in the morning, skin sagging, and didn't even bother to hide it. It made me realize that we like to organize the people in our lives into tidy little compartments, keeping them there to make ourselves feel safe, so seeing my coworkers *there*, like *that*—ripped from our emotionless cubicles and conference rooms, wiping snot on their shirtsleeves and their eyes red and raw—felt unnatural and wrong, driving home the realness of it all.

I opened the back door and stepped onto the porch, the cool breeze feeling good on my face. It was warm in there, stuffy. Too small a house for too many people. Then I walked over to the porch steps and sat down, placing the champagne on the ground, and put my head in my hands.

"Isabelle?"

I swung around, hand to my chest, realizing I wasn't alone. Ben was standing just to the side of the house, hidden behind some bushes, although I recognized his voice as soon as I heard it.

"Ben," I said, standing up. "What are you doing?"

He lifted his arm, a cigarette lit between his fingers, and shrugged.

"I didn't know you smoked."

"I don't."

I took a few steps forward, glancing through the windows at the back of the house. Nobody was looking outside; they were all too busy mingling, gathering near an appetizer table arranged with plastic trays of sweaty cheese and baby carrots the texture of ashy elbows. They were eying the family pictures that cluttered up the walls—Allison on a soccer field, in a graduation cap, a wedding gown—shaking their heads and muttering the same recycled lines.

"Ben," I said again, stepping off the porch and onto the grass, closer to him. We were hidden then, behind the house and beneath the trees. Nobody knew we were out there; nobody could see. "I'm so sorry. I don't even know what to say."

"Thank you," he said, sighing. He leaned his head back, his eyes on the sky. "I just had to get out of there. Away from . . . everybody."

"I get that."

"You have no idea how many people I've had to talk to over these last few days," he said, looking back at me. His eyes looked so tired, like he hadn't slept in a week.

"I can imagine," I said, taking another step closer. And I *could* imagine. I had been through it before; or, at least, something similar.

"And the entire time," he said, taking another drag of his cigarette, the tendons in his neck bulging, "I was just thinking about how badly I wanted to talk to you."

I stopped mid-stride, unsure if I'd heard him correctly.

"I know I probably shouldn't say that, especially here . . . but fuck, Isabelle. I don't care anymore. I don't. Life's too short."

There was a crash from somewhere inside, loud, like someone dropping a glass. I heard a sob erupt and peeked around the corner of the house, seeing a flutter of bodies through the window running to something—or rather, *someone*—on the ground. It was Allison's mom, I realized, crumpled into a heap on the floor. She was kneeling in a pile of shards—a broken wineglass—with bloody knees, crying.

I motioned to the back door, mouth half-open, like he should get back inside, but Ben didn't flinch. He didn't move. He just kept looking at me, kept talking.

"These last couple years with Allison have been tough," he said. "She had a problem, Isabelle. A problem I didn't know how to handle. I tried to help her, but—"

He stopped, pinched the bridge of his nose. The cherry-red tip of his cigarette was dangerously close to his skin, and I was sure that he could feel it. The burn of it, right between his eyes.

"I came home from the office Monday night and found her on

the bathroom floor. She was pale. Her eyes were open. That's not the first time she had, you know . . . but this time, the way she looked, I just knew that she was—"

I didn't wait for him to finish his sentence. Instead, I closed the rest of the distance between us, wrapping my arms around him.

"It's okay," I said. "It's not your fault."

I could imagine that, too. How he was feeling. Being the one to blame.

"I wanted to tell you so many times." I could feel the warmth of his breath on my neck, the stale smokiness, and I realized that this was the closest we had dared to get since that night at the oyster roast. The first time since then that we had ever really touched. "All those times we were talking, and I was avoiding going home, avoiding having to deal with it, I wanted to just tell you all of it. Get it off my chest. We weren't happy, Isabelle. We weren't good together anymore."

"It's okay," I said again, because I didn't know what else to say.

"I *tried*," he said, pulling back from me. The way he was looking at me, so desperate, I could tell that he wanted me to believe him. He *needed* me to believe him. "I tried so hard to make it work. I mean, you know, all those times that we were together, I wanted to . . . but, obviously, I *didn't*—"

"I know you tried, Ben. You don't have to convince me."

I pulled my hands from his back and placed them on his cheeks, holding him tight. I looked into his eyes; our faces, inches apart, and before I knew what was happening, the space between us closed. Ben's lips were on mine, moving frantically, his hands pulling at my hair. I felt his cigarette drop to the ground, skimming my arm on the way down, and our kiss was long and hard and desperate, the culmination of six months of wanting, wondering, remembering what it had been like that first time on the water.

I had forgotten where I was in that moment, what I was doing. Allison's mother on the ground inside, too distraught to care about the glass cutting into her flesh. All of my coworkers—my future, my career—one small step away from finding us out, from ruining it all. But I didn't care about any of it. All that mattered was that I was with him, finally.

He was *mine*, finally.

"*Ben?*"

I heard the back door open, the creak of the hinges. A pair of footsteps stepping out onto the porch, feet from where we were standing.

"*Ben, are you out there?*"

In an instant, Ben separated himself from my arms, peeling his hands from my hair and wiping his lips, removing any traces of me from his skin. One second, we were intertwined, knotted together, whole—and the next, he was gone.

"Yeah, out here," he said, jumping up onto the porch without looking back. "Just getting some air."

I heard the slap of a hand against his back. That same voice, swathed in worry.

"You okay?"

"Yeah," he said, clearing his throat. "Yeah, all good."

I heard Ben walk back inside, his shoes on the hardwood, but knew, somehow, that the person who disrupted us was still there. I could feel him, lingering, just on the other side the wall. I pushed myself farther back into the bushes, feeling the branches scratch at my skin, getting tangled in my hair, and held my breath, waiting to be found. He took a few steps forward, and I watched the back of his head emerge as he walked toward the steps, hands punched into his pockets, before looking down at the ground—at my champagne glass, sweating in the heat, little bubbles exploding to the surface. Then he leaned down, picked it up, and inspected the smudge of lipstick on the rim.

I turned around and ran.

CHAPTER THIRTY-ONE

NOW

Waylon and I spent the rest of the weekend recording. It's starting to come more naturally now: those conversations that once felt scripted and forced flowing effortlessly, like we're two old friends, hunched over coffee, making up for lost time.

It's Monday morning now, and I watch as he shuffles around the kitchen with a mug in one hand and a piece of toast in the other. It reminds me of Ben and me, just barely over a year ago. The easy chaos of a weekday morning. The natural rhythm of two lives intertwined, growing together like vines: me, planting a kiss on his cheek as he brushed his teeth; Ben's fingers grazing my back as I perched on the edge of the bed, lotioning my legs. Helping him shave those hard-to-reach nooks on his neck, my razor pushing into his soft spots.

"I'm going to swing by the station first," Waylon says, wiping a smear of peanut butter from his lip. "See if I can catch Dozier first thing."

"Sure," I say, blinking away the daydream. "Sounds good."

I told him about my neighbor this weekend, too. About the confrontation on his porch and my sighting of him at the vigil; the old man in the rocking chair with a direct view into my yard. I still don't have any evidence, any proof, but I desperately need some other angle to focus on after seeing myself on that laptop screen.

I *need* to believe there's another explanation, another answer, outside of the one that's starting to swirl in my mind like an apparition taking shape in the dark.

"Call you after?" he asks. "Maybe we can meet for lunch?"

I smile and nod, waving him out of the house and exhaling slowly as soon as the door shuts behind him.

I walk over to the table now and open up my laptop, launching another baby monitor video and forcing myself to watch. I appreciate his help—really, I do—but there are still some things I'd rather do without him. Like these videos. I need to watch more of them, and I'd rather do it without Waylon watching, too.

My chest tightens now as I watch myself place Mason in his crib. I start to fast-forward and the clock ticks dutifully ahead: nine o'clock, ten o'clock, midnight, two a.m. I stare at the little crack of moonlight beneath the closed door, waiting for another movement. Another shadow. Finally, I let myself exhale as soon as the sun starts to come up, illuminating his bedroom, and the clock strikes six.

The video stops. I've made it to morning. Nothing happened.

I lean back into my chair, thinking. I just can't shake that image from my mind: me, standing in Mason's nursery, staring ahead at nothing. I was under the impression that my sleepwalking had stopped once I left for college. I remember being terrified when I moved into the dorms, imagining myself waking up naked in the hallway or hovering over some random boy in bed. Running a bath in the communal showers—silently slipping beneath the water, bubbles rising to the surface until suddenly, they stopped—or, God forbid, forgetting that I was sleeping nine floors aboveground and getting the urge to open up a window and climb outside. But none of that ever happened. It slowed down considerably once I hit my teens, like the doctor had said it would, and by the time I was out on my own, it seemed to go away completely.

Only apparently, it didn't.

And then there's the other thing that's been bothering me; the other little detail that seems like nothing—but at the same time, seems like something, too. When Ben and I met, I looked like Allison—half a decade younger, sure, but the resemblance was there. I didn't see it at the time. I was so entranced by her, by everything about her, that I couldn't possibly recognize myself in her in any conceivable way. Her age intimidated me; her body intimidated me. She was a *woman*, and I, a girl. Fresh on the job, fighting a naive crush on my boss, inferior to her in every way that mattered—but now, after eight years of time, I look in the mirror and I can see it: brown hair, olive skin. The almond shape of our eyes and the lank hang of our arms by our sides, long and skinny, like we don't quite know where to put them.

And now, whoever this new girl is looks like *me*.

Ben clearly has a type, and I can't decide if that makes me feel better or worse. Maybe this new girl is nothing more than a rebound, a quick fling to help him get over a failed marriage and a lost son . . . but then does that mean that *I* was just a rebound, too? A rebound from Allison? I guess it isn't unusual to have a type—lots of guys have a type—but for some reason, it reminds me of those people who buy the exact same dog when their other one dies. Instead of trying to grieve and move on, try something new, they instead decide to just replace it entirely and recreate their former life. Pretend that nothing even happened.

I know that's not fair, but at the same time, I can't help but wonder now what he was thinking when we met each other that night at the oyster roast: he was unhappy, Allison was unhappy, their home life a wreck. He had been out on his own and found himself quite literally colliding with the younger, bouncier, perkier version of her. How it must have felt for him that night, looking at me and imagining that he was out with his wife, his *happy* wife, a wife who was interested in him again, flirting with him again, hanging on his every word. A wife who didn't have to drown her dissatisfaction with their life in pills; a wife who met him for coffee and cocktails and threw secret winks in his direction.

So that's what he had seen in me; I had always wondered. It wasn't *me* that he was attracted to. It wasn't that at all. I had just reminded him of *her*—only I was still shiny and new, a model upgrade, not yet broken by the torments of time.

Or at least, that's what he thought.

I shake the idea from my mind and click out of the video I was watching, selecting another one. Then another. I work my way through an entire week, then decide to watch a few a bit closer to the time of Mason's disappearance: two months before. So far, I haven't seen myself again, and I start to wonder it was just a onetime thing. I'm halfway through another video—it's just after one in the morning in this one, and Mason is lying on his back, breathing deeply—when I hear Roscoe perk up on the other side of the living room. He starts to bark, and I look up to see the shadow of a man approaching the front door.

"Coming," I yell, hitting *Pause* before standing up from the table.

I'm expecting it to be Waylon, not quite comfortable enough in my home to let himself in—after all, he's only been gone for an hour, just enough time to drive to the station, get shut down, and drive back empty-handed—but when I open the door, that's not who I see.

"Good morning," Detective Dozier says, hands on his hips. "Mind if I come in?"

CHAPTER THIRTY-TWO

For a second, I'm too stunned to speak. Dozier is not supposed to be here. He's supposed to be at the station, with Waylon, talking about my neighbor.

"Got your voice mails," he says when I don't respond. "And your emails. Figured I'd swing by on my way to the station as opposed to calling you back."

"Oh, thank you," I say, finally finding my voice. "Yes, please come in."

I open the door wider, and Dozier steps inside, offering Roscoe his hand to sniff.

"So, what's this about your neighbor?" he asks, getting right to it. "Seventeen-forty-two Catty Lane?"

"Yeah," I say, taking a seat on the couch. I gesture for him to sit, but he keeps standing. "He's not really my neighbor, exactly—he lives on the street parallel to mine—but I noticed the other day that he has a direct view into my backyard. He can practically see Mason's window from his porch."

I look down and realize that I'm clenching my fists tightly. I uncurl my fingers, flex them a few times.

"When I tried to ask him about it, he got very defensive," I continue. "Basically chased me off his property, like he didn't like the fact that I was snooping around. He wouldn't even tell me his name."

Dozier shifts on his feet, moving the weight from one foot to the other. I watch as he chews on his own lip like a toothpick, as if turning something over in his mind.

"I talked to him once before, last year, and he didn't raise any red flags," I continue, pushing on. "But there's just something about the way he *spoke* to me—"

"I'm going to stop you right here," Dozier interrupts, holding up his hand. "I thought we made it clear that you're not to be interrogating anyone on your own anymore."

"I wasn't *interrogating* him," I say. "I just wanted to ask—"

"—if he kidnapped your son without any probable cause or proof?"

"No," I say, getting agitated. "But I don't understand why he wouldn't at least be open to *talking* to me, unless he has something to hide . . ."

"Maybe because the last time you tried to '*talk*' to someone, you broke his nose."

I stop, my mind back in that grocery store. To that old man in his apron and my fists flying, connecting so hard with his face. The wet crunch of cartilage and his old, leathery hands cupped over his head, shaking like a kid in a tornado drill. The tissue-paper skin of his arms already streaked with bruises, and the blood trickling down his chin, thick and sticky as it pooled on the ground and seeped into the tile cracks.

"I didn't mean to do that," I murmur. "I told you that already."

"Yeah, well, you did. So maybe you shouldn't be surprised when folks get a little skittish when you show up unannounced. Why were you on his porch in the first place?"

I hesitate. Part of me doesn't even want to tell him about the man I saw before. I can still picture his brown robe and stringy gray hair;

the way he had stared at me, through me, his eyes fogged over with cataracts, like he hadn't even seen me at all.

That man wasn't like the other times, though. I know he wasn't. He wasn't just a shadow or some blurry figure dancing in my peripheral vision; a noise my sleep-deprived mind had simply made up and cast out into the world. An imaginary friend.

No, this man was *real*.

"There was someone else," I say at last, forcing myself to continue. "I was walking my dog around the neighborhood. Late—like, one in the morning—and there was an older man sitting on his porch."

I wait for Dozier to respond, but instead, he remains silent.

"He was just *sitting* there," I continue. "Staring into nothing. I've never seen him before. And why would he be out there so late at night? What if he was out there the night Mason was taken? What if he saw something, or—"

"Do you make it a habit to walk around your neighborhood at one in the morning?" the detective asks, cutting me off. "Seems a little strange, even with the dog."

I exhale, pushing my palms into my face. This conversation is reminding me of last March, the way this man had pushed me to the absolute edge. The way he was somehow able to make everything I said sound bad, wrong. Guilty.

"I have trouble sleeping, okay?" I drop my hands into my lap and look at him, glaring. "I would think you would, too, considering my son is still missing, and you still haven't found him."

We're both quiet, staring at each other, until Dozier sighs. He walks toward me, finally, and sits on the edge of the couch, taking care to keep a few feet of distance between us. Like I'm a disease he doesn't want to catch.

"It's highly unlikely that man saw anything on the night of the disappearance," he says, his hands on his thighs. "He doesn't live there."

"How do you know that?" I ask, a prickle in my chest. "Do you know the man who does?"

Dozier is quiet, staring at me, and I can tell he's keeping something from me. Something big.

"I can find out on my own," I continue. "It'll just be easier if you tell me yourself."

The detective sighs, pinching the skin between his eyes. Finally, he speaks.

"The man who owns the house is Paul Hayes," he says at last. "We know who he is because he's out on parole—but he's been a perfectly law-abiding citizen for years. His parole officer visits him once a month, and I can assure you: He lives alone. There is nobody else in that house. I don't know who you saw, but he doesn't live there. He wasn't out there the night Mason was taken."

"Paul Hayes," I repeat, testing the name out on my tongue. It sounds vaguely familiar again, probably from when I met him last year. A forgettable name for a forgettable person. "What's he out on parole for?"

"Nothing violent. Some drug offenses."

"Can you go talk to him?" I ask, remembering what Waylon said about the case he solved. That girl found in the basement; the proof hiding in his own house. "Maybe get a warrant—?"

"No, I can't get a warrant," he snaps. "Jesus, I can't just question anybody about a kidnapping without some kind of probable cause. And *seeing someone* on his porch at night is not probable cause."

I don't like the way he said that—*seeing someone*—as if it belonged in air quotes. As if it didn't actually happen; as if I'm just making it up, or worse, as if I somehow imagined it.

"Is there anything else?" he asks.

"Yes," I say, my voice sharp. "There is something else. The email I sent you—"

"Right," he says, standing up from the couch with a groan. "I took a look at the article and didn't see any suspicious comments."

"Well, that's the thing," I say, standing up, too. I walk over to the table and sit back down, grabbing my laptop and pulling the article up. "The one I wanted you to look at . . . it disappeared. Why would someone write a comment and then delete it?"

"What did it say?"

"It said '*He's in a better place.*'"

Detective Dozier eyes me quietly before letting out a sigh and walking into my dining room. I avoid his eyes as he takes in the wall, the pictures and map and article clippings cluttering up every surface.

"Christ," he mutters. It's probably triple the size it was the last time he saw it, expanding slowly like a bleeding stain.

"Why would someone write that?" I ask again, ignoring him. "Why would someone *say* that?"

"There are a lot of reasons," he says at last, leaning over the table to look at my screen. "Maybe it was some well-meaning religious fanatic who realized how insensitive their comment was and deleted it. Or maybe you misread it. Was this it?"

He points at the screen, to the very last comment: *Such a bizarre case.*

"No," I say, shaking my head. Remembering. "I didn't misread it. It said '*He's in a better place.*'"

"Look," he says, straightening back up again. I watch as he walks over to the entryway, scratching Roscoe's ears with one hand as he opens the door with the other. "There's nothing I can do about any of this. You're inventing clues where they don't exist, and you're pulling resources away from other angles. Do you have any idea how many times you called me last week?"

We're both quiet. I can feel my cheeks starting to burn, the mental image of Detective Dozier seeing my name on his cell phone screen and willfully ignoring it searing in my mind.

"Leave Paul Hayes alone," he says at last. "And as always, I'll call you with any developments."

He's decided that this visit is over, then. That, once again, I've wasted his time. He's made it halfway out, pulling the door shut behind him, when something comes over me that I can't control, rising up from the pit of my belly like stomach acid.

"I didn't kill my son!" I yell after him. "I didn't hurt him."

I don't know why I say it, but in this moment, it feels like I have to. It's the same way I feel every time I'm standing onstage, taking in all those looks from the audience: doubtful, distrusting. Like they're just waiting for me to fail, cameras out, ready to document it for their own sick pleasure and plaster it across the internet for the world to see. Or maybe it's the way this man has been dismissing me for over a year—the way he looks at me with smug eyes and a smirk, like he knows something I don't—or meets all my questions with groans and sighs instead of actual answers. Like he doesn't believe he'll ever catch the person responsible—because, in his mind, the person responsible is *me*.

Or maybe—after seeing myself on that laptop screen and all those memories of Margaret that are suddenly so raw and real—maybe I need to believe it, too.

"I didn't do anything wrong," I say, quieter now, embarrassed at the sound of my own voice.

Detective Dozier stops mid-step and turns around slowly. His hand is still hanging off the knob as he looks at me, eyebrows raised, a tug of satisfaction on his lips, like he's just won some kind of dare between us.

"I never said you did."

CHAPTER THIRTY-THREE

THEN

I'm sitting on the edge of my bed, still in my nightgown. I shut the window earlier, even though it's still hot in the house—even though, without the breeze, the air is sticky and still. I can't stand the smell anymore: the smell of the marsh. The smell of death, the way it comes creeping through the cracked windowpane, snaking its way beneath my nostrils like a finger beckoning me close.

"You're going to have to listen to me very carefully," Dad says now, his voice urgent and low. I can't bring myself to face him, sitting next to me on the bed, so instead, I stare at the carpet. "Izzy, the police will be here any minute. They're going to want to talk to you about what happened last night."

"But I don't know what happened last night—"

"That's right," he says. "You don't know. You were sleeping."

I look up at him, eyebrows bunched. His unspoken words hang heavy between us, an implication that it would be wise to do exactly as he says.

"But sometimes, you know . . ." I stop, look back down at my lap as I try to work out how to phrase it. "Sometimes, I get up and do things—"

"Not last night," he says, shaking his head. "Last night, you were asleep the whole time. You don't even need to bring that up."

"But when I woke up—"

"When you woke up, you came downstairs and found your mother and me seated at the kitchen table," he interrupts. "And that's when we told you what happened."

"But what *did happen*?" I ask, my voice painfully shrill. I'm tired of dancing around it; tired of speaking in code. I have a feeling, deep down, that I know what the answer is, but I just need to hear him say it. "Dad, what happened to Margaret?"

"She's . . . gone, Isabelle. She died."

I knew it from the way my parents had looked at me in the kitchen—my mother, those waxy eyes, and the way she pushed past me so angrily. I knew it from the moment I rolled over and noticed Margaret missing from bed, really. It was like an instinct, barely there. Like the world was somehow different, smaller, without her in it. After all, death haunts this place—it always has. In a way, it almost feels like it's been picking us off, one by one. Like it's some kind of toll, and our debt is not yet paid.

I hear the sudden slam of car doors outside, signaling the police have arrived. Dad gets up quickly and pats my leg, looking down at me one last time.

"Only speak when spoken to," he says. "Don't say anything unless it's in response to a question."

I nod.

"Exactly as I said," he repeats. Then he slips into the hallway and shuts the door behind him.

I've been listening to the noises downstairs for a while now: the murmuring, the whispers. The sound of people walking around the house, inspecting things. Finally, I hear a knock on my door—a gentle, polite pounding that says: *I don't need your permission; I'm coming in anyway.* It's nothing more than a courtesy, I know. An opportunity for me to steel myself, steady my breathing.

I glance at the door.

"Isabelle, sweetheart, this is Chief Montgomery." My dad pokes his head inside before pushing the door open. I see another man beside him: tall and lanky with a head the shape and shine of a cue ball. "He's here to ask you a few questions."

I nod, look down at my hands clasped in my lap, and repeat Dad's lines in my mind over and over again. It doesn't feel like a lie, really, because I don't know what happened—I wouldn't even know if I *was* lying—but somehow, it doesn't feel like the truth, either.

"Hi, Isabelle." Chief Montgomery walks across my bedroom, taking a seat next to me on the mattress. I hear the springs creak, feel my weight tilt toward him. "Do you mind if I sit here?"

I shake my head, even though he's already sitting.

"Can you tell me what you remember about last night? Anything unusual happen?"

I look up at the man, the way his forehead seems to connect seamlessly with his scalp, both shiny and sleek with sweat. He reminds me of a copperhead Margaret and I found in our backyard once: the pointy nose, the slit-like eyes. Margaret wanted to keep it, give it a name, but Dad decapitated it with a shovel without a second thought. I'll never forget the *crunch* it made when that metal made contact; the mucusy strings of blood and entrails that hung out of its neck like soggy noodles. The way the body kept moving for a minute, writhing around on the ground like it didn't even know it was dead.

I glance at my dad, register his gentle little nod.

"Nothing unusual," I say, and that's the truth, sort of. The air conditioner was out, and Margaret had slept in my room. That was kind of unusual. "We had a bath, then we got into bed."

"Okay," Chief Montgomery says. "And around what time was that?"

I shrug. "Nine?"

"Did you get out of bed for any reason? To go to the bathroom maybe, or get a drink of water?"

I glance at my dad again, then immediately back down to my lap. "No. I was asleep the whole night."

"Okay," he says, nodding. "Okay, and what about Margaret? Did you see her get out of bed?"

"No," I say again. "I was sleeping."

"Did you hear anything?"

"No."

"Not even through that window?"

I look up at the man; he's pointing at the wall, my window, facing the marsh.

"No," I say again. "It was closed."

"Why was it closed? It's hot in here." He pulls a handkerchief out of his pocket and wipes his head, like he wants to emphasize the fact that he's sweating. Immediately, I see little beads of it squeeze back to the surface, like his scalp is made of mesh. "Surely you could have used some breeze, right? And if the window was open, maybe you might have heard something in the water? Splashing or yelling?"

"No," I say again. "It wasn't open. I . . . don't like the smell."

Chief Montgomery nods. "Okay," he says, the sweat trickling down his neck now. "Okay. And about what time did you get up this morning?"

I want to look at my dad again, but something tells me I shouldn't keep doing that. That I should keep my eyes straight ahead, trained on the man in front of me.

"Seven?"

"Are you always such an early bird?"

"I guess."

"And was Margaret awake when you got up?"

"I'm not sure."

He shifts on the mattress, crossing his legs, and I don't like the way the movement is making me slide closer to him again. Our legs are touching, and I want to scoot back, but at the same time, I'm afraid to move.

"Isabelle, I'm gonna need your help on this, okay? I hear you and your sister were close."

I nod—*were*—and before I can look away, I feel a tear escape, making its way down my cheek. I lift my arm and wipe it away with the back of my hand.

"What happened this morning after you woke up? Is there anything unusual that you can remember? Anything at all out of place?"

I think about getting up, unsteady and slow, the overwhelming smell of the marsh in my bedroom that has since aired out. The water on the carpet that squished between my toes, now close to dry. Running into the bathroom, finding towels on my floor; towels that my dad picked up and dropped into the washing machine, tidying up behind him. The fact that I was wearing a different nightgown from the one I fell asleep in, or the dried mud I felt smeared behind my ear. I lift my hand now and touch that same little patch of skin. It's clean. Before the police got here, I had scrubbed it raw. Erased the fingermarks like I had tried to erase the footsteps on my carpet.

Like if I could just make them disappear, it would mean that they were never even there to begin with.

"No," I say at last. "Nothing out of place. I went downstairs, into the kitchen, and found my parents. And that's when . . . that's when they told me about Margaret. That she had an accident."

"Okay." He nods. "Okay, sweetheart, that's all I need. You did great."

He pats my knee with his hand before standing up and walking back toward my father. Then they both smile in my direction before stepping into the hallway and shutting the door behind them.

I stay seated for a while, staring at the wall in front of me, my heart pounding in my chest. I've never liked to lie. It always makes me feel so wrong, so ashamed, but earlier this morning, when Dad was walking me through it, he had said that sometimes a lie can be a good thing if it's done for the right reasons.

It reminded me of a lie I told for Margaret once, sometime last year, after she had broken my mother's crystal vase. She knew not to touch it—it was an antique; like so many other things in this house, off-limits—but she did it anyway, standing on a barstool on her tip-toes, reaching for it with outstretched hands. She had just picked Mom some flowers from outside, but before she could display them, her right foot slipped, sending the thing crashing down onto the tile, shattering everywhere. Mom was angry, of course—*furious*—but I knew Margaret didn't mean it. She didn't *mean* to break anything. So right then, in the middle of her scolding, I stepped forward and took the blame.

Maybe this was like that, I reason. A good lie. Maybe Dad wants me to lie to protect Margaret. But somehow, deep down, I know that's not right. I know it's not Margaret he's protecting.

Somehow, I know that it's me.

CHAPTER THIRTY-FOUR

NOW

I can't keep watching these videos—not after that visit from Dozier. I feel rattled, restless, like my veins have morphed into live wires buzzing with electrical charge.

I'm having a hard time processing everything he just told me: that that comment could've been a figment of my own imagination; that Paul Hayes lives alone. I suppose it's possible he had company—that maybe that old man on his porch was visiting for the week, someone completely harmless—but still. Why was he sitting out there in the middle of the night? Why had he ignored me? Had he even seen that I was there?

And, even more terrifying: Was *he* even there?

I shake my head, pace around the floor for a bit, trying to relax. I'll go back to the house tonight, see if he's still there. Maybe I should bring Waylon with me, just to be sure that he sees him, too. And if he does, I'll know. I'll know I'm not crazy.

I grab my phone and open up Facebook, typing in his name: Paul Hayes. I quickly realize that there are a lot of Paul Hayeses out there—an attorney in Texas with a wide-brimmed hat; an Oklahoma teenager with a giant truck. There are even a few right here in

Savannah, holding up deer and fish and other dead things, but none of them are him.

I open up Instagram next, do the same search, and scroll.

Nothing. Not a single thing.

I lower my phone, chew on the inside of my cheek, and think. To the outside world, Paul Hayes seems not to exist—and suddenly, I wonder if that's on purpose. I wonder if he was forgettable for a reason. When I talked to him last year, knocking on that door with Mason's poster in hand, he had been the perfect combination of unremarkable: polite but not overly friendly, cooperative but not especially helpful. Like someone who didn't want to raise any flags. Someone who wanted to disappear into the shadows.

Someone with something to hide.

I suppose it isn't a crime to like your privacy, but still. He has a record. He's out on parole. He was at the vigil. His porch has a direct view into my backyard.

It's something—a lead, definitely. And one that I need to know more about.

I also need to know more about my sleepwalking. I need to find out if it means anything, and—I swallow, close my eyes—if I could have done something again. Something I don't remember. I look down and dial Dr. Harris's number next, listening to the ringing before it flips to voice mail. Then I leave a quick message, asking to be penciled in as soon as possible.

I hang up, but before I can put my phone down, I feel it start to vibrate in my hand.

"Waylon," I say, answering immediately after seeing his name on the screen. "You'll never guess—"

"Hey, Isabelle," he interrupts, sounding breathless and excited. "Just got a few words in with Detective Dozier."

I stop, my mouth hanging open as I glance at the clock. Dozier just left here a few minutes ago. There's no way he could have gotten to the station that fast.

"Oh," I say, feeling my cheeks flush with red, my heartbeat rising. "And how did that go?"

"Great. He's being cooperative, but he did say he doesn't know anything about your neighbor. I'm sorry."

I open my mouth to respond again, but the words don't come out.

"I'm heading to lunch a little early," he says, oblivious to the thoughts racing around in my mind. "Still want to meet?"

I'm stunned, standing in place, trying to work through the implications of this conversation. What it all means.

"Isabelle?"

"Yeah." I finally manage to croak out a word, although right now, lunch with Waylon is the last thing I want to do. "Yeah, sounds good."

"Great," he says. "Meet you at Framboise in thirty. I'll tell you all about it."

The line goes dead, and I stand in silence, the phone still pushed to my ear. Then I swallow, lower my arm slowly, a blanket of dread descending over me as I look around my house, at all of Waylon's things cluttered around the room: his jacket flung over the dining room chair, his suitcase stacked in the hallway corner. His mug on the counter, drips of coffee that touched his lips still staining the rim. There are pieces of him everywhere, these microscopic clues of another life in my home like dust on furniture, visible only when you catch a glimpse in just the right light.

And that's when the gravity of it all fully hits me.

Waylon sought me out on that airplane. With a rush of certainty, I know it in my bones. He was looking for me, *specifically*; maybe he even went to TrueCrimeCon to meet me. He had found me sitting there, that empty seat next to me, and introduced himself. Handed me his card. Then he came here and gave me a taste of what he knew I wanted: someone to listen, someone to understand. Someone to *care*. It was only a bite, though. Only enough to satisfy the craving. And then he threatened to go, leaving me desperate: a junky in need of just one more fix, so I had offered my home to make him stay.

Now this man who came into my life just one week ago has managed to weasel his way in so completely, I realize there is no way it wasn't orchestrated. There is no way it wasn't planned.

I think about the violence again, like I have so many times over this past year. About how sometimes, it presents itself as a shotgun blast, loud and messy, spraying gore against the wall—but other times, it's as quiet as a whisper: a handful of swallowed pills or a scream underwater. A stranger slipping into a window at night before leaving without a trace. But then there are the other times, too, when it comes masked as something else. When it's invited inside, stepping politely through the front door wearing a disguise: an ally, a friend.

I thought Waylon cared. I thought he wanted to help. But now I don't know why he's here. I don't know what he wants.

Now I know that he's lying. I know that he has a secret, too.

CHAPTER THIRTY-FIVE

On my way to Framboise, I get another phone call. This time, it's Dr. Harris, calling me back.

"Isabelle," he says, seemingly happy to hear from me. I've been avoiding him, I know, for months now. There's an expectation with doctors that with their help, you should be getting better; that all your problems should slowly dissolve like salt in water, leaving nothing behind but the bitter taste of what used to be. But clearly, I'm not. They're not. "Sorry for missing your call. I was with a client."

"Yeah, hi," I say, holding my phone between my cheek and shoulder. I'm in the car, ten minutes from the restaurant. "That's okay. I was just wondering if I could make an appointment—"

"Yes, your voice mail requested *as soon as possible*. Is everything okay?"

"I'm fine," I lie. "I just have some questions for you. Wanted to pick your brain."

"Does this afternoon work? I've had a cancellation."

I look at the clock in my car; it's already past noon. "What time?"

"One thirty?"

I drum my fingers against the wheel. I want to hear what Waylon has to say—no, I *need* to hear what Waylon has to say—about his fictional meeting with Detective Dozier, his lie regarding Paul Hayes. I need to know what he's after, why he's here. Why he's lying to me. But at the same time, I know I'll see him tonight, too. There's no avoiding that now. No avoiding him.

"Sure," I say, deciding on the spot to cancel lunch and take this appointment instead. After all, as much as I'm afraid of all the reasons why Waylon may be lying to me—of what he's doing in my house, my life—I'm more afraid of what I saw on that laptop screen. "I'll see you at one thirty."

Once I arrive, the office feels familiar yet foreign, like walking into your own home in a dream. I used to come here so often—twice a week every week, starting last July—that I knew it inch by inch. But now so many little things have changed, it doesn't feel *quite* right. I know they're supposed to be subtle alterations, a slow redecoration over the past six months, but all at once, it feels jarring, like seeing the drastic changes in a child after too much time apart.

All of it is making me feel uneasy, like I'm in the wrong place.

"How are you sleeping?" Dr. Harris asks now, leaning forward. His hair is a bit longer than it was the last time I saw him, the old stubble on his chin grown out into the beginnings of a beard. "Any better than before?"

"Yes, better," I lie. "Much better."

"That's fantastic," he says, pleased with himself. "Are you following my protocol? Getting enough exercise, cutting out alcohol and caffeine—"

"Yes," I lie again, because I don't want to rehash this with him. I need caffeine to get anything done during the day; without it, I might as well be a zombie. And alcohol . . . well, it feels like I need that, too, sometimes. Just for different reasons.

"Have you been creating a relaxing nighttime routine like we talked about? Cutting out electronics, stressful triggers—"

"Yes."

The lies are coming too easily now, but how am I supposed to create a *relaxing nighttime routine* when I live the way that I do—always alone, always on edge, always waiting for Mason to come home? My entire existence is a stressful trigger; my house the scene of a crime that remains perpetually unsolved.

"Cutting down on daytime naps?"

I think about all my little microsleeps; those minutes or hours of unaccounted-for time. About blinking my eyes, finding someone staring at me—Waylon, or a stranger—concern in their eyes. But it's not as if I'm doing that on purpose. As if I have any control. So again, I nod.

"How about the sleeping pills?" he asks. "Have you been taking those?"

"On occasion," I say. "But the strength still seems a bit low."

"You're on the highest dosage."

"I know."

Dr. Harris eyes me, shifting in his chair.

"So, what is it you wanted to talk to me about?" he asks, spinning a pen between his fingers like a baton. "You mentioned you had some questions."

"Yes. Not about insomnia, though. About sleepwalking, actually."

"Ah," he says, leaning back with a playful grin. "You used to be a sleepwalker, correct? I remember discussing that."

"When I was a kid. It used to happen pretty frequently."

"That's not uncommon in adolescence."

"What triggers it, exactly?"

"Oh, lots of things," he says. "Fatigue, irregular sleep schedules. High fever, some medications, trauma, genetics, stress. Most of the time, though, it just happens."

"For no real reason?"

"Yes," he says. "During stages three and four of deep sleep. It's called *disassociated arousal*. Some parts of the brain are asleep while others are still awake."

"I was just wondering," I say, looking down at my lap. More and more, this is feeling like that morning with Chief Montgomery: him, sitting too close in my bedroom, and me, hiding the truth. Diverting my eyes. Too afraid of what he might find there: my secret, my lie, curled up somewhere deep in my pupils like a hibernating animal. "Is it possible for someone to do something bad while they're sleepwalking? And not know it? Not remember?"

"Define *bad*," he says, resting his chin in his hand. "Sometimes people urinate in their closets, for example, or venture outside. Have entire conversations, even. That can be embarrassing."

"No, I mean, can they do something . . . dangerous," I ask, looking up at him. "Violent."

"It's rare," he says, speaking slowly. "But sometimes people will try to drive cars or climb out of windows, and that can of course be very dangerous—"

"What about to other people?"

Dr. Harris stops talking. His eyes narrow. "Why are you asking?"

"I think maybe I've started again." The story I developed in the car on the way over flows from my lips so naturally now, just the way I practiced. "I woke up the other morning and there were some things rearranged in my living room, things I don't remember moving. It was a little unsettling."

I remember all those mornings when I was younger, finding my belongings out of place: my shoes in two different spots, my hairbrush in the laundry room. The way I would pick them up, eye them curiously, as if they had sprouted legs in the night and roamed around the house on their own.

"I'm sure it was," he says. "But rest assured, you have nothing to worry about. Just keep your doors locked so you don't wander outside, maybe set an alarm. About two percent of children go on to become adult sleepwalkers, so considering your history, I'm not exactly surprised."

"Okay," I say, nodding. "That's good to know. So no one has ever . . . I don't know, *killed someone* in their sleep, then?"

I smile, let out a little laugh, trying to signal that I'm kidding. That I don't actually believe it to be possible. That I haven't been thinking it, wondering it, ever since I was a child but instead just erased it from my mind—like those footprints, that mud—pretending the thought was never even there to begin with.

"*Homicidal sleepwalking*," Dr. Harris says, smiling back. "Believe it or not, it has happened. But again, it's very rare."

I feel that familiar pain in my stomach, like someone's taking a meat grinder to my insides, turning my organs to chum.

"The most famous is the case of Kenneth Parks," he continues. "For the murder of his mother-in-law and attempted murder of his father-in-law in 1987."

"What did he do?"

"Drove fourteen miles, let himself into their house with his key, and bludgeoned her to death with a tire iron. Then he tried to strangle his father-in-law before getting back in his car and driving away."

"All that while he was *sleeping*?"

Dr. Harris shrugs. "Five neurological experts seemed to think so. He was acquitted."

"How could that be possible?"

"The subconscious mind is both beautiful and mysterious," he says, tapping his forehead with his pen. "The upper frontal lobe is the most evolved part of the brain, where moral teaching lives. When we sleepwalk, that part of the brain is fast asleep. So a sleepwalker could do things, *terrible* things, that they would never do if they were awake. They can't differentiate between right and wrong."

I swallow, nodding along, trying to act interested but detached. Like this is a simple curiosity and nothing more.

"It's like your body is on autopilot, but of course, most cases aren't quite that extreme," he continues. "The sleepwalker might be going about their regular routine, perhaps—like attempting to drive to work, shave their neck—and accidentally kill someone, or themselves, in the process."

I think back to Mason's nursery—to me, a shadow drifting down the hall, stopping in front of his door. Opening it, entering his bedroom, the way I had done so many times before.

"Or maybe they become startled and attack a bystander," he continues. "That's where the saying comes from: *Never wake a sleepwalker.*"

Back in my bedroom, lying there with Margaret. Her wide eyes staring into mine, her face pushed into that pillow.

"Did you wake me?" I had asked, that flare of embarrassment creeping up my neck like flames licking at walls.

"Mom said not to. It's dangerous."

"It's not dangerous," I had said. *"That's an old wives' tale."*

"Would the person remember?" I ask now. "Doing something like that?"

"Unless they wake up mid-attack, not usually, no," he says. "A sleepwalker rarely remembers their episode in the morning—though sometimes, they can. It's like recalling a dream."

I clear my throat and stand up from the chair quickly, desperate to get out of here.

"Thank you," I say. "That was very helpful."

"You sure that's everything?" he asks, standing with me. "I still have another thirty minutes before my next appointment."

"Yeah, that's everything. I just wanted to make sure, you know, that it was safe."

"For the most part, perfectly safe," he says, stuffing his hands in his pockets. I nod, turn to leave, and feel his eyes on my back as I make my way to the door. "But Isabelle—?"

"Yeah?" I ask, swinging around. My hand is on his doorknob; I'm almost gone.

"You know what's more dangerous than sleepwalking?"

"What's that?"

"Sleep deprivation," he says. "Really. It leads to all sorts of issues."

"I know," I smirk. "I'm aware."

"I'm being serious," he says, eying me again, unsmiling, like he isn't quite sure if he should let me leave. "Forget the lethargy, the memory problems, the sensory disruptions. If it gets severe enough, it can lead to hallucinations, delusions. Really bad stuff."

"I know," I say again, biting my lip.

He looks at me for a beat more, like he's trying to send me some kind of message, until finally, he sits back down, placing his hands on his desk.

"Just try to get some sleep, okay? Promise me."

"Sure," I say, opening the door and stepping into the lobby. I'm afraid of how easily they're coming now, the lies, rising up from the pit of my belly and gurgling out of my mouth like the black algae spewing from that wide, stone mouth. "I promise."

CHAPTER THIRTY-SIX

After Allison's memorial, Ben came over. He didn't tell me he was going to; I didn't ask. But when I heard a knock on my door that night, late, I knew I would find him standing on the other side it. I never questioned how he knew my address, and honestly, I didn't care. I just opened the door and took a step back, letting him in like I had let him into my life so many times before. Without question.

I remember he was still wearing his suit—the suit he had put on that morning, the suit he had worn as he buried his wife—and within minutes, it was being peeled off by me. His jacket slumped to the ground, left in a heap next to the shoes I had walked three miles home in, their heels worn down to stubs and *my* heels bloody and raw. There was a clumsy kind of urgency to it, my fingers fumbling their way down his buttons, like tripping off the edge of a cliff. Like if we didn't just leap into it at that very moment—minds blank, bodies on autopilot—we would come to our senses and back away slowly. We would stop, think about what we were doing, and realize how horribly wrong it all was.

But we didn't. We didn't stop.

Afterward, we lay together in silence, fingers intertwined, in bed.

I still slept on the same sad little mattress from my childhood bed-room, Margaret's smell seeped somewhere deep into the threads like a stain. Lying there with Ben made me feel too juvenile, too young, remembering the way my sister and I would pull the covers over our heads and tell each other stories with flashlights, trying to drown out the whispered arguments or full-blown screams coming from some-where down the hall.

"You know we can't tell anybody about this," Ben said after a couple minutes of quiet, his hands in my hair. I was trying to ignore the wedding band I could still feel on his finger. The cool pinch of it on my skin. "Not yet."

I looked at him, my eyes tracing his profile in the dark.

"With work," he clarified. "I could lose my job. You could, too."

"Oh, right. Of course."

"We'll find a way," he said, kissing my forehead before rolling over and standing up with a groan. "With time."

I remember watching him pull on his boxers and walk into the bathroom, my eyes drinking him in as if I were preparing for another drought without him. I didn't know how to feel in that moment. There had been a question lingering in the back of my mind all day, this unspoken seed of doubt that planted itself the moment Ben had pulled me to him on the side of that house, its spindly roots snaking their way through my brain, digging in deep and growing wild. Ever since his fingers wove themselves into my hair and his lips attached to mine, I couldn't help but wonder: If Allison *hadn't* died, would this have ever happened?

If she hadn't died, would Ben have ever chosen me?

Maybe this was just his grief talking. Maybe he couldn't bear the thought of being alone, going home to an empty house—the same house where he had found her, sprawled across the tile, a hollow bot-tle of pills in her palm and the crusts of dried spit caked to her lip. I imagined him standing in my doorway, those dark puddles beneath his eyes like dirty rainwater collecting in the street. Maybe tomorrow morning he'd wake up, clear his throat, and glue those same eyes to the floor, pronouncing this a mistake: something, like that first night together, that we should never speak of again.

After all, Ben had been faced with making the choice between Allison and me before, and every single time, he chose her. He chose her that night at the oyster roast when he walked away from me and never came back. He chose her during all our secret evenings together, nursing his beer, his fingers peeling at the damp label before standing up, nodding his head, and leaving me alone with nothing but a pile of scraps on the bar top. When Allison was alive, he chose her instead of me over and over and over again, that much had been painfully clear. So in a way, as I lay there in the dark—imagining Allison being lowered into the dirt, her tan skin now pale and lifeless; those lips that had once breathed a secret into my ear pursed and still—a part of me was glad. Because I knew that Ben wouldn't have to choose anymore. The choice had been made for him.

Really, he never even had a choice at all.

CHAPTER THIRTY-SEVEN

I told Waylon I had a stomach bug. That was my excuse for missing lunch—and my excuse for locking myself in my bedroom all day, pretending to sleep it off.

I want to talk to him, I do. I need to hear his lie about visiting Dozier at the police station, try to work out what it is that he's doing here. What he wants. But I need to figure out my strategy first. I need to figure out how I'm going to respond; if I'm going to confront him, demand answers, or simply play dumb, keep up the charade, and see where it takes me.

I grabbed my laptop as soon as I got home, slipping quietly into my room and crawling into bed, biding my time. Listening to the sound of him tiptoeing around the house on his own: the flush of the toilet, a cleared throat. I could sense him outside my bedroom door on occasion, hovering; I pictured his hand floating above my doorknob, considering whether or not he should knock before deciding, finally, to pull it back and walk away. I can't help but wonder what he's been doing with free rein of my home: sifting through my mail, maybe, or poking around in the trash. Trying to steal an intimate look into my life by analyzing which brand of condiments I buy or what appointments I have scrawled in my calendar.

People tend to stash their dirtiest secrets in the most common of places.

All the while, I've been watching more recordings from Mason's baby monitor, methodically working my way through each day. I've seen myself a few more times, moseying into his nursery in the middle of the night: stopping, staring. But that's it. I don't move any closer than mid-room; I don't do anything other than just stand there, swaying a little, until at some point, I turn around and walk back out.

It's around two in the morning in the video I'm watching now, and there I am again: standing in a pair of waffle-knit pajamas, arms rigid at my sides, long hair flowing over my shoulders like snarled seaweed. It's unsettling, seeing me there. My sleepwalking caught on camera. But so far, I haven't done anything alarming. Every time I see myself walk inside, I feel my stomach clench; but then, every time I turn around and walk back out, it relaxes again, like a muscle being pricked with a needle.

Eventually, I start to wonder if maybe they're right. All of them. Detective Dozier accusing me of inventing clues where they don't exist; Dr. Harris saying it's normal. *I'm* normal.

I start to wonder if maybe this is perfectly harmless. Maybe I have nothing to worry about after all.

I hear a sound from the living room and hit *Pause*, my body on screen frozen in time. It's the creak of the couch as Waylon stands up, turns off the TV, and tosses the remote onto the cushions. It's late now, well after midnight, and I hear him walk down the hall, past my bedroom and into the guest room, shutting the door behind him.

I hold my breath, listening. Hearing the shuffle of his feet next door, the flick of the light switch. The squeak of the springs as he climbs into bed. I imagine him pulling the covers over his chest, his body growing heavy, relaxing into the mattress.

And then I wait.

After twenty minutes, I slide out of bed and pad across the room toward the door. Roscoe perks up, and I hold out my hand, silencing him before he can make a noise. Then I push my ear to the wood, listening some more. I hear no signs of life; no noises coming from his room.

Only then do I decide that it's safe.

I open my door and creep into the hallway, the house completely dark. Roscoe jumps from the bed and we walk into the kitchen together. Everything looks normal—there's a single bowl hanging upside down in the drying rack, traces of Waylon's solitary dinner; the vague scent of citrus from my dish soap lingering in the air—until I glance into the dining room, my eyes landing on the table. Waylon's laptop and recording equipment are set up the way they were before; just beneath it, his briefcase leans up against the wooden table leg.

My eyes dart over to my closed guest room door, then back to the table.

I creep over to it, easing myself into a chair in the dark. Then I lean over and grab his briefcase, hoisting it onto my lap. Thankfully, it isn't the kind that locks, so I open the flap and peer inside. There's a notebook; a few folders full of papers. I grab his wallet and flip it open, eying his driver's license.

At least he wasn't lying about his name. I had Googled him, of course, but the proof is right here—Waylon Spencer—along with his picture and an Atlanta address.

I flip the wallet closed, toss it back into the briefcase, and grab a handful of folders next. I open the first one and realize it's the case file I gave him just last week. Everything seems to be there— undisturbed, untouched—so I move on to the next one, flip it open, and freeze.

It's another copy of Mason's case file. But this one looks much, much older.

I pull the file out and place it on the table, my fingers tracing their way down the fraying edges. There are pen marks and coffee stains;

notes scribbled in the margins and sections highlighted with dried-out markers. There's the *MISSING* poster and the interview transcripts; the sex offender registry and crime scene photos. It's obvious that he's pored over it; read every word—not only once, but multiple times. I continue to flick through the pages, my eyes scanning all the same things Waylon had seen that first day in my dining room, acting as if he were taking it all in for the very first time.

Suddenly, I remember the way he had tried to hand it back to me, like he didn't even need it.

"*Keep it,*" I had said. "*I have my own copy.*"

Apparently, so did he.

"Why does he have this?" I whisper, feeling the worn paper between my fingers. Why would he have his own copy? I suppose it's not *impossible*—journalists can always get their hands on these things—but why wouldn't he tell me? Why would he pretend?

I think back to that first recorded conversation again—how I had repeated myself, telling him things he already knew, and the way he had been so convincing. Asking the exact same questions with feigned curiosity; nodding his head, eyebrows bunched, like he didn't already know the answers I was about to repeat.

He's a good liar, just like me.

I close the folder and stuff it back into his briefcase, placing it on the floor in the same spot as before. Then I pick up the headphones and place them snug over my ears. I can hear my heartbeat pounding loudly, my breath heavy and hoarse. I look down at the stereo and press *Play*, starting whatever recording he was just listening to in the exact spot where he left it.

"*That seems hard for me to fathom.*"

I feel a punch in my gut—I know that voice. It's Detective Dozier, and already, I know whose voice I'm going to hear next.

"*Well, it's the truth.*"

It's mine.

This isn't my conversation with Waylon. He isn't editing anything we've worked on together. This is an interview recording from the police station. This is one of the early ones; one of the very first when they had separated Ben and me.

When I had been questioned—no, *interrogated*—alone.

"All right, let's go over this one more time." Dozier's voice leaks through the speakers and into my ears, sending a familiar chill down my spine. I can still picture his eyes—those eyes that were so calloused and hard. So disbelieving. I can still see the way he was leaning against the table between us, drumming his fingers across the wood in a calm, steady rhythm. Like he had all the time in the world. *"You woke up at six o'clock."*

"Yes, that's correct."

"And you didn't think to check on your son until after eight?"

"I . . . I thought he was still sleeping. I didn't want to disturb him."

"Does he always sleep until eight?"

"No . . . no, usually he wakes up earlier."

I flinch at the sound of my own voice. I can hear it shaking, a little tremble in my throat.

"What time does he usually wake up?"

"Around six thirty."

"And you didn't think it was strange that you didn't hear a peep from his room at all? Almost two hours after he's normally up?"

"I was just hoping, I guess, that maybe he was sleeping in."

"And why were you hoping he was sleeping in?"

"Um, well, he can be fussy sometimes, so I was hoping . . . I guess I wanted to take advantage of—"

"I'm sorry, did you just say you wanted to 'take advantage of' the fact that your son seemed to not be waking up?"

"No, sorry, I didn't mean it like that . . . I just meant—"

I rip the headphones off and place them on the table, pushing my head into my hands. *Goddamnit.* I knew those interviews had been bad, but now, listening to them back, they're even worse than I remembered. I can still feel the adrenaline coursing through my veins, the fear making my fingers shake like a junkie during withdrawal.

Detective Dozier's eyes drilling into mine, trying to pierce me so deeply that I would finally crack.

I try to piece together what this all means—Waylon having a copy of the case file already; listening to these recordings of Dozier grilling me, hard. Logically, I know this could all be research for the podcast. It seems unusual that he would hide it from me, but at the same time, this is his job.

Either way, it's not incriminating enough to approach him with. I need something more.

I look at his laptop next, glancing back to his closed bedroom door, then down to the keyboard, tapping *Return*. It isn't password protected, miraculously—maybe he was just on it, and it hasn't been asleep long enough to lock—and I watch as the screen and keys illuminate in the dark. My heart thumps hard in my chest as I start moving my fingers across the track pad, navigating first to his desktop. There are various folders organized alphabetically: *Finance, Interviews, Personal, Research.* I don't have time to scour his entire computer—he could walk into the hallway at any second and catch me here, snooping through his files—so I click on *Research* first.

After all, it seems like Waylon has certainly done his research.

I find various subfolders inside, each one labeled by episode and season. My eyes skim across every one until I reach the bottom of the list—to the very last folder, simply labeled *X.*

I click on the *X* folder, my eyes bulging when I see what's inside. There are pictures of me—dozens of pictures—in various stages of life. There's my headshot from *The Grit* and a wedding photo of Ben and me; our first family picture, with Mason between us, and even a few selfies of us I had posted to Facebook years ago. At the very bottom, my eyes linger on a candid of Ben and me at a bar; it was taken from across the room, the two of us caught in an intimate moment together, leaning in close. Unaware.

My hand hovers over my open mouth, shock bolting me in place.

Suddenly, I hear a creak from the guest room and I jump, twisting around fast. I half expect Waylon to be standing behind me, watching me in the dark, but still, I'm alone. I hold my breath, my eyes on his closed door, imagining his unconscious body flipping over on the old mattress and sinking in deep, making the box spring groan.

Finally, after a few seconds, it feels safe enough turn back around.

I click out of the *Research* folder, ready to shut the laptop and leave it just as it was, until I decide to check one more thing. I launch a browser window and navigate to his Search History next, knowing I only have a few more minutes, and quickly skim down the list of his most recently viewed websites. Most of them are innocent—email, news—until I come across the same TrueCrimeCon article I had been reading last week.

I suppose it isn't unbelievable that Waylon would be reading it—he is working on my case, after all, and he was *there*—but now, I think about that comment again.

He's in a better place.

It disappeared just after our first meeting together: before our dinner at Framboise, it was there, but when I got home, it wasn't. I file the thought away and keep skimming, getting ready to call it quits, when all of a sudden, I can feel the air exit my lungs.

This is it. This is the *more* I was looking for.

It's an article from *The Beaufort News*, my hometown newspaper. Waylon was reading it recently, just yesterday, and my hands shake as I click on the link and watch as it loads. The article is old, scanned and archived from 1999, and I feel a prickle of tears as the headline appears.

DAUGHTER OF CONGRESSMAN HENRY RHETT TRAGICALLY DROWNS IN MARSH

CHAPTER THIRTY-EIGHT

THEN

I hear the slam of a door and leap from my bed, run down the hall, and lean over the staircase. I can see them through the front door window: Dad and Chief Montgomery, huddled close on the porch, talking. Then I run back up the stairs, two at a time, and unlatch the window at the front of the house, pushing it open slowly.

"I appreciate you doing this, Henry. I know it wasn't easy."

A warm blast of early afternoon air hits me along with the chief's slippery voice, traveling through the hall like oil on water. I crouch down low and listen.

"Yeah, sure, no problem," Dad says, exhaling. I can't see his face, but I imagine his thumb and forefinger rubbing the bridge of his noise, the way he does when he's stressed out or deep in thought. "I know you're just doing your job."

"I'll write up the official report later today," he says. "Accidental drowning."

"Thank you."

"And Henry . . ." The chief stops, hesitates, like he's not sure if he should continue. Like he's overstepping some kind of boundary, blurring the lines between personal and professional. Finally, he exhales, decides to push forward. "I'm so sorry about all of this. Your family . . . you're good people. All of you. You've been through hell."

I hear my dad sniff as a little wet choke erupts from his throat. The sound makes me uncomfortable. I don't think I've ever heard my dad cry before; he's never even come close.

"Thank you," he says again, clearing his throat.

"It's not your fault," the chief continues. "Over four hundred kids under the age of six drown in pools every year, mostly in June, July, and August. It's hot, Henry. Hotter'n hell."

My dad is quiet, but I can picture him nodding along, dabbing at his eyes with the handkerchief he keeps stuffed in his back pocket.

"Your air-conditioning is out. She probably just thought she'd take a dip, cool off. Outgoing tide could have swept her up quick."

"Yeah," my dad says. "Yeah, I know."

I slide the window shut and walk slowly back to my bedroom, feeling a daze settle over me as I process what I just heard. It makes sense, their story. It is hot, Margaret was hot, complaining about it constantly. I remember her in the studio, the sweat dripping from her neck and her cheeks a fiery red. I remember her in that bath, ice water prickling her skin. She had asked to sleep outside, looked longingly out that window, ached for the wind whipping off the water to bring her some sense of comfort, of relief—but still, I know it's a lie. I *know* Dad is lying, because Margaret never would have wandered out there alone: deciding to take to the marsh, submerge herself in the water until she was too deep to turn back. She would have never done that on her own.

But she would have done it with me.

I remember her coming into my bedroom that night: climbing into my arms, pushing herself close, even when she was afraid. Margaret followed me constantly; it didn't matter when or where. She was a quiet little body trailing me around like a shadow—and shadows don't move on their own.

I lift my hand to my neck, touch the area behind my ear that I had scrubbed clean. It stings. The skin feels red and raw like carpet burn, and I close my eyes, trying to think. Trying to talk to her, summon her, wherever she is. I need her to tell me what happened, what I should do, the way we did before: pinching our eyes shut, trying to recreate that feeling of prickling skin on your neck. Of knowing you're not alone.

Even though it's still sweltering, I feel a trail of goose bumps erupt down my spine.

When I woke up this morning, there was water on the carpet, the bathroom floor. Damp towels growing musty in a heap and a clean nightgown replacing the one I had fallen asleep in. Fresh mud caked to my skin.

I think of my mother, the way she had looked at me in the kitchen: anger and sadness, her shoulders stiff and her mouth a thin cut across her face. The way she had stood up, brushed past me, and slammed the door behind her. She knew, and my father did, too. Maybe they had wandered out there, unable to sleep after Margaret told them about the footprints, and found us outside together in the dark, our white nightgowns glowing in the moonlight. Me, standing at the edge of the marsh, while Margaret floated gently beside me, face down, her hair splayed across the water like a blot of ink, expanding slowly.

I picture them running across the grass, yelling her name. Pulling her from the water, her wet, limp body no longer too hot but, suddenly, too cold. Mud clinging to her skin, her hair. That terrible, awful smell.

I imagine my mother carrying her inside, laying her delicately on the kitchen tile. Shaking her shoulders, begging her to wake up—or maybe just pretending that she was still asleep. Maybe she couldn't handle those wide, unblinking eyes so she had simply pulled her lids shut with her fingers and prayed for them to click open on their own, just like that doll's.

And then there's my father, leading me inside, just like that night of the fire: my hand in his, entirely unconscious, as he stripped off my clothes, patted me dry. Led me back to bed with unseeing eyes.

I can picture it, I can: Margaret, waking up next to me as I flung myself from the sheets, tossing my legs over the mattress in the dark. Following me down the hall, down the stairs, into the backyard. Working up the courage to reach out, grab my shoulder, as I approached the edge of the marsh.

"*Did you try to wake me?*" I had asked.

"*Mom said not to. It's dangerous.*"

"*It's not dangerous. That's an old wives' tale.*"

She listened. Margaret always listened to me. To everything I said.

"*I won't hurt you,*" I had told her. And she nodded her head, believing. Trusting.

It was a promise I couldn't keep.

CHAPTER THIRTY-NINE

NOW

I can barely breathe as I sit in the silence, Waylon's laptop glowing in the dark like that spring tide moon. I continue to stare at the headline, the memories pummeling over me like water from a broken dam, until I hear a low growl from somewhere across the house.

I slap the laptop shut and twist around, relief flowing through me when I realize it's just Roscoe pawing at the back door.

"Oh God," I whisper, my head feeling airy and light. "I'm sorry, buddy."

I stand up and walk back into the kitchen, guilt washing over me as I realize he hasn't been outside all day. Then I open the back door and let him out, deciding to step into the backyard with him. I need some air.

I slide the door shut behind us and take a deep breath, trying to steady the shaking in my hands. It's muggy out tonight, a stifling damp in the air that hints at impending rain. Roscoe sniffs around, his senses in overdrive after an entire day stuck indoors, and I guess mine are, too, because everything seems to be somehow intensified tonight, like I'm looking at the world through a microscope. I can hear the unified croak of the toads in the marsh a few blocks east; the cicadas, nature's white noise, suddenly deafening in my ears.

I pace around a bit, my eyes adjusting to the dark, and think.

Waylon is looking into Mason's case, that much is the truth, but it seems like he's been looking into it for far longer than I thought—and more than that, it seems like he's looking into *me*. The case file and recordings are one thing, but the pictures and article seem to be something else entirely. It seems more personal, more targeted.

All I know is I can't trust him anymore. I can't trust him to help.

I need to start finding some answers on my own now, without him, and suddenly, my neck snaps up. I have an idea.

I walk over to Mason's window and move a little to the right, to the exact spot that I had seen peeking out between the trees as I sat in that rocking chair just four days ago. I realize now that if Paul Hayes can see into my backyard from his porch, then that means, standing in the right spot, I should be able to see his porch from here, too. I look across my backyard, past the fence, through the gap in the foliage, and squint. It's dark outside, but I have the light from the moon, the stars glowing bright against a cloudless sky. There's a streetlight near his house, the one that shines almost directly onto his porch, and that's when I see it: a subtle alteration in the air like the shifting of a shadow or the gentle sway of a rocking chair.

He's there.

Moving quickly, I let Roscoe inside and shut him in my bedroom, grabbing my cell phone and leaving again through the front door. Then I walk around the block, making my way toward 1742 Catty Lane.

I approach the house, my heart beating hard in my chest, and think about Dr. Harris's words.

Hallucinations, delusions.

I think about what Detective Dozier told me just this morning: that Paul Hayes lives alone. I think about that comment I had seen—

that I *thought* I had seen—and how, suddenly, it was no longer there. But was it even there to begin with? Honestly, I'm not sure anymore. I'm not sure about anything ever since I saw myself on that laptop screen, standing over Mason's crib in the dark. I don't know what I'll do if I get to Paul's house and find that the porch is empty; if that rocking chair is just moving on its own, being pushed by the phantom legs of the breeze. I can't really stand to think about it. But the closer I get, the more confident I feel: He's there. I can see him so clearly, staring straight into the void. That same weathered face, old, like leather left out in the sun; bulging eyes like cloudy marbles.

This man, whoever he is, feels like my best shot right now. My only shot.

I slow down once I reach the porch, casting Dozier's warning to stay away into the recesses of my mind. Then I turn to face him, clearing my throat.

"Hi," I begin, suddenly unsure of what to say next. "We met on Wednesday night, when I was walking my dog. Do you remember?"

The man continues to stare, still in that same bathrobe, his hands clenching the armrests. They are so boney, so frail. I'm about to open my mouth again, prod him some more, when slowly, his gaze turns toward mine.

"Oh, yes," he says, his voice soft and wet. "I remember."

I exhale, smiling weakly. I knew this man was real. I *knew* he was. Suddenly, I feel ridiculous for even doubting it.

"I hope you don't mind. I know it's late, but I just wanted to ask you a few questions. I tried stopping by during the day on Friday, but—"

"We didn't meet on Wednesday," he says. His voice is so fragile, so quiet, I have to take a few steps forward, straining to hear. "You seem to be the one who doesn't remember. Or maybe you'd just like me to forget."

I take another step forward, confusion settling over me.

"I'm sorry . . . have we met?" I ask. "I can't seem to place you—"

The man continues to rock, his eyes back on the street again. I catch a quick twitch in his lips, and I wonder if maybe he's senile.

"Lots of times," he says, and although his voice is soft, it seems entirely lucid. He doesn't seem confused. "You're Isabelle Drake."

The shock of hearing my name on his lips, my *full* name, causes me to stumble a bit, as if the words themselves had reached out and shoved my shoulders back. It is entirely possible that he knows who I am—after all, the whole town knows who I am—but this seems to be more than that.

The way he says it feels like I should know who he is, too.

"When have we met?" I ask now, eying him carefully. "I really don't think we have."

"Couple years ago," he says. "You used to walk by at night."

I can feel my eyes widen as I try to make sense of what he's saying. I never used to take Roscoe for walks at night; that just started recently, after Mason was taken. After Ben moved out. After I stopped sleeping.

"I'm sorry, I think you're mistaken—"

"No, I'm not." He shakes his head before letting out a low, wet cough. "You live right there." He nods his head in the direction of my house, then looks back at me. "I may be old, girl, but I'm not crazy."

I think of what Dr. Harris told me earlier: how sleepwalkers can have entire conversations, sometimes, without even realizing. How their movements can seem so lifelike, so lucid.

"Keep your doors locked so you don't wander outside."

It had happened with Margaret before: sitting on the floor together, playing with dolls. Her not even realizing I was sleeping.

"What did we talk about?"

"Not much," he says. "You introduced yourself the first time, then after that, we just nodded to each other, exchanged waves."

"That can't be right—"

"That's why I was surprised to see you the other night," he continues. "It's been a while. Didn't think you'd be coming back—not after everything that's happened, anyway."

I think back to the way he had looked at me before; his eyes blank, staring. So he had seen me after all. He had just been confused when I introduced myself, acting as if we were strangers. As if we had never met before.

"And when did this stop?" I ask. "Me walking by? When was the last time?"

"I think you know the answer to that," he says, that chair creaking louder.

"Let's pretend I don't."

"It's been a year," he says, nodding to himself. "Almost to the day, in fact."

"A year," I repeat. "And you're sure about that?"

"Oh, I'm sure. March of last year."

"And why are you so sure?" I ask, the ground beneath me starting to sway.

The man turns to look at me, finally, his cataracted eyes like two crystal balls and an amused look on his face, like we're rehashing some kind of inside joke that I don't understand. I suddenly have the distinct feeling that whatever this dance is between us is something we've done before. Something he very much enjoys.

"Because," he says at last, a twitch of a smile appearing on his lips, "you had your kid with you that time."

CHAPTER FORTY

I push myself back into my bedroom and slam the door with too much force. Roscoe perks up, confused, and I know I'm being loud enough to wake up Waylon, but right now, I don't care.

Nothing matters anymore. Nothing matters but this.

The images are swirling around me like bathwater slowly circling its way down the drain: those dirty footprints on the carpet and the fingermarks beneath my ear; the open window and the smell of the marsh and that stuffed dinosaur covered in mud. It's getting harder and harder to separate fact from the fiction; dream from reality. Then from now.

Margaret from Mason.

I hear a knock at my door, cautious and slow, and turn to the side. Waylon is in the hallway.

"Isabelle?" he calls. "Is everything okay? I thought I heard the door—"

I curse beneath my breath and consider staying quiet, letting him just wait for a while before being forced to walk away. I can feel him on the other side of the wall, hesitant. Five seconds go by, then ten, but I can still see his shadow beneath the door, unmoving. He knocks again.

"Isabelle," he says, firmer now. "I know you're awake."

Roscoe jumps off the bed, walks over to the door and starts to scratch. I sigh, lean my head back, and take a few steps forward, steeling myself before I thrust it open.

"Hi," I say. "Sorry. Didn't mean to disturb you."

"Why were you outside?" He looks disheveled, his hair a nest of tangles and his eyes coated with sleep. There's a strange intimacy to seeing people teetering on the edge of consciousness like this, knowing that they're vulnerable. Like the first time a new partner unwittingly falls asleep in your bed and you lie next to them in the dark, watching the gentle rise and fall of their chest, the bare skin of their neck. Knowing that, in those precious moments, they are completely defenseless. Completely exposed. "It's"—he glances around, looking for a clock, but unable to find one—"I don't know, two in the morning?"

"I just had to get some air," I say. "I've been shut in here all day."

I can tell he doesn't believe me, but it's the best I've got.

"Is everything okay?" he asks. "I feel like there's something you're not telling me. You're . . . sweating."

I lift my hand to my forehead, feeling the cold slick of my skin. I had practically run home from Paul's house, too afraid to turn back around. To see the gaze of that man on my back; to face the accusations I could see twirling in his eyes.

"I'm fine," I say. "It's just this bug."

"Do you need me to take you to the doctor? You really aren't looking good . . . no offense."

I glance to the side, to the mirror hanging above my dresser, and almost recoil at my reflection. He's right. My skin is sallow and pale, like I just ingested something rotten; my eyes are sunken in, exposing the gentle slope of my skull. His expression is making me remember the way Dr. Harris had looked at me earlier today—or, I suppose that was yesterday; it's all starting to blur together now—that same sense of concern.

"You know what's more dangerous than sleepwalking? Sleep deprivation."

"I'm fine," I repeat. "Really."

"Okay." He looks at me, unconvinced, and I think I see a flicker of sadness appear on his features before it disappears just as fast. Or maybe it's pity. The thought of how easy it was for him to snake his way into my life like this; how he only needed to say the right things at the right times in order for my guard to drop completely.

He takes a step closer to me, and I flinch.

"Isabelle . . . you know you can trust me, right? You can tell me if there's something else going on?"

I don't know how to respond to that. I don't know if I can trust him after what I discovered—but I don't know if I can trust myself, either. So instead, I look at my feet, my eyes drilling into the carpet. I can hear the tick of the clock in the living room and Roscoe's tongue working its way over his fur as he lays on my bed, a methodical licking. The gentle buzz of the overhead light, like a swarm of flies circling something dead.

"What did Dozier tell you?" I ask at last, my voice a whisper.

"What?"

"At the station." I look up, trying to read his expression. Trying to stay firm and focused when, really, the fear coursing through me makes me feel like I might faint. "Today. You said you talked to him."

"Oh," he says, rubbing the back of his neck. "Yeah. Let's not get into that right now, okay?"

"But you said—"

"Not now," he repeats. "It can wait. You need to get some sleep."

I exhale, nod, knowing that there's no point in trying to convince him. It is two in the morning, after all—most people would be asleep at this hour.

Most people.

"Okay," I say, my eyes stinging at the thought of waiting until morning—*later* in the morning, I mean—to finally find some answers. "Okay, sounds good. I'll sleep."

Waylon smiles, oblivious to the fact that once he leaves, once the door shuts behind him, nothing will change.

I'll still be here, awake, only without him, I'll be alone.

"Well, good night," he says, turning around and flipping off the light.

I shut the door quickly and listen as Waylon retreats into his own room—then I hear the gentle click of the lock and realize: I don't think I've ever heard him lock the door before. I wonder if it's because of me. If it's because he's afraid of me—afraid of being alone with me in the dark—the way my own mother was.

I make my way back to bed and crawl beneath the covers, glancing at my laptop and pulling it toward me. I tap at the keyboard until it comes back to life, and there I am, just as I had left it: there's me, standing in Mason's nursery, the video on *Pause*. I stare at the frozen image on the screen, my body moving through some kind of mindless rhythm, like a wind-up doll walking on its own, and I wonder: If I was going into Mason's nursery like this, night after night, I suppose it's possible I was going outside, too.

I try to imagine myself walking down the hall, passing his nursery, and opening the front door instead, roaming the streets of my neighborhood, like some kind of restless spirit walking a familiar, comforting path. I think of those footprints on my carpet again; the fact that I had done that exact thing before—but even if that's the case, there's no way I would have brought Mason with me. I've seen myself enough times on these videos to know: I've never touched him. I've never even gotten closer than mid-room. That man must be confused. He must be lying to me, playing with me, trying to make me believe something that just isn't true.

I hit *Play* again, resuming the video, watching as my body continues to sway like laundry on a clothing line being pushed by the wind. I observe the way Mason kicks his little feet in his sleep, the entire screen glowing in a strange, night-vision gray, making me look like I'm an animal in the dark, wandering into some kind of trap. Finally,

I see my legs move: a step, and then another. I wait for myself to turn around, to walk back toward the door, but instead of walking out the way I came, I start to walk closer. Closer to Mason.

I lean forward, the light from the laptop making my eyes burn. I watch as my body approaches his crib and stands, silently, above him, peering down—then as I lean forward, my arms outstretched.

No, I think, unable to look away, unable to move, as my unconscious body picks up my son, his little feet kicking in the air as I hoist him up, bring him close. Hold him tight against my chest.

I slap my laptop shut, too afraid to see what comes next.

CHAPTER FORTY-ONE

A month after Allison's memorial, I left my job at *The Grit*.

Ben found a way, just like he promised, and it involved me going freelance. I would continue writing for them on a project-by-project basis, then when we went public with our relationship, it wouldn't look as bad. It wouldn't look like a boss and his employee; it wouldn't have started when Allison was still alive.

We had connected *afterward,* of course. After Allison was dead. After I was already gone.

Our wedding was small, intimate. It didn't feel right to Ben to have a grand reception, and I tended to agree. It was his second marriage, after all, less than a year after Allison's death. And besides, I didn't have many people I wanted to invite.

To be honest, I didn't have anyone at all.

We exchanged vows in Chippewa Square, the cobblestones providing a makeshift aisle, our altar an archway of sweeping trees. I wore white, a simple summer dress, and remember grinning widely every time a random passerby would whistle as they caught a glimpse. After so many months of secrecy—of trying to ignore each other at the office; of being out in public together, but not really *together*—it felt good for the world to acknowledge us.

To acknowledge me.

After the ceremony, we went to dinner, just Ben and me. We ate pasta and drank two bottles of rosé, laughing and beaming and utterly giddy at the thought of spending the rest of our lives together. We had moved into our house just a few days earlier, but the furniture hadn't been delivered yet, so we spent our wedding night in an improvised bed made of blankets and throw pillows laid out across the living room floor. I remember the mismatched candle collection flickering from the mantel, the flower petals he had ripped from my bouquet and sprinkled across the carpet. It was passionate and romantic and emotional and real.

It was the happiest night of my life.

We had talked about children, of course. Neither of us wanted them. Ben was too busy. His priority was work, it always would be, and he knew that would make him absent: one of those fathers who was never really there. I understood that—appreciated it, even, having grown up with one myself—so I told him I never saw myself as a mother, either. And that was the truth. It reminded me too much of Margaret: of what had happened when another life had been left in my care.

Of how badly I had failed the first time.

But then something inside me started to change. It was a slow revelation, barely there, that took years to take root, like a helicopter seed drifting away before planting itself in open soil. I was enjoying freelancing, for the most part, but it was different from *The Grit*. I didn't have an office or coworkers; I spent almost all of my time alone. I got to travel a bit, here and there, but mostly I was home, spending the majority of each day glancing at the clock, counting down the hours until Ben would walk back through the door, and I would finally have some company.

And then, of course, there was Ben. The subtle changes that took place in him, too. The way he stopped eying me as I slinked around the house in my barely there bathrobe, his eyes cast down at his computer instead. The way he seemed to get home later and later, our once-fresh marriage suddenly grown stale. Before, he seemed so excited by me. So *alive*. But now that he had me, I felt myself starting to tarnish in his eyes, like a piece of fine jewelry left alone for too long. I tried to tell myself that that was just marriage—an inevitable, slow decay that took place as the years stripped us of our spontaneity and spark—but I didn't want to accept it. I didn't want to accept that, only four years in, things had already stalled.

I didn't want to accept that after everything we had gone through together—after losing Allison, and my job, and all those other little casualties that felt like they were offered up in the hopes of something *more*—this was it.

I remember that morning so vividly; the morning that seed finally sprouted into something wild and alive. It was like an invasive weed I could no longer contain, snaking its way through my brain and taking over everything. I had been thinking about it for a while, really. I had been thinking that maybe a baby wouldn't be so bad—in fact, maybe it would be *good*. Maybe it would nudge Ben to stay home a little more; to shift his priorities. Maybe it would help bring us back together—and maybe, *maybe*, it would be my chance to take care of someone after I had failed to take care of Margaret.

My chance to make up for my past.

So one morning, I walked into the bathroom and shut the door behind me, the silent click of the lock making my heartbeat rise to my throat. I can still picture myself standing over that toilet and pushing my birth control pills through their foil casing, one by one, and into the water, like they were some kind of ceremonial sacrifice. The tickle of anticipation in my stomach as I flushed, watching them spin in circles until they disappeared altogether. Ripping Ben's clothes off as soon as he got home and lying in silence together afterward, wondering. Waiting. Trying to somehow feel it happening beneath my skin.

And I felt guilt, yes. The shame for lying and even a little twinge of embarrassment at having stooped to something so devious and low—but also the thrill of having some semblance of control over my life again.

Of making a decision for myself for once.

To be honest, I didn't really think it would happen—or at least, not that fast. But it was only a matter of months until it hit me: a wave of nausea so intense that my arm shot out to the side and grasped the kitchen counter with a grip so tight it was startling. I remember closing my eyes, pursing my lips. Forcing the vomit to glide back down my throat before running into the bathroom and collapsing onto the floor.

I remember reaching slowly for a test, the still-full box wedged and ripping, where I had hid it in a dusty corner like a mousetrap, ready to snap at my fingers.

"Ben?" I had yelled, my eyes boring into those two pink lines, unsure if they were real. "Ben, can you come in here?"

But then, I remembered: He wasn't there.

Months went by, and things continued to change, only not in the way I had hoped. I watched as my skin pulled and stretched and dimpled like Play-Doh; as my ankles swelled up and my belly button popped. I smiled as old coworkers placed their palms on my stomach, feeling the kicks and commenting on my glowing skin, but all the while, I felt like I was hiding something: a dirty little secret they couldn't possibly understand. Because I could still remember that moment in the bathroom, the initial reaction that flared up so quickly, like that first bout of nausea I pushed down just as fast. I remembered what it was like to sit on that tile, test in hand, my eyes drilling into those two pink lines as the silence of my house, my life, echoed around me like a scream underwater—somehow both strident and smothered at the exact same time.

Before the tears and the excitement and the joy kicked in, I felt something else first. Something I didn't expect.

As sudden as a blink, barely there, I felt a stab of regret.

CHAPTER FORTY-TWO

There's coffee in the kitchen. I heard Waylon get up this morning, shuffle down the hall, and put on a pot. I heard the sputter of the water, the screaming steam. The clank of ceramic mugs as he pulled them out of the cabinet and set them on the counter, pouring himself a cup and walking into the living room. The scent trailing behind him before branching off and wafting down the hall, under my door, looking for me.

I've been sitting in my bed all night, that image from the laptop branded into my mind: me, grabbing Mason out of his crib in the dark. Holding him tight against my chest as he wriggled and writhed, that little stuffed dinosaur still clutched in his fingers.

I've been thinking about that old man's twitchy smile and cloudy eyes as he stared straight into mine, daring me to remember.

I creep out of my bedroom slowly, hesitantly, like a drunk emerging from slumber after a boisterous, bleary night.

"Morning," Waylon says, tipping his mug at me. "Did you get some sleep?"

"Yeah," I lie, avoiding his eyes. "Sorry about last night. Disturbing you."

"Don't be. Are you feeling better?"

I ignore him, grabbing the pot and pouring myself a mug, pushing my palms into the warmth so hard it hurts. Then I walk into the living room and join him on the couch, pulling my legs beneath me like a toddler.

"So, can we talk about it now?"

Waylon laughs, placing his mug on a coaster as he shakes his head slowly.

"Getting right to it, huh?"

"Well, that is why you're here, isn't it? To help me find my son?"

There's a flutter of something behind his expression: that millisecond of preparation that always presents itself just before someone steels themselves to lie. It's easy to spot, as long as you know where to look: the tension in the jaw, the hardening of the eyes. It disappears just as quickly as it came, but still. It was there.

"Of course it is," he says, leaning back and picking up his mug again, fidgeting. "I just thought you'd want a second to wake up first."

"I'm just curious, is all. It seems like you've had more luck with Dozier in a week than I have in a year."

"Sometimes fresh blood helps."

"I see that."

Waylon looks at me, his fingers pulling at a fraying thread on the couch.

"He told me he'd be open to letting me listen to some interview recordings, maybe use a few for the show," he says at last. "I've read the transcripts, anyway."

He takes a sip of his coffee and smacks his lips, clearly satisfied with his answer. And that much is true, I suppose—only he's omitting the fact that he already has them.

"Which interviews?" I ask. My cup is still untouched, steaming in my hands.

"I'm not sure yet. There are days of footage to sift through. I'm going to swing by later. Pick them up."

I nod, remembering those entire afternoons spent in the police station. The empty water bottles at my feet and my tired reflection in the mirror on the wall, feeling the eyes of all the people behind it, watching. Remembering my voice from last night, leaking through the headphones like marsh water rushing through a cracked window. An open mouth.

"Can I come with you?" I ask.

"I'm not sure that would be a good idea."

"Why not?"

Waylon exhales, pushing coffee-scented breath out through his lips.

"Look," he says at last, crossing one leg over the other. "I really appreciate everything you've done here . . . letting me stay at your place, how cooperative you've been. It's been above and beyond."

"But?"

"*But*," he repeats, steeling himself, "I don't want the integrity of the podcast to be at risk."

"The *integrity*—"

Waylon holds up his hands, stopping me mid-sentence. "If anyone were to find out that we've been working on this together, my credibility would be shot. There's no way anyone would see it as objective. I mean, I'm sorry to say this, but—"

"But I'm a suspect," I interject. "And you need to treat me as such."

"Yes," he says. "Well, no. I'm just saying that it can't *appear* like I'm taking sides."

"If you were really concerned about your integrity, you never would have agreed to stay here in the first place," I say, standing up from the couch. "So why don't you tell me what it is you're really after?"

Waylon is quiet, his fingers tapping away at the side of his mug. "I'm not sure what you're trying to say."

"I know you lied to me about seeing Dozier yesterday. I know because he was here."

Waylon perks up, his eyes growing wide.

"He must have come by after I left—"

"And I know you lied about Dozier saying he doesn't know my neighbor, too, because he does know him. He told me his name," I say, the anger and the betrayal pushing me forward. "So stop with your bullshit about *credibility* because you and I both know that you have none. Why are you here?"

"I'm . . . I'm here to help," he says, though it's starting to sound less convincing. Like even he knows that there's no use lying anymore. "I'm here to figure out what happened to your son—"

"*Bullshit.* I went through your stuff last night. I saw everything you've been hiding. Why are you here?"

He's quiet, his lips pursed tight as we stare at each other from across the couch in a silent standoff. Just as I'm starting to think he'll never talk, he bows his head and blows a tunnel of air out through his lips.

"Isabelle, you've seen the evidence," he says at last. "You've seen it all."

"So?"

"So you know what the evidence says. Whoever took Mason . . . they came from inside the house."

I look at him, blink a few times. The implication, of course, is clear. I know what he's trying to say.

"The evidence doesn't line up with the idea of a forced entry."

"But there was an open window—" I start.

"But no footprints on the carpet," he interrupts, finally looking up at me. "If someone came into your house through that window, there would have been dirt on the carpet. Mud, grass, *something*."

"That's just one thing that could easily be explained," I say. "He could have taken his shoes off—"

"Why didn't Roscoe bark?" he continues, pressing on. "He barks when he sees strangers. Someone would have heard him. You would have woken up. Why was he quiet?"

"He wasn't . . . he wasn't in the nursery," I say, even though I know it's a bad answer. He would have heard it, anyway. "Maybe he was asleep."

"He was quiet because nobody broke into your house, Isabelle. I know it, you know it, the cops know it. There was no intruder."

I think of Detective Dozier and the way he's always brushing me off; the way he looks at me like he knows something I don't. The way he never seems to give me the time of day.

So I was right, then. That's what he thinks. That's what they all think.

"You really believe that?" I ask, trying to keep my voice level. Trying to keep myself from crying. "This whole time you've been here, every conversation we've had . . . ?"

We're both dancing around it, avoiding having to say it outright, but from the look in his eyes, he knows what I'm asking: *Do you think I killed my son?*

"Yeah," he says at last, his eyes on mine. "Yeah, I do."

I should have seen this coming. I'm a storyteller myself, after all, and a storyteller never goes into a story without *actually* knowing the story. Without having an idea of what it is you want to tell. You don't go in blind, searching for answers. You *have* the answers—your answers, at least; the answers you want—and you go in searching for proof.

From that very first conversation on the airplane, this has been Waylon's angle. *I* have been his angle. I thought he was different, I thought he cared, so I let him in, told him things. Things I've never told anyone. But that was his game all along, wasn't it? That was his goal: to get me to relax, open up, by cooking me dinner and pouring me wine; by listening to me so intently and never pushing too hard.

But all along, he believed it. Just like everybody else.

Isabelle Drake is a baby killer.

"Get out," I say, pointing at the door. "I want you out of my house."

Waylon is quiet, his lips still parted, like he wants to fight back. "I want you out *now*."

Finally, he nods before standing up silently and walking into the guest room. I hover by the couch, arms crossed tight against my chest and the sting of tears in my eyes as I watch him pack his things. It hurts: the betrayal, the lies. The fact that I had finally allowed myself to feel listened to, to feel heard. To feel like I'm not in this alone.

But that's not what hurts the most.

It's the fact that, even after getting to know me, Waylon still believes there's a meanness in me, buried deep. That there's something nocturnal that slithers out in the dark; something with a bloodlust that needs to be quenched. He really believes that I walked into Mason's nursery that night and did something to him, something terrible. Something so bad my own conscious mind has blocked it out, refusing to remember, the same way I did something to Margaret.

But still, that's not the worst of it.

The worst of it is that now, with a startling certainty, I believe it, too.

CHAPTER FORTY-THREE

I'm downtown near *The Grit*'s office, the oak trees lining a long street of historic brick condos. They're expensive, I can tell. The types of houses people buy not for the house itself but for the connotation of it. The types of houses that exude money and status—sort of like *The Grit* itself, I guess. So in a way, it makes sense that Ben has chosen to live here. It fits the image.

I reach his stoop and climb the steps, glancing at my watch. I was hoping to catch him before work, on his way out, but I might have missed him. If he's not here, I'll just have to wait. Then I take a deep breath and ring the bell, hearing the buzz from inside, my hands punched into my pockets. After a few minutes of silence, I get ready to turn around, walk down the steps, and try again later, when suddenly, the door flies open.

Ben is laughing, like he's mid-conversation, and I watch as his smile fades as he takes me in.

"Isabelle," he says. "What are you doing here?"

"Do you have a second? I was hoping we could talk."

"Uh, no," he says, glancing over his shoulder. "No, not really. I'm running late for work."

"It's important—"

"*Ben?*" I hear a voice from somewhere inside. It's a woman's voice, young and flirty, and I bow my head, trying to hide my reddening cheeks. It's her. "*Ben, are you out there? Who is it?*"

"Nobody," he calls over his shoulder. "Just a second."

We stand in silence, both of us too embarrassed to look the other in the eye. *Nobody.* I've walked in on something, I can tell. A Tuesday morning spent together, and I wonder if this is just a coincidence—if maybe they drank too much last night and stumbled back here together, deciding to crash at his place instead of calling a car—or if she lives here, too. If he just bounced that quickly from me to her, the same way he did from Allison to me.

I poke my head to the side, trying to catch a glimpse into his home.

"So, what is it, Isabelle?" he says, leaning on the doorframe, trying to obscure my view. "What brings you here this early on a Tuesday morning?"

"I just had some questions," I say. "About, you know, that night . . ."

"Jesus," he says, lowering his head. He's pinching the skin between his eyes, hard, like I'm a migraine he's trying to fight off. "Are you kidding me?"

"It's important—"

"Isabelle, you need to *let this go.*"

"Are you saying that because that's what's best for me?" I ask. "Or because you think I don't want to know the truth?"

Ben stares at me, his head cocked to the side. "What does that mean?"

I think about all the other times he's looked at me like this—on Dr. Harris's couch, his hand on my knee; in our living room at dusk as I stood planted by the window, my eyes glassed over—searching my expression for something long-since lost: a flicker of recognition, maybe. A glimpse of knowledge. A memory lodged somewhere deep in my subconscious, trying to claw its way out.

"I think you know what it means," I say. "Look, Ben, if you're trying to protect me or something—"

I stop, my mind back in Beaufort again. On my father and the way he had looked at me, too. The way he had covered for me, lied for me, because the truth, he knew, would kill me. Maybe that's why Ben has been so adamant about trying to get me to move on. Maybe that's why he's been trying to convince me to stop searching, stop hoping.

Because he knows it's pointless. He knows the truth.

"If you know something about what happened and you're just afraid to say it . . . please," I say, pleading now. "I have to know. I can't wonder like this forever. I can't—"

Before he can respond, the door opens wide, and a woman appears behind him. She's wearing one of his work shirts—a white button-up, the collar half popped—her dark hair tied into a bun on the top of her head. She's smiling politely, barefaced and beautiful, as she puts her hand on his shoulder and pushes herself into view.

"Hi, Isabelle," she says. "It's good to see you."

I stare at the woman in the doorframe and register Ben's shoulders tighten at her touch. I wonder if he sees it, too. How alike we are. The Cupid's bow of our lips; the angled cheekbones, the same shade of hair. I wonder if he sees it, if he's embarrassed, or if it's entirely subconscious. If he doesn't even realize that I feel like I'm staring straight at us, half a decade ago, when I was the one wrapped in his clothes, making him breakfast. Making him laugh.

"Isabelle, this is Valerie," he says at last. "Though I've heard you two have already been acquainted."

"Valerie," I repeat, taking in her dark eyes and open smile. At first, I don't know what he's talking about—I don't know what he means by *acquainted*—but then I notice her dimples, those two identical chasms in her cheeks hugging her lips like a pair of parentheses. "From the church."

I think back to the cathedral on the night of Mason's vigil: the wanderers and worshipers, and the way I had closed my eyes and drifted away for a while. Opening them back up again and finding everyone gone before walking into the back room. The way the light from inside had spilled out onto the sidewalk like the moon on water, and the bargain coffee brewing in the corner making my eyes feel tight. Those cheap metal chairs arranged in a sad circle on the floor and the woman who had greeted me. Invited me to stay.

"I didn't really get the chance to introduce myself before," she says to me now, thrusting her hand out in my direction. "Properly, I mean."

I look down at it, remembering the man who had interrupted us then, shuffling inside just as her lips had started to part. I can't bring myself to take it.

"Valerie, hon, we'll just be a second," Ben says after a prolonged silence. I can tell that she wants to stay—she wants to make this right between us, whatever *this* is—but instead, he gives her a kiss on the head and steps onto the stoop, closing the door behind him and leaving her inside.

"So," I say at last, crossing my arms after a beat of uncomfortable quiet. "The therapist."

"Isabelle, come on." He sighs. "Not now."

"I have to admit, I didn't expect this cliché from you," I continue, a glimpse of anger starting to surge in my chest. I can taste it again—blood, pennies, the metallic tang of rage forcing itself up my throat. "But then again, who am I to talk? I did marry my boss."

"That's enough," he says. "I tried to get you to go with me. I *tried.*"

I think back to those chairs again, trying to imagine Ben sitting in one of them. The vulnerability of it. It seems so out-of-place for him, so wrong, and I feel a sudden pang of guilt at the thought of him entering that room for the first time alone. I picture the nervous fidget in his fingers as he tried to find the words; his voice, usually so commanding, starting to crack.

The realization lodges itself in my chest like a knife wedging into my rib cage, cold and sharp: I should have been there with him.

"So we were still together," I say instead, imagining him leaving the house every Monday night and spending it with her, as I stayed seated at the dining room table, my rabid eyes consuming all those pictures on the wall. I had practically forced them together, driving him into the arms of someone who could actually help.

"We weren't still together and you know it," he says. "We hadn't been *together* for a long time. Not really."

"That's news to me," I say. "I guess it's kind of like how you and Allison weren't together, either. *Not really.*"

Ben stares at me, and I can tell that took him by surprise. I've never brought up Allison like this before. I've never insinuated that what he did to her—what *we* did to her, together, behind her back—was wrong on so many levels.

"So, what, did she hold you and let you cry and make you feel better when I couldn't?" I ask. Ben is still silent, staring at me, but I can't stop. I want to hurt him, even though it isn't fair. Even though none of this would have happened—*none* of it—if it weren't for me.

"You should know that we didn't get together until recently," he says quietly. He's matching my anger with pity, which makes it even worse. "That is the truth. Not until after I stopped going. After I moved out."

"How kind of her to wait."

"*I* reached out to *her*," Ben says. "Okay? She didn't initiate anything. She didn't do anything wrong."

We're both quiet, and I can feel my heart thumping hard against his ring, still dangling against my chest. I have the sudden urge to rip it off and throw it at him, but admitting that I've been holding on to it like this is something I still can't bring myself to do.

"Would you have moved out if Mason wasn't taken?" I ask instead. I need to get it out before I have the chance to reel the words back in; before I can change my mind and crawl back into the shadows, choosing ignorance over a truth that will surely kill me. "Or did you move out *because* he was taken?"

"Isabelle, don't do this to yourself."

"Did you leave because I did something to him? Something I don't remember?"

He looks at me, his mouth half open like he wants to respond, but at the same time, he can't.

"Answer me."

Ben sighs, looking down at his shoes. Finally, he shakes his head.

"I think you should go home," he says at last, turning around and opening the door. I can see Valerie inside, perched on the edge of a barstool, sympathy in her eyes. "Whatever it is you're looking for . . . you're not going to find it here."

CHAPTER FORTY-FOUR

As much as I hate to admit it, Ben is right.

I'm not going to find what I'm looking for here. I have to start from the beginning—and the beginning isn't the night Mason went missing. It isn't the night Ben and I met.

The beginning is back in Beaufort. The beginning is the night Margaret died. *That* is the beginning—the tip of the first domino. The cataclysmic butterfly flap that sent my entire life into motion. I can't ignore it anymore. I can't pretend to believe my father's lies, pushing down all the evidence I had seen for myself: the nightgown, the carpet, the mud. Because I've known, for a while now, how it looks. Where it points.

Not only with Margaret, but with Mason, too.

I've known, I've just refused to see it. I've refused to turn on the light. But the fact of the matter is, I can't live my life in the dark anymore. I can't. It's been too long.

I'm in the car now, driving north along the coast. Home is less than an hour away, and still, I rarely go back. Only when it's absolutely necessary. I haven't called, haven't given my parents warning of my arrival, because to be honest, I don't want to commit myself to it. I want to give myself the option of pulling up, seeing that house—*my* house—looming large behind that wrought-iron gate and simply turning around and driving back to Savannah, because I know the mere sight of it, the memories, might be strong enough to change my mind.

I drive across Port Royal Sound, my eyes skipping over the vast ocean, and into downtown, passing so many landmarks—all of them, in some way, a backdrop to my youth: Bay Street, teeming with tourists, where Margaret and I used to go for ice cream on warm Saturday nights. Pigeon Point and that old wooden playground where we would walk each weekend, the two of us holding hands as we crossed the busy street. I remember the slide, particularly. That shiny metal and the way the sun would make it as hot as a stovetop, but we didn't seem to care. We would still rush up that ladder, over and over and over again, and glide down on our backs, our stomachs, our sides. I remember the skipping of our bare skin as our shirts rode up, our bodies squealing all the way down as they stuck to the metal like eggs on a frying pan. That tinny burn and the red welts on our fingertips that would eventually crust and peel.

I drive past the cemetery next, an unavoidable landmark, and look the other way.

Finally, I get to my street. I slow the car considerably, practically crawling toward the cul-de-sac, like a prisoner making his way to the gallows, stalling for time. My house sits at the very back of it, the endpoint of the road. Go any farther and you'd drop into the sea.

I pull off to the side, park on the grass, and climb out of the car, the whiff of salt and mud hitting me as soon as I open the door. The gate is still there; the plaque, still there, although by now, the ivy has grown so thick that you can no longer read the inscription. The jasmine is supposed to be in bloom this time of year, its nutmeggy smell infiltrating the air, but the tiny white blossoms, usually thin and spindly like starfish bleached from the sun, are brown and crusty instead, their pedals flaking off like dried skin.

Even the plants can't escape the death of this place.

I make my way to the house slowly. To anybody else, it would be such a serene view, but to me, the memories prevail. I see that giant oak tree with limbs like fingers, and the statues that seem to take on lives of their own. The dock that juts into the marsh, its boards now mangled and cracking from saltwater and neglect. The massive willow in our front yard, its vast network of roots erupting from the trunk and growing over the grass in all directions before burrowing beneath the driveway like varicose veins, gnarled and throbbing and cracking the pavement.

There's a sickness in this property: something wicked that's been pulsing through the house for centuries. Even as a girl, I could feel it. I could feel it traveling through us all.

I exhale, reach my hand through the bars, and unhook the latch. Then I walk toward the front door, knowing that they're home. I can smell the fresh lavender of their laundry detergent billowing out through the air vent; I can see their cars parked in the back, even though I know nobody ever drives them. Growing up here, there's just something about this place—a sensation, a *feeling*—that's been ingrained in me, buried deep, like a splinter wedged fast into the skin. I've spent my entire life trying to ignore it, trying not to bother it, and in time, it seemed to just become a part of me: something wrong inside that's stuck so deep, my body just learned to live with it. Grow around it like a tumor.

But here, now, I can feel it flaring up again, the mere sight of this place hitting it in just the right way.

I push my finger into the bell now and hear the noise on the other side, bouncing off the walls, the empty space. I wait, trying not to fidget, knowing that, once they answer, I'll be face-to-face with my parents for the first time since Mason was taken. Finally, I hear the twist of the lock; the old hinges creaking as the heavy door lurches open. I hear my father's dry throat clearing—a habit he picked up from smoking and has never been able to drop—and say a silent *thank-you* that it's him I'll have to face first.

"Hey, Dad." He looks up at me, obviously surprised to see me standing there. I flash him a meek smile, shrug a little, and look down at the ground, studying my shoes. "Mind if I come in?"

CHAPTER FORTY-FIVE

THEN

It's been six months without Margaret, and somehow both everything and nothing has changed.

We lowered her into the ground at Beaufort National Cemetery. I remember standing there, dressed in black, the little white headstones aligned in perfectly spaced straight lines. They reminded me of fangs, small and pointy, or of standing inside a giant shark's mouth, lost amidst the endless rows of jagged teeth. All of us nothing more than scraps of flesh snagged against their serrated edges.

The pastor had called it an honor for her to be buried there among some of our nation's bravest soldiers—Dad was a veteran, after all, which meant that one day, he would join her there, too. I didn't see it as an honor, though. I saw it as a cruel *dis*honor, because burying her there implied that there was something valiant about her death— something heroic and necessary—when in reality, she died by choking on dirty marsh water, facedown in the mud.

It was raining, I remember, but nobody had thought to bring an umbrella, so we just stood there, the three of us, water dripping off my mother's ringlet curls as we watched the tiny casket being lowered into a pit of sludge. Her doll was in there, too, tucked beneath her arm.

Mom couldn't stand the thought of Margaret being buried alone, but there was something eerie about it to me, imagining those porcelain eyes still open as the casket was being closed, enveloping them both in darkness. The fact that time would go on, Margret's body would decay and rot and turn into nothing but bones, and there, still wedged into her armpit, would be Ellie, her baby—eyes open, lips grinning, buried alive.

After it was over, we drove home in silence, each of us retreating to our own quiet corners of the house. Mom couldn't stop crying; Dad couldn't stop drinking. He retired a few months later, deciding to stay home with Mom and me indefinitely. Maybe Margaret's death forced him to realize how much of her life he had missed; maybe the publicity of her drowning was too hard to avoid, the questions too hard to answer, so he decided to just shut himself in.

Or maybe Mom made him. Maybe she was too afraid to spend any more nights with me alone.

In some ways, life has gone on as if nothing even happened, like stubbing your toe and trying to walk through the pain with tears in your eyes. School started up again in August, the way it always has, and I just went through the motions as if everything were fine. As if Margaret's little backpack weren't still suspended next to mine in the mudroom, partially zipped shut with her favorite sweater peeking out. It was like we all wanted it there for her, just in case she clawed her way out of that coffin and came walking back from the graveyard, wet and shivering and covered in mud, looking for something to keep her warm. Her bedroom remains untouched, though Mom insists on leaving the door shut. Dad says it's because she can't stand to see it: her little bed, her pink walls, her white mesh canopy dangling like a cobweb from the ceiling. Sometimes, I stop in the doorframe and try to imagine what it must have felt like for her to open her eyes and see me standing there, rigid and staring, a silhouette in the dark.

How afraid she must have been.

In other ways, though, life after Margaret has been unimaginably different. Holidays have come and gone and we've just ignored them all, pretended they didn't exist, as if disregarding the passage of time would make the fact that the world was moving on without her a little less real. Everything reminds me of her now: the taste of sweet tea, the smell of the marsh. The quietness of the house every morning as I make my way downstairs, the deafening silence amplified even further by the fact that she isn't here to fill it with her footsteps, her laughter, her voice.

Mom's stopped painting, her third-floor studio slowly morphing into a room for storage. Dad's home constantly, his cheeks, once perfectly smooth, sprouting wiry little hairs that have slowly grown into a fully formed beard peppered with gray. We have visitors on occasion: Chief Montgomery checking in, the neighbors offering casseroles and condolences. The tourists poking their heads through the bars feels even more ominous now, like it isn't the history they want to see, but something darker. A week after Margaret died, a bald man with oval glasses started coming over twice a week, listening to Mom cry. He nods his head and scribbles notes on a legal pad as she talks—or, more often, just sits in silence, tears dripping from her chin—leaving her with various bottles of pills that keep multiplying on the countertop.

The biggest change, though, seems to be with my sleep—or, rather, my lack thereof. I used to be such a deep sleeper; I used to fall asleep in an instant, like the closing of my lids signaled to my brain that it was time to shut off, too. Parts of it, anyway. But now I lie awake, unblinking eyes on the ceiling, watching as my room morphs slowly from dusk to dawn. It's like my brain wants me to remember something; it won't shut down until I remember. And when I do fall asleep—finally, after hours of violent fits and bursts—I have the same dream, always.

Every single time, I dream of her.

I dream of the two of us outside, the glow of the moon making our nightgowns shine as we stand at the edge of the water. I dream of her hand in mine, fingers tight, her neck twisting as she stares at me in the darkness.

Her eyes wide, trusting, before she turns back around, faces the marsh.

And then she takes a slow step forward, her toes sending a ripple through the water as I stand back and watch her go.

CHAPTER FORTY-SIX

NOW

I've grown used to uncomfortable silence in this house. After Margaret, that's all there ever was.

Dad offered me a drink when I first walked in. "We have whiskey, wine . . ." His voice trailed off before he could finish. He was embarrassed, I think, when he realized it wasn't yet noon.

"Coffee," I said. "Please. Thanks."

We're in the living room now, the three of us sitting in opposite corners. I'm perched on the edge of the couch—the kind of couch that's purchased for aesthetic alone, the cushions the consistency of cardboard, and the upholstery a clean, crisp white—while my parents are in two armchairs on either side of the fireplace. There's a tray of cookies between us arranged in an ornate circle. My mom brought them out—mostly, I think, to give her hands something to do, an excuse not to touch me. I know they're just going to sit there, growing stale. That she'll brush them all into the trash once I leave, slap the lid shut, like my presence alone somehow rendered them spoiled.

"I got your card," I say at last. "And the check. Thank you."

"Sure," my dad says, smiling. "It's the least we could do."

"You didn't have to, though. I mean, I don't *need* it—"

He waves his hand as if brushing off a gnat.

"How's Ben?"

I look at him and notice his set lips and clenched jaw. He's uncomfortable, grasping for conversation, a mad scramble in his mind that I'm sure began the moment he opened the door and saw me standing on the other side of it. He's never liked to talk about problems; neither of my parents have. Politics and religion were always welcome in our house, but emotions and feelings and all those other sticky subjects were simply buried beneath piles of money and presents until they disappeared altogether.

"He's fine," I say at last. Of course, they don't know we're separated. I never told them. "Busy with work."

"Good," he says, nodding. "That's good."

I set my coffee on the side table. I haven't taken a sip since I sat down. I'm too afraid of sloshing the liquid over the side, staining the couch. Old habits die hard. Then I glance at my mother, at the way she's sitting rigid in her chair like she's strapped into a straight jacket. Her hands are clenched tight in her lap, one ankle hooked around the other the way we learned in cotillion. They've changed so much since Margaret died. My mother used to see the world in such vibrant colors. I remember the way she would look at me with such wonder in her eyes—her head lolled to the side, fingers tickling at her chin, like I had come into this world as a piece of artwork, commissioned by her steady hand, and somehow sprung myself from the canvas. Took on a life of my own. But now it's like her world has faded into black and white.

Whenever she looks in my direction, those same eyes skip over me completely, like I'm nothing but empty space.

"So what can we do for you, Izzy?"

My dad squirms in his chair, crossing and uncrossing his legs. He's changed, too. His booming voice has withered into a whisper, jittery and unsure. He used to command attention every time he walked into a room, but now it's like he looks for the nearest corner and hides there, tries to blend into the wallpaper.

"I was actually in the neighborhood," I lie. "For work. I'm writing a story."

"Oh, that's great, sweetie."

He doesn't ask what it's about; I knew he wouldn't. Sometimes, I wonder if it bothers them: the fact that my life moves forward when Margaret's came to such an abrupt and violent ending, like a car careening into a wall. My job, my husband, my son. All reminders of what she wouldn't have. What I took from her.

But then again, maybe it brings them some semblance of comfort that I've managed to destroy those things on my own.

"How are you, honey?" my mother finally asks, the addition of her voice both sudden and startling. "How are you holding up?"

I look over at her. There's that question again. The question nobody really wants you to answer.

"I'm . . . you know," I say, giving her a pinched smile. "Not great, honestly."

"Any updates with the case?"

My dad cuts in, and I can feel the shift of power in the room again, almost like the way a storm cloud alters the pressure in the air, making it harder to breathe. They had met Mason, of course—I would never keep my parents from meeting their grandson—but by the time he came into this world, the distance between us had grown so vast, there was nothing we could do to cross it. I remember them stepping into my home for the first and last time, glancing around as if they were in a museum, too afraid to touch anything. Tiptoeing around rogue toys and dirty laundry the same way I had always navigated their antique vases and breakable things with a sense of acute awareness, though that sharp tang of irony seemed to have gone over their heads completely. Ben had ushered them toward me as I nursed Mason on the couch, my old button-up stained and sour, and I'll never forget the way my mother blushed when she saw me like that, her eyes darting to the ground like she was embarrassed for us both. The entire visit, my father had been the one to hold him, smelling his head and pinching his cheeks, while she sat silently by his side. At one point, he had thrust Mason toward her, gesturing for her to take him, and I felt a spasm in my chest as she looked at him, then up at me, muttering a quiet *Excuse me* before standing up and walking back outside.

Like her own grandson would make her break out in hives.

She had been thinking about Margaret, I'm sure. About how she should have been there—or, more likely, about how it should have been her baby we were all in town to see. I'm sure she had been imagining her singing to that doll, hushing to her sleep. Bouncing her on her knee in the kitchen.

Margaret would have been such a good mother. A better mother than me.

"No, not really," I say at last. It dawns on me now: I wonder if they've suspected it all along. Mason's disappearance. I wonder if they heard the news, saw my face on the television screen, and thought to themselves: *It happened again.*

I wonder if they pictured me at night, holding him in the dark the same way I must have held Margaret's hand. If they've been protecting me now the same way they protected me then: through silence, secrets. Lies.

"Well, keep us posted," my father says, like we're talking about a job interview. We've never really gotten the hang of how to interact with one another since Margaret left us. Without her around to pad our interactions, they've felt jagged and awkward, like old friends bumping into each other at the grocery store. Exchanging pleasantries while biting our tongues, tasting blood, racking our brains for excuses to leave.

"I passed the cemetery on my way here," I say, looking for an opening. "Have you been to visit recently?"

I catch a glimpse of a shudder roll through my mother's body, like she was hit with a sudden blast of cold. My father cocks his head, like he doesn't know what I'm talking about.

"I might stop by later," I continue. "I haven't been, you know, since—"

"We go every Sunday," my dad interrupts. "After church."

"That's good."

Silence again. My mother is scratching at the fabric of her armchair, her nails digging into the expensive threads. I catch my dad stealing a glance at the grandfather clock, probably wondering how a minute could possibly move so slowly.

"You know we don't talk about it much," I say, unable to peel my eyes from the carpet. This is where we used to lie: Margaret and I, stomachs on the oriental, flipping through issues of *The Grit* and sounding out the words together. Revealing stories of another world, another life, imagining ourselves ripped from our own and implanted into the pages. "That night, what happened. We've never actually talked about it—"

"What's there to talk about? It was a terrible accident."

I look at my mother—still silent, still scratching—and back to my dad. That air of authority has crept back into his voice just a little bit. Just enough for him to signal that this conversation is off-limits.

"It was." I continue pushing forward. "But I think it might help me if we could just *talk* about it. Mom asked how I was doing—"

"Okay," he says, leaning forward, resting his chin on his palm, like he's a psychiatrist, studying me. "What would you like to talk about, Isabelle?"

"I have . . . memories, I guess, of that night. Some things that have been bothering me. Things that don't make sense."

My parents shoot each other a look.

"Like, when I woke up that morning . . . there was water on the carpet." I force myself to continue, hawking up the words like vomit stuck in my throat. "I was wearing a different nightgown from what I fell asleep in. There was mud—"

"Isabelle, what is this about?" my dad asks, his voice suddenly softer. "Why are you dragging all this back up?"

"Because I need to know what *happened*!" I shout, louder than I intend to. My voice seems to echo off the walls, the grand piano, a pitchy whining vibrating off the strings. "I *need* to know—"

"Your sister had an accident, sweetie. It was nobody's fault."

I remember the way he had coached me that morning, reciting those same words over and over again. The way my mother had looked at me, head tilted to the side, her eyes cloudy with a waxy shine like she thought I was a ghost.

"But I feel like I was there. I *remember*—"

"Don't do this," he says, the exact same words Ben had said to me this morning now echoing up my father's throat. "Isabelle, don't do this to yourself."

CHAPTER FORTY-SEVEN

I forgot how the sun sets here. Slowly, at first, the turquoise gradually morphing into a slathering of peaches and yellows and tangerines bleeding together like watercolors—and then, quick as a blink, it's like someone lit a match and set fire to the sky, the blaze traveling across the canvas as if it were drenched in kerosene and left to burn. I'm on the dock now, watching as the sun dips below the horizon. With dusk reflecting off the water, it almost feels like I'm sitting in it, right in the middle: a room on fire with flames above and below me, swallowing me whole.

"Stay for dinner," Dad had said, changing the subject as quick as a whip crack. I didn't want to, but at the same time, I did, so I glanced at my mother, looking for a hint of permission in her gaze.

She gave me a twitch of a smile, a small nod, and so I agreed.

The kitchen looked different, our old cobalt backsplash replaced with subway tile, simple and white. Some of it had to be renovated after that summer fire, of course, but the rest, I knew, was an attempt to erase the memories, the past. There were tiny pots of herbs set against the windowsill: basil and rosemary and parsley and sage, giving the air a woody smell, like freshly mown grass. I watched as

Mom clipped at the leaves with little silver scissors, collecting a heap in her palm. I don't remember her cooking much, but she seemed to know what she was doing.

I had been chopping lettuce for dinner, a cleaver in my grip and my eyes somewhere distant, when Mom placed a hand on my shoulder, startling me back to the present.

"You know I love you," she said, her voice shaking. It seemed like an attempt at reconciliation; a moment of forgiveness I never felt I deserved. "You know that, right?"

I stand up from the dock now, brushing the pollen from my jeans. Despite their attempts at redecorating, at erasing the memories of Margaret, I can still see her everywhere here: In the kitchen table where she used to sit, singing to her doll in that high-pitched voice. In the copper skillets hanging above the stove, the same ones I used to make her omelets in, sliding the eggs onto a plate and placing it in front of her. Watching her eat. In the backyard where we use to sit with those statues, sweet tea in hand, and here on the dock, especially, water lapping against the pilings like a soft, ceaseless nudge.

It's getting dark outside, the moon fingernail thin, and I start the long walk back up the dock. I agreed to stay the night after shooting my neighbor a text to check on Roscoe. Maybe it's because I don't want to go home, feel the restored emptiness of my house without Waylon in it, or think about how all those people at the conference had been right all along. How they had somehow seen me more clearly than I've ever been able to see myself.

Or maybe it's because, after all these years, it finally feels like the icy wall my parents have erected between us since Margaret's death is slowly starting to melt. That in coming here, I had extended an olive branch. That I was apologizing, for the very first time, for what I did—and in return, they were apologizing for leaving me so alone.

For seeming to forget that I'm their daughter, too.

I walk through the backyard, past the statues and the rose bushes and the giant stone birdbath with a dead palmetto bug floating on its back. Then I step through the back door, the house quiet and still. My parents retreated to their bedroom an hour ago—partly, I think, because we ran out of things to say—and I walk into the kitchen again, emptying the bottle of wine we opened earlier into a fresh glass. Then I walk up the stairs, down the hallway, and into my old bedroom.

They've redecorated here, too, a new queen in place of the child-hood bed I took with me to Savannah. It looks like a proper guest room now, though I know they don't have any guests. I resist the urge to peek into Margaret's room—to see if they've erased that, too—and instead place my wine on the bedside table, stripping off my clothes and changing into the pair of pajamas Mom laid out for me on the mattress.

Then I sit on the floor, cradling the wine against my chest, and wonder how I'll spend the next ten hours alone in the dark.

Just like when I was a child, the house seems to come alive at night. I can hear it breathing—the draft in the hallway like a long exhale; the pop of the floorboards a cracking neck. Margaret's voice: *You ever feel like we're not alone?* I creep out of my bedroom and glance at the stairs: the third floor. Where we used to paint, Margaret and I, the French doors swung open and a warm breeze like breath on our necks.

I start to climb, remembering the way we used to huddle on the balcony, mugs of hot chocolate cupped in our hands anytime the tem-perature dropped below fifty. Margaret making wishes on shooting stars or pointing hungrily at the water anytime we saw the breach of a fin or the skid of shrimp dimpling the glassy surface.

I reach the landing and look around, the giant open room now housing old furniture covered in sheets like banished ghosts. Mom's easel is still in the corner, facing the floor-to-ceiling windows like she was just mid-paint, and I can picture her eyes flicking back and forth between the canvas and the backyard, swirling her brush against the various colors of her palette, its own abstract work of art. That thin slab of wood tells the stories of paintings past: the pink she used to color Margaret's flushed cheeks, the green of my father's armchair, the blue of the rising tide.

I walk the perimeter of the room, holding the glass below my chin like a security blanket, trying to make out the shapes in the dark.

In the back corner, I come across a pile of paintings perched against the wall, so I sit on the hardwood floor, legs crossed, and start thumbing through them. Some of them are finished—a bowl of fruit on the kitchen counter, the creeping jasmine swallowing the bricks of our front gate—while some she abandoned midway through: the rough outline of a face, lines disjointed. Eyes lifeless and blank.

I flip through a couple more, smiling at the ones I recognize, when suddenly, I stop.

There, in the back, is the one I had seen that summer: me in my white nightgown, standing at the edge of the marsh—only now I realize what I had seen before wasn't finished. Now that girl is flanked by two other bodies: one with brown hair cascading over her shoulders and the other, so small, with locks the color of caramel candy. The three of them are holding hands, walking into the water together, that spring tide moon lighting the way.

And that's when it hits me.

The girl I had seen in the painting—the girl Margaret had pointed to and assumed to be me—wasn't actually me at all.

And she isn't wearing a nightgown. The one in the middle: She's wearing a robe.

"Isabelle."

I jump at the voice behind me, knocking my wineglass over with my knee. Then I spin around, the red liquid spilling across the floorboards like blood, and register a body in the dark before me. It's my mother, the glow of the moon illuminating her face; tears streaming down her cheeks like rain on a window.

"Isabelle, honey, let me explain."

CHAPTER FORTY-EIGHT

I like to think of our memories like a mirror: reflecting images back to us, something familiar, but at the same time, backward. Distorted. Not *quite* as they are. But it's impossible to look our past straight in the eye, to see things with perfect clarity, so we have to rely on the memories.

We have to hope they aren't somehow warped or broken, bending reality to fit the way we wish things were.

"I was sick," my mother says to me now, stepping forward in the dark. Her arms are outstretched, and I crawl back, afraid to let her get too close, my palm pushing into the shattered glass on the floor. "Isabelle, honey. I was very, very sick."

The memories of my mother have always been dreamlike and hazy: her in those gossamer white robes, with curls like a lion's mane and that trancelike gaze. It's like I wanted to see her in the most flattering light, her sharp edges buffed out and airbrushed to perfection: an angel or a goddess or something not entirely human. Not entirely real.

"What do you mean, sick?"

I'm trying to ignore the stinging cut in my hand; the trickle of blood I feel dripping down my wrist.

"It started when we lost Ellie."

"Ellie?" I ask, unable to mask my confusion. "Margaret's doll?"

I think of all the times she was there with us, porcelain eyes watching over everything. Virtually every memory from those final months has her in it: Margaret singing to her in the kitchen or nestling her between us in bed that last night, my mother's hands on our cheeks.

"*My girls,*" she had said. "*My two beautiful girls.*"

And then Margaret: "*You forgot Ellie.*"

Suddenly, like the cock of a shotgun demanding attention, I feel the pieces starting to slip into place.

I think of the strangeness of my mother's laugh every time Margaret mentioned that name; her sad little smiles and the way she would clear her throat and walk away before she retreated to her bedroom and shut the door behind her, leaving us alone for hours on end. The distant look in her eyes when she gazed out the window, like she was staring at something the rest of us couldn't see.

"Oh my God," I say, finally remembering. *Really* remembering. Like that splinter, buried in deep, the pain comes shooting back again, almost bringing me to my knees.

I think of the gentle slope of her stomach beneath that flimsy white robe, still slightly swollen, like a balloon deflating slowly. Losing its shape.

"*Yes, well. Of course we can't forget about Ellie.*"

But we did. We forgot about her—or at least, *I* forgot about her. Eloise, *Ellie,* my second sister. The one who died before she could even take her first breath.

I remember it all now, not fragmented like a dream or a nightmare, but in sudden, startling clarity: my mother's screams as they echoed down the hall, and Margaret coming into my bedroom, her little eyes peeking through my cracked door the way she always did when she was afraid. Scampering into my bed and the two of us huddled beneath the covers together, flashlights shining, telling each other stories to try to drown out the noise—and then the deafening silence that followed, almost like the house had stopped breathing, too.

I remember working up the courage to creep out of my room, finally, my eyes landing on my father as he paced outside their bedroom, brown bottle in hand. I could see my mother in bed, covered in blood. Sheets staining red as she held something limp and lifeless in her arms and the sudden sound of her fragile voice traveling down the hall.

"Hush little baby, don't say a word. Mama's gonna buy you a mockingbird."

I see her in the kitchen, weeks later, fingers twisting through Margaret's hair as she bounced that doll against her hip.

"Have you named her yet?"

And then Margaret's answer, followed by the sudden stillness of my mother's hand, like her veins had frozen to ice; her face, sad and pale, like she had seen a ghost.

"Ellie," she had said, that proud smile tugging at her lips. *"Like Eloise."*

"Eloise," I say now, the name suddenly so familiar. I had even seen her nursery once. The door was perpetually closed the way Margaret's was, too, eventually, like it was easier to just walk right past it and pretend she never even existed. But I had seen it—*we* had seen it—Margaret and I, during one of those long, summer days when we wandered around the house unsupervised. We had peeked inside, looked at her crib. Trailed our fingers along that little white rocking chair sitting motionless in the corner and read her name—*Eloise*—embroidered onto everything.

That's where she got it: Margaret. That's where she got the name.

I can't even imagine how that must have felt for my mother: Margaret naming her own baby after the one my mother had just lost. Singing that exact same song to her over and over and over again, pushing on a bruise so it could never really heal. It wasn't intentional, I know, but Margaret was always listening, always remembering. Always mirroring what she saw the rest of us do, rocking her own little Ellie in her arms, silent and still.

"Were you depressed?" I ask now, tears in my eyes. "Mom, of course you would be—"

Looking back, I realize now that my mother was here, with us, but she wasn't actually *with* us. Not really. Margaret and I were always on our own: making ourselves breakfast in the morning and wandering around the house at night. Playing near the water and walking to the park alone, hand in hand, crossing busy streets of traffic without a parent in sight.

Always in our nightgowns, even long after morning had passed.

It seemed so idyllic back then, like some kind of fairy tale. There's no way we could have known what was happening, what was really going on. Like the Lost Boys of *Peter Pan*, calling out for mother, our freedom was an illusion.

What it really was, was neglect.

"No," my mother says, shaking her head, a sad little squeak erupting from somewhere deep in her throat. "No, it wasn't that. It was something more than that."

Losing Ellie was the moment we lost my mother, too. The moment everything changed. Even then I felt it, though I didn't understand. That feeling of death that was always there, always present, swollen and bloated and hovering over everything like it was just biding its time, waiting to claim one of us next. The strangeness of it, of *her*, settling over the house, like we had all morphed into those plush fabric dolls, buttons for eyes, moving through the motions like nothing had happened.

Like none of us were really *us* anymore.

"I tried to tell your father that something wasn't right," she continues. "That I was feeling things, *thinking* things, that were starting to scare me."

I suddenly remember the sound of my mother's voice that night, seeping through my father's office door as I stood on the other side of it, listening. The little beg that erupted from the back of her throat.

"You don't know what it's like. Henry, you don't understand."

I always thought she was talking about me walking through the house at night: eyes open, body rigid. *It's dangerous to wake a sleepwalker.* I always thought she was saying that he didn't understand what it was like living with *me*, dealing with *me*. That she was afraid of *me*.

But that wasn't the case. That wasn't the case at all.

She was afraid of herself.

CHAPTER FORTY-NINE

"What did you do?" I whisper, the reality of what my mother is trying to tell me making the blood turn solid in my veins. "Mom, what did you do?"

I can hear the thumping of my own heart in my ears, like holding your nose and plunging underwater; I watch as she hugs herself, those long, thin fingers digging into the skin of her arms, and think back to that final night with Margaret again. It had been so hot, *too* hot, our bodies sticking together with sweat in my bed. I think about the way she had whined in the bathtub—"*How much longer?*"—and my mother's fingers trailing across the cool water, leaving behind little ripples in her wake, like the fin of a shark barely breaching the surface.

"*Not much longer,*" she said. "*We'll be comfortable soon.*"

"*By morning?*"

And then that smile again: sad and resigned, like someone so far past her breaking point. Someone who knew, deep down, she was about to do something wrong. Something terrible.

"*Sure. By morning.*"

I stare at my mother from across the room now, finally letting the pieces fall into place. She lets out a little wet choke, lower lip trembling, and something about the way the moonlight is hitting her face through the windows wiggles another memory free. It's that dream again; that dream that kept repeating itself in the months immediately after Margaret died. But it wasn't a dream at all, was it? Instead, it was a memory that emerged disjoined and unclear, like a reflection in a shattered mirror, fragments reflecting back to me as I lay in bed, restless and thrashing.

Dr. Harris had told me, after all, that sleepwalkers can sometimes remember: "*It's like recalling a dream.*"

It's of the two of us outside, Margaret and me, the glow of the moon making our nightgowns shine. Standing at the edge of the water, hand in hand, Margaret twisting her neck to stare at me as if asking permission before turning back around and facing the marsh. It always stopped there, the dream, but now I can see the rest of it: Margaret taking a slow step forward and sending a wave of ripples toward my mother, standing before us, water lapping at her calves. That white robe dripping, translucent against her skin, as she stretched out her arms and beckoned us forward.

That little smile on her lips, and her eyes glassy and gray, filling with tears.

"Why?" I ask, remembering how Margaret had stepped forward while I hung back, watching—seeing, but not really *seeing*. How she had trusted me. How I had let her go. "Why would you do that? Why Margaret?"

"It wasn't about Margaret," she shakes her head. "It was about us. All of us."

"I don't understand—"

But then I see my mother's hand resting on Margaret's cheek in the kitchen, staring at us like we weren't even real.

"*I wish you could stay my babies forever.*"

"I tried one other time," she continues, taking a step forward. "I left the gas on the stove overnight. I remember hoping it would be quick. Thinking it was the right thing to do, even. That we would just go to sleep and wake up together—*all* of us, somewhere else, and everything would be okay."

She's quiet, her eyes somewhere far away, remembering.

"Something caught fire before the carbon monoxide could spread."

I remember rousing awake in the front yard, the sight of those flames licking up the walls as I blinked my bleary eyes. The heat on my skin as my father squeezed my hand and led me back to bed.

"He knew," I say now, not a question but a statement—because suddenly, it all makes perfect sense. "Dad knew."

"I can't blame him," my mother says. "Things were different back then. People didn't like to talk about it."

My mother had come to him, and he hadn't listened. She had lost a child—held her dead baby in her arms, singing to it softly as if it could somehow hear—and still, week after week, he left her alone, vulnerable and afraid.

"*Maybe if we could get some help,*" she had asked, that desperate voice traveling beneath the office door. "*If I could get some help.*"

And then my father, his voice tough, like a callus on your palm: "*No.*"

"Yes, you can," I say now, my eyes on hers in the dark. The fear I had just felt seconds earlier is quickly being replaced with something new, something different. "You can blame him, Mom. You asked him for help. You set our house on fire, and he didn't do anything. He didn't *listen.*"

She shakes her head, her gaze cast down to the floor like she's still so ashamed. It's always so easy to blame the mother.

A *bad* mother. A *neglectful* mother.

"He kept saying it was an accident," she says. "That I didn't do it on purpose."

"An accident," I repeat, remembering the way he kept reiterating it after Margaret, too, almost like he needed to believe it himself.

"He didn't want to believe that things had gotten that bad," she continues. "It was hard for him, too, honey. And he was a congressman, Isabelle. The whole family line . . . they have a reputation. He was afraid of how it might look."

I don't know how to process this. I don't know what to think: my father, valuing his job, his reputation, above the safety of his family—but at the same time, it doesn't surprise me, either. Not really. Everything in our lives had always been for show: The way Margaret and I were dressed in matching outfits and the expensive furniture arranged just so. The giant house and the manicured lawn and the way strangers would ogle at us through the gate as if we, too, were on display. As if we existed for their consumption alone, satiating their curiosity as we played the part: children in the yard, mother tending to the garden.

Our life like a picture, too perfect to be real.

"It was hard," she continues. "He was gone all the time, working, and I was always alone with you girls. Alone in my head."

I think about my mother and those stories she told: the feelings on the back of her neck, prickling at her skin, like being watched. The meaning she had assigned in an attempt to make sense of what was happening in her own head: someone trying to send her a message, maybe. Someone telling her to do things, terrible things, she never would have done on her own.

Suddenly, I remember all those moments with Mason, too: letting my mind wander to that dusty corner of the brain where mothers are never supposed to go. The late nights, the shrieking, the overwhelming urge to make it stop by any means necessary. Those dirty little thoughts that would worm their way into my awareness in the dark, and the way I would let myself indulge in them, like sneaking into the pantry and gorging myself sick: a vile, frenzied feeding.

And then the fear that crept in like a slow injection. The way I would force myself to put him down, back away slowly. Convince myself that it was normal. Because it *is* normal, isn't it? Feeling that way? But how could you possibly know? How do you know if it's something more? Something dangerous?

And if it is . . . how do you stop it?

CHAPTER FIFTY

I left as soon as the sun came up, my car winding down the drive-way with those stone statues in my rearview: the baby, the angel. The woman with the sickness. I wasn't sure if I could face them in the day-light: My mother, for what she told me. My father, for what he did—or rather, what he didn't do.

"I always thought it was me," I had said, a numbness settling over me as the comprehension set in. I watched as my mother cocked her head, like she didn't understand. "I always thought I was the one who led her out there. That maybe I was asleep, and she followed me. That she tried to wake me, and I . . . I did something—"

And then I realized: I never really said it. Not outright, anyway. I told them I had memories from that night that didn't add up: the water on the carpet, the clean nightgown, the mud on my neck. I told them I wanted to know what happened—what *really* happened—and they had glanced at each other from across the living room, like they were afraid that their mask was slipping. That their secret was about to be revealed.

Their secret. Not mine.

"Honey, no," my mother had said, shaking her head. Tears streaming. "No, you didn't do anything wrong. I had no idea you thought that."

"How could I *not* have thought that?" I yelled. "Margaret was always following me around. I was always waking up in strange places. I've spent my entire life thinking that."

I glance to the side now, at the thick folder resting on my passenger seat. My mother had handed it to me after we descended the steps together in a wordless daze, promising its contents would help explain the rest. I can't bring myself to open it, not yet, so instead, I keep driving, my body on autopilot. I don't even know who's responsible; I don't even know who I should blame. It was my mother's hands that shook Margaret from sleep, taking her in one arm and me in the other, eyes open but empty, as we wandered into the dark. It was her hands that beckoned her into the water, forefingers curling, promising her that it would be okay. That relief was coming. That we would be comfortable soon. Her hands that held her down, fought the thrashing, reached out to me next, once the movement had stopped.

That touched my neck, smearing those three fingers of mud, like she wanted to feel my heartbeat for the very last time, a gentle pounding that would soon slow to a stop.

It was her hands, but it wasn't *her*. Not really. I know it wasn't.

I wonder what it was like for him, my father, snaking his arm across the bed to find nothing but empty space where her body should have been. Bolting upright, blinking in the dark, instinctively knowing that something was wrong. I imagine him throwing on his robe and running into the kitchen, expecting to find her there: tampering with the stove, maybe, or stalking the halls the way she sometimes did when she couldn't sleep. Checking outside and hoping to see her standing by the marsh again, barefoot, before coming back in and leaving dirty prints on the carpet. Making the floorboards pop as she roamed around, watching us sleep.

But when he got out there, he realized what had happened.

What he had *let* happen.

He saw the three of us beneath the glow of the spring tide moon: two of us, standing, and the third, the smallest, facedown in the water, still as a piece of driftwood floating with the current.

I turn into Beaufort National Cemetery now, just as the sunrise starts to bleed across the horizon, and pull into the empty lot. The air is dewy, a permanent floral aroma from all the arrangements laid on each grave. I wind my way through the headstones—even though I haven't been here since the day we buried Margaret, I could never forget where she is—and finally, when I reach her, I kneel down on the turf, feeling the damp seep through the knees of my jeans.

I stare at her headstone, an immaculate white marble, her name, birthday, and death day etched into the surface.

Margaret Evelyn Rhett
    May 4, 1993—July 17, 1999

Next to her, there's another one, nearly identical.

Eloise Annabelle Rhett
    April 27, 1999—April 27, 1999

Two pitifully short amounts of time.

I exhale, lean back on my feet, and squeeze back a tear. Everything makes sense now: Margaret questioning me about the footprints that day on the water, her head tilted to the side.

"Is it because of what happened?"

I had started sleepwalking right after we lost Ellie, the trauma of what was going on in our house triggering something inside me that I could never understand.

Margaret understood, though. Somehow, she knew.

"We're not supposed to talk about that."

Because we weren't. We never talked about anything. Even to this day, my parents prefer secrets and silence to uncomfortable conversation. They never even mentioned it to us. They never even explained what happened; never allowed us to understand or grieve. They simply closed the door to her nursery and continued on as if everything were fine, letting my memory wash her away.

I think about how my mother couldn't look at me the morning after Margaret died—or any day *since* that morning—and the man who came to the house and talked to her. Let her cry. The way my father had held out Mason, and the way she had just stood up, walked away, like she didn't feel she deserved it.

Last night, as we were making dinner.

"You know I love you. You know that, right?"

My mother never hated me; she never blamed me. She hated herself. She killed Margaret, her own daughter, and she had tried to kill me. And because of that, she wouldn't let herself near me. She wouldn't let herself be my mother again.

I suppose I should be grateful my father got there in time—that he ran into the water and scooped Margaret into his arms, putting himself between my mother and me before she could do it again. That he had cleaned me, changed my clothes, and led me back to bed the way he had done so many times before when he found me wandering around the house at night. That he had coached me in the morning, told me exactly what to say.

That he had quit his job, gotten my mother the help that she needed—but only behind the fortressed walls of our home.

Only in secret, where nobody else could see.

It would have been the end of him, after all. Everything he and his father and his grandfather had worked toward would be gone in an instant if the world found out what my mother had done. The Rhett name would no longer be cemented in history as something regal and refined; instead, it would be synonymous with death, just like the house itself.

I think about the way Chief Montgomery had barely even pushed me that morning, like he only needed me to recite a few lines. How he and my father had huddled together after, whispered on the porch steps, crafting the perfect story: just a tragic accident. A summer drowning. The wrong side of the statistic. Deep down, the chief must have known it wasn't true, but still, he let himself believe it. It was the story he had wanted to be real. The one that was easier to accept. And so my father had nodded, sniffed, and created an alternate reality that was just easier for everyone to swallow. Then he held on tight to his secret, his lie—not to protect me, though, but to protect my mother. Himself.

All of us.

CHAPTER FIFTY-ONE

I stay at the cemetery until the legs of my jeans are soaked through with damp. Then I stand up, make my way back to the car, and unlock it, sliding into the driver's seat.

I eye the folder again, reaching out and touching the flap. My broken skin is bandaged over from the cut from the wineglass, and I can feel my heartbeat in my palm, thumping hard in my hand. Then I take a deep breath and pull the folder onto my lap, flipping it open and scanning the pages of notes that doctor had taken as he listened to my mother cry.

Her official diagnosis was *postpartum psychosis*, a *"very rare, severe yet treatable condition that can occur after the birth of a baby,"* exacerbated even further by the trauma, grief, and isolation following the death of said baby. Words like *delusions or strange beliefs, inability to sleep,* and *paranoia and suspiciousness* leap out at me from the page, branding themselves into my brain.

All of it had been there. All of the signs, the symptoms, if only someone had cared enough to look.

There's a sense of relief knowing that I was wrong about Margaret—knowing that it wasn't me who led her out there, held her body down in the dark—but still, the uneasiness isn't gone. It's just something new now. Something different.

Postpartum psychosis is considered a clinical emergency, I continue to read. *Symptoms wax and wane, meaning a woman can be lucid enough to hold a conversation, then suffer hallucinations and delusions just hours later. There is a five percent suicide rate and four percent infanticide rate associated with the illness, and the risk of developing postpartum psychosis is higher in women with a history in their family, such as a mother or sister—*

I slap the folder shut and toss it back onto the passenger seat before turning out of the cemetery and finding my way back to the highway, letting my mind wander as I drive. The thought makes me sick: That maybe I did something to Mason in the same way my mother did something to Margaret. That maybe I really had acted on those thoughts, peeled myself from bed that night, and wandered into his bedroom the same way my mother had wandered into mine.

Or maybe, just *maybe*, I could be wrong about this, too.

It feels good to let myself believe it, if only for a second: That if I didn't hurt Margaret, then maybe I didn't hurt Mason, either. That maybe there's another explanation, another reason, that absolves me of any guilt.

I could talk to Dr. Harris, perhaps, ask him more veiled questions in another desperate attempt at answers. Or I could go back to Paul Hayes's house and try to figure out, again, who that old man is. What he knows. Maybe he's lying about seeing me walking around at night, Mason wrapped in my arms. Maybe he's just trying to confuse me, scare me. Get me to stop asking questions. I decide it's better than nothing, because right now, I'm back at square one. Waylon isn't on my side anymore—he made that perfectly clear yesterday, sitting in my living room, accusing me of murder—which means, once again, I'm back to being alone.

Back to trying to find my son without the help of the police, the public. Ben.

There is something about Ben, though, that's been tickling at my

subconscious. Something about our meeting yesterday that felt familiar, though I can't put my finger on why. Maybe it was the surreality
of staring at Valerie up close, at finding myself so swiftly flipped into
the role that Allison once held—no longer *the other one,* but now, *the
old one.* The one he had discarded for something shinier, better, like
a malfunctioning toy. The way she had sashayed into the archway,
her tanned skin visible behind the translucency of his shirt, like she
had just rolled out of bed—*his* bed—and grabbed it from the floor,
plucking it from the spot where he had abandoned it the night before
in a fervent frenzy and shrugged it over her shoulders.

The way she had called to him from the kitchen, her singsongy
voice floating through the halls.

"Ben? Are you out there? Who is it?"

And his response, like a swift kick to the stomach: "Nobody."

I've been driving on autopilot, these familiar roads of home leading me back to the city, but suddenly, the scenery around me seems
to get brighter, sharper. The edges magnified with a startling clarity,
like I've ingested some kind of drug.

I know what it is. I know what was nagging at me. I know what
it was about yesterday that made me feel so uneasy.

It was those words. Valerie's words had dislodged another memory from somewhere deep inside me: the guilt, the shame, of being
pushed into the bushes at the memorial as Ben peeled himself from
me, jogged up the porch steps, and discarded me like his cigarette,
still smoldering in the grass. The fear of holding my breath and letting
the branches claw at my hair, cut at my cheeks, like a gnarled hand
pressed tight against my mouth. Dirty nails digging into my skin,
keeping me quiet.

The panic that swelled in my chest as I watched that man saunter
into the backyard, hands in his pockets.

"Ben? Are you out there?"

Watching his shoulders tense as he spotted my glass, champagne
still fizzing, and the smudge of lipstick on the brim as he lifted it

up, inspected it, like he had found some kind of clue. I hadn't seen his face—I ran before he had the chance to turn back around, face the house, and find me hiding there—but I heard him. I heard his voice loud and clear. It was a voice I didn't recognize at the time, but now, I would recognize it anywhere. It's a voice that has been so prevalent in my life for these last two weeks, ever since he introduced himself on that airplane, sat across from me at my dining room table. Rang loudly in those giant headphones clamped tight around my ears.

That man was Waylon.

I grip the wheel harder, my foot like lead pushing down on the pedal. Even after all these years, I feel sure of it in a way I haven't felt sure of anything. All this time, Waylon's voice felt familiar. I knew I had heard it before—I *knew* it—I just couldn't figure out from where.

But now, I know. He was there, at that house. This is what he's been hiding. This is Waylon's secret. This is what he didn't want me to know.

He knows Ben.

I throw my car into park on the side of the road and dig out my phone. Does Ben know he's here? Did he send him to me for some reason? To extract information, maybe? Another way of keeping tabs?

I launch a new browser and type his name into the search engine, my fingers shaking as I pound at the screen. The page fills with articles about the podcast, interviews with true crime forums, mentions of the Guy Rooney case and his involvement in getting it solved. None of this is helpful, so this time, I refine my search: *Waylon Spencer and Benjamin Drake.*

When the results load, I feel the breath exit my lungs.

I remember us sitting at dinner together, the tension in my chest as I told him about Ben, our past. About what happened to his wife and how her death was our birth. The clank of my fork as I dropped it, hands shaking, recounting the way she had died.

"Doesn't any part of you think that her death was very . . . convenient?"

That very first night in my dining room and the light from outside growing dimmer by the minute. Staring at that wall, tasting
blood on my tongue from my torn cuticle.

"*Why do you do this for a living?*" I had asked, not at all prepared
for the answer.

It was because of his sister's murder.

His sister, Allison.

CHAPTER FIFTY-TWO

I click on the first article that pops up: Allison's obituary. My eyes flicker over the blocks of text, skimming past the funeral details and the requests for donations in lieu of flowers and the sugarcoated description of her passing—vague, innocuous words like *unexpectedly* and *peacefully* and *in her sleep*—until I hit the very last line.

Allison is survived by her husband, Benjamin, her parents, Robert and Rosemary, and her younger brother, Waylon.

I navigate back to the results and click on another article—a wedding announcement—and swallow as the headline loads: BENJAMIN DRAKE & ALLISON SPENCER. There's a picture of the two of them together—that same one he had proudly displayed in his office, on the hull of a sailboat, her giant, oval-shaped diamond reflecting the glare of the sun above—and it makes my stomach squeeze. I never knew her maiden name; I had never even thought to ask. We never talked about her. She was the one topic that was always off-limits, before and after our marriage, like if we just ignored her existence entirely, it would absolve us both of any wrongdoing. Any guilt.

I had learned that from my parents, I suppose.

I can't help but notice how perfect they look together in this picture: young, vibrant, happy. The way we once were, too.

It's not a common name, Waylon, but I have to be sure. I have to be absolutely positive. So I keep scrolling, skimming past quotes from Allison's parents and ceremony details until I reach a family picture at the very bottom—and there it is. There *they* are. All of them, together.

Ben, Allison, Waylon, their parents. One big, happy family.

I drop my phone in my lap. This confirms it: Waylon and Allison Spencer. They're siblings. Waylon is Allison's brother. He was there, at her memorial, huddled in that room that I refused to step inside. Accepting condolences alongside Ben, his brother-in-law. Walking into the backyard as we embraced, unknowingly stumbling into something incriminating and wrong.

"What happened to her?" I had asked, embarrassed at the aspect of me never once wondering what Waylon's story was. We all have one, I suppose. A story. A series of events that twist our lives along some uncharted path. A sequence of births and deaths, beginnings and endings. Love and loss. Joy and pain.

"That's the question," he had said. *"The one case I've been working on since I was twenty-three years old."*

Except Allison's death wasn't a mystery. It wasn't some cold case that garnered national attention; her parents weren't at TrueCrime-Con, selling their souls for eyes. It was a dismally drab death, the way most of them actually are. Allison overdosed. They found the pills in her stomach, the empty prescription bottle in her limp, lifeless hand. Her name on the label. Ben had found her like that, sprawled across the bathroom floor with saucers for pupils and blue-gray skin.

At least, that's what he said.

I pick my phone up again and dial Waylon's number, too jittery to care about the way we left things. Maybe I had misunderstood what he was saying. Maybe—after seeing myself on that laptop screen, after talking to that man on the porch, after uncovering the similarities between Margaret's death and Mason's disappearance and planting myself at the center of them both—maybe I had only heard what I had wanted to hear.

"Nobody broke into your house, Isabelle. I know it, you know it, the cops know it. There was no intruder."

Maybe I had already come to my own conclusion at that point: That I was responsible. That I did something wrong, something terrible. Something I couldn't remember. But just like with Margaret, maybe I was wrong. Just like with Margaret, maybe I wasn't searching for answers, not really. Maybe I already *had* my answers—that I was to blame—and I was just searching for proof.

Any scrap of proof that confirmed what I already believed: That I was a bad mother. That I failed my son, just like I had failed my sister.

"Isabelle?"

Waylon answers slowly, curiously, like he's wondering if I really meant to call. Like he thinks I dialed the wrong number and he's afraid to hear my voice on the other side of the line. I glance at the clock in my car—it's still early, well before rush hour—and realize that I might have woken him up.

"Waylon," I say, trying to calm the tremor in my throat. "What you said to me yesterday—"

"I know, I'm sorry," he interrupts, his voice breathy and hoarse. I picture him lying in a cold motel room, bed-head hair sticking out in all directions as he fumbles for the lamp in the dark. "I feel terrible about it. I was too harsh—"

"Do you think I hurt Mason?" I cut him off. "Do you think I killed my son?"

"*What?*" The sharp intake of air, the change in tone, tells me everything I need to know. It's like my words were a bucket of ice water thrown across his face, startling him awake. "Isabelle, no. Why would you think that?"

I exhale, relief flowing through me.

"I know who you are," I say. "You're Allison's brother. Allison Spencer. Allison Drake."

The line is silent. I can hear him breathing, thinking, wondering what to say next.

"I'm not mad," I continue. "I just . . . I need to know what you're doing here. And what you think you know about Ben."

There has always been chatter about Ben, I suppose, the same way there has always been chatter about me. The parents are the two most logical suspects, after all, but I had always dismissed it. Always sided so strongly with Ben. We had been together. We had been asleep the entire night, limbs like tentacles intertwined in the sheets.

But then again, Waylon had asked about that, too.

"So your husband could have gotten up and you wouldn't have noticed?"

I remember Margaret sliding her little body beneath the dead weight of my arm. Me, waking up in the morning without any memory of her arrival. Without a clue as to what had happened in the night. Before the insomnia, I was always such a heavy sleeper . . . so how do I really know that he was there all along? How do I *really* know that he didn't get up, slip out from beneath the covers, and do something in the night? Something he's keeping from me?

Maybe some part of me had always wondered, the way I so desperately hoped that our stories aligned. The way I had strained to hear what he was saying on the other side of that wall being interrogated on his own, like there was some flicker of distrust between us that I never wanted to acknowledge. The way I never asked about Allison—about what happened to her, what he thought about it all, like I didn't even want to know.

Maybe, somewhere deep in the recesses of my mind—the same place where I had exiled those thoughts about Mason and those memories of my childhood, my mother, Eloise; the ones that hurt to think about and were easier to just ignore, or even better, recreate into something altogether different, molding them like putty in my hands until they looked the way I wanted them to—maybe, I had thought it then: the convenience of her death, the unanswered questions. The easy lies he constructed, jumping so quickly from her to me.

"It's not what I think I know," Waylon says at last, his voice measured and calm. "It's what I *do* know. He was my brother-in-law for ten years, Isabelle. I know him better than anybody."

"He was my husband for seven," I respond. "I think I know him pretty well, too."

"That's what Allison thought."

I hesitate, drumming my fingers against the steering wheel. For the first time, I try to put myself in Allison's shoes. I try to make myself imagine it: how it would feel if Ben did to me what he did to her. What *we* did to her. If he lied about his whereabouts, spent hours on end with another woman at some dimly lit bar, looking at her the way he had once looked at me: chin tucked low, an intensity in his eyes. A playful grin tugging at his lip, like he was imagining the two of us together in some other, private place. If he texted her late at night, after I was asleep, our naked bodies pressed together but in two entirely different places. If I woke up in the morning and climbed on top of him, oblivious to the fact that he was picturing her instead of me.

In this light, it actually seems worse than cheating. It's more calculated, more cunning. More manipulative.

"So, what?" I ask. "You actually think he killed her? You actually think he's capable of *murder?*"

"Isabelle," he responds, his voice clinical and cold, as if he's delivering a diagnosis that he knows will be the end of me, "I *know* he killed her."

CHAPTER FIFTY-THREE

Mason was six months old when I approached Ben about working again.

I never consciously *stopped* working, really, it just seemed to happen without me even realizing. Ben took the news of my pregnancy well—he was surprised but excited, the way I said I was, too—but still, he was busy. The work never eased up, his schedule never thinned, so it was *my* identity that had to shift, a slow, gradual, seemingly inevitable progression, like aging, that I didn't really notice was happening until I woke up one morning, looked in the mirror, and hardly recognized the face staring back.

I had tiptoed from *writer* to *freelance writer* to *working mother* to, at last, just *mother*. And I loved Mason—I *loved* being his mother. I loved spending my days belly-down on the carpet, reading him stories or watching him squirm around on the floor. I loved watching him learn how to flip over, hold up his head. The awe in his eyes as he opened them wider and discovered the world around him. That initial feeling of regret was gone, and I did come to see it as my second chance, reminiscent of Margaret, getting to take care of him the way I once took care of her.

It was starting to get easier, motherhood—or at least, more manageable—but still, something was missing.

I often thought of that passion I had as a child: my fingers dancing over that plaque in our yard, my eyes tearing through magazines, drinking up words, as fast as I could. Sometimes, I would dig up old issues of *The Grit* and flip through the pages, eying my byline, rereading my own words like I was dredging up the last drops of something delicious through a straw before I hit the bone-dry bottom. I could almost hear the frantic slurping of me trying to get one last taste of the person I used to be before it dried up forever.

I decided, before bringing it up, that I would see what was out there first. Besides, maybe I didn't have it in me anymore. It had been almost a year since I wrote anything, so I scoured through my old contacts, grazed the most recent articles of some of my favorite magazines. I spent Mason's midnight feedings flipping through social media, my phone alight in the dark, and finally came across an article about a boiled-peanut salesman in North Carolina who had recently lost his entire operation after a propane tank exploded in his backyard. It was covered on some small local news station—he had lost over ten thousand dollars' worth of equipment—and I could just imagine the piece, something bigger: a feature on his family, who had been in the little-known industry for decades; a behind-the-scenes tour of his backyard business that went up in flames. The history of the food, its overlooked origins, maybe even a fundraiser set up to help him get back on his feet. It would be like the stories I wrote for *The Grit*, the stories I loved: meaningful and muddy and real.

I pitched the idea to a regional magazine, they loved it, and they offered me three thousand dollars, plus travel, to get it done.

"That's more than I've ever made doing freelance," I had said after I explained the idea to Ben. I had been sitting on the bed with Mason, bouncing him on my leg, as Ben stripped off his tie after work. "With that kind of money per story, I could make a real career out of this—"

"We don't need money," he had said. "You know that."

"Well, it's not *just* the money—"

"How long would you be away?" His expression was blank, un-readable. Mason was getting squirmy, and as if it proved his point, Ben gestured to him. "He's still so young."

"A week, tops," I had said, moving him from one knee to the other. "Maybe only a couple days. I think you can handle it."

I had smirked, teasing him, but he didn't smile back.

"Or I could just go every morning and come back at night, but that would be a lot of driving—"

"No," he said, unbuttoning his collar and flexing his neck. "No, you should do it. If that's what will make you happy."

"I *am* happy," I said. "I just . . . I guess I just need something for myself, too. You have the magazine—"

I stopped, felt my cheeks start to burn. We had danced around *The Grit* just like we had danced around Allison: best to pretend it didn't exist. Best to believe that I had left of my own volition, even though sometimes, when I thought about Ben still reporting to that big, beautiful office each morning—walking past my old desk, some-body else's body in my chair and bylines on the wall; sharing coffee with my old coworkers, my friends—I felt an overwhelming twinge of sadness. Like a death I had never fully mourned.

"You should do it," he repeated, walking over to me. I smiled, stretched out my neck, and gave him my lips to kiss—but instead of greeting them with his own, he grabbed Mason, took him from me, and turned back around, disappearing into the hall. "Like I said. Whatever makes you happy."

CHAPTER FIFTY-FOUR

I pull into a metered spot on River Street and walk the few blocks to The Bean, a hole-in-the-wall coffee spot I know Ben would never visit. It's too grungy for him, the kind of place where you pour your own creamer when it's still in the carton, sweating in the corner alongside fossilized packets of sweetener and mismatched spoons. Waylon hadn't left town yet—he got a hotel room yesterday, after I kicked him out, too shell-shocked from our confrontation to make the drive home—and when I step inside, he's already there, waiting for me.

"Hey," I say, dropping my purse onto the empty stool. There's an awkwardness to our interaction, like reconciling exes, but I try to push through it. "I'm just gonna—"

I gesture to the bar, but he shakes his head, pushing a mug in my direction like a peace offering.

"This one's for you."

"Thanks." I smile, sliding into the seat. I grab the coffee and take a sip.

"I'm sorry I lied to you," he says, his fingers bouncing across the table. "Or I guess a more accurate way of stating it is *willfully omitting the truth*. Either way, it was shitty."

I smile again, nod my head, and think about the strange little bow he had greeted me with when he first stepped foot into my home. The way his eyes had scanned around the room, looking for traces of Ben, and how he had ducked down low at Framboise, trying to make himself smaller. He must have been terrified, I realize, stepping into those situations and not knowing what he would find. If Ben had been there with me, his cover would be destroyed.

"So," I say, drumming my fingers against the mug, "where should we start?"

"From the beginning, I guess." Waylon exhales, rolling his neck like he's preparing for some kind of fight. "Allison and Ben met in high school. He was a few years older than her, and I think she liked that— the attention of an older guy. How it made her feel older herself."

I picture Ben as a teenager, roaming the high school halls the same way he roamed around the office or up on that rooftop: with purpose and poise. He was popular, I'm sure. Letterman jackets and pockets of friends flanking him on either side. I picture him catching Allison's eye at her locker, shooting her a wink and a grin. The way she probably looked around before mouthing: "*Me?*" Like she couldn't possibly believe that his attention was directed at her.

"I can relate to that."

"He eventually went away for college but came back every weekend to see her," he says. "He proposed pretty much as soon as she turned twenty, got married when she was twenty-one. She never dated anyone else. My parents loved him."

"And you didn't?"

"I *mean* . . . " He shrugs. "I was a kid when we met. He used to suck up to me in that boyfriend kind of way, but I always felt like I saw through him. Like his whole *perfect person* persona was an act."

Ben was always good at making himself the most well-liked person in the room—the way he always knew just what to say and when to say it, moseying through a crowd with an easy confidence and perfectly placed hand that seemed to pull people toward him like gravity.

Kids don't fall for that kind of thing, though. They always seem to sense something the rest of us can't.

"Anyway, Allison was always such a vibrant person. She loved to argue." He smiles. "She wanted to be a lawyer."

"I didn't know that."

"Oh, yeah, and she would have been great at it, too, but she followed him to college—a big journalism school, because that's what *he* wanted—and by the time she graduated, Ben had talked her out of it. Law school was expensive; he was a few years in at his job and had finally saved enough for them to start enjoying it. It was like she just shrunk herself down to make more room for him."

I feel the familiar sting of tears in my eyes. I can relate to that, too. The way I had justified it at the time, as if my leaving *The Grit* and my life slowly dwindling down to nothing wasn't *his* choice, but *ours*. I remember gossiping about Allison that night of the party, Kasey's champagne breath in my ear. Judging her for being unemployed, staying at home. Her body gliding next to his like an oversized accessory, unaware of the fact that she had a passion worth pursuing. Something she was good at, something she loved.

Just like me.

"It just sucked to watch," Waylon continues. "But it wasn't like he was *all* bad. I couldn't point to anything inherently wrong about their relationship. It seemed like he treated her well when I saw them together. He made her laugh. I figured that if he made her happy . . . I don't know. I should just stay out of it."

"Relationships are complicated," I say, blowing on my coffee to give myself something to do.

"Yeah, but that's the thing," he says, shifting in his chair. "I was nine when we met. Allison and I were seven years apart, so I didn't know what a *healthy relationship* looked like. But as I got older—as we both got older—Ben and I started growing into two completely different kinds of guys. And I realized that whatever a healthy relationship was . . . that wasn't it."

I'm quiet. I decide to let Waylon keep talking, let him tell me what he knows, before I chime in again.

"Anyway, the years went by, and Allison kept shrinking. She tried to talk to him a few times about going to law school, getting her own thing going, and he would guilt trip her out of it every single time. It was like she was just this thing meant to check a box in his own life and not even live her own."

I remember that night, when I had decided to go back to work. The touch of unease as I had brought it up, like I knew I was flirting with fire. The way Ben had taken Mason from me afterward, like a punishment. A warning of what was to come.

"Whatever makes you happy."

I did it anyway. I went to North Carolina, I wrote the story. I started working again, part-time, traveling once or twice a month. It ignited a spark in me that I knew I needed—I *knew* I couldn't be a good person, a good mother, without first being good to myself—but now I wonder if it had ignited something in Ben, too. Something dangerous. I had made him a father when he never wanted to be one in the first place, and then I started leaving him alone with Mason for days at a time. It was as if all those small little acts of defiance had lit some kind of fuse, and we had been inching closer and closer toward the explosion without me even realizing.

"One night, I was in town visiting family," he continues. "I decided to go into the city for a drink, so I walked into this bar and saw Ben sitting there by himself. It was late, a couple hours after he should have been done with work. I figured Allison was there with him, maybe in the bathroom or something, but just as I was walking over to say hi, another woman sat down next to him."

I feel the heat crawl up my neck. I already know where this is going. All of those late nights together, nursing drinks for longer than necessary because neither one of us wanted to walk away. Waylon is looking at me now like he's seeing me again for the very first time. Like he's remembering the way I had sauntered back to that table, my fingers grazing Ben's shoulders, touching the bare skin of his neck and pretending it was an accident. The way I would willfully ignore his left hand, the gold band he would always fidget with, spinning it around his finger, like if he wore it down enough, it might just dissolve. Disappear on its own.

"It was you."

"Waylon, I'm sorry." I push my hands into my neck, trying to cool it down, but the warmth from the coffee only makes it worse. I can feel my cheeks burning, physical proof of the shame I feel radiating out from my every pore. "I promise you, though, we didn't do anything. *Nothing* happened—"

"It's not that," he interrupts, waving his hand. "I watched you, though, for the entire night. I watched you interacting. And he treated you the exact same way he treated Allison—the way he touched your arm, the way he leaned over his beer when you were talking. I could tell he made you feel special, just like how he made her feel. It was like you were interchangeable to him. You even *looked* the same."

I glance across the café, trying to find something to fix my gaze on to keep myself from crying. I remember that picture I had seen on Waylon's computer now—Ben and I, sitting close at that bar, caught on camera unaware.

I have never felt more naive, more foolish, than I do right now.

I remember thinking that we were different—Ben and I, *we* were different from *them*—but that's just not true. We were the same. Allison and I were the same to him. Interchangeable.

"There's no way you could have known," Waylon says now, reading my mind again. He reaches across the table and touches my hand. "It's not your fault."

"It is, though," I say. "I knew he was married—"

"You were young," he says. "You can't help the way someone makes you feel. And he's good, Isabelle. He makes everyone feel like that."

"So, what happened next?" I ask, although I'm becoming increasingly confident that I don't actually want to know. Waylon's expression confirms it: the way his shoulders tense, his lower lip quivers before he bites it, hard. I watch as his eyes grow damp and distant, and he pulls his hand from mine, wiping them angrily, before returning his focus on me.

"She got pregnant," he says at last. "And then a couple of weeks later, she died."

CHAPTER FIFTY-FIVE

I can still feel it: the stick of the tile against my thighs. The sweat on my fingertips as I gripped the toilet, and the vomit in my hair, tangling the strands together like gum. My back against the wall as I sat on the bathroom floor, alone, staring as those two pink lines appeared in my hand. They were faint enough to make me question it—I remember tilting my head, squinting, like it was some kind of mirage that might disappear with just the right angle—but I knew, in my gut, that they were there. That this was real.

And then that single, fleeting second of regret.

The truth was, nothing about our life had panned out the way I thought it would. Ben and I weren't the same people we were when we'd met—at least, I wasn't. Not anymore. Making a baby together had felt like a final attempt at making it work, a last-ditch effort to turn it all around, and while I know now how crazy that sounds, finding your life unraveling like that makes you feel pretty desperate to weave it into something beautiful and whole before it disappears altogether and leaves you with nothing.

After all, I had given up so much for him. Losing him, too, would have felt like losing everything.

But sitting there on the tile with that test in my hand made it truly sink in: the reality of what I had done. The reality of *forever* with Ben—of another human being tying us together for eternity. The possibility that it might not change things for the better—and in fact, it might make it all worse. Those were the thoughts racing through my mind during that single second, and I wonder now if that's how Allison felt when she found out, too: trapped. Trapped in her house, in her marriage, and now, in her own body. That one, final thing that was snatched away from her and claimed by somebody else.

Or maybe she was elated. Maybe she thought it would be a fresh start. Maybe she pushed down the bad thoughts like another bout of nausea, swallowing their putrid taste and plastering on a smile. Hoping that their problems might finally be solved.

"Allison never would have overdosed pregnant," Waylon says now, eyes quivering. "She *never* would have done that."

"Are you sure she knew?" I ask. "Nobody at the office knew."

"She knew. She told us. It was really early, but she was the most open person on the planet. She could never keep a secret."

I remember her hand on my arm, her lips on my ear. The whip of the wind on that rooftop and the combination of all three making my skin crawl like something had burrowed beneath it.

"To be quite honest, this dress squeezes me in all the wrong places."

I remember how she had been carrying a flute around the rooftop, but her breath smelled like mouthwash instead of champagne; how her fingers rested gently on her stomach, as if she wanted me to know. She wanted *someone* to know.

"Waylon, I hate to say this . . ." I trail off, wondering how to word this delicately. "She was clearly struggling, maybe unable to think straight—"

"She wouldn't have done it, Isabelle."

I pinch my lips, nod, and think of my mother. I think of how she wouldn't have done what she did, either. Not if somebody had been there to help. Not if somebody had listened. Nobody understands what it's like to be locked inside the mind of a mother: the things you think that you aren't supposed to; the beliefs that burrow themselves deep into your brain like a parasite, making you sick.

But at the same time, I can't help but wonder.

All those years, I thought Allison's death had saved Ben from making a choice—a choice between us two—but now I realize something that should have been obvious: Since when did Ben ever sit back and let life happen to him? Since when was he ever *not* in control? Ben didn't do that. He never left things to chance; he never played a passive role in his own life, the way he expected us to. So maybe he *was* making a choice—maybe, in the end, his choice was going to be me. But then Allison had called him into the bathroom one day, the same way I tried to five years later. She had showed him the test and wrapped her arms around his neck, squeezing, and he'd had the realization that he was stuck, too.

That the choice had been made for him, and it wasn't the one he wanted.

"He was done with her, Isabelle. She wasn't the same girl she was when he proposed—and how could he expect her to be? He had taken everything from her that made her *her*."

I remember the way he had looked at me that night on the roof, his head bent low. His wife was pregnant, he *knew* she was pregnant, and still, he did it anyway. Now all those moments we spent together when she was home alone suddenly look so different, like peeling back expensive wallpaper and finding black mold underneath.

"At the memorial, I snuck away into Allison's bedroom on the second floor, just to get a breath," he continues. "To get away from it all. I looked out the window and that's when I saw you two tangled together on the side of the house. At her *memorial*."

I can feel the humiliation leak through my veins like someone injected me with it. The slow crawl, like venom, from my toes to my legs, my stomach, my chest. My face burns as I imagine the shock, the rage; Waylon's hands gripping the windowsill as he watched us defile his sister's memory in her own home. Flinging his body down the stairs, out the door, intentionally making us stop.

"And that's when I knew it," he says. "Seeing you two together at the bar, then again at the memorial. He fucking killed her."

"Waylon, I'm so sorry—" I start, pushing my fingers so hard into my mug that I can feel the skin burning: a sharp, hot singe.

"I'm not asking you to apologize," he says, shaking his head. "That's not why I'm here."

"Then why are you here?"

"Because I want him to pay. There wasn't enough evidence with Allison, but when I heard about Mason going missing, I knew it. I knew he did it again."

I think about the case file in Waylon's briefcase. The interview recordings he had been listening to and all those pictures of me, of *us*, hidden on his laptop.

He wasn't looking into me. He was looking into Ben.

"What about the article?" I ask, remembering the other thing I had found there. "The one about Margaret on your laptop. That had nothing to do with Ben—"

"I was curious," he admits, looking ashamed now, too. "I've known about you for years, ever since I saw you that night at the bar, but I didn't actually *know* you. I knew Ben married you and had a kid with you, but I was trying to understand you a little better. Trying to see if you were someone I could trust, if I could tell you who I was and what I thought about Ben. But every time I asked about your past, you clammed up."

I think about him nudging me along at Framboise or in my dining room, always peppering in those personal questions that I shut down so fast.

"After you told me your maiden name was Rhett, I Googled you and found the article." He shrugs. "I'm sorry. I didn't mean to pry."

I nod, tapping my nails against my mug, thinking. There's still one thing, though, that doesn't add up. One thing I can't bring myself to accept.

"Why would he hurt Mason?" I ask at last. "Sure, maybe he didn't want to be with me anymore . . . but why him? Why our son? He didn't do anything wrong."

"How do you think it would look if Ben had two wives commit suicide?" Waylon asks, eyebrows raised. "Harder to get away with, I think. Besides, do you really think he wanted to be a single dad?"

I think about the clench in his jaw as he thought about me leaving, working, the burden of parenthood placed solely on his shoulders for only a matter of days. I think about how quickly things had dissolved between us after Mason disappeared—how I had wanted to work on our marriage, on us—but he had decided almost immediately that it was over, almost as if his decision had been made long before that point.

"No," I say at last. "No, he wouldn't want that."

Ben never wanted to be a father. He never wanted Mason. I knew that going into it, of course, but lots of people have a change of heart when it comes to parenthood—I know I did, that twinge of regret evaporating completely the moment I looked into those bright green eyes. Ben was a loving father on the surface of it, but still, I had cornered him into a life he never wanted.

He wasn't used to not getting his way.

"Right," Waylon says, leaning back. "I just thought that by coming here—by talking to you, getting inside your house, your head—I might be able to figure it out. Finally find enough evidence to put that asshole away and stop him from hurting anyone else."

I don't want to believe it, but at the same time, it makes sense. Nobody broke into our house. The evidence just isn't there. But Ben would have known that the battery in the baby monitor was dead. Ben would have been able to walk into the nursery without waking up Roscoe or making Mason cry. Ben would have been able to open the window from the inside, try to stage an intrusion, before walking out the front door without leaving any prints.

Ben would have been able to come home after, slide under the covers, and wind his arms around my waist, pushing himself close. Pretending that he had been there all along. The realization makes me sick, and that's when I taste it again: metallic, like blood, thick and sticky and dripping over everything.

Burning my throat, painting my tongue. Coating everything in red.

CHAPTER FIFTY-SIX

I sit in my car, idling, the exhaust billowing out as I slump down in the driver's seat and stare at his blind-drawn windows. I blink a few times, trying to fight off the sudden heaviness of my eyelids, and imagine what he's doing right now, without me, the way I have so many times before.

What *they're* doing.

It's still early, about thirty minutes before the office opens, and she's there. I know she is. I saw two silhouettes outlined against his bedroom curtains earlier, pushed together before peeling apart. One long, slender arm grabbing at his waist, like she wasn't quite ready for him to leave. They're probably eating breakfast right now, sipping their French-pressed coffee in silence, his hand on her thigh as he skims the news—the same way he had handled Allison, his touch barely there as he pushed the small of her back around the restaurant, like she was a possession he didn't want to misplace.

I glance at the clock now—he should be leaving soon—and as if on cue, the front door swings open. After all this time, I still know his routine by heart. I watch Ben step out, briefcase in hand, as Valerie appears on the porch steps behind him. It's still strange, seeing them together. Watching my husband engage in these easy interactions with another woman, almost as if I'm looking at my own life through a fun-house mirror: one that distorts my features, turning me into somebody else. She's in his slippers and an oversized T-shirt, her hair a perfect mess, and it takes me a second to recover from how effortlessly she seems to fit into his clothes, his life.

How easy it is for her to slip into my skin and take my place.

Back when I found out about her, there was a certain bitterness in my mouth when I thought about Valerie—it was like sucking on a lemon and feeling that pinch in my jaw, making me wince—but now I realize that makes me a hypocrite. She's kind and compassionate— she's *me*, eight years ago—and I can't help but wonder what would have happened if someone had warned me then about who Ben was, what he was capable of, before I had gotten too involved. If someone had explained to me the way men like that work: how we're just pawns in their game, their gentle hands steering us in the direction that's most beneficial for them.

Using us, sacrificing us, a strategic power play masked as romance.

I wonder if it would have made a difference, if I would have listened, or if I would have just shrugged them off and continued on with my life.

Probably the latter, but I have to try.

I slouch lower as Ben hops down the steps and takes a right, heading toward the office, and stay reclined for another few minutes, making sure he doesn't come back. Finally, after stealing one last look in the rearview, I dig my hand into my purse and pull out my eye drops, giving myself one more convincing kick of life before turning off the ignition and unlocking the door.

I'm about to step out, my foot hovering over the concrete, but almost immediately, I see Valerie on the porch again and I slam the door shut. Her earlier outfit has been replaced with a shirtdress and sandals, and I watch as she locks the front door, skips down the steps, and slides herself inside the car parked just a few feet from mine.

Before I can think twice, I crank my own car, fasten my seat belt, and follow as she pulls out of the space and drives down the road. Then I tail her at a distance until she pulls into a little residential neighborhood on the opposite side of town.

This must be her house, I think as I watch her ease into a street spot and let herself into a little white cottage. It reminds me of my first apartment, how childish it seemed when I came home after a night with Ben. My inexperience amplified after being in the presence of someone older, more successful. More mature. Valerie's home has the appearance of someone who tries—there's a wrought-iron rocker on the porch, a few spindly plants in plastic potters, a pollen-caked rug that's bleached from the sun—but also someone who clearly thrifts for furniture or picks up discarded couches on the side of the road, reupholstering them to hide the stains. I remember being her age, trying to stitch together a life from scraps. I wonder if she's ever brought Ben here. I wonder if she felt embarrassed, the way I did, as I watched him take in my Ikea desk and mismatched chairs and plastic silverware washed and saved from takeout bags, his teeth gnawing at his lip telling me everything I needed to know.

I step out of my car and walk across the street, approaching her home. Then I take a deep breath, climb the stairs, and knock twice before I can change my mind. The door swings open almost immediately, and I register the shock on her face when she sees me standing there, my arms dangling awkwardly by my sides.

"Isabelle," she says, trying to mask the surprise in her voice. "What are you doing here?"

"I was wondering if we could talk. Just for a couple minutes."

"How do you know where I live?"

I'm quiet, trying to decide how to answer that. *Because I followed you here* doesn't sound like the best way to convince her to let me in, so instead, I keep talking.

"There are some things you should know," I say. "Things about Ben."

"I'm . . . I'm sorry," she stutters, clearly trying to shake off the shock. "I'm sorry, but I think you should leave." She starts to close the door, but before she can, I stick my foot over the threshold, wedging it open.

"It's important," I say. "I'm worried about you."

"*You're* worried about *me*?" she asks, her eyes growing wide. "Isabelle, no offense, but I think you should be worried about yourself."

"Is that what Ben told you?" I ask, leaning forward. "That we weren't happy for a long, long time? That he tried to help me but he could never get through? That he's a good person and deserves to be happy, too?"

I see her expression waver, just for a second, and I know I've hit a nerve. I imagine Ben showing up to therapy, alone, eyes misty as he described me to her the same way he had described Allison to me on the side of that house: my hands on his cheeks, heartstrings pulled so tight they felt like they might snap. Painting a picture of me that cast me in the worst possible light: a broken woman, a lost cause. Someone he had tried to save.

Valerie's eyes are on mine now, and I can see the questions swirling in her pupils. The questions I know she wants to ask. She's curious about me the same way I had been curious about Allison. I think back now on that moment when Valerie and I first met—the moment I had stumbled into that room in the church and taken her by surprise. I think about the way she had looked at me and invited me to stay, almost as if she wanted to know my side of it, too.

"He's not who you think he is," I continue. "I just want to talk."

I try to put myself in her shoes, wondering: If I had found Allison on my doorstep one morning, offering herself to me the way I am now to Valerie, would I have taken the opportunity? Would I have betrayed Ben for just the smallest peek into their lives together—a glimpse behind that carefully closed curtain that he would never allow me to push aside? After all, I had imagined it so many times: her, *them*, the way I'm sure Valerie has imagined us.

I think of Allison's fingers on my arm, her lips on my ear. The goose bumps that erupted across my skin, the intrigue of being so close to someone I had spent so much time daydreaming about, wondering about. Obsessing about.

I would have done it. I would have let her in.

"Valerie," I say, resting my hand on hers. She flinches, like she had expected my touch to burn, but after a few more seconds of silence, I can see her resolve melt. Like wax turning to liquid, malleable in my fingers, the curiosity overcomes her, the way I knew it would.

Then she cracks the door back open, her eyes on the floor, and gestures for me to come inside.

CHAPTER FIFTY-SEVEN

I step into the living room and take a seat on the edge of a slipcovered couch. The house is small but homey: a fireplace with a cluttered mantel, string lights illuminating a collection of candles and books stacked high in both corners. There's a glass coffee table in the center of it all and a series of pictures clipped to a string with clothespins against the back wall.

She seems fun, eclectic. So incredibly young.

Valerie sits in a chair on the opposite side of the table, eying me from across the room. She doesn't seem scared or suspicious; instead, she seems a little on guard, like I'm some kind of rabid animal she isn't quite sure how to handle.

Like I might lash out and bite.

"First of all," she says, crossing one leg over the other, "I just wanted to say that I'm sorry, Isabelle. I told Ben that it felt too soon . . ."

She stops, diverts her eyes to the floor, fully aware of the role she holds in this relationship of ours.

"You just have a lot going on," she continues. "And I'm sorry if the addition of me is making it worse."

I'm quiet, not quite sure how to respond to that.

"Thank you," I say at last. "That means a lot."

"So, what is it that you'd like me to know?"

She leans back in her chair, and I get the distinct feeling that she's about to read me like one of her patients. Like she's inherently wary of what I'm about to divulge and she intends to analyze whatever comes out of my mouth next.

"There's no easy way to say this," I start, trying to keep my leg from bouncing. "But I just want to make sure you know what you're getting yourself into. With Ben."

"Okay," she says. "And what am I getting myself into?"

"Did you know he was married before? Before me, I mean."

"Allison," she nods. "Yes, I've heard."

I try not to show my surprise at the mention of her name. For some reason, I assumed Ben would have hidden that from her. Less baggage.

"And did you know she died?"

"Yes. I've seen my fair share of suicide in this line of work, unfortunately. It's tragic."

"Well, an overdose," I clarify. "Accidental or . . . otherwise."

Valerie looks at me, her eyes squinting as she tries to dissect what I'm saying. "You really think it was an accident?"

"Honestly?" I ask, steeling myself. "I'm not convinced she did it at all."

She tilts her head to the side, like she's trying to decide if I'm joking.

"She died right around the time Ben and I started to get involved," I continue, talking faster. "Did Ben tell you she was pregnant? Did he tell you he never really wanted kids?"

Valerie blinks, expressionless, and I wait for a response, for *something*, but nothing ever comes.

"In hindsight, it doesn't seem like a coincidence," I go on, realizing she isn't going to budge. "Especially now, with the disappearance

of my son . . . and *you*, showing up right after . . . not that I am placing *any* blame on you, of course. But Ben had motivations for both
Allison and Mason to be out of his life. We can't just ignore that."

I watch as she lets the information settle over her, absorbing every
word.

"I just wanted you to know everything up front," I finish. "So
you can make the right decision for yourself."

"Wow," she finally mutters, shaking her head. "That's . . . a lot
to take in."

"I know. I know it's hard to process—"

"Do you understand what you're saying?" she asks, cutting me
off. "Isabelle, listen to what you're saying. Listen to how it sounds."

I feel a familiar twist in my stomach, that same stabbing pain that
flared up every time Ben or my mother or Detective Dozier looked
at me the way Valerie is looking at me right now: with suspicion,
distrust. Fear.

"I know how it sounds," I say. "But Valerie, he's dangerous."

"No," she says, shaking her head. "No, *this* is dangerous, Isabelle.
You spinning these insane theories is dangerous. You're going to hurt
someone again."

I feel a catch in my throat, because I can't deny that. She's right.
I have hurt someone before. I have already lost myself in the quest to
find answers, abandoning reason and logic in an effort to find someone to blame.

But this time isn't like that. This time, it feels *right*.

"I was just trying to hear you out, give you a chance, but you need
professional help," she continues. "Real, serious help, Isabelle. And I
can't do that for you. Given our personal ties, it wouldn't be right. I wish
I could, but I can't."

Valerie stands up, a silent cue that it's time for me to leave.

"Ben warned me about this," she says, almost like an afterthought.
"You're exactly like he said you were."

"And how did he say I was?" I whisper, my heart pounding in my chest.

"Deeply troubled," she says at last. "Practically unhinged."

I squeeze my fingers, feeling the stinging cut in my palm, and finally allow myself to process what I've become over these last twelve months: not even human, really, but a nocturnal animal. A shell of a thing crawling through life with hazy eyes and a mind hinging on madness, like I'm one small stumble away from losing it completely. I've tried not to spend too much time worrying about how it must look from the outside, but now I let myself see it all through Ben's eyes: that collage in my dining room and the way I sit there for hours, staring. Imagining. Thinking through scenarios and convincing myself they could be real.

Lying awake in the dark or wandering around the neighborhood at night; running around blind, looking for someone, *anyone*, to take away my blame.

"Look, Isabelle. I'm sorry," Valerie says at last, sighing. "I really am. But you are looking for answers in places where they just don't exist."

I pick at my nails, eyes cast down to the floor. I've heard that so many times. Suddenly, I think of my father, creating that story about Margaret's death because it was just easier for everyone to accept. I wonder if that's what Waylon did, too. If he simply created a story he needed to believe: that Allison never would have done it. That she never would have taken her own life. Maybe he's been spending the last eight years trying to prove it, dedicating his own life to learning about death because the truth of his own sister's is too painful to accept.

Maybe he's just looking for someone to be responsible, the way I am, too. Maybe we're both so desperate for answers, we're willing to believe anything.

"I won't tell Ben you came here," Valerie says. "He would be heartbroken if he found out you were thinking about him like this."

I nod my head gently, too ashamed to meet her gaze. Then I stand up and take one more glance around the room, ready to apologize and step back outside, when something in the corner catches my eye.

It's that wall of pictures. I realize now, standing closer, they're almost entirely of Ben.

I walk toward the wall, away from the door, and scan them all hanging there, one by one. I see Valerie and Ben sitting in the grass downtown, Spanish moss draped behind them like a stage curtain being whipped back. There's another of them in the stands of a concert, colorful lights dancing across a stage in the distance, and one more of them lying on the beach, their sunglasses reflecting a phone held high in the sky.

"Isabelle," Valerie says, trying to nudge me along. I can hear her walking closer, sidling up behind me. "I don't think it'll help for you to look at those."

But I don't turn around. I can't turn around. I'm too focused on Ben and the varying shades of stubble on his cheeks; on Valerie's subtle highlights slowly growing out, a finger of dark roots pinching at her scalp. Visible signs of the passage of time that shouldn't be possible for a relationship this new.

"You didn't meet at that grief counseling group."

It seems so obvious to me now, I hate myself for not seeing it sooner. After all, we had a story, too. Ben and I. But it wasn't real. It was something he had concocted; something he had created to paint himself in the most flattering light. Our relationship had started long before we announced it to the world, and I remember that first night together after the memorial now, the two of us tangled between the sheets of my childhood bed. The sickness that settled in my stomach after he stood up and walked away, like I knew I had just consumed something that was bound to hurt me.

"You know we can't tell anybody about this. Not yet."

I twist around now and look at Valerie, standing right behind me, eyes wide and afraid. He really did do to me what we did to Allison.

Ben and Valerie were together long before we were apart.

"How long?" I ask, taking a step closer. "How long have you been together?"

Valerie shakes her head, a little quiver in her lip, and takes a step backward, putting some distance between us.

"How long?"

"I felt so bad for the longest time," she says at last. "Doing what we did behind your back. But the things he told me about you . . ."

I remember that feeling: the justification of it. The guilt, the indignity, overridden by the stories I told myself. The stories about Allison I decided to accept in order to make myself feel better: that *they* weren't *us*. It's a form of self-preservation, really. We are nothing but what we choose to believe, but it's all a mirage, bending and warping and shimmering in the distance, changing its form at any given second.

Showing us exactly what we want to see when we want to see it.

"How long?" I repeat, my resolve settling back in and hardening in my stomach. "How long have you been with Ben?"

The house is quiet in a silent standoff. Finally, she sighs.

"Two years."

Two years. *Two years.* For two entire years, Ben has been seeing someone else. Before Mason was taken. Before he even took his first steps.

I count back in my head now, trying to determine how old he would have been.

"Six months," I say, muttering to myself. Mason would have been six months old when they first got together: the age he was when I started working again. When I took off for a few nights every month, driving to North Carolina and Alabama and Mississippi, trying to chase those little moments of meaning that were ripped from me all those years ago.

"You were always leaving," Valerie says now, still trying to justify it. "He was lonely, Isabelle. You left him and your son for days on end—"

"*He* was lonely?" I say, a sudden burst of anger surging through me. "Is that what he said? He said that *I* was always leaving? That *I* was the one who was never around?"

"I saw it," she says, her voice suddenly sharp like venom. "I saw the way he had to take care of Mason by himself. Don't deny it."

"You saw it—" I whisper, the room starting to spin. "Oh my God. He brought you to our house?"

I take a few steps closer, into the center of the room, my mind racing.

"He brought you to our house, around our son, and he was growing up," I say, speaking faster. "Mason was growing up, just starting to talk. Pretty soon, he would have started saying something, right? Saying something to me about the other woman who came over when I wasn't there?"

I think about that story I always tell to the audience; the one meant to ease the tension and elicit a laugh. Mason and Ben and the mobile above his crib; how he would try to sound out the words— Tyranto*snorious*—getting better and better every single time.

"Don't you think Ben thought about that?" I ask. "Don't you think he *realized*—"

I stop, stare, understanding settling over me slowly. All of these little pieces that never added up, never made sense, until now. I can feel the blood drain from my face, like someone ripped out a plug from beneath me, bleeding me dry.

The truth is right here, right in front of me. I have literally been staring at it, at *her*, this entire time.

"What did you do?" I ask, my voice a whisper. "What did you do to my son?"

Valerie is quiet, eying me. It really is striking how alike we look, especially at a distance. The tanned skin of her arms, her legs; the coffee-brown shade of her hair and the wide, unassuming eyes. I imagine her walking down the street at night, late, leaving my house at the end of a few days spent with Ben. She would have parked somewhere far away, I'm sure, to keep a cover from the neighbors. Ben would have insisted—for appearances' sake. Always for appearances' sake. And I can almost picture it: her, striding past that streetlight, feeling the life leaking from her skin with every single step, knowing that I was on my way home to him. Knowing that we would be sleeping together that night while she was in this sad little house, alone, her eyes on the ceiling and her mind on us. It was the same way I felt when Ben would stand up from that barstool and return home to Allison: the gut-wrenching knowledge of being something he kept hidden, secret, like a dirty habit he only broke out at night.

And then: the creak of a rocking chair. The realization that she wasn't alone. A glance to the side and an old man sitting on his porch, cloudy eyes on her.

"I'm Isabelle," she would have said, stopping, smiling. Letting herself believe it. Letting herself shed her own skin and slip into mine for just one more second. Letting herself be *me*, Ben's wife, the way I had always wanted to be Allison. Like if she just said it out loud, willed it into existence, it would somehow be true. "Your neighbor, Isabelle Drake."

CHAPTER FIFTY-EIGHT

"I don't know what you're talking about."

Valerie is still looking at me, unwavering, and I can feel the bile claw its way up my throat.

"Yes you do," I say, my voice trembling. "You took my son."

I imagine her letting herself into my home with her key—the key Ben had given her, swiping it from beneath our mat that day and slipping it into her palm, closing her fingers—and the quiet stillness of the house as Roscoe ambled up to her in the dark. He would have recognized her after an entire year of her coming over; she wouldn't have been a stranger anymore. I can imagine the hushed whispers as she calmed him back to bed, rubbed behind his ears. Her footsteps down the hall, into Mason's nursery. Creeping into his bedroom, covering her fingers with the fabric of her sleeves, and sliding the window open. Letting in a cool, damp breeze as she picked him up and carried him back out the front door, locking it behind her.

I wonder if Mason felt safe with her. I wonder if that's why he didn't scream.

"Some people just aren't fit to be mothers," she says at last, like that's an explanation I should somehow understand.

"What did you do to him?"

I try to imagine it, those little tastes of a life she got with Ben—a *real* life, not the hidden, secret thing she had—before they were ripped away from her over and over and over again. The adrenaline pumping through her chest that very first time she stepped into our home, trailed her fingers across my vanity. Ran my brush through her hair, leaving her own strands tangled in with mine and smiling at the knowledge that I would never know. Looking into my mirror and seeing her own reflection, her confidence growing as she flipped through my closet, tried on my clothes. Imagining herself in the pictures with Ben instead of me.

"Neither of you wanted to be parents," she says. "Not really. Not when it came down to it."

I imagine her lying in our bed, fingers dancing across Ben's bare chest. Mason's cries erupting from the other room—and him having to get up, leave her there.

He was always a fussy baby.

"There are so many people out there who would love to have a child," she says. "You have no idea, Isabelle. People would kill for it, but it's not for everybody."

She didn't want to share Ben anymore. She didn't want to share him with me, with Mason. With anybody.

"Tell me where he is," I say, hands shaking. I take a step forward, closer to her. She's backed up against the coffee table now; there's nowhere left to go. "If you tell me, I can forget about this. I can forget about you."

"It's for the best," she says. "For everybody."

I take another step, closer. "Tell me where he is."

"Ben told me what you did to your sister," she continues. "It was only a matter of time before you did something to your son, too. You know that, right?"

"Tell me where he is!" I shout, a blinding rage coursing through me. It feels just like that last time—my arms, my hands, tingling with

adrenaline; the roiling anger building and building right before I lost control.

"*It's okay,*" she says, smiling. "Isabelle, he's in a better place."

I hear those words, and I suddenly see it so clearly: Valerie on her computer, reading that article, staring at that picture of me onstage. My bloodshot eyes soaking in the scowls and the stares for just the tiniest chance at the truth. Looking out at the audience, pleading into the microphone, and eventually, just absorbing the whispers so deep that finally, I believed them, too.

I think of Valerie knowing that—knowing the truth, what she did, what she took from me—and still typing that comment anyway, dangling it in front of me before coming to her senses and erasing it forever.

I think of her looking at me in that church, head tilted to the side as she gestured to the candles flickering in the dark. The pity in her eyes—the nerve, the *arrogance*—and suddenly, I feel my body lunge at her before I can even realize what I'm doing, those words ringing loudly in my ears.

He's in a better place.

I feel the sudden jolt of impact, our bodies tangling together and falling in unison until we collapse onto the coffee table and it buckles beneath us, the sound of glass shattering mixed with a sickening skull crack.

CHAPTER FIFTY-NINE

TWO DAYS LATER

Thump-thump-thump.

My pupils are drilling into a spot in the carpet. A spot with no significance, really, other than the fact that my eyes seem to like it here. I listen to the thumping, the beating, the steady thrum of a heartbeat in my ears. A rhythmic echo, like slipping beneath the bathwater and listening to it pulse.

Thump-thump.

I look up, blink a few times, the spot dissolving into the carpet again.

"Isabelle?" *Thump-thump-thump.* "Isabelle, I see your car outside."

I realize now that someone is at the door, knocking. Roscoe is barking, his tail wagging heatedly against the hardwood floor, and I squeeze my eyes shut, trying to squelch the stinging. Then I stand up from the couch and make my way over.

"That's enough," I say, patting down his ears. My chest squeezes as I reach for the door, even though I already know who it is. Even though I've been expecting it, expecting *him*, while I've watched the world go by through my window like a time-lapse video for the last two days.

"Detective Dozier," I say, cracking the door open and registering his familiar frame on my porch: the heavy limbs and hardened eyes. "Good to see you."

"Yeah, hi," he says, hooking his thumbs through his belt loops again. "I've been out here for five minutes. You didn't hear me knocking?"

"I was asleep," I lie, plastering a smile on my face. "Sorry."

"Mind if I come in?"

"Sure." I extend my arm out and open the door wider before walking back into the living room and taking a seat on the couch.

"What happened there?"

I follow his gaze and look down at the gauze on my hand. It's still wrapped tightly around my palm, a little spot of dried blood soaked through the bandage.

"Wineglass," I say, holding it up. "Cut it pretty bad."

"Huh."

He continues to stare, his eyes darting back and forth between my face and my hand.

"So, what can I do for you?" I ask, trying to change the subject.

"There's been a . . . development," he says at last. "In your case. Wanted to come by and tell you myself."

I look up at him, eyes tight, like I just opened them underwater in a bathtub full of chlorine. I've spent the last forty-eight hours in a strange jumble of numbness and nerves, like my body doesn't quite know how it should respond. I've felt this way ever since I stood up slowly in Valerie's living room, the crunch of glass beneath my shoes and the raggedness of my own breath amplified around me. Ever since I looked down at her lifeless body and those shards from the table, sharp and piercing, like dozens of daggers scattered across the floor.

Ever since I gazed into those wide-open eyes, glassy like porcelain, and the puddle of blood expanding beneath her. The absolute stillness of her chest.

"And what's that?" I ask, even though I already know.

"I'm sure you've seen the news," he says, taking a step forward. "About the murder of Valerie Sherman."

"Yes," I say, nodding. It's been all over, of course: the latest craze. A young, attractive woman found dead in her home, in a pool of her own blood. "Burglary gone wrong, I heard."

"That was the original theory," he says. "Broken coffee table, the house in disarray. But the more we looked at it, the more it seemed off. Staged."

I clench my fingers. "Staged?"

"Like someone was trying to fake a break-in," he continues, eying me. "Similar to cracking open a window to try to fake a kidnapping."

I can feel my heart hammering in my chest, my palms getting slick with sweat.

"Why are you telling me this?"

"As I'm sure you know by now, Valerie was in a relationship with your husband. Had been for quite a while. While you two were still married."

"Yes," I say, nodding. "Yes, I'm aware."

"We found pictures of him in the home," he says. "Other . . . *belongings* that appear to be his."

I'm quiet, letting him continue. Only speak when spoken to, a trick my father taught me.

"After her death hit the news, we got a phone call from a client of hers," he says at last. "Valerie was a therapist. She ran a weekly grief counseling group out of the cathedral downtown. Had quite a few regulars."

I nod.

"According to this client, he saw the two of you interacting on the night of Mason's vigil."

I remember that man who had shuffled in, breaking up our conversation before it could even start. The apology in his eyes as he hobbled past, taking a seat. Eying us quietly from the corner, listening.

"Did you know who she was then?" Dozier asks. "Her relation-ship with your husband?"

"No," I say, the first authentic thing I've said all day. "No, I didn't. I had no idea."

"So you just happened to confront your husband's mistress less than two weeks before she was found dead in her home?"

"I don't know what to tell you," I say. "Coincidence, I guess."

His eyes dart down to my hand again, then back at me.

"Is this why you're here?" I ask at last, trying to sound exasper-ated. Trying to act as though the idea of me having anything to do with this is ridiculous, impossible. Too far-fetched to even entertain. "To question me about a murder?"

Dozier stares at me for another second before he lets out a sigh, shaking his head.

"No," he says at last. "I'm here because that client also gave us a name."

"A name," I repeat, trying to hide my confusion. This isn't how I expected this conversation to go. "Whose name?"

"The name of a woman who also used to attend the group but stopped coming after Mason's disappearance," he says. "A woman who was unable to have children."

My eyes are drilling into his now, remembering those words Val-erie had said. The justification for what she did, as if she were doing the world a favor.

"There are so many people out there who would love to have a child."

"He didn't think much of it at first, but after learning about Val-erie's death and then hearing about her affair with your husband, he decided to call it in."

It takes a second to register, but finally, I realize what he's trying to tell me: A woman going missing at the exact same time as Mason. A woman who wanted kids and couldn't have them. A woman who knew Valerie.

"So what does this mean?" I ask, edging myself to the very end of the couch. "Who is she?"

"I don't want you getting ahead of yourself," he says, holding his palm out. He digs his other hand into his back pocket, pulling out a small picture. "It could be nothing, but we're looking into it. Does this woman look familiar to you? Or does the name *Abigail Fisher* ring a bell?"

I grab the picture and stare at the woman: her mousey brown hair and unassuming eyes. She looks a little older than me—mid-forties, maybe—and I massage the name in my mind, trying to place it. I've sifted through so many names over these last twelve months—and that's when my neck snaps up, my eyes on my dining room. I stand up and walk toward the table, the TrueCrimeCon attendee list still tacked up on the wall.

"Abigail Fisher," I say, my finger tapping hard against the name when I find it. I try to tamp down the hopeful beating in my chest, but the excitement is palpable in my voice now. A giddiness I can't contain. "Right here. Abigail Fisher. She was at the conference."

I look at Dozier, then back down at the picture, and that's when I realize: the eyes. I've seen those eyes before. I remember the way they grew so damp and distant, tears glistening as she watched me on stage, mouthing my every word.

"Oh my God," I say, rushing over to my laptop and throwing it open. I remember pulling up that article and studying the picture of the audience; the way the camera flash had made their eyes glow, turning them into something ethereal and strange.

The way that woman's gaze had made me physically shiver, like my body was reacting to some kind of danger my mind couldn't yet understand.

"Abigail Fisher," I say again, my heart thumping too hard in my chest as the article loads. Once it does, I twist around and tap at the screen, my fingers dancing wildly, watching Dozier's expression shift as he processes it, too: his gaze moving from me to the audience, then zeroing in on her. His eyes darting back and forth between the woman in the front row and the woman in the picture he gave me.

The room is quiet for a beat longer, the hugeness of this moment settling over us both. Finally, after all this time, we have a face. A name. A chance.

"Abigail Fisher," he repeats, nodding his head in a resigned rhythm. "That's her."

CHAPTER SIXTY

ONE WEEK LATER

I hear a buzz and glance up, watching as the bulky metal door swings open. My eyes are stinging. Not from sleep, though—or rather, the lack thereof—but from the cheap, fluorescent bulbs above me. From the harsh light of this place.

"Isabelle Drake?"

I glance at the prison guard in front of the door and I raise my hand, smiling meekly. The gash on my palm has healed slightly now, no longer a gaping wound but a thin, puckered scab. I can still see Dozier's eyes on it, on *me*, trying to piece it all together in my living room that day. Trying to assemble all the clues into the perfect pattern to make a picture form.

"Last thing," he had said, swinging around as I escorted him to the door. He couldn't stop staring at it: that bloody cut on my palm. He was thinking, I'm sure, of Valerie's lifeless body over that mountain of glass; of those shards, sharp and jagged, and the temper he had seen in me himself. The way it could flare up at any second, leaving me in a blind rage.

"Valerie took a lot from you," he said, shifting his weight from one leg to the other like he was suddenly uncomfortable. "How does that make you feel?"

I stared at him blankly, the understatement of the century.

"She took my son," I said, gesturing to the picture still in his grasp. "How do you think it makes me feel?"

"We don't know that yet," he responded, though I could see it in his face: the certainty already setting in. The perfection of it: A woman who wanted a child more than anything and another woman who wanted one gone. He could picture it, I'm sure, the way I was, too: Valerie listening to Abigail cry every Monday night, lamenting the unfairness of it all. Yearning to be a mother, the desperation in her voice, while Valerie thought of Mason and all the lies Ben had told her about me being unfit, unworthy. Imagining how his disappearance would solve just about everything.

"*It's for the best,*" she had said. "*For everybody.*"

Dozier sighed, and I could hear his tongue clicking around in his mouth, his fingernails scratching against the fabric of his pants. Fidgeting, deciding.

"I'll keep you posted," he said at last, and I knew, in that moment, that my plan was going to work.

I stand up now and watch as the guard escorts Ben into the visitors' area, trying to imagine how different I must look to him after only one week. I caught a glance of myself in my hallway mirror as I was leaving to visit the prison: the life has flushed back into my cheeks, like someone dripped red dye into water and let it expand, creeping to the edges. Turning everything pink. My eyes are wider, brighter, more alert, and the shadows beneath them are beginning to fade like a healing bruise.

But Ben: He looks different, too.

"How are you doing?" I ask, tilting my head as we both take a seat. I can see it now, finally, what everyone else had seen in me: The exhaustion etched so deep in his face and the new wrinkles that have practically appeared overnight. The way his skin looks sallow and pale, like something slowly dying. "Are you getting any sleep?"

Ben looks at me and runs his hands down his cheeks, his fingers pulling at the stubble. I can't help but stare at the handcuffs on his wrists, pinching his skin.

"Isabelle," he says at last, his voice hoarse. "I didn't do this."

I think back to that morning at Valerie's. To standing up, looking around. Her lifeless body beneath me, and the gravity of what I had done settling over everything. To blinking my eyes, trying to clear the dark spots from my vision and the spinning in my head. The realization that it would come back to me—that it would *always* come back to me. The scorned wife, the desperate mother. The crazed woman who simply lost it in a frantic quest for answers.

"They found your ring beneath her couch," I say now. "Right next to her body. Your DNA was all over her, Ben. Beneath her nails. It doesn't look good."

"Because we were together that *morning*," he says, frustrated, ripping his hands through his hair like he's repeated that same statement so many times before.

I remember the twitching of my fingers as the last bits of adrenaline left my body, like an overworked muscle starting to give out. How they had snaked their way beneath the collar of my shirt as I stared down at her, thinking, twisting Ben's ring between them like I had done so many times before.

The ring with his name etched across the surface. The ring nobody even knew I had.

"That ring," he says now. "I don't know how that ring got there, Isabelle. I have no fucking clue. I don't even wear it anymore. Maybe she took it from my condo or something, I don't know."

"Did you find out what she did to Mason?" I ask, my voice soft. "Because if you did, I wouldn't blame you. I would have done the same thing."

"*No,*" he says. "Jesus, Isabelle, I swear. I had no idea. Look: I'm sorry, I am. I'm sorry for everything. But I didn't *kill* anybody."

I look at Ben, my husband, and marvel at how well it all came together: the story I created, woven into reality as I stood in Valerie's living room, rubbing the ring against my shirt and rolling it across the floor. As I picked at the evidence, the facts, and pieced together a narrative to explain it all away. I knew how it would look once the police found it there, ripped off in a struggle and lost in the dusty corners beneath the couch.

A married man and his mistress. I knew how the story would unfold.

"It's easy to blame the boyfriend," I say, Waylon's voice pulsing in my ears like the steady thrum of heartbeat: *I want him to pay.* "Just like it's easy to blame the mother. But you know what still doesn't make sense to me, though? What I can't figure out?"

"What's that?" he asks, irritation dripping.

"How did Valerie know the baby monitor was dead?"

I take in the sharp clench of his jaw; the subtle clank of the chains as his leg shifts beneath him. The bob of his throat as he swallows, readying himself for a lie.

"She knew it was there," I continue. "She had been to our house before and she never once went into his nursery. I would have seen her on my phone."

"I don't know," he says, his voice low. "I have no idea."

"But she had to have known it wasn't recording that night. It's almost like someone mentioned it to her."

Ben is silent across the table, his eyes on mine.

"Like someone told her which night to show up."

I can feel the heavy air between us, and I know, in my gut, that I'm right about this, too. I can picture them lying in our bed together during one of my nights away. I can hear Mason's cries erupting from beneath the door and Ben sighing, leaving, muttering something about how I had let the batteries die and couldn't be bothered to change them. Valerie, stretched out alone, the wheels in her mind starting to spin, and his voice the grease they needed to keep turning.

"Tell me about Allison," I say at last, leaning forward, because he needs to understand why he's here. "How did she die, Ben?"

I can see the color drain from his face; his skin, somehow, growing even paler.

"What do you mean?" he asks.

"You know what I mean."

"She killed herself. Isabelle, she—" He stops, swallows, twists his head slightly. "You don't think I did something to her, too, do you?"

I try to imagine it: Ben, forcing Allison to swallow those pills. Crushing them into a powder and slipping them into her coffee, maybe. Hiding them in her food.

"Izzy," he pleads. "Jesus, I've never *killed* anyone."

I don't think that's how it happened, though. After all, Ben's words are his weapon. They always have been. He's always known that the best way to control someone is by planting an idea in their mind and making them believe it was theirs all along. He's always been good at sprinkling the bread crumbs, one by one, until all those little steps have taken you somewhere else entirely—a place that you don't even recognize anymore. A place so far gone, you can't find your way back. He's always known how to suffocate someone from the inside out; how to starve them, drown them, push them so close to the edge that when they look down and see nothing but empty air beneath them—when they dangle their foot off the ledge and feel themselves starting to fall—the idea of it might actually feel good.

And that deserves to be punished, too, doesn't it?

I imagine Allison during all of those late nights, pregnant, knowing her husband was out with somebody else. Feeling the same loneliness that I had felt, the same regret, and seeing her life flash through her mind like a movie: Ben, pointing at her in the high school hall and deciding that she was his. Pulling her in and giving her everything she wanted before steering her life onto a different path and leaving her there, stranded and alone, just as another life had started to grow inside her.

I imagine her walking into the bathroom, tears in her eyes, one hand on her stomach and the bottle of pills he left out on the counter, staring at her like a quiet dare. Picking them up and holding them in her hand, knowing that he left them there on purpose. Knowing what he wanted her to do—and, slowly, starting to think that she might want to do it, too.

After all, the violence always comes to us in ways we could never expect: quickly, quietly. Masked as something else. Ben has always known that you don't have to pull the trigger to get away with murder—sometimes, all you need to do is load the gun and let it go off on its own.

CHAPTER SIXTY-ONE

EPILOGUE

"Tell me a story."

I can still hear her voice, Margaret's voice, as she lay on her belly on our living room floor. I can see her legs kicking in the air and those glossy pages splayed out in front of us like a real-life storybook: stories of other people, other places. Being transported into their skin as I read the words out loud, imagining what it might feel like to be someone else. To live another life.

"You're good, though. At telling the story."

Waylon and I on that airplane, my eyes pinched shut as he stared in my direction. The floor beneath us vibrating as we took off into the air.

"It's not a story," I had said. *"It's my life."*

But aren't all of our lives just stories we tell ourselves? Stories we try to craft so perfectly and cast out into the world? Stories that become so vivid, so real, that eventually we start to believe them, too?

I had started spinning my own story at the age of eight, a web of lies that became stronger and more intricate as life went on. Those microscopic threads sticky and strong, trapping everything good and devouring it whole. There was something wrong with me. Something dark and toxic traveling through my veins. Something evil that that house had injected me with, a deadly venom that turned my eyes to stone. It started as a single sentence muttered to me in the morning— *"It scares me when you do that"*—and had morphed into something bigger, messier. Something that defined my very existence.

Those footprints on my carpet, my body acting in ways my mind couldn't control. All-consuming, like marsh fog in the morning, rolling across the yard and swallowing me alive.

Sometimes, the stories we create are about ourselves. Sometimes, other people. But as long as we believe them—as long as we can convince *others* to believe them—they keep their power. They remain true.

I glance up at Waylon now, that green light blinking between us, and feel the weight of the headphones around my ears. We've covered it all, finally: Ben and Allison and the way the police were never quite convinced of her suicide. How Dozier had always suspected him but never had the proof he needed to convict. How he had always watched from a distance after that, especially after our son went missing, pushing himself into the trees at the vigil. Interrogating his wife to learn what I knew.

Trying to catch him in a misstep. A lie.

I think about how Dozier had looked at me last week, his eyes darting down to my bandaged hand. He knew what happened to Valerie—deep down, he *knew*—just like Chief Montgomery knew what happened to Margaret. What *really* happened. But he didn't want to know that, not really. He didn't want to know the truth, what actually occurred, but instead wanted to hear what was easier to believe. So he had asked me all the right questions, listened to me recite my lines, then shaped a reality in his mind that was better, more convenient, than the one that really existed, holding his own lie tight against his chest before watching it wriggle away, like something slippery in his hands.

We talked about Ben and Valerie and the plan they hatched together; his ring beneath the couch, and how he had used her to find his way back to a childless life before killing her when it was over and staging it as a burglary to keep his secret safe. Kasey agreed to be interviewed, too, talking at length about how Ben was quietly controlling. How she had watched me change, slowly, long before Mason vanished, and how he had alienated me from everyone in my life until he was all I had left.

After the news of Ben's arrest broke, Paul Hayes visited my house, too, asking me to keep a secret of his own.

"That man you saw is my father," he said, a nervous tremor in his throat. "He's been living with me now that he's nearing the end, but we both have records. Pasts that I'm not proud of."

I remembered again what Dozier had said: the drug charges and his time in jail. It was against the terms of Paul's parole to harbor another criminal, even though they're family, so he kept his father stashed in the house, blinds drawn and windows dark, hidden away each day until the sun dipped down and it was safe to come back out.

"Dad told me he saw you that night," he said, shaking his head. "All this time, I thought it was you, but I couldn't turn you in without turning us in, too."

I think of him slinking back at the vigil; the hatred in his eyes as he found me sitting on his porch. He thought I was a murderer. He thought I murdered my own child and his father was the only person on earth who could prove it. He must have been racked with guilt, watching me get away with it every single day and knowing that he and he alone could bring me to justice—but in the end, he chose family, protecting himself and his father through silence and lies.

And then there's my own family, too: My parents, who have since reached back out in an attempt to mend the brokenness between us. My mother, and the quiet guilt she constantly carries; my father, and the shame he feels for failing us so badly. They had already lost two daughters, after all. They didn't want to lose a third. It'll take time, I know, getting to know one another again—forgiving them for everything they did and didn't do—but at least it's out in the open now: Margaret and Ellie and the terrible things that happened in that house.

The memories that none of us wanted to remember—but, now that I do, will be impossible to forget.

I remove my headphones and watch as Waylon flips the switch, turning the green light off. It'll be out into the world soon, our story, pulsing through the ears of others—and then it'll be true. It'll be true because they'll believe it to be, bending the facts to fit their feelings. Finding fragments of truth in all the wrong places. Forcing them together to reveal a picture that was never even there in the first place.

"You feel good?" Waylon asks, wrapping the cords around his wrist and nestling them back into the case. "About all of this?"

I glance outside, the setting sun casting an orange light across the sky. Just three weeks ago, the sunset used to signal the start of something—the start of another long, lonely stretch of night—but now it feels like the end. The end of a nightmare that I've finally managed from wake up from.

"Yeah," I say, nodding. "Yeah, I do."

"Everything you did," he says, "it was worth it."

I smile before walking Waylon to the door, opening it wide as we say our goodbyes. Once he's gone, I turn back around and take in the renewed silence of my house: Roscoe on the floor, napping quietly, dusk streaming through the windows as dinner warms on the stove. I peer into my dining room, thinking about all those names and pictures and article clippings that I've since torn down; all the conferences and calls to Dozier. The leads I chased blindly in the dark.

That comment that had appeared and vanished again.

He's in a better place.

That's how it all ended: that comment. Even after it was deleted, they were still able to trace it—and it brought them not to Valerie's place, but to Abigail Fisher's, a nondescript little rental she had moved into halfway across the country. And that's where they found her, waiting, almost like she was relieved to get caught: sitting in a little nursery set up with toys and dinosaurs and piles of books.

All the things a child would need to be happy, healthy. Loved.

I still think about how it must have been for her: a childless woman just trying to grieve and move on—but she couldn't. She couldn't move on. Instead, she held on to it, refusing to let it go, pushing it around and around until Valerie approached her one night, late, and told her a story.

A story about a boy with an unfit mother. A boy who would be better off with somebody else.

In a way, I understand it. I really do. Nothing about grief makes sense: the things it has us do, the lies it leads us to believe. Valerie simply told her what she wanted to hear, and she let herself believe it—that it was for the best, for *everybody*—so she swallowed her guilt and her fear as she met her that night, late, fingers digging into Mason's little body as he was passed between them in the dark, his stuffed dinosaur slipping from his grip and getting stuck in the mud.

Then she strapped him into her car seat and took off fast, disappearing into the night.

I walk down the hall now, toward Mason's nursery, and approach the door that I've always kept closed. I touch my hand to the knob the way I've done so many times before—too afraid to twist it, to peer inside, to catch a glimpse of everything I had lost—but now I do. I open it gently. I let myself look. And there he is, just as I've imagined it so many times before: There's Mason, sitting up in his bed, cracking that toothy little smile when he sees me. He's holding that same stuffed toy, the mud cleaned off before being removed from evidence and returned back to us, a gentle reminder of the life with me I know he's probably forgotten.

He was gone for an entire year, after all. An entire year that I will never get back.

And that could have been the end of it: Abigail Fisher driving fast down the interstate, moving them both into a new home. A new life.

Mason growing up with another mother, his young memory erasing me completely, little glimpses coming to him only as a foggy dream, a distant echo. Something fractured and broken and warped with time. He might have been happy, even, whatever story Abigail told him planting roots and turning true—until she started seeing me in the news each day, begging for him back. Until the doubts had crept in, forcing her to come to my talks and listen to me speak. Until she started seeing me not as the monster Valerie had made me out to be but as a heartsick mother desperate for her child—so she memorized my speech and cried as I told it, knowing she had made a mistake, but still, trying to convince herself that the story had been true. That she did what was right.

That he was in a better place.

AUTHOR'S NOTE

If you haven't made it to the end of the story yet, I ask that you stop reading this now and finish first—what comes next will surely spoil everything.

Before this book existed on paper and it was still just an idea in my head, the idea was basically this: What would it feel like to be trapped inside the mind of a sleep-deprived mother who, deep down, believed that the disappearance of her child was somehow her fault? When I started wondering *why* she would believe that, it hit me like a truck: It's because mothers—and, honestly, women in general—are conditioned from birth to feel guilty about something. We *always* think things are our fault. We always feel the need to apologize: For being too much or too little. Too loud or too quiet. Too driven or too content.

For wanting children more than anything or for not even wanting them at all.

I won't lie to you: I was afraid to write a book about motherhood without first being a mother myself. I make some strong statements in this novel, and I was worried about making those statements without coming from a place of personal experience. There are many things about motherhood that I simply cannot understand, and in those in-stances, I relied heavily on research, as well as speaking to friends and family members who *are* mothers to help me sort through it all. And while I acknowledge that there are certain emotions and experiences that I cannot fully appreciate yet, I also believe that every woman can understand the unspoken expectations of it: the *weight* of motherhood that seems to be ever-present throughout our entire lives from the very moment we're given our first doll. Not only that, but because of the judgment that emanates from others once we make a decision of our own, oftentimes, we feel like we can't even talk about it.

We feel completely alone in an experience that's shared by so many.

When I came to that realization, I just wanted to stuff this book full of different types of women: flawed, complicated, messy women who will surely draw scorn for their various decisions—but really, that's the point. Isabelle is, in many ways, my attempt at showcasing the damage societal pressures and expectations can have on a single person. Is she the perfect mother? No. And does she make mistakes? Yes. She struggles, as do all mothers, and feels extreme guilt over thoughts and emotions that she doesn't even know are normal—but how *could* she know if nobody ever talks about it? Despite it all, though, she loves her son fiercely—however, that love will never be enough to save her in the court of public opinion... or even in her own mind, for that matter, so accustomed is she to absorbing every-one else's blame.

When it comes to Isabelle's mother, I tried to tread lightly and respectfully on a topic so fragile. I did a lot of research on postpar-tum psychosis, and the character of Elizabeth was informed, in large part, by Andrea Yates. The more I read about her, the more her ac-tions shifted in my mind from horrifying to heartbreaking: She was a mother at the end of her mental rope. She asked for help, never received it, and was villainized for what happened as a result. Of course, what she did was both tragic and terrifying—but at the same time, it could have been avoided, too, if only the mental health of mothers wasn't something we so easily shrugged off or pretended not to notice. The same can be said for Elizabeth.

Allison, Valerie, Kasey, and Abigail are also women in this story with complicated emotions that lead to their own varying decisions: good and bad, right and wrong—but mostly, I think, somewhere in the murky middle. In real life, we are so rarely afforded the luxury of things being in simple black and white, so I try to stay true to that in my stories, too, by making each character as multifaceted as possible. For that reason, I hope they inspire some enlightening conversation—or, at the very least, gave you an entertaining read.

Finally, if you are concerned about your own mental health or the mental health of a loved one, please know that there are resources available to help. A good place to start would be the National Institute of Mental Health website: www.nimh.nih.gov/health/find-help.

ACKNOWLEDGMENTS

I have a complicated relationship with the Acknowledgments page.

On the one hand, I love nothing more than calling attention to the many, many people who play a role in bringing a book to life. I never knew how much of a team effort publishing a book truly was before I entered this industry, and let me tell you: it feels downright dishonest to only list one name on the cover. But on the other hand, it is impossible to list every single name, and it pains me to think that I'm leaving someone out—so, with that said: Please know, whoever you are, that if you touched this story in any way, I am incredibly grateful.

To my agent, Dan Conaway: This story wouldn't exist without you. You changed my life and gave me the freedom to keep writing. Thank you so much for that.

To Chaim Lipskar, Peggy Boulos-Smith, Maja Nikolic, Jessica Berger, Kate Boggs, and everyone else at Writers House: You continue to be amazing and I consider myself so lucky to be in your company. Thank you for all your hard work.

To my editor, Kelley Ragland: Thank you so much for every conversation that helped to steer this story on the right track. To Allison

Ziegler, Sarah MeInyk, Hector DeJean, Madeline Houpt, Paul Hochman, David Rotstein, and everyone else at Minotaur, St. Martin's Publishing Group, and Macmillan: Thank you for your tireless efforts. A massive thanks also goes out to Andy Martin and Jen Enderlin for giving me the chance.

To my UK editor, Julia Wisdom, and all of the folks over at HarperCollins UK, including but not limited to Lizz Burrell, Susanna Peden, and Maddy Marshall: Thank you so much for bringing another one of my books—and me!—overseas. It's a dream come true.

To my film agent, Sylvie Rabineau, at WME: Thank you for everything you do to bring my stories to the screen. I am so thrilled to be working together again.

To the librarians, booksellers, bloggers, reviewers, bookstagrammers, book clubs, and the online reading community: I don't even know what to say. When I was writing the acknowledgments for *A Flicker in the Dark*, I didn't yet understand the massive influence you all would have on my work and my life. This time around, I understand—and I am so grateful. Thank you for embracing my writing, stories, and characters; thank you for sharing the books you love with others and for allowing me to connect with so many wonderful readers all over the world. I owe so much to all of you, so thank you.

To independent bookstores everywhere, especially Buxton Books, Itinerant Literate, and The Village Bookseller right here in Charleston: Thank you for lifting up a local who grew up dreaming of one day seeing my name on shelves like yours.

To my husband, Britt: I thought you were supportive the first time around, but these last twelve months have shown me how truly lucky I am. Thank you for supporting me, no matter what, and for always being down for an adventure. I love you so much.

To my parents, Kevin and Sue, for continuing to be my number one fans. Please don't think my fascination with dysfunctional families has anything to do with our own.

To my sister, Mallory, for once again giving me the most valuable feedback on that bad first draft. Growing up with you gave me the sister memories I needed to make this story come alive. Thank you for letting me follow you through life like a (not-so-quiet) little shadow.

To Brian, Laura, Alvin, Lindsey and Matt, and the rest of my wonderful family: Thank you, as always, for your enthusiasm and support.

To my friends, near and far, who have encouraged me constantly ever since I shared this weird secret of mine: Thank you for always being there. I wish I could name you all, but I feel the need to at least name the ones who have gone above and beyond to make me feel supported and loved: Rebekah, Caitlin, Ashley, Erin, Kolbie, Jeremy, Kaela, Justin, Tina, Noah, Eli, Laura, Abby, John, Bobby, Reid, Peter, Mégane, Jacqueline, and Caroline.

To Mako, for keeping me company.

To Douglas, for the inspiration.

And finally, my readers, to whom I owe the world: If you picked this book up after *A Flicker in the Dark,* thank you for sticking with me. If this was your very first story of mine, thank you for giving me a chance.

OXFORD COUNTY LIBRARY